The Spy Who
Haunted Me

The Spy Who Haunted Me

Simon Green

The right of Simon R. Green to be identified as the author
of this work has been asserted by him in accordance with
the Copyright, Designs and Patents Act 1988.

First published in Great Britain in 2009
by Gollancz
An imprint of the Orion Publishing Group
Orion House, 5 Upper St Martin's Lane,
London WC2H 9EA
An Hachette UK Company

This edition published in Great Britain in 2010
by Gollancz

1 3 5 7 9 10 8 6 4 2

A CIP catalogue record for this book
is available from the British Library

ISBN 978 0 575 08855 9

Printed and bound in the UK by CPI Mackays, Chatham ME5 8TD

The Orion Publishing Group's policy is to use papers
that are natural, renewable and recyclable products and
made from wood grown in sustainable forests. The logging
and manufacturing processes are expected to conform to
the environmental regulations of the country of origin.

www.orionbooks.co.uk

You don't have to be afraid of the dark.

I mean, yes: it is full of monsters . . . and vampires and werewolves and aliens and mad scientists, and everything else that's ever put the fear of God into you. Plus a whole bunch of people who are stranger and scarier than any mere monster could ever be. But my family exists to stand between you and them; every day, and all through the night. The Drood family has protected you and all Humanity from the forces of darkness for some two thousand years now; and we're very good at it. My name is Drood, Eddie Drood. Also known as Shaman Bond, the very secret agent.

I face down the monsters, so you don't have to.

But don't expect a knight in shining armour. I do my best, but sometimes . . . the night can be very dark indeed.

CHAPTER ONE
The crime of the century

In the early hours, when it seems like the dark will go on forever and the dawn will never come, the night people come out to play. They swarm through the empty London streets, trailing long multi-coloured streamers and brandishing champagne bottles, howling with laughter and singing the bits they remember from popular songs. They always wear the very best, even if it is stained with booze and food and dusted with various powders; and they all look like film stars or supermodels or personalities . . . It's only when you get right up close you can see the bloodied and worn-down feet, the haunted eyes and the desperate smiles, and hear the lost lonely strain in their laughter. For the night people, parties go on forever. There are all kinds of Hell.

I had left Leicester Square tube station and was heading unhurriedly into Covent Garden. I was just Shaman Bond that night, my easy-going, relatively harmless cover identity, dressed well but casually with nothing to distinguish me from a hundred other late-night revellers. I've been trained not to stand out, to blend into any crowd, to have a face that no one will remember ten minutes later. An agent's face. I come and I go and do what I have to, and no one ever knows. If I've done my job right.

It was an early morning in late September, a pleasant enough night. The moon was full, the stars were out, and the street lamps glowed like tarnished gold. Long black limousines cruised past, transporting high-class hookers with silver hair and artificial smiles to expensive rendezvous at the best hotels. Black-leather couriers on powerful motorbikes carried important secrets back and forth, from embassy to embassy or industry to industry. And a gang of knobbly-looking kobolds in Westminster Council uniforms were chatting and swearing cheerfully as they hauled dead trolls out of an open manhole, and dumped the distorted bodies into the back of a waiting refuse truck. There's a lot goes on in London streets at night that most Londoners are better off not knowing about.

The kobolds nodded easily to me as I passed, and I smiled easily back. Night people can always recognise their own kind. Kobolds perform necessary repairs, clean up the night's various messes and deal very sternly with the various unnatural vermin that thrive deep down under the streets of London. Trolls, albino alligators, intelligent rat colonies, the inhuman spawn of slumming alien deities. That sort of thing.

You wouldn't be able to see them, because you don't have the Sight: the practised ability to See the world as it really is, in all its awful glory. Even I can't bear to See it for long. The Sight is one of the advantages of being a Drood. It comes from the golden collar I wear around my throat – a torc, in the old language. The torc is the secret weapon of the Droods. It makes us strong enough to go head to head with monsters and demons, and kick their nasty arses.

Further down the street, two large bottle-green reptiloids were having a slapping match over the unformed soul they'd ripped out of some squashed piece of roadkill. They'd clearly fallen on hard times, and actually backed away when they saw me coming. I left them to it. Eddie Drood might have felt obliged to do something about them, but I was Shaman Bond that night, and I didn't want to break cover. Cover identities are very important for a Drood field agent. I've spent years building up my public face, my public life, one careful step at a time. Droods come and go, but no one ever sees our faces. We protect the world, but we're not dumb enough to expect it to be grateful.

I'm only Eddie Drood when I'm at home, with the family. Or when I'm in action. Anywhen else, I'm Shaman Bond, so I can walk through the world just like you. Drood field agents are ninety-nine per cent urban myth, and we like it that way. Makes it so much scarier when we do choose to show ourselves.

So who is Shaman Bond? I'm glad you asked. He's an easy-going, vaguely feckless, borderline criminal man about town. Always a part of the scene, but never tied to anyone or anything. Everybody sort of knows him, even if they're not too sure what he actually does to hold body and soul together. If anyone should ask, he'll wink and smile, and change the subject. There are a lot of people like that, in the long reaches of the night. Shaman knows his way around, is on nodding acquaintance with a surprisingly large number of the people who matter, and is always ready to consider some dodgy venture or clandestine scheme; particularly if his funds are running low. The perfect cover for turning up anywhere, and listening to gossip.

I think mostly I prefer being Shaman Bond. No duties or responsibilities, no pressure . . . and Shaman's a nice guy. Eddie Drood doesn't always have that option.

Half a dozen Grey aliens were clustered around a strange piece of non-human technology, that shimmered and sparkled under the heavy light of the street lamps. The Greys were wearing designer sunglasses, presumably so they wouldn't be recognised. Otherwise they were entirely naked, dull grey skin slipping and sliding over their inhuman bone structure as though it wasn't properly attached. I made a mental note to check with my family that the Greys' permits were in order, and just what that particular bunch were up to.

There had almost certainly been a memo about it, but I'm always at least a month behind. You wouldn't believe how much paperwork is involved in being a very secret agent. And don't even get me started about claiming expenses . . .

I headed deeper into Covent Garden, and before and behind and around me blazed layer upon layer of ghosts. Of people and places, buildings and events, all of them trapped in repeating loops of time. Reminders and remainders, recordings of the Past, piled on top of each other like the layers of an onion . . . Because no matter how many layers you peel away there's always one more underneath. London is very old, and absolutely littered with things that won't stay dead. Even if you hit them with a really big stick.

No one paid me any attention. One of the first things they teach you as a field agent is how to walk unseen in plain sight. To be average and anonymous, just another face in the crowd. You could walk past me in the street and not even notice I was there. It's all in the training. You too could give the appearance of being nobody in particular, not worth a second glance, if you were prepared to put in the work.

My current mission was important, but frustratingly vague. The safety of England hung in the balance, but no one could tell me why. Something important was being planned by foreign elements, some dark and dangerous scheme aimed at the very heart of London; but no one could tell me what or who or when. And of course *foreign* could mean exactly that, or it could mean elves or aliens or unnatural forces from outside our reality. The family precogs are always right, but they see the future through a glass darkly, and they're vague when it comes to useful details. Some warnings have been so obscure they only became clear in hindsight.

The Tower of London, they said. *Our greatest treasure is at risk. England endangered. The crime of the century . . .*

Vague, or what?

But the family takes this stuff very seriously, so I was sent to investigate. London is my territory. London, also known as the Smoke; and everyone knows there's no smoke without fire. So there I was, Shaman Bond again, out and about to talk to people in the know, and hopefully discover what the Hell was going on and put a stop to it. I couldn't simply call up the golden armour from my torc and go crashing into places as Eddie Drood, field agent, protector of the innocent and brown-trouserer of the ungodly. They'd scatter and head for the hills. But people would talk to Shaman Bond. They like him.

I've gone to great pains to make him likeable.

You get to London's infamous Hiring Hall by walking down a side street that isn't always there, knowing the right passWords to say in the right places so the guard dogs won't turn into hellhounds and rip the soul out of you, and finally by going through a left-handed door that will only open if it likes the look of your face.

You'll soon know if you've been black-listed: the door handle will bite your hand off. And no, you don't get to complain. No one asked you to come.

The Hiring Hall's been around since the time of Elizabeth I; indeed, supposedly the first stalls were set out on the frozen surface of the River Thames in 1589. They had real winters in those days. Like all successful businesses, the hall has grown tremendously down the centuries, and though the jobs and services on offer in the Hiring

Hall may have changed some since those early days, they haven't changed in principle. It's still all about money and power and influence. Love and hate and especially sex. At the infamous and just a bit scary Hiring Hall, jobs are available, services and skills are on offer, deals are made and people are screwed over on a regular basis.

The Hiring Hall has been owned by the same family since Shakespearean times. No one ever says the name out loud, but here's a clue. The company is called 'Pound Of Flesh Inc', and their motto is 'We always take our cut'.

I walked down the side street, said all the right Words (including '*Good doggy*'), and pushed open the nicely anonymous door. The handle recognised Shaman Bond and remained just a handle. Inside the hall it was all noise and chaos, and the raucous clamour of business being done. The Hiring Hall is long and large and contains wonders, and everyone who is anyone has had a stall there at one time or another. The stalls are packed tightly together, constantly jostling for those extra few inches, lining all four walls for as far as the eye can see and a bit further. The great open space in the middle was packed with a deafening, jostling mob of the unnatural and the ungodly, the criminal and the rogue and the defiantly free-thinking, all looking for temporary gainful employment, certain very select and secret services, and the chance to do somebody else down. The din was appalling, the smell not much better, and the sheer spectacle of both people and prospects more than enough to overwhelm the unseasoned visitor.

Want to hire a murderer, or arrange your own death? Sell your soul, or someone else's? Do you have a plan to steal fabulous items, or an urgent need to dispose of them? Then you've come to the right place. But watch your back, always read the small print, and count your testicles afterwards.

All around me there were ghosts looking for suitable houses to haunt, werewolves offering to track down the missing or gone to ground, vampires hidden behind romantic glamours offering themselves as gigolos or assassins or means of assisted suicide; and the usual cluster of ghouls, amiable as always, ready to clean up natural disasters or chemical spills. (Ghouls can stomach anything.) Shaman Bond has been known to pick up the odd job here, so no one was particularly surprised to see me. Shaman specialises in supplying secrets and unusual information, for an only slightly extortionate fee. The family research department tells me what I need to know, I pass it on to my customers, and everybody's happy. And if the family occasionally wants to distribute some false information or black propaganda where it'll do the most damage, well, everyone knows you take your chances when you come to Hiring Hall. Shaman Bond has a better reputation than most, and that's all that matters.

I eased my way through the milling crowd, nodding and smiling, showing my best face to friends and enemies. The Hiring Hall is neutral ground to one and all, strictly enforced by the dozen or so animated brass golems standing round the walls. (And by other, less obvious but quite spectacularly nasty devices hidden away in unexpected places.) It doesn't matter whether it's blood feuds, tribal hatreds, centuries-long vendettas or dogmatic diversity – they all get left at the door if you want to do business in Hiring Hall.

I allowed the currents in the crowd to take me where they wanted, while I took a good look around. It seemed everybody had a stall out today: governments and religions, independent contractors and middle men, service providers and every kind of bad business you could think of. Including some very big names you'd almost certainly recognise. There were even a few stalls representing the smaller countries in the world, offering specialised services and opportunities, desperate for a chance to play with the big boys.

And, of course, there were stalls for every spy and intelligence agency in the world. Not the Droods, of course. We're urban legends, remember?

But the CIA was there, and the KGB (or whatever initials they're hiding behind these days), Vril Power Inc, the Vatican (represented by a big butch nun from the Salvation Army Sisterhood), the Tracey Brothers, Druid Nation (*Let's put the fear back into Halloween!*), and a rather familiar face manning the MI13 booth. I wandered over and smiled at the balding, middle-aged figure of Philip MacAlpine, once one of England's top spies. He saw me coming, and if anything looked even more put upon. I came to a halt before him, and he actually sighed loudly.

'Hello, Phil,' I said. 'What are you doing here?'

'I could ask you the same question,' he growled. 'I take it you are here as Shaman Bond, and not—'

'Quite,' I said. 'Please don't mention the name on the tip of your tongue, or I will be obliged to rip out that tongue, throw it on the ground and stamp on it.'

He sniffed loudly. 'That's right. Kick a man when he's down. This is your fault, you know. I had a perfectly good position at MI5, with seniority, and tenure. I had my own office, *with a window*! And then they sent me after you.'

'And I kicked your arse all over the place,' I said pleasantly. 'I remember.'

He glared at me. 'You killed over a hundred of my people. Good men and women, just doing their jobs.'

'They were trying to kill me at the time,' I said. 'I've always taken that very personally.'

He sniffed again. 'Thanks to you, and the failure of that mission, I got promoted sideways, into MI13. No seniority, no tenure, and I have to share an office with three other operatives and a rubber plant. Overseeing the weird shit that none of the other MI offices want to deal with. You know what they've got me doing here? Public relations. Handing out leaflets and badges and application forms. Shoot me now, you bastard.'

'Don't tempt me,' I said.

'I had a career! I did important things! I couldn't tell anybody about them, but still . . . It's not fair.'

'I let you live, didn't I?' I said reasonably. 'What's MI13 up to these days? Anything interesting?'

He shrugged. 'Same old same old. Watching the aliens watching us, making sure they play nice and don't stray outside the negotiated limits. There's word of a Mothmen breakout down in Cornwall. I think they're attracted to the lighthouses. When I'm finished here, I'm supposed to be putting together a team to go down to reason with them and/or kick their heads in. Could I interest you . . .'

'I'm spoken for,' I said. 'Don't suppose you've heard of any current threats to the Tower of London, have you?'

'Nothing recent.' MacAlpine studied me. 'Is this something I should be concerned about?'

'Of course not,' I said, smiling. 'I'm on the case.'

I could tell he was about to say something indiscreet, so I nodded goodbye and let the currents of the crowd carry me away. I don't like to spend too much time with any of the intelligence agencies when I'm being Shaman. Part of his usefulness as a cover identity is that Shaman never allies himself with any cause or faction for long, and therefore is welcome anywhere. Shaman Bond is a chancer, a hustler, a useful extra hand and a reliable backup. Always on the scene, but never aspiring to be a major player. A man who knows things, and people, but can be relied on to keep his mouth shut. And ... a bit dull and boring, when necessary, so no one ever wants to get too close.

The usual faces were making themselves known. I bumped into one of the scene's main fixers, the infamous Middle Man. Tall and elegant, wearing a bright green kaftan and smoking a slim black cigarillo in a long ivory holder. Handsome enough, in a ravaged-by-time sort of way, with flat black hair and more than a hint of mascara. His fingernails had been painted jet green. He was accompanied by two Thai teenagers in bright red leathers, who might have been brother and sister or something even closer. The Middle Man knew me as Shaman Bond, and as Eddie Drood, but didn't know they were the same person. I know a lot of people like that. It would probably complicate things, if I were a complicated person.

'Shaman!' said the Middle Man, gesturing lazily with one long languid hand. 'How nice! On the prowl for Madam Opportunity, are we? The creditors pressing close again? How very tiresome for you.'

'You know how it is,' I said. 'It's an expensive world, for those of us who want a little fun out of life.'

'Oh, I know, I know, dear boy. I swear the money evaporates out of my pockets when I'm not looking.'

'Particularly when you gamble as much as you do,' I said. 'And so badly.'

The Middle Man glared at his Thai boy. 'Have you been telling tales out of school again, Maurice? I shall have to be very strict with you later. You know you like that ...'

We chatted a while, but when he didn't so much as raise an elegantly painted eyebrow when I mentioned the Tower of London, I made my excuses and moved on. The next familiar face made a point of bumping into me. Leo Morn might be good company, but he's always on the prowl and on the scrounge. I swear he came out of the womb trying to cadge a cigarette off the midwife. Leo is tall, slight, long-haired, pale and interesting, and looks like he ought to be starring in a particularly gloomy Tim Burton film. Dressed all in black, he appeared so frail you half expected one good breeze would carry him away. But, as with so many of the people I know, appearances can be deceptive. Leo Morn has hidden strengths, and a heart of solid granite.

He was looking for tracking work.

'Still playing bass with that punk folk band?' I said, and he grinned wolfishly.

'Of course! Got some really good gigs lined up.'

'Are you still having to change the name of the band regularly, so clubs will hire you twice?' I said innocently.

He scowled. 'We are ahead of our time! We're currently called Angel's Son. Got a sweet gig at Moles, in Bath, end of the month. Drop in, if you're in the area. Catch us while you can. I doubt we'll be there long.'

'No offence, Leo,' I said, 'but on the whole I think I'd rather stick skewers in my ears.'

'For someone who didn't want to give offence, I'd have to say you came pretty damned close there,' said Leo.

I wished him luck and he stalked off. People got out of his way; they could smell the wolf on him.

Next was Harry Fabulous, handsome, charming, deeply fashionable, and all of it as fake as his constant smile. Harry showed no interest in the stalls, moving instead from one potential customer to another like a shark in good fishing waters. Harry would steal the shirt off your back, but do it so charmingly you'd end up apologising to him that it wasn't of better quality. Harry Fabulous: conman, thief, grifter, and your go-to man for absolutely everything that was bad for you.

'Shaman! Dear fellow!' said Harry, showing me all his teeth in his most professional smile. 'Good to see you out and about again. Haven't seen you since . . . ah well, not in public, eh? What have you been up to?'

'You'd never believe me,' I said solemnly. 'How about yourself, Harry? How's business?'

'Oh, busy, as always.' His smile faltered for a moment, his eyes briefly far away. 'Had a bit of bad business with an angel in the Nightside, and now I find it necessary to do good works for the sake of my soul. You know how it is. Could I interest you in something a bit special, for an entirely reasonable price? I can get my hands on some very tasty smoked black centipede meat, or some full-strength Hyde, or even some prime Martian red weed, a very cool smoke . . . No? How about some Yeti's Tears? Kirlian boost? Deep Speed, from the House of Blue Lights?'

'Think I'll pass,' I said firmly.

'Then I must be off,' he said briskly. 'You know how it is, old boy. Things to see, people to do . . . I think I spot a tourist over there, just begging to be relieved of everything he owns.'

And off he went, sliding so smoothly through the crowd he hardly made a ripple, a smile on his lips and honest larceny in his heart.

Standing alone, apparently lost in thought in the middle of his own personal and very private space, was the Notional Man. Everyone was giving him plenty of room, because no one in their right mind wanted to get too close to him. He might notice them. The Notional Man was a human being reduced (or perhaps evolved) to its most abstract form. You see him most clearly out of the corner of your eye, but even then more as an impression than any definite shape. I don't know what he uses for a body these days, but it sure as Hell isn't flesh any more. He's a projection, an idea of a man – immortal, invulnerable and capable of thinking round corners you didn't even know were there. Some say he lost a bet, with God or the Devil, and some say he did it to himself and now can't undo it. Either way, the Notional Man comes and goes as he pleases and no one knows how or why. A tragedy or a triumph, and quite possibly both. The only thing that everyone can agree on is that he's mad, bad and dangerous to know, so we're all very polite to him.

I'd never seen him in Hiring Hall before.

He turned his abstract head in my direction, and I felt the impact of his gaze. He knew who I really was. He knew everything he wanted to know. He didn't walk towards me, he was suddenly there, right in front of me. I did my best not to jump or flinch away. Up close, he was even more disturbing. It hurt my eyes to look at him directly; everything about him was *wrong*. Like a circle with straight lines, or a room with too many angles. He had height and breadth and depth and other things too. I could feel myself shaking.

His voice exploded inside my head, and I cried out. He was sound and colours and deafening images. The Notional Man had moved beyond speech into something that might have been the other side of telepathy. All I could tell was that he was looking for something, or someone, but he couldn't make me understand what. Blood spurted from my nostrils, and welled up from under my eyelids. And then, just like that, he was back where he had been before, and the only person inside my head was me.

A passing Man In Black offered me a paper tissue, and I nodded gratefully, mopping at the blood on my cheeks and pressing the tissue against my throbbing nose.

All in all, a fairly typical encounter with the Notional Man. The Droods have received several requests to terminate his existence with more than usual extreme prejudice, on the grounds that he's just too damned worrying; and we're seriously considering it, if only for the challenge. The trouble with the Notional Man is that he's pure and potent, as much a concept as anything else, and totally beyond any human capacity to understand or manipulate. And who wants a god you can't understand or appease, and doesn't give a damn whether you worship him or not?

I checked the paper tissue. There was no blood on it. Neither, when I checked, was there any blood on my cheeks, around my eyes or drying inside my nostrils. Typical.

I strolled on through the crowd. Exchanged words, shook hands, kissed cheeks. I like being Shaman Bond. All right, he's not really real, as such, but I feel so much more comfortable being him than I do being Eddie Drood. Shaman can be strong or silly, wise or foolish, exactly as he chooses, and it doesn't matter a damn whether he screws up. He doesn't have the fate of Humanity resting on his shoulders.

He has friends. A Drood only has family, and enemies.

Shaman Bond is more than the mask I hide behind in public. He's the man I might have been, if my life had been my own.

The CIA's stall, as always, was very big and bright and colourful, complete with flat-screen images, all the latest gadgets and gizmos, an American flag standing tall and proud, and a real eagle squatting on a perch glaring suspiciously at passersby. The CIA would recruit anyone who showed an interest, and did a thriving trade in souvenirs and memorabilia, and there was never any shortage of cash in hand for information and gossip . . . but really they were there to establish their presence. To remind us they were always watching. I recognised another familiar face behind the table, and wandered over.

Nickie Carter is old school CIA, fourth or maybe even fifth generation in the spy game. A pleasant-looking brunette in her early twenties, Nickie wore a smart powder-blue suit and a professional smile, and looked like the successful product of some famous business school. She also knew fifty-seven ways to kill you with a single finger, and some quite disgusting things she could do with her mouth. We once spent a lost weekend in Helsinki together, on the trail of someone who turned out not to exist, as such. The job's like that, sometimes.

She only knows me as Shaman Bond. Which is just as well, or she'd probably feel obliged to try and kill me.

Nickie smiled sweetly at me. 'Shaman, honey, looking good! Sorry about that enforced rendition attempt last year; some damned fool higher up the food chain got it into his head that you were a player in the Manifest Destiny group. I tried to tell them, but no one ever listens to a mere field agent any more. It's all computers these days, all trends and predictions. Damn bean-counters . . .' She gazed at me. 'How did you manage to avoid us, Shaman?'

'Nice to see you again, Nickie,' I said. 'Aren't you going to introduce me to your friend?'

Nickie smiled fondly at the elderly gentleman sitting beside her, staring off into the distance. 'Of course. This is a colleague of mine, Shaman. May I present to you one of the living legends of the CIA, Stephen Victor, on his farewell tour of Europe.'

I knew the name. A definite major player back in the seventies, with a quite extraordinary way with the ladies. A one-man honey trap, by all accounts; women from both sides of the Cold War couldn't wait to jump into bed with him and tell him every secret they knew. He couldn't be that far into his sixties, but he looked twenty years older. He had a great noble head, a bit gaunt, with a mane of silver-grey hair, but though his mouth was firm enough, his eyes were vague and far away. He had that slightly rumpled look of a man who'd been dressed by someone else. He smiled in my direction when Nickie cued him with my name, and he shook my hand with a firm manly grip, but there was no one home behind his eyes. Just a shell of the man he'd once been, trotted out for public consumption. He let go of my hand and went back to staring at nothing again.

'He's here to visit some old haunts, meet a few past friends and enemies,' said Nickie. 'In the hope he can squeeze some last few secrets out before he's retired. Poor old thing. Can't even put him out to stud. Don't worry, Shaman, we can say what we like. He's deaf as a post.'

'I suppose it comes to all of us, in the end,' I said.

'Not if I can help it,' Nickie said firmly. 'The moment I start forgetting how many beans make four, I firmly intend to take up bungee-jumping over live volcanoes. Go out with a little style, while I'm still me. Look at the state of him ... doesn't know whether it's Tuesday or Belgium. I'm his nurse as much as his bodyguard. The last time he was in London, our ambassador introduced him to the Queen. And he propositioned her.'

'Really?' I said. 'How did Her Majesty respond?'

'No one knows,' Nickie said darkly. 'But Prince Philip had a Hell of a lot to say afterwards.'

I grinned, excused myself and wandered off again. Stephen Victor, the great seducer of his generation, reduced to a bag of bones in a crumpled suit. Was that all I had to look forward to? Was it my future, if I lived that long? A relic of the past, my triumphs and achievements faded into some vague respectful legend? Another prematurely aged agent, lost in memories of the past? No. The odds were I'd die young and die bloody, like most field agents.

I looked around me. Agents from all the major countries and powers were represented, buying and selling information and influence, and probably discussing a little discreet murder and sabotage on the side. Unusual to see so many out at once ... not that anyone would say anything. The Hiring Hall doesn't care who or what you were, as long as you pay the rent on your stall on time.

On the whole, the big boys don't bother much with Shaman Bond. He's too small-time to interest them. Occasionally someone will decide they want to know what he knows, and turn the dogs loose on him. But somehow Shaman always seems to know about these things in advance, and sidesteps their traps and blandishments with equal ease. Sometimes the big boys like to order him about, to remind everyone who's in charge, and he usually goes along with it. It's amazing what you can learn by keeping your eyes and ears open. When you're nothing but small fry, hired help, the important people will often speak quite openly in front of you, as though you're not even there.

I spent the best part of two hours cruising through Hiring Hall, walking up and down in it, talking with everyone and politely avoiding murmured offers of employment in secret jobs and dubious schemes ... and at the end of it I was no wiser. It wasn't as though I had much to go on; all the family precogs had was a threat to the Tower of London, and a general sense of danger and urgency. I've always felt that most precogs would benefit greatly from a good slap round the head.

I mentioned the Tower of London to the better connected rogues and scumbags in Hiring Hall, but all I got in return was vague words and vaguer promises to let me know if they heard anything. Something was in the air, some big job; but no one knew anything for sure. No one had a name, or a even a direction to point in.

I had been hinting, as broadly as possible, that I was in the market for a bit of action, no risk too great. I'd even let it be known I was quite definitely up for a bash at any symbols of authority; but while there was no shortage of offers, none of them sounded right. *I owe some people*, I would say. *People not known for their patience or understanding.* And familiar faces would nod and smile, and say they quite understood, and suggest all kinds of interesting opportunities (some of which I made a mental note to deal with later), but none of them what I was there for.

Until finally it was dropped in my lap, through an anonymous tip. Now, it's not easy to be anonymous around a Drood; we can See through most glamours and disguises, and we're almost impossible to sneak up on. Nevertheless, this quiet voice whispered in my ear, soft as a dove's fart: 'If you're interested in the Tower of London job, you need to speak to Big Oz. Over there, by the Universal Exports stall.'

'Who are you?' I said quietly, careful not to look around. 'Why are you telling me this?'

A breath of laughter, warm on my ear. 'Perhaps because even the most unrepentant villain can, much to his own surprise, turn out to be a patriot.'

I waited, but there was nothing more. I looked around, but there was only the crowd, shoving and jostling and shouting each other down, doing business. I considered the situation. Big Oz? Really? If the Emerald City was mounting an operation in London, I should have been informed. Unless it was in one of those damned memos I hadn't got around to yet . . .

But no. It turned out the man I'd been pointed at was Big Aus, a fanatical republican Australian. I introduced myself, and he crushed my hand in a big meaty fist. He was a large man, broad in the shoulder and wide in the belly, wearing a suit that looked like he'd ordered it from a photograph. He had a broad cheerful face, with sharp piercing eyes and a ready smile. He knew my name and reputation, and said he was very pleased to see me.

'Call me Big Oz,' he said. 'Everyone does. And you are a sight for sore eyes, Shaman. I'm a man short for a really sweet scheme, and you fit the part perfectly. Dame Luck must be smiling on me today. You want in? You're in!'

'Hold it,' I said quickly. 'It's nice to be wanted, Big Oz, but I'm not agreeing to be a part of anything until I know what it is I'm getting into. And what the money's like.'

'Of course! Of course! Wouldn't want a fella who was willing to dive in blind! We can't talk here. You come along with me, to this nice little watering hole I know round the corner. The rest of the gang's already there, waiting for me to fill the last gap with the right man. You'll love them – they're real characters, like you. Come with me, Shaman, and I will tell you how we're going to make ourselves really bloody wealthy, and stick it to the whole bloody British Monarchy. We are going to pull off the crime of the century, and help make God's Own Country of Australia the republic she was always meant to be!'

Big Oz took me firmly by the arm and escorted me to a tacky little theme eatery a few streets away from the Hiring Hall – an almost unbearably twee faux-Irish chain called the 'L'il Leprechaun'. I knew of the chain, but had never thought I'd actually be required to eat in one. The L'il Leprechauns have about as much in common with real Irish cuisine and culture as a plastic shamrock, and even less dignity. If the real Little People ever find out what's being perpetrated in their name, they'll declare a fatwah on the whole damned chain.

The eatery was decked out in loud primary colours, the tables were shaped like great flattened-off mushrooms, and there were pots of gold in which to stub out your herbal cigarettes. Cartoon leprechauns gambolled cheerfully across the walls and ceiling, and even peeped playfully out from behind the big stand-up menus. Most of the food, and even some of the drinks, came in shades of green. I made a mental note to steer well clear of the beefburgers. A sulky waitress done up as a Bunny Colleen, complete with sprayed-on freckles, tottered over on high heels and led Big Aus and I to a table at the back, where three other people were already sitting.

I knew them, and they knew me. Big Aus had heard of me, in the way most people have heard of Shaman Bond, but these three were very familiar faces. I don't know that I'd call them friends, exactly, but we'd worked together in the past, at one time or another, to our mutual profit, and we moved in the same social circles. I pulled up a chair so I could sit with my back to the wall, while Big Aus dropped his great weight on to a plastic chair with such impact that it actually shuddered beneath him.

As always, Coffin Jobe looked like he'd just been dug up out his grave and then hit over the head with the shovel. He was a tall, thin, sad affair, wrapped in a long grimy coat with food stains down the front, topped with a scarf to keep the cold out. He wore heavy old-fashioned spectacles, with the type of thick lenses normally employed to fry ants with the help of the sun, behind which his gaunt face had the kind of pallor usually only found on things that live at the bottom of the sea. Coffin Jobe was cursed with an unusual affliction. Like narcoleptics, who have a tendency to fall suddenly asleep and then wake up again, Coffin Jobe is a necropleptic. He has the tendency to suddenly fall down dead, and then get over it. A serial resurrector, as it were. He's been dying and coming back to life again on a regular basis for some years now, and no one knows why – least of all him. (Though there are those who say he's doing it in order to get used to being dead, so he can develop an immunity.) However, as a direct result of his many assignations with the Other Side, Coffin Jobe can See the world with more than usual clarity. This has made him very useful on many a criminal endeavour, as there's no one better at spotting hidden traps and unexpected dangers.

He's also as crazy as a sewer rat on amphetamines, but you have to expect that. People make allowances.

I've always suspected that Coffin Jobe can See the torc around my throat, and therefore knows I'm really a Drood; but he's never said anything. He'd never betray a friend and a confidant. Not unless there was really serious money involved.

The Dancing Fool, on the other hand, would sell his own granny for the promise of a bent penny. He was the fastest fighter in the world, and made sure that everyone knew it. He could move so fast you didn't even know you'd been hit until the ground jumped up to slap you in the face. All the best martial arts are based on dances; he claimed his was based on an old Scottish sword dance. He practised the deadly martial art of knowing exactly what an opponent is going to do before they do it. He called it déjà fu. He liked to style himself as an international assassin, but really he was just hired muscle. He was talented enough, but not all that bright, and was cursed with a terrible temper. When the red mist descended, he was a danger to anyone around him, including his own allies. A broad, bluff Scottish type, he wore clan colours I knew for a fact he wasn't entitled to, and affected a lilting Highlands accent.

He also had no sense of humour. You could tell that from his clothes.

And finally, there was Strange Chloe, a disturbing young lady with a permanent scowl and a stuck-out lower lip. A Goth, of course. In fact, a Goth's Goth. Dressed in black, complete with fishnet stockings and a black velvet bow holding back long jet-black hair, her stark white face was dominated with dark makeup and stylings she'd actually had tattooed in place. The eyelids in particular must really have hurt. Strange Chloe had a mad on for the entire world, so much so that when she really concentrated, the world actually crumbled under the force of her gaze. She could make walls fall down, rivers evaporate, and people crumble into dust; and she did. Fortunately, she lacked the energy to get into any real trouble, and hadn't the ambition necessary to make herself a major player.

For which the rest of us were very grateful. She did just enough to get by, and spent most of her time sulking in bed.

I couldn't help feeling that the quality of her life would improve greatly if she got her ashes hauled on a regular basis. But it would be a brave man who tried.

So: a man who could See traps, a thug for hire and a woman who could make things go away just by looking at them. Not a bad crew.

Strange Chloe fixed me with a thoughtful glower. 'What are you doing here, Shaman?'

'Shaman knows secrets about the Tower of London, Chloe,' Big Aus said smoothly.

'Such as?' said the Dancing Fool. He did his best to sound tough, but if he was really tough he'd never have put up with his nickname.

'I know more than most people,' I said easily. 'Including a whole bunch of stuff that no one but the Tower staff are supposed to know.'

'How?' said Coffin Jobe, trying hard to sound like he cared. He doesn't really have any social skills any more, but he does try.

'Because I'm Shaman Bond,' I said. 'I know things. So, what is this caper about, O my brothers? Are we after the Crown Jewels?'

'Hardly,' said Big Aus. 'It would take more than our combined talents to get anywhere near them. Only one man ever got his hands on the Crown Jewels, and that was one Colonel Blood, back in 1671. The guards caught up with him before he even made it to the main gate. Word is he died slowly and very nastily for his pains. No. We're after something just as important, but not nearly as well defended.'

'Should we be talking about this openly, in public?' murmured Coffin Jobe, staring sadly around him through his oversized lenses.

'Relax,' said Big Aus. 'No one who matters would be seen dead in a dump like this. And listen to the racket! With so many people coming and going, ordering meals and chatting together, and that bloody awful piped Riverdance music, we could discuss kidnapping the Queen and selling her organs on ebay and no one would hear us. The safest place to conspire has always been in public places. It's the secret meetings in out-of-the-way places that always attract the authorities' attention.'

'What are we after?' I said.

Strange Chloe grinned suddenly. It didn't suit her. 'The ravens, Shaman. We're going to murderise the Tower ravens.'

I frowned, looking back and forth to make sure they were serious. 'Are we talking about the old legend, that if the ravens ever leave the Tower of London England will suffer a great disaster?'

'Got it in one!' Big Aus said cheerfully. 'But it's more than a legend, sport. I've done the research. The threat is taken so seriously that ravens in and around the Tower have to have their wing feathers clipped to make sure they can't fly away.'

'How very practical, and indeed British,' murmured Coffin Jobe. 'Does anyone else feel that draught?'

'We're going to use our various abilities to get us close to the Tower, take care of the guards and then kill the ravens,' said Big Aus.

'Aye!' said the Dancing Fool. 'A powerful blow against the treacherous English!'

'Pardon me if I'm being a bit slow here,' I said. 'But where's the profit in this? The hard cash, the old champagne coupons? Kidnapping the ravens for ransom, yes, I can see that; but ... killing them?'

'I'm providing the backing for this little venture,' Big Aus said sharply. 'Myself and a small consortium of like-minded Australian patriots. We're going to strike a blow against England in general and the Monarchy in particular. Humiliate Parliament and the bloody Queen, all at the same time! That's worth ten times what we're fronting, in the name of the republican cause.'

Strange Chloe sniffed airily. 'It's something to do. Could be fun. Will I get to kill lots of people?'

'Almost certainly,' Big Aus assured her. He reached out to pat her hand, and then reconsidered and pulled his hand back again.

'Burgle the Bloody Tower, and make the English establishment look like idiots,' said the Dancing Fool. 'A plan with no drawbacks.'

'I like it when lots of people die suddenly,' Coffin Jobe said wistfully. 'I don't feel so alone then.'

The Dancing Fool glared at him. 'Why don't you go and haunt a house somewhere?'

'Because I frighten the ghosts,' said Coffin Jobe.

He might have been joking, or he might not. It's hard to tell, with Coffin Jobe.

As it happened, I knew for a fact there was no truth to the legend about the ravens. If there was, the Droods would have their own guard on them. My family has a long history of knowing what's really dangerous, and what isn't. The whole raven thing is just a story made up to give the tourists a bit of a thrill. But this little caper still needed stopping. Big Aus was right about one thing; if the ravens were killed, those popular symbols of Queen and Country, right in the heart of London, it would make everyone look bad. Very definitely including the Droods, for letting it happen on our watch. Might give other people the idea we didn't have our eye on the ball; and we can't have that.

Still, the situation was ... complicated. Big Aus I didn't know from Adam, except he was slightly better dressed. The other three, however, while not exactly friends, were still people Shaman Bond knew. We had history together, some good, some bad. I couldn't warn them off, without raising everyone's suspicions; as far as they were concerned, this was easy money. So on top of putting a stop to the scheme, and taking down Big Aus, I also had to find a way of doing it that wouldn't involve seriously hurting my associates, or revealing I was really a Drood.

Great. Wonderful. Terrific.

And I wasn't entirely convinced by Big Aus. The more time I spent with him, the more convinced I became that the man was playing a role. He might well be the bluff Australian republican he claimed to be, but I couldn't help feeling there was more to the man than that. And much more to this caper than killing ravens. So I'd let things run as long as possible, to see what would happen ... and then rely on my skills and abilities to slam the brakes down hard the moment things looked like getting out of hand.

I was authorised to kill Big Aus, if necessary. And the others. I try very hard not to kill, on any of my missions. I'm an agent, not an assassin. But sometimes it's the job.

Big Aus leaned forward across the table, and looked at each of us steadily in turn. 'Does anyone have any problems they'd like to discuss? If so, speak up now, or forever hold your peace. Because once you're in, you're in all the way.'

'I find I don't care much about anything but hard cash since I started dying on a regular basis,' Coffin Jobe said sadly. 'At least with enough money I can be miserable in comfort.'

'The Hell with bloody England!' said the Dancing Fool. 'Let it all fall down!'

'And I don't give a toss,' said Strange Chloe. 'Go for it.'

And then they all looked at me. I smiled. 'You know I only ever ask one question: how much does the job pay?'

Big Aus told me, and I didn't have to fake my interest. He was offering serious money, far more than the caper warranted. Which probably meant he didn't expect us to be around afterwards to collect our pay. Which was ... interesting. I gave him my best smile.

'I'm in. The game is on. Shall we order now?'

'You must be joking,' said Big Aus. 'I wouldn't even use the toilet in a place like this.'

He had a point.

The Big Plan, as outlined by Big Aus, turned out to be refreshingly simple and straightforward. My job was to provide information about the hidden and deadly protections set in place outside and inside the Tower, and then Coffin Jobe would use his more than mortal gaze to walk us past and through them. He said he could actually See the shut-down Words implicit in any magical protections, and I hoped he was right. The Dancing Fool would use his déjà fu to deal with any human guards we ran into and Strange Chloe would look harshly upon the ravens. And then we would leg it for the nearest horizon. Big Aus, it seemed, was just along for the ride.

'I'm paying for this,' he said flatly. 'And part of what I'm paying for is a ringside seat.'

I sat back in my chair, apparently lost in thought, and surreptitiously studied the others as they told each other how easy it was going to be, and how much fun, and the great reputations they'd make for themselves. The usual stuff. Sometimes I swear they're just a bunch of big kids. I took the time to review the information about the Tower of London that the family had supplied me with earlier. The Drood researchers know all there is to know about ... pretty much anything, really. And enough to fake it about everything else. That's their job. By the time Big Aus had calmed the others down and turned back to me, I was ready to sound like an expert and blind them with details.

'The best time to approach the Tower will be in the early hours of the morning,' I said confidently, 'when the human guards are at their lowest spirits and there are no tourists to get in the way. Nothing like innocent bystanders to screw up the most well-laid of plans.'

'Right,' growled the Dancing Fool. 'The less uncontrollable factors, the better. Go on, Shaman.'

'Thank you,' I said dryly. 'First off, you should know there isn't just one Tower of London. There's a whole bunch of them. Over a dozen, in fact, set together inside a high stone wall, like a veritable castle. And we are talking seriously thick stone walls, baptised with human blood by their builders to give them strength, and with executed criminals buried down in the foundations so the dead will hold them up for ever. Builders took pride in their work, in those days.

'The original Tower of London was the White Tower, built on the orders of William the Conqueror back in the eleventh century. The one most people think of when they say "Tower of London" is actually the Bloody Tower, dating from Tudor times. That's where traitors to the realm were kept before execution. But there's also Flint Tower, St Thomas's Tower (which contains the Traitors' Gate entrance), and Whitechapel Tower, which holds the Crown Jewels. Each of these towers stand host to secrets and treasures undreamt of by the everyday public; and they are very heavily defended.'

'You're just showing off now,' said the Dancing Fool. 'Stick with what matters, Shaman.'

'My feet are cold,' Coffin Jobe said wistfully.

'You want research, you get research,' I said. 'The ravens have their own lodging house, inside the castle complex, for shelter during particularly inclement weather. Which means if we want to be sure of getting them all, we're going to have to get inside the castle. Which will mean getting past the human guards, the Yeomen Warders. Never call them "Beefeaters", by the way; apparently that started out as an old French insult, and the Warders are still very sensitive about it.'

'Well, Hell,' said Strange Chloe. 'We wouldn't want to upset them.'

'No, we wouldn't,' I said sternly. 'Our best bet lies in sneaking in and out, without anyone knowing we were there until it's too late. The Yeomen Warders are all military men, including ex-SAS and combat sorcerers. They don't choose just anybody to guard England's treasures. And then there are the magical protections, the proximity mines and the shaped curses. Are you still with us, Jobe, or are you dead?'

'Resting my eyes,' said Coffin Jobe. 'I hope someone is writing this down. I'll never remember it all.'

'Nothing on paper!' Big Aus said quickly. 'Carry on, Shaman. You're doing fine.'

'It's the ghosts we have to worry about,' I said. That got their attention. 'These aren't the usual memories recorded in time, played back to haunt the present. I'm talking about actual spirits, lost souls, damned and bound to this world by terrible magics. All the executed traitors, condemned to defend the Towers of London for eternity, for their crimes. To serve and protect England as they failed to do in life, until Judgement Day itself, if need be. Some of these ghosts have been around a really long time, and they have grown strange and awful. Nothing like centuries of accumulated guilt and grievance to make you ready to take it out on someone else.'

'I can See ghosts,' Coffin Jobe offered quietly. 'But that's all.'

'And I can only fight what I can touch,' said the Dancing Fool, scowling. 'No one said anything about ghosts.'

'And I can only affect the world of the living,' said Strange Chloe. 'That's it. Game over. The caper is off.'

'Wait, wait,' said Big Aus, flapping his hands about. 'Shaman, tell me you have a suggestion.'

'Of course,' I said. 'That's what you're paying me for.' I had to be careful here. I was skirting territory and information that Shaman Bond shouldn't really have access to. 'Traitors weren't executed in the Bloody Tower; they were killed on Tower Hill, well outside the castle complex. Executions were public matters in those days; public entertainments. The source of power, to control the ghosts, will be buried deep inside the hill. Probably something very old, and very nasty. Nothing we're equipped to deal with ... So, if you want to avoid being detected by the ghosts, the best way is ... not to be there.' I grinned at their confused faces. 'I'm pretty sure I can get my hands on a certain very useful item that will hide us from the ghosts' view. For a while, anyway. Long enough for us to sneak in, do the dreadful deed and then get the Hell out of there.'

Of course, I didn't actually need such a device. My torc made me invisible to anyone or anything I wanted to be invisible to, and I was pretty sure I could extend that protection over the others, for a while. Or until I found it necessary to drop it.

'How long will it take you to acquire this device?' said Big Aus.

'I can have it by this evening.'

'This is going to cost extra,' said Big Aus. 'How much, Shaman?'

I told him, and he winced. It had to be big enough, to make sure he'd take the device seriously.

'All right,' he said. 'But if it doesn't work, I'll take it out of your hide!'

'If it doesn't work, we'll all be dead,' I said.

'We'll hit the ravens tomorrow,' Big Aus said forcefully, rubbing his hands together. 'We go in early, like Shaman said. Five a.m. Straight in, do the necessary, and straight out. No messing. And don't be late getting there, any of you, or we'll start without you.'

And just like that, we were committed to the crime of the century.

I got there first, of course. To check out the lie of the land, and make sure no one else was planning any surprises. You can't be too careful, in this game. So I was there on the open causeway by Traitors' Gate at three a.m., two good hours in advance. I stood alone on the great grey flagstones, hidden behind my torc's glamour, invisible to all. Hopefully including the ghosts. You can never tell with the dead; they follow their own rules. I hunched my shoulders inside my long duster coat, and folded my arms tightly to keep out the cold wind blowing steadily off the River Thames.

It was only a short walk from Tower Hill tube station, through mostly empty streets. No one about but the usual revellers, old gods and self-made monsters on their way to the next party. Things flapping high up in the sky, and voices declaiming long-forgotten languages in ancient tunnels deep under the earth. The usual. I looked the towers over carefully with my Sight, and the whole place blazed with dazzling arcane energies. Layer upon layer of old magics and deadly protections, proximity mines floating unseen in mid air, just waiting to hit you with all kinds of nasty medicine if you were dumb enough to approach with bad thoughts in mind. The shaped curses under the flagstones were harder to spot, lying in wait like trapdoor spiders. The huge old walls containing the towers were solid in more than three dimensions, and the towers themselves were half buried under spells, like so much crawling ivy. There were bright lights and terrible sounds, and the whole place stank of blood and horror and despair.

That was the ghosts, of course. I couldn't See them without dropping more of my defences than I was comfortable with, but I could feel them the way fish know when there's a shark in the water.

I turned my back on the castle complex, and stood looking out over the Thames. Old river, dark river, with its own sad secrets. Boats came and went, not meant for everyday eyes. Undines ploughed through choppy waters, darting in and out of dim memories of all the vessels that had travelled up and down the mighty Thames in their day. Everything from Roman triremes to a flower-bedecked barge bearing a young Queen Elizabeth I. She looked over at the Bloody Tower, where she'd spent so much of her youth, and I swear for a moment she looked right at me. I bowed to her anyway, just in case, and when I looked up she was smiling at me. A young woman with all her life ahead of her. Dust and less than dust, for centuries now. And then she looked away, and was lost in the Past again.

There were mists on the water, and lights in buildings like beacons against the dark, and always the sound of distant traffic. I could see Tower Bridge, that so many tourists confuse with London Bridge, and the lights of planes flying low above the city. It was three o'clock in the morning, the hour that tries men's souls, and I still had two hours to kill. I stamped my feet to drive out the cold, and did *The Times*' crossword in my head. Cheating a bit when necessary.

I watched the sun come up over the city, long strands of crimson bleeding across the dull grey lowering sky. I thought about the ravens. They might not be as important as Big Aus thought, but I couldn't let anything happen to them. So how far should I let this caper go, before I interfered? Pretty far. No way was this just about ravens. Big Aus was planning something more, had to be. Raving republican or not, no one fronts this kind of money to kill a few birds and embarrass England and the Monarchy.

So what was Big Aus up to? There were all kinds of treasures, objects of power and dangerous secrets tucked safely away in the

27

towers; but they were very well guarded. Including the Crown Jewels. No one steals what is England's. Least of all poor old Colonel Blood, who took a long hard time dying, only to find that death was no release. His spirit was still here, damned to guard the very treasure he tried to steal. Never a good idea to piss off English royalty. They have a nasty sense of humour.

I stuck my hands deep into my coat pockets, and let my fingers close over the useful devices the family Armourer had rushed to me for this operation. I'm a great believer in having a few aces hidden away in useful places. The best defence against other people's surprises is to have some of your own ready to go at a moment's notice.

As five o'clock drew nearer, one by one the others appeared out of the early morning mists to join me as I lowered my torc's invisibility. Coffin Jobe, peering about him with his sad, preoccupied eyes. The Dancing Fool, big and scowling. Strange Chloe, glaring about her as though the morning cold and gloom was a personal insult. And Big Aus, wearing a very expensive overcoat, and grinning broadly.

'It's cold and damp and dark and bloody cold,' said Strange Chloe, glaring at me like it was my fault. 'I hate being up this early. It's not natural.'

'Savour your anger, Chloe,' said Big Aus briskly. 'Nurse it in your heart, and hold it ready for when it's needed. I want to see feathers flying in every direction. Are we ready to go?'

'Why did we have to be here so early?' said the Dancing Fool, his hairy legs shaking visibly beneath his kilt. 'Tourists won't be around for hours yet.'

'Because it's so much more dramatic!' said Big Aus, still grinning. 'If you're going to commit the crime of the century, you have to do it with style! History expects it of us! Great affairs must be conducted in a great manner. Some day this could be a major motion picture . . . Besides: ghosts are always at their weakest around the dawn, when the night is busy becoming day. Everyone knows that.'

'I didn't,' said the Dancing Fool. He looked at me. 'Did you, Shaman?'

'Of course,' I said. 'But then, I know everything. Unfortunately—'

'I knew he was going to say that,' Coffin Jobe said quietly. 'Didn't you all know he was going to say that?'

'Unfortunately, this is the Tower of London,' I said. 'And these are not your everyday ghosts.' I looked at Big Aus. 'Great affairs? Hollywood? Crime of the century? What's so great about killing a few birds?'

Before anybody could say anything, Coffin Jobe dropped down dead. No warning. His eyes rolled up in his head, he stopped breathing and he collapsed, his long body folding up with practised ease so that he hardly made a sound when he hit the flagstones.

'You prick!' said Strange Chloe.

'He does pick his moments,' the Dancing Fool agreed.

We gathered round the dead body, and looked at each other. The first aid manual doesn't cover situations like this. I did wonder whether we should try slapping his cheeks, or calling his name, or pounding on his chest with a fist, but you only had to look at Coffin Jobe to know he was dead, and beyond all such encouragements. I've buried people who looked less dead than he did. And then Coffin Jobe sucked in a harsh rattling breath, his long arms and legs twitched spasmodically, and his eyes snapped open. He sat up cautiously, shook his head a few times a bit gingerly, as though he half expected something to rattle, and then he rose to his feet, avoiding offers of help.

'Wow,' he said, smiling gently. 'What a rush!'

'You get off on being dead!' said Strange Chloe. 'Oh please, Jobe, teach me how to do it!'

'It isn't the dying,' he said. 'It's the coming back to life. Oh, yes!' He realised we were watching him, and smiled a little shame-facedly. 'Ah. Sorry about that. So embarrassing.'

'Are you going to do it again?' said Big Aus.

'Almost certainly.'

'I meant during the job!'

'Oh, no. I shouldn't think so. I think it's based on stress ... Are we ready to start now? I am.'

'Damn right,' said the Dancing Fool, scowling unhappily about him. 'I feel naked, standing out here in public. I prefer to work from the shadows. I am one with the shadows, and the dark.'

'Never knew an assassin who wasn't,' I said. 'Relax, everyone. You've been covered by my newly acquired device since you got here. No one can see us any more: not the living, the dead, or the towers' defences. We should be able to walk right through them.'

'"Should"?' said Strange Chloe. 'I really don't think I am comfortable with that word, under the circumstances. I want to hear you being a lot more confident about this before I take one step closer to Traitors' Gate.'

'We learn by doing,' I said cheerfully.

'And if you're wrong about this?' said the Dancing Fool.

'Then you get to say, "I told you so" in the few seconds before we are killed suddenly and horribly in violent ways.'

'I've never liked your sense of humour, Shaman,' said Coffin Jobe.

'You wound me,' I said. 'Come along, children. Destiny awaits. Maybe they'll get Johnny Depp to play me. The ravens are inside, tucked up snugly in their lodging house. The Yeomen Wardens are on their rounds, and at this point are as far from the lodging house as they ever get. Jobe, front and centre. You're on. Can you See the ghosts?'

He looked mournfully at Traitors' Gate, his eyes very big behind the heavy lenses. His gaze moved slowly along the great stone wall rising up before us, he started to say something, and then he suddenly fell down dead again. The Dancing Fool swore loudly, Big Aus made a frustrated sound, and Strange Chloe kicked Coffin Jobe in the ribs.

'I don't believe it!' she said. 'He's done it again!'

'Stop kicking the dead man, Chloe,' said Big Aus. 'Major bad karma. It isn't his fault, after all.'

We gathered around Coffin Jobe's body again, and waited and waited, but he didn't come back. We finally did kneel down beside him, and tried slapping his cheeks and calling his name, but there was no response. The colour had dropped out of his face, and his open eyes were fixed and staring. Finally everyone looked at me, because I'm supposed to be the one with the answers. So, very reluctantly, I pushed my Sight all the way open; and Saw ghosts.

They were everywhere, hundreds of them, men and women and even children, walking on the ground and in the air, stumbling and gliding out of Traitors' Gate, most still carrying the memories of their death wounds on their insubstantial bodies. Some had heads, some didn't. The horrible trauma of their violent deaths had carried over into how they thought of their bodies. Some were still bleeding from wounds that would never heal, while others bore the torture marks of rack and wheel and fire. Traitors all, condemned to suffer long after their deaths.

They were screaming and howling and crying out, ghostly voices from far away, thick with rage and despair and horror at what had been done to them. And some wept, never to be comforted, troubled for ever by their crimes and betrayals. They burst out of the high stone wall like maggots from a wound, and crawled headfirst down the cracked grey stone like shimmering lizards.

Half a dozen of them had grabbed hold of Coffin Jobe's soul, and were preventing it from returning to his body. Jobe looked quite different in spirit; a large, even muscular form. The man he remembered being, before his affliction ate away at him. He fought the ghosts fiercely, his soul blazing brightly on the night, stronger than it had any right to be; but still he was no match for the ghostly defenders of the Towers of London. They seemed more like beasts than men, tearing at his soul with hands like claws. And more ghosts were coming. Coffin Jobe looked right at me, and cried out for help; and then the ghosts Saw me too.

A great astral shout went up as the ghosts looked in my direction, and Saw me Seeing them. The closest ones surged right for me, mouthing ancient curses, though their voices seemed to echo from miles or years away. Their eyes burned with more than human hatred and misery, their horrid forms radiating menace. I stood my ground, and reached into my coat pocket for the weapon the Armourer had provided, for just such a situation. I took the jade amulet out and showed it to the ghosts, and another great shout went up. They knew what it was.

I said the activating Word in a loud carrying voice, and the mellow bomb detonated in my hand. And for fifty feet straight ahead of me, the world was full of happy thoughts, good intentions and positive emotions. Enforced mellowness, saturating the night. I was immune, of course, but it hit the ghosts like a hurricane, driving them back. They couldn't stand the happiness. They fled, shrieking horribly. Some were crying. Even the ones holding on to Coffin Jobe fled back to the safety of the towers, and he looked at me, smiled briefly, and then dropped back into his body. I shut down my Sight, slamming my mental barriers back into place. I'd Seen enough for one night.

I bent down over Coffin Jobe as he started breathing again, and surreptitiously hit him with a nerve pinch. He'd sleep for a good hour or more now. I smiled inwardly. One down, more or less unhurt. Three to go. I shut down the mellow bomb, and slipped it back into my coat pocket.

'Well at least he's breathing again,' said the Dancing Fool a bit dubiously. 'I suppose that's an improvement.'

'What, rather than not being even a little bit alive?' said Strange Chloe. 'Yes, I'd say so. But he's no use to us like that. Maybe I should—'

'No you shouldn't,' Big Aus said quickly. 'Kicking the Hell out of him does not help.'

'It helps me.'

'I didn't hear that,' Big Aus said determinedly.

'I said, "It helps me!"'

'Can we hold back on the whole shouting thing?' I said. 'My device is keeping us unseen and unheard, but only as long as you don't push it. There's no need to panic; just leave him here. I can See well enough to get us inside.'

The Dancing Fool looked at me suspiciously. 'And you never mentioned this before, because?'

'Because we had Coffin Jobe,' I said. 'And you know I don't like to reveal my secrets unless I have to.'

Big Aus looked down at the unconscious Coffin Jobe. 'I'm not sure I like the idea of leaving him here . . .'

'We can pick him up on the way out,' I said. 'And besides, what's the worse that could happen to him? Someone might kill him? I think he's pretty used to that by now. So: are we going in, or not?'

'We go in,' said Big Aus. 'No way are we giving up, not when we're so close. Show us the way, Shaman.'

I led them towards Traitors' Gate, indicating which flagstones they should avoid treading on. We had to approach the gate by a slow, indirect route to avoid the protective magics floating unseen in the air. I made the others hop on one foot, crouch down and rise up, and even walk backwards. Mostly for my own amusement, but occasionally because there were real traps to be avoided. Coffin Jobe would never have been able to get them in. There were wards present that would have fried his mind just for looking at them, and places where only knowledge of the right passWords kept us alive. But eventually we came to Traitors' Gate, and I led the way through the great stone maw that was the only entrance into the castle complex. A gateway into horror, death and worse than death for all too many people. I kept my Sight strictly focused, so I wouldn't have to See things I didn't want to, but even so my skin crawled the whole time. It's not easy walking through a place you know can kill you horribly, in a hundred ways, if you let your concentration drop.

I could still feel the screams, even if I couldn't hear them.

Once through the gate and into the enclosed cobbled courtyard, it was calm and quiet. The ghosts were outside, the Yeomen Warder patrols couldn't see or hear us, and all that stood between us and the ravens was the locked door of their lodging house. I froze as I heard approaching footsteps, and gestured urgently for the others to stand still, and silent. Half a dozen Yeomen Warders came walking out of the shadows, chatting quietly. I cursed them silently. Dealing with the ghosts had taken longer than I'd thought, and the patrol had come round again. The bright red and gold uniforms looked quaintly old-fashioned, but the men inside them were hard and competent and experienced. One of them had a raven perched on his shoulder, and was feeding it grapes that looked very much like eyeballs.

'That's a raven?' Strange Chloe said quietly. 'That's it? I was expecting something a bit more special, not an oversized crow!'

'Don't show your ignorance,' I said firmly. 'Ravens are the Rolls Royce of the crow family.'

'Are you sure they can't see or hear us?' said the Dancing Fool, shifting uncertainly from foot to foot.

'Are they rushing towards us, yelling terrible oaths and shooting at us with great big shooty things?' I said. 'Then no, they can't see or hear us.'

'Let the Yeomen open the lodging house for us,' said Big Aus. 'And then we kill them.'

'Ravens, or Yeomen Warders?' said the Dancing Fool.

'The ravens,' I said quickly. 'Spill human blood in this place, and you'll set off every alarm they've got.'

'No,' Big Aus said flatly. 'Kill them all, ravens and men, and anyone else who gets in our way.'

I decided this had gone far enough. I would have liked more time to take care of my friends before I had to take down Big Aus, but the secret of a field agent is to be flexible. So I pulled my concealing glamour back into my torc, and let the others suddenly appear in the courtyard. The Yeomen Warders reacted immediately, producing big guns out of nowhere and yelling for us to surrender. The Dancing Fool howled an ancient Scottish battle cry and charged the guards, moving so quickly I could barely follow him. He was in and among them in a moment, somehow never where their guns were pointing. With déjà fu, he could actually dodge bullets. I'd seen him do it.

The Yeomen Warders couldn't lay a hand on the Dancing Fool, for all their skill. He knew what they were going to do almost before the thought had entered their heads, and he moved like the trained dancer he was: every move calculated and graceful, fast and brutal. But the sounds of combat brought more Yeomen Warders running into the courtyard, charging forward to join the fray.

The Dancing Fool was one of the best fighters I'd ever seen, but in the end he never stood a chance. Out-numbered and surrounded, the only futures left for him to see were the ones where the Yeomen Warders inevitably beat the shit out of him. He went down still fighting, but he went down and did not rise again. Battered and bruised, the Yeomen Warders stood over his unconscious body, breathing hard.

Strange Chloe might have saved him. With her anger raised, her terrible scorching stare could have raked through the massed guards like a machine gun. But of course I couldn't allow that. So I moved in behind her while her whole attention was fixed on the fight, and then showed her the same nerve pinch I'd shown Coffin Jobe. Strange Chloe sighed once, her knees buckled, and I caught her and lowered her carefully to the cobbled ground. I didn't want her hurting herself. I straightened up, feeling rather pleased with myself. Three of my colleagues safely taken out of the game, with none of them realising it was down to me.

I could probably have taken the Dancing Fool down too, before he got to the Yeomen Warders; but I never liked him much.

It was only then that I looked around for Big Aus, and the smile froze on my lips as I discovered he was nowhere to be seen. I raced over to the ravens' lodging house, but the door was still firmly locked. The ravens were safe. But Big Aus wasn't there. Well, of course he wasn't there; he'd never really been interested in the ravens.

Everything he'd said, everything he'd done, had been a cover for something else.

His crime of the century.

I glared quickly about me, and caught a glimpse of a dark figure slipping silently into the stone passageway that led to Whitechapel Tower. Immediately I was off and running after him, knowing for sure now what it was he was after. And I'd made it possible, through my involvement. I got us in here, past the ghosts and the traps. I gave the Dancing Fool to the Yeomen Warders, thus holding their attention. But even so . . . I still couldn't believe Big Aus thought he could get away with this.

I subvocalised my activating Words, and the golden armour held inside my torc shot out to cover my whole body in a moment. To the Yeomen Warders I must have seemed to appear out of nowhere as I dropped the no-see-me glamour. A golden statue of a man, smooth and seamless, glowing in the half–light as I raced through the stone passageway faster than any normal man could have managed. When I wear the Drood armour I am supernaturally fast, and strong, and impervious to harm. The great secret weapon of the Drood family, whereby we are able to take on gods and monsters and beat the living crap out of them, until they remember their place.

More human guards appeared before me, crying out startled orders to halt and be recognised, but I was through and past them before they could even react. Combat sorcerers waved their arms and shouted harsh Words, but their magics shattered harmlessly against my golden armour. An automatic weapon opened fire from an upper window, but my armour absorbed the bullets, or let them pock-mark the old stone wall behind me. Half a dozen guards came together to block the entrance to Whitechapel Tower, determined to keep me out, and I didn't have the time to stop and reason with them. They didn't know the Australian fox was already in the henhouse. So I ploughed right through them, throwing them aside with my armour's more than human strength, hoping I didn't hurt them too badly.

They really should have known better than to try and stop a Drood about his duty.

I pounded up the stone steps two at a time to the great chamber at the top of Whitechapel Tower, but by the time I got there Big Aus had already entered the Jewel House, and was smiling happily at the Crown Jewels laid out behind the enclosing iron bars. He looked round as I lurched into the Jewel House, took in my golden armour, and laughed breathlessly. I stood very still, just inside the doorway, peering about me through the featureless golden mask that covered my face. (I could have put eyeholes in the mask, but I never did. I could see perfectly well through the mask, and besides, a featureless face mask spooks the Hell out of the bad guys. Mostly.) Big Aus gestured grandly for me to enter, and I did so, my golden feet thudding loudly on the bare stone floor. Big Aus backed away, putting the Crown Jewels between us. The crowns and the diadems, the diamonds and rubies, the glorious regalia of centuries past.

Enough wealth to make any man a king.

Big Aus grinned at me, his dark eyes full of mockery. 'So Shaman Bond is a Drood. Didn't see that one coming. But it doesn't matter. Not even a Drood field agent can stop me now. I chose my team so very carefully: greedy enough to go where even angels would be too sensible to tread, and dumb enough to swallow that nonsense about the ravens. After all, the Tower could always get more ravens ... I talked enough about my plans, in all the right places, that I knew one of my team would turn out to be a Drood in disguise. I was the one who sent your family the anonymous tip in the first place, to make sure you'd get involved. Didn't think it would be you, though, Shaman. No offence, but you never struck me as smart enough.'

I didn't say anything. Just kept moving around the great circular display, so he had to keep retreating before me.

'I needed a Drood, you see,' said Big Aus. 'I'd never get past the defences here without a Drood's help. I thought the Dancing Fool was the Drood. He was a fighter, and surely no one could really be that dumb and that arrogant ... Anyway, you played your part wonderfully. Got me past the defences, drew off the human guards, and bought me enough time to get to the Crown Jewels. I'm obliged to you. Really.'

'The jewels are defended,' I said. I couldn't stand the smugness in his voice any more. 'And while you might have got in, you'll never get out.'

'Of course I will,' said Big Aus. 'You can't stop me. I am prepared. Even for a Drood.'

And suddenly there in his hand was an aboriginal pointing bone. A small discoloured human bone, baptised in blood and murder magic. An aboriginal shaman who knew what he was doing could point it at things that shouldn't be in this world, and make them disappear. Big Aus stabbed the pointing bone at me, and something slammed against my armoured chest like a cannonball. The sound echoed through the Jewel House, as though someone had struck a great golden bell; but I didn't move. I felt no impact, inside my marvellous armour. I advanced slowly on Big Aus as he stabbed the bone at me again and again, and every time the impact and the sound was less.

Big Aus shrugged quickly, stuffed the pointing bone back into his pocket and gabbled something in a language I didn't understand. Which worried me a bit, because my torc was supposed to translate every language I heard, or at the very least supply best-guess subtitles. These words were so old, so ancient and separate, that they pre-dated the Druids who eventually became the Droods. Big Aus really had done his homework.

I was almost within arm's reach of him. I showed him a golden fist, with spikes rising up from the knuckles. He wasn't smiling any more, his voice strained by the uncivilised words, his broad red face shining with sweat. He back-pedalled so fast he was almost running, but he still stayed close the Crown Jewels, refusing to be driven away. And then he spat out the last few words, and a snake as big as all the world appeared out of nowhere and wrapped itself around me.

It was huge beyond bearing, its coils big as tube trains, super-imposed on the Jewel House but no less real for that, twisting slowly as the coils tightened around me. It wasn't a real snake, of course. This was the spirit of a snake, an ancient ur-spirit in snake form, called back out of the Dreaming by Words that should never have been spoken. I couldn't believe any aboriginal shaman would have willingly surrendered these Words to Big Aus. No matter what he was promised. Spirits like this should never be summoned back into our limited physical world; they always have their own agenda.

Big Aus was chanting more Words now, at the iron bars

surrounding the Crown Jewels. Protective spells sparked and sputtered and went out, and the metal bars dropped and ran away like melting candle-wax. I could See it all through the coils of the Snake, and I had had enough. It might be a ancient spirit made flesh, perhaps even an elder god let into the world from which it had been driven long ago; but it was still just a snake, and I was a Drood. Through the golden mask I could See its life-force, flowing through the massive coils like a river of burning light. I thrust my armoured hand deep into the unnatural snake-flesh, closed my golden fist around the life-force, and *squeezed*. The Snake screamed once, and then vanished, disappearing into the safety of the Dreamtime.

And I was left alone with Big Aus.

He looked at the Crown Jewels, defenceless before him, and then at me. 'You can't stop me,' he said defiantly. 'I've prepared too long for this. I have weapons and devices enough to stop even a Drood in his tracks, and a teleport spell already set up to take me and the jewels out of here.'

'You might have the weapons,' I said. 'But I know the right Words.'

And I spoke aloud the Words the family Armourer had sent me, written in his own hand on a one-time-only sheet of parchment. Words that disappeared even as I memorised them, because they were too dangerous to be read by anyone who wasn't family, and protected. Old Words, powerful Words. I'd really hoped I wouldn't have to use them, because they were a Summoning to forces best left undisturbed. And the first principle of magic is, do not call up what you cannot as easily put down.

But needs must, when the Devil drives. I spoke the Words, and one by one they came: the old kings and queens of England. Their spirits bound by their own will to answer the call, in this place, to serve England again in her time of need. Kings from Athelstan to Canute, Henrys and Richards, Queens Mary and Elizabeth and even poor Anne of the Thousand Days. They stood tall and proud in their crowns and regal robes, surrounding Big Aus. He looked from face to pitiless face, mumbling his useless words of power, and then they closed in on him, and he screamed. And just like that, I was alone in the Jewel Room.

The kings and queens of England had returned to their rest, with one new ghost condemned to defend the Towers of London for all eternity.

I went down the curving stone stairs, back through the stone passageways and across the open courtyard, and then out through Traitors' Gate. No one tried to stop me, or ask questions. If a Drood field agent was leaving, then the trouble was over and that was enough. Outside on the causeway, the sun was up and morning had come. It looked like being a good day, for England.

CHAPTER TWO
Summoned to judgement, summoned to tourney

So. Previously, in the Secret Histories . . .

My family used to be ruled over by a matriarch, my grandmother, Martha Drood. But I discovered that the family had become corrupt and divided under her rule, and that she was party to an old and terrible secret at the heart of the Droods' power. So I turned against my family, brought my grandmother down, destroyed the awful Heart from which our power came, and took over running the family myself. I replaced the alien Heart with an interdimensional traveller that preferred, for inscrutable reasons if its own, to be called Ethel, and I did my best to change the way the family did things, introducing democracy for the first time.

I organised free and fair elections to decide who should run the family; and they voted overwhelmingly for Martha Drood.

I did consider killing her, blowing up the family home, scattering the Droods to the four corners of the Earth and generally acting up cranky, but basically I couldn't be arsed. They'd made their choice, let them live with it. I had overthrown the Zero Tolerance faction within the family, destroyed the evil Manifest Destiny conspiracy outside the family, and saved Humanity from the invasion of the Hungry Gods. I just didn't have it in me to fight another war.

Besides, Martha did have the experience, and she had mellowed, and the Heart was gone, so . . . I let her get on with it. I went back to being nothing more than a field agent again, with no more crushing duties and responsibilities and decisions; which was, anyway, what I'd always wanted.

I was still part of the Matriarch's advisory Council, to which she was, technically, obliged to explain herself and if necessary answer to; the family insisted. Thanks a whole bunch, family. And if Grand-mother should go to the bad again, I could always kill her, burn the place down, scatter the family, etc.

The advisory Council consisted of myself, my uncle Jack the Armourer, my cousin Harry, and William the Librarian. But not my girlfriend, the wild witch of the woods, Molly Metcalf. Even though she had served with honour on the previous Council, during the Hungry Gods War. In the end the Droods wouldn't accept her in a position of authority over them, because she wasn't family. If she were to marry me, that would be different, of course. But Molly is a free spirit, and not the marrying kind. So she left The Hall and returned to her own private wood. I could have gone with her. I wanted to. But I had my duty, to my family and to the world, and through everything that's changed I still believe in the importance and necessity of what I do.

Molly understands. She'd never been happy in The Hall anyway.

I have my own room in The Hall, with a good view, and I also happen to possess a handy little item called the Merlin Glass, that allows me to jump straight to where I'm needed. It's also a direct doorway to Molly's wild woods. I spend as much time there as I can. Distance and family and duty are not enough to separate or divide us.

Molly and I love each other. In an ever-changing world, it's the one certainty I can rely on.

I was always happiest working alone, as a field agent, my only responsibility to the job and to the mission. All the time I was running the family, I couldn't wait to put it behind me and go back to my old job. Which only goes to show. Always be wary when the fates give you what you ask for. It means they're setting you up for something really bad . . .

So, anyway; after the Tower of London affair, the family called me back from London. *Come home*, they said. *You're needed. Most urgent, most secret, get your arse back here right now. But don't use the Merlin Glass.* 'Most urgent' and 'most secret' means the fat is already in the fire and melting fast, and not using the Glass meant . . . Someone was watching. I got my new car out of its garage, and set course for the south-west countryside of England. It was a pleasant enough run, down the motorway and then into the narrow roads and winding lanes that lead to a house you won't find on any map. The Hall has been home to the Droods for generations, and we take our privacy very seriously. Anyone who comes looking for us won't find us. Or if by some unfortunate chance they do, no one will ever see them again.

We might protect you from the monsters in the dark, but we don't like to be bothered. We're your bodyguards, not your mother.

My new car, a Rover 25, had been carefully chosen to be anonymous and everyday. It was bright red; in fact, it was so red it was *Red!* Every time I got into it I was reminded of the old adage about a car being an extension of a penis extension. I was tempted to paint the bonnet purple and sculpt some veins down the sides. Do I need to tell you I didn't choose this car?

Still, it came complete with extras, courtesy of my Uncle Jack. Armed, armoured and faster than a rat up a drainpipe, this particular Rover 25 could do 300 m.p.h. in reverse, fly at Mach two, and even, in an emergency, go sideways. The Armourer was very keen for me to try that out, but I didn't like the look in his eye when he said it. He's still mad at me for messing up his beloved racing Bentley. The Rover 25 had the usual hidden weaponry, protections and nasty surprises for the ungodly, plus an ejector seat that could blast an unwanted passenger straight into the next dimension but three.

The gateway to the massive grounds surrounding The Hall is only there if you're a Drood; to the rest of the world it's a very solid stone wall. I aimed the Rover 25 at the wall and put my foot down, and the car sailed through, the ancient stonework brushing briefly against my face like so many cobwebs; and then I was driving up the old familiar path that led through the long rolling grounds to The Hall . . . and everything that was waiting for me.

The sweeping green lawns stretched away in all directions for as far as the eye could follow, maintained by sprinkler systems that contained more than a touch of holy water, just in case. My family has a lot of enemies, but anyone who comes after us where we live deserves every nasty thing that happens to them. Robot machine guns rose smoothly up through the grass from their concealed bunkers, to track the Rover 25 as it passed, but I didn't take it personally. I was being considered and identified by a hundred invisible security systems. We Droods haven't survived as a force for good all these centuries by taking anything for granted.

Winged unicorns frolicked gracefully overhead in the clear blue sky, so pure a white they left shimmering trails behind them; while down below aristocratic swans drifted unconcerned across the smooth dark waters of the lake. There are undines in there too, but they mostly keep themselves to themselves. Two really ugly gryphons were humping enthusiastically up against a large Henry Moore statue, and getting muck and mess on it. I didn't give a toss. Never did like that statue: ugly great thing. And the roses were out again, blossoming red, white and blue.

The Hall stood tall and broad and firm on the horizon, heavy with the weight of history and obligation and sacred cause. A huge manor house in the old Tudor style, with four wings added on somewhat later, plus other things too. Strange lights burned in many of the windows, accompanied no doubt by the usual odd noises and the occasional rumble of an explosion. We're a lively family. I passed the old hedge maze, giving it plenty of room and a distrustful glance. It covers half an acre, and is fiendishly intricate in its layout, but we never use it. The maze was designed and built in Georgian times to hold and contain Something, but no one now remembers who or what or why. When your home contains as many marvels and wonders as ours, a few things are bound to fall through the cracks. Sometimes literally. Now and again we throw in someone we don't like very much, just to see what will happen. So far, not one of them has ever come out again.

A rocket-assisted autogyro blasted off from one of the landing pads on the roof, leaving a long contrail behind it, while someone in a jet-pack glided in for a landing. And no, in case you were wondering: no one in this family has used a broomstick for centuries. The Droods live very firmly in the present, not the past.

I slammed the Rover 25 to a halt in a shower of flying gravel and parked the car right outside the front door, just because I knew I wasn't supposed to. I stepped out of the Rover and looked the old place over. It hadn't changed in the six months I'd been away, but that was the point of the Drood family home; it never changed. Like the family, it maintained; sometimes in the face of everything the world could send against it. The car door locked itself behind me, and I heard the defences powering up. Good luck to anyone who tried to move it; my car had a few protections even the family didn't know about.

I like to keep my family on their toes; it keeps them from taking me for granted.

I headed for the front entrance, and the huge door immediately swung open before me, revealing the cold, grim face of the new Sarjeant-At-Arms. The old Sarjeant went out in a blaze of glory during the Hungry Gods War, and the new guy didn't have his brutal and despised predecessor's effortless air of menace and imminent violence. He tried hard, though. He was squat and broad and muscular, and in his immaculate formal butler's outfit, looked very much like a nightclub bouncer at a funeral. His face was dark and craggy, and had clearly never once been bothered by a smile. Not surprising, when you considered the importance of his duties. Not only was he the first line of defence against any attack on The Hall, he was also responsible for internal discipline within the family. A good Sarjeant-At-Arms may be respected, even feared, but never liked. It's probably part of the job description. Thou shalt not be popular. The Sarjeant maintains family discipline by enforcing every law with open brutality.

He does not spare the rod with the children.

The new Sarjeant-At-Arms' name, never used any more in public, was Cedric. There's something about certain names that pretty much ensures that particular child will be teased and bullied by his peers all through childhood. Sometimes I think the parents do it on purpose, to ensure their precious progeny will grow up tough and hard. With a name like Cedric, the guy was destined to be Sarjeant-At-Arms some day. That, or a serial killer.

He stood firmly in the doorway, deliberately blocking my way. He glowered at me, his arms folded tightly across his impressive chest. I considered him thoughtfully. While I was running the family I was exempt from family discipline, but now I was just a field agent again ... I was still exempt, as far as I was concerned. I've never got on with authority figures. Even when I was one. I'm a firm believer in rules and discipline within the family, as long as they don't apply to me. I was tempted to hit the Sarjeant with my one remaining mellow bomb. I quite liked the idea of seeing Cedric sitting naked on the lawns, hugging the gryphons and singing show tunes to them. But I had promised myself I'd be good, at least until I'd found out what was so important that I had to be summoned back so urgently.

And how deep I was in it.

'Hello, Cedric,' I said. 'Getting much?'

'Move the car,' he said. His voice was little more than a whisper, and all the more menacing for it. His cold, unwavering gaze would have reduced a lesser man to tears.

'You move it,' I said cheerfully. 'Really, I'd love to see you try. Anyone who tries to shift that motor against its will, dear Sarjeant, will almost certainly find bits of themselves raining down all over the lawns, covering a wide area.'

'Parking in front of The Hall is against the rules,' said the Sarjeant. He really did have a very impressive stare. Probably would have worked on anyone else.

'So am I,' I said. 'Now shift your incredible bulk out of my way, or I'll tell the Matriarch you were mean to me. I'm here to meet with her and the Council.'

'I know,' said the Sarjeant. 'And you're late.' He leaned forward slightly, his great form towering over me. 'I don't care who you are or what you've done; you mess with me and I'll make you permanently late. You'll be the late Edwin Drood.'

'See, there you had to go and spoil it,' I said. 'Never hammer a threat into the ground, Cedric.'

His expression didn't change, but he stepped aside to allow me to pass. I strode in with my nose in the air, back into The Hall that was my home, like it or not. Back into the cold embrace and dangerous entanglements of my beloved family.

I made my way unhurriedly through the long corridors and passageways, the great open chambers and galleries, surrounded on all sides by the acquired loot of ages. To the victor goes the spoils, and we have spoiled ourselves. The Hall is stuffed full of accumulated treasures, including masterpieces of art and famous statues by immortal names. Gifts from grateful governments, and others. Or perhaps tribute to the secret masters of the world. Presented equally prominently were suits of armour and weapons from centuries past, and not a few from the future, all with their own legends and histories, all of them bright and gleaming and ready for use at a moment's notice. There were fabulous carpets and rich hanging drapes, and long shafts of sunlight poured like slow time through tall stained-glass windows.

They were waiting for me in what used to be called the Sanctity, a great cavernous chamber that once contained the Heart, that gave the family its armour and its power. A single massive diamond as big as a bus, with a million gleaming facets, the Heart turned out to be an other-dimensional fugitive from justice that fed on pain and horror and death; until I destroyed it. These days the Sanctity is empty, and the family's armour and power derives from another extra-dimensional creature, with rather more friendly motives. She insists on being called Ethel; though God knows I've tried to talk her out of it. Ethel manifests in the Sanctity as a soothing shade of red, suffusing the whole chamber with its happy presence and the scent of roses.

The Council table was of ancient oak and set in the middle of the chamber. It would have looked small and even insignificant in such a setting, if not for the importance of the people sitting at it. I strolled across the chamber, head held high, maintaining an ostentatious serenity under the accusing weight of their stares. My footsteps echoed loudly in the quiet. I sat down in the single empty chair, and smiled easily around me.

'So. Who's got the cards?'

They didn't smile. Not all the Council were there: only the Matriarch and the Armourer. Martha Drood sat straight-backed in her chair, tall and elegant and more regal than any queen. She had been a famous beauty once, and you could still see the force of it in her strong bone structure. She wore country tweeds, twin set and pearls, and her long grey hair was piled on top of her head in the style of times past. My grandmother – though she'd never let that get in the way of doing whatever needed to be done. She'd tried to have me killed, but we'd got over that; mostly. She had to be in her early seventies now, but there wasn't an ounce of weakness in her.

She studied me with calm, calculating grey eyes, waiting for me to acknowledge her, so I deliberately nodded cheerfully to the Armourer.

A bald, middle-aged man with thick tufty white eyebrows and a permanent scowl, Uncle Jack looked sulky and put-upon, as he always did when called away from his beloved Armoury. Devilishly talented when it came to creating dangerous and devious devices, he couldn't be bothered with people skills any more. He used to be a field agent, and a great one in his day, but he rarely left the Armoury now.

'I prefer things to people,' he once told me. 'You can fix things when they go wrong.'

The long lab coat wrapped around his spindly frame had presumably been white once, but it was now disfigured with rips and tears, chemical stains and burns, and the occasional splash of someone else's blood. And what might have been mustard. Under the lab coat, the Armourer was wearing a grubby T-shirt, with the legend 'Weapons Of Mass Destruction R Us'. He had large, bony, engineer's hands, and kind eyes.

'Hi there, hi there, hi there!' said Ethel, her words seeming to burst out of everywhere at once. 'Welcome home, Eddie! Great to have you back; everyone else here is so stuffy! They don't know how to have fun, the great bunch of stiffs. The Hall is always so much more lively when you're around. How was London? How was the Tower? Did you bring me back a present?'

'I never know what to get you,' I said. 'You're so hard to buy for, but then I find that's true for most immaterial other-dimensional entities.' I ignored Ethel's giggles and looked at the Matriarch. 'Where's the rest of the Council? Are we waiting for them?'

'No,' said Martha, her voice calm and even and utterly devoid of any kind of warmth. 'For the time being, we are the Council. Your cousin Harry is out in the field, with his partner Roger Morningstar, infiltrating one of the more dubious Paris nightclubs in pursuit of the notorious Fantom. I can't believe that madman's on the loose again so soon after we put him away. If the French authorities can't build a prison strong enough to hold their most notorious and appalling criminal, I shall have the Armourer build them something special. And make them pay through the nose for it.'

'I thought we blew the Fantom up last year?' said the Armourer, frowning.

'We did,' said the Matriarch. 'It didn't take. Harry and Roger will be back when they can.'

'And William?' I said.

'The Librarian is hard at work, in the Old Library,' said the Armourer. 'Hardly ever leaves the place. Got a cot set up in there, and a chemical toilet, and has all his meals sent in.'

'Normally I wouldn't allow such behaviour,' said the Matriarch. 'But we need him.'

'It's not healthy,' the Armourer said firmly. 'I mean, I love my Armoury, but at the end of the day I lock the door behind me and go home.'

'William is doing good and necessary work,' the Matriarch said firmly. 'And that is all that matters.'

'To us,' said the Armourer. 'But what about him?'

'Hush, Jack.'

'Yes, Mother.'

I nodded glumly. 'I did hope he'd improve, after I got him out of that asylum for the criminally insane and brought him home, but the Heart really did a number on his head. Give him time, he'll bounce back. He's a tough old stick.'

'Of course,' said Martha. 'He's a Drood.'

'And we're never more dangerous than when we're crazy!' said the Armourer, waggling his bushy eyebrows.

'Jack!'

'Sorry, Mother.'

'So,' I said thoughtfully. 'Just the three of us. How cosy.'

'Four!' said the crimson glow reproachfully.

'Sorry, Ethel,' I said. 'Four. Now ... what is so important that I have to be dragged all the way back here, with absolutely no advance warning? And why did I have to drive down? Why couldn't I transport myself directly here through the Merlin Glass, like I normally do?'

'We can't risk word of this getting out,' the Matriarch said steadily. 'I've never entirely trusted the Merlin Glass. I mean, look who made it. You did bring it with you?'

'Of course,' I said. 'It's safely locked in the boot of my car.'

'Good,' said the Armourer. 'That means no one can listen in through it.'

'I see the family's paranoia is well and thriving,' I said. 'Look, either someone gives me a really good reason for my being here, or I am driving my nice little car straight back to the more civilised comforts of London. I am not in charge of the family any more, and only a member of the Council when I absolutely have to be; I am a field agent again, and I like it that way. I have just saved the Crown Jewels from being stolen, protected the whole of England from a terrible disaster, and I am owed some serious down time.'

Give the Matriarch credit, she didn't so much as blink an eye at my tirade, even though no one else in the family would have dared talk to her in such a way. 'Have you finished?' she said calmly.

'Get to the point or I'll set fire to your shoes,' I said.

She smiled thinly. 'So I'm only in charge of running this family when it suits you, Edwin? I don't think so. You accepted the result of the election. You stepped down, in my favour. You gave up overall duty and responsibility, in return for your ... independence. You agreed to accept my authority as Matriarch; or do you now intend to remove me by force? Again?'

'Depends,' I said darkly. 'Why am I here?'

'First, there is urgent Council business that must be discussed,' said the Matriarch a bit triumphantly, and I could have wept. She was going to do this her way, and all I could do was go along. Because she was in charge now, and because she really wouldn't have summoned me so urgently unless it was important. She didn't want me back, undermining her authority and setting a bad example, any more than I wanted to be here.

The Matriarch nodded to the Armourer, and he sat up straight in his chair and launched into a prepared speech. 'There are a great many questions left over from the Hungry Gods War,' he said, scowling more deeply than ever. 'We never did find out who the traitor and damned fool in the family was, who first summoned the Loathly Ones into our reality and opened a door for the Many-Angled Ones, the Hungry Gods. We're sure now it wasn't any accident. The traitor insisted on bringing the Loathly Ones through, to use as weapons during World War Two, when there were many other, and far safer, options. So why did he do it?'

'There is ... some evidence suggesting the traitor may still be alive, and a part of this family,' said the Matriarch. Her voice was very cold now. 'He would have to be over a hundred years old, and extending his life through unnatural means. It seems ... he has killed another member of the family, and taken over their identity.'

'How is that *possible?*' I said, actually shocked. 'When we're crammed together in this place, how the Hell could he do it without being noticed? One of the reasons I was so glad to get out of The Hall was because of how closely we all live on top of each other.'

'No clues, no hard evidence, not even any real theories,' the Armourer said grimly. 'Nothing definite, just ... whispers. But whoever he is, he's still making trouble. We're pretty sure he started the Zero Tolerance faction in the family, and founded and manipulated the Manifest Destiny group outside it. That faction still has its supporters in the family, muttering that we should be more proactive against our many enemies. Don't look at me like that, Eddie. I know better than to believe such nonsense; but it's what some people are saying.'

'Fools,' said the Matriarch. 'We protect Humanity by keeping its enemies off balance, playing one against another. We stick to the old ways because they work, and have done for centuries.'

'Still,' I said, thinking hard. 'A traitor, very old and very powerful, embedded deep inside the family. Like we don't have enough problems. Are there any family members left who were active during the thirties and forties? They might be able to help us.'

'Don't look at me,' said Martha. 'I was but a child, in those days. William is currently looking through family records in search of gaps or anomalies.'

'Droods don't tend to live long lives,' said the Armourer. 'We live hard, we carry heavy responsibilities, and we burn out early. Which is why I've been thinking about a new kind of device – a whole new way to call up the recently dead and ask them questions.'

'No, Armourer,' said the Matriarch, very firmly.

'All right, my last try was a bit of a disaster, but this one would work! I'm almost certain we could reach departed Droods from the thirties—'

'I said no, Jack!' The Matriarch glared at him until he lapsed into rebellious silence. 'It is against family policy to encourage ghosts, or we'd be hip deep in revenants by now. You know very well that even the most dearly departed cannot be trusted. The dead always have their own agenda.'

'There's always been a few manifestations in The Hall,' said the Armourer. 'Why don't we try them? I mean, Jacob may be gone, but there's still the headless nun in the Old Gallery . . .'

'Good luck getting her to answer questions,' I murmured.

'All right then, what about—'

'*The dead are out of bounds,*' the Matriarch said loudly. 'We will move on. We still don't know who killed Sebastian. Or rather, what was left of him after he'd been infected and possessed by a Loathly One. He died in one of our most secure holding cells, inside an isolation tank.' She gave the Armourer a hard look, and he fidgeted nervously in his seat. 'I was given to understand those tanks were impregnable.'

'They are!' said the Armourer. 'I designed them myself. Be fair, he didn't escape, did he? Whoever killed Sebastian walked right through our defences, past our surveillance systems, scientific and magical, without setting off one alarm; and apparently was able to murder Sebastian without entering the isolation tank. My people have gone over the whole damned area with every investigative tool we've got, including several I invented specially, and turned up nothing. Of course, if my best isn't good enough for you . . .'

'Don't sulk, Jack. It's unbecoming in a man of your age. And sit up straight; you're slouching again.'

'Yes, Mother.'

'Edwin . . .'

'Don't try pulling rank on me, Grandmother. I'll slouch if I want to.'

'I was about to say it always come back to there being a traitor in this family. Someone with access to our secrets.'

'Secrets,' I said. 'Could this traitor be the same traitor who gave up the secrets of The Hall's defences, so the Heart could be attacked? We never did find out who was behind that. And given what we now know about the sick and evil nature of the Heart, could those attacking forces have been good guys all along?'

'Ethel?' said the Matriarch.

'I keep telling you,' the disembodied voice said reproachfully,

'I really don't know. I know many things. Secrets of the universes. If you know what pyramids were really for, you'd spit and go blind. But the Heart made a lot of enemies before it came here. Destroyed whole worlds, whole civilisations, for its pleasure. I wasn't the only one trying to track it down, for justice and vengeance.'

'And your first contact with this dimension was through the Blue Fairy,' I said thoughtfully.

'Yes. He went fishing through the dimensions, and happened to catch on to a very small part of me.'

'He opens dimensional doors,' the Matriarch said slowly. 'And we brought him here, into The Hall, during the Hungry Gods War. On your recommendation, Edwin.'

'He betrayed my trust,' I said. 'But he couldn't be our traitor.'

'Why not?' said the Armourer. 'What do we really know about him? A half-elf, product of an elven father and a human mother. We have a pretty good idea of who the father was, but I don't think anyone ever identified the mother. Could she have been a Drood? It would help explain why the Blue Fairy was so desperate to steal a torc from us.'

'I once discovered the Blue Fairy lurking in the Old Library,' I said. 'Maybe he was looking for evidence of his family roots.'

'We need to talk with William,' said the Matriarch. 'Ethel, establish a communication link, please.'

'Oh sure! No problem! I love doing stuff like this. You know, the material laws of your dimension are really easy to mess with. Basically because they're not so much laws, as local agreements. I could—'

'No, you couldn't,' I said quickly. 'Contrary to anything you may hear us say, we actually do like things the way they are. Just give us a window to the Old Library, please.'

Ethel sniffed. 'You're so unadventurous. And you never did get round to explaining this sex thing you all do.'

'*Later*, Ethel. The window, please.'

The air shimmered before us, and a pair of heavy plush velvet purple curtains appeared. There was a loud trumpet fanfare from nowhere, followed by a roll of drums, and then the curtains opened dramatically to reveal a view into the Old Library. Hard to tell where, exactly; one tall stack of dusty old bookshelves looks much like another. The light was a dull golden glow, like a patina of age impressed upon the air itself. William appeared abruptly before us, thrusting his angry face at us like one of those three-dimensional images gone feral. With his heavily lined face, fierce eyes and lengthening grey hair and beard, William looked like an Old Testament Prophet, one of those who specialise in predicting really bad things happening any time soon.

'There is absolutely no need to ring an incredibly loud bell at this end when you want to talk to me! I am crazy, not deaf! You know I don't like loud noises. Or squirrels.'

'Report your progress, Librarian,' said the Matriarch, cutting across what promised to be a lengthy diatribe.

William scowled at her. 'Say "please".'

The Matriarch sighed. 'Edwin, would you like to be head of this family again?'

'Say "please" to him, and get it over with,' I said.

'Oh very well. Please,' said the Matriarch.

'Didn't sound like you meant it,' William said cunningly. 'Say "pretty please".'

'Pretty please!'

'Very good, Matriarch! Now try disestablishmentarianism in Krakatoa East of Java.'

'William . . .' I said.

He pouted. 'No one knows how to have fun in this family. All right: progress report.' He cleared his throat and blinked his eyes a bit vaguely. 'I'm still putting together a list of all the books missing from the Old Library. Some quite important volumes and documents are not where they should be. Mostly to do with our own family history—'

'That's it?' said the Armourer. 'That's all you've done? You've had months!'

'Don't shout! I'll have a mood swing. You know I'm still not properly myself yet.' The Librarian clasped his hands together tightly, perhaps so we wouldn't see how badly they were shaking. 'Being in the Old Library helps. I feel safe here. Secure.'

'We have prepared a very comfortable room for you in East Wing,' said the Matriarch. 'It's got a view. Not much of a view, perhaps, but still . . .'

'No! No!' William shook his head jerkily. 'I'm not ready to be with other people. Not yet. Had enough of that in the asylum. It's easier to be me when I'm not ... distracted. I like it here, among the books. I trust them. You know where you are with books.' He stopped and looked around him uncertainly for a moment. 'Though sometimes I see things out of the corners of my eyes. Might be real. Might not. I don't take chances any more ... Eddie, good to see you again! Always good to see you. Yes. Did you want something?'

'The books that have gone missing from the Old Library,' I said patiently. 'You said they concerned Drood family history.'

'One hundred and twenty-seven items, so far,' the Librarian said instantly. He was immediately more precise and focused, once he was on safe ground again. 'Books, folios, even original manuscripts. Some I can only identify from their titles, or from gaps left on the shelves. No idea about the actual contents. We really must assemble a proper index, as a matter of urgency. There are some gaps on the shelves I can't explain at all.

'My first thought was that the books might have been taken by the Zero Tolerance faction, to hand over to Truman's Manifest Destiny group, but I am told a thorough search of their abandoned bases has failed to turn up a single volume. So I've been working on the assumption that the traitor in our family is responsible. Perhaps he intended to sell them to our enemies, perhaps they contained clues to his true identity.

He stopped again, to look jerkily about him. 'This is the Old Library,' he said slowly. 'Long thought lost, and destroyed. Not the Library I used to run, before the Heart destroyed my mind ... No. This is an old place, older than you think. Older than anyone thinks. Listen to me, Martha. I may not be the man I once was, and I may have trouble with my memory, but I am not crazy. Even if I sometimes play it, just to watch that vein throb in your forehead. I can say I am not crazy with some confidence, because I have been crazy and I know what it feels like. This ... is different. There's something in here, with me. Hiding in the stacks, in the shadows, in the gaps ... Watching. Waiting. I don't know what it is, or how long it might have been here. Maybe it's always been here. Sometimes I think it's a good thing, sometimes not.

Maybe there was a good reason why the Old Library had to be lost ... And maybe, just maybe, when we reopened the Old Library, we woke it up again.

'I'm pretty sure there's something inside the Merlin Glass, too. You should be careful, Eddie. Check the reflection for things that shouldn't be there—'

He broke off as his young assistant, Rafe, appeared beside him in the window. Rafe had been made family Librarian in William's absence, but immediately stood aside on William's return. Rafe was the first to admit he wasn't in William's league. He patted William comfortingly on the shoulder. Rafe had a kind, almost clerical face, and a first-class mind when he concentrated.

'There you are,' he said chidingly to William. 'I take my eye off you for ten minutes ... You didn't take your medication again this morning, did you?'

'Turns my piss blue,' grumbled William. 'Never trust anything that turns your piss blue.'

Rafe looked out of the window at me. 'Is this anything I can help you with? The Librarian really isn't strong, you know. He should be having his rest period now.'

'I am not a child, Rafe,' said the Librarian. 'I do not need a rest period.'

'All right then,' Rafe said patiently. 'Why not come and have a nice sit down? I've just made a fresh pot of tea.'

'Are there Jaffa Cakes?' said the Librarian.

'Of course there are Jaffa Cakes. And a few chocolate chip cookies.'

'That's more like it!' said the Librarian cheerfully. 'Nothing like a good cup of tea to sharpen the wits and clean out the kidneys. I shall address my thoughts to the problem, Matriarch, and inform you when I have an answer.'

He marched away, not looking back. Rafe watched the Librarian go, and sighed quietly.

'He has his good days, and his bad days. He has a remarkable mind, when he's himself. The work he's done here has been exceptional. We're months ahead of where I thought we'd be. But, he's still—'

'Distracted,' said the Matriarch.

'Well, yes. Sometimes. But he is a lot better than he used to be. Really.'

'Of course, Rafe,' said the Armourer. 'We understand. Can you tell us anything about the missing books, or the identity of our possible traitor?'

'Nothing that William wouldn't already have said. I really thought we were on to something when we discovered the Zero Tolerance faction had had access to the Old Library, but Callan's been very definite that he hasn't found anything in the Manifest Destiny bases he's been through.'

'Keep looking,' said the Matriarch. 'And keep an eye on William.'

She gestured sharply, and Ethel closed the window. She didn't bother with the curtains or flourishes this time. Perhaps even Ethel could sense when the Matriarch really wasn't in the mood.

'How is Callan, these days?' I said carefully.

'Recovering,' said the Armourer. 'He's adapted well to his new torc, but we're keeping a watchful eye on him. No Drood has ever survived having his torc ripped off him before.'

'There's no denying he's been behaving oddly,' said the Matriarch. 'But then, Callan always did. He insisted on returning to the field the moment he was physically capable, and none of us had the heart to say no. But since then, he's been a driven man. Working every hour God sends – either to prove to us that he's still the man he used to be, or to prove it to himself.'

'The family has always asked a lot of us,' I said.

'Only when necessary,' the Matriarch said immediately. 'For the good of the family, and the world.'

'At least tell me Callan's not out there on his own,' I said.

'Of course not!' said the Matriarch. 'We partnered him with Subway Sue, another of our spiritually walking wounded. Each of them thinks they're there to look after the other, and so far it seems to be working. They're currently down in Tasmania, investigating a new outbreak of Devil worship.'

'He sent us a postcard,' said the Armourer. 'Quite a rude one, actually. I'll show it to you later, Eddie.'

'It is vital to the family that we recover the stolen torc,' the Matriarch said forcefully. 'We cannot allow our most powerful weapon to remain in the hands of an enemy.'

'The Blue Fairy said he was taking it to the Fae Court,' said the Armourer. 'And the only direct route to the world of the elves these days is in Shadows Fall.' The Armourer shuddered briefly. 'Don't know which of those places disturbs me the most.'

'Well somebody's going to have to go and get it,' said Ethel. 'I can't reach the torc myself, and it's not for want of trying. It's part of me and I want it back. But I can't reach into the elven realm; it's too *different*. And believe me, I know from different. The Fae Court would put my teeth on edge. If I had any.'

'Hold everything!' I said. 'If that's why you called me back, you can forget it. I am not going to the Fae Court. It's dangerous! Besides, they hate me!'

'They hate everybody,' said the Armourer, not unreasonably. 'They're elves.'

'Yeah, but I killed a whole bunch of elf lords and ladies on the M4, remember? I appear before Oberon and Titania, and they'll turn me into something. Probably something soft and squishy that squelches when it moves. You do remember that attempt on my life, Grandmother? You did arrange it, after all.'

'I have apologised,' said the Matriarch. 'I don't see what else I can do.'

'No,' I said. 'You wouldn't. Look, for this you need a diplomat. Someone they'll talk to. Or at the very least listen to.'

'Trust me,' said the Matriarch. 'I would never send you on any mission where diplomacy was necessary.'

'Even when you say something nice, it sounds like an insult,' I said. 'Come on, people, you've been round and round the bushes so many times you've worn a trench in the ground. Why am I here?'

The Matriarch and the Armourer glanced at each other. 'Forgive us for coming at this in such a roundabout way,' the Armourer said finally, 'but we thought it important you understood and appreciated the situation the family is in. Traitors within, enemies without, and far too many questions we can't answer. On top of that, we're stretched far too thin. We've had to send out too many new field agents, to replace those who died during the Hungry Gods War. Often without proper training, because there just wasn't time. Many of them are going to die, but we had to send them anyway because we have to re-establish our presence in the world. Remind everyone that the Droods are still a force to be reckoned with.'

'The family cannot afford to be perceived as weak, or divided,' the Matriarch said. 'For the moment, most of the world governments are still impressed, if not actually grateful, that we were able to save the world from the invading Hungry Gods. So everyone's behaving themselves and playing nice. But it won't last.'

'And the usual troublemakers are still out there,' said the Armourer. 'Dr Delerium, the Kali Corporation, the Djinn Jeanie. So when someone comes forward, and offers us the name and current identity of the traitor within the family . . . we have to take them seriously.'

'We have received . . . a communication,' said the Matriarch, her thin mouth compressing, as though tasting something bad. 'From Alexander King, the legendary Independent Agent. Yes, I thought you'd recognise the name, Edwin. The single greatest spy the world has ever known.'

'Damn right!' I said, sitting up straight in spite of myself. 'You used to tell me stories about him when I was a kid, Uncle Jack. Hell, everyone knows stories about the Independent Agent!'

'Impress me,' said the Matriarch. 'Show me you paid some attention during your lessons. What do you know about Alexander King?'

'There have always been other intelligence agencies in the world,' I said, 'doing the same work as us. Some political, some religious: the Regent of Shadows, the London Knights, the Salvation Army Sisterhood. And any number of individual agents, playing the great game for their own reasons: the Walking Man, the Travelling Doctor, the Old Wolf of Kabul, John Taylor in the Nightside . . . But the best of them has always been Alexander King. He's taken on every rogue organisation, faction, and individual of mass destruction, and run rings round all of them. He's worked with or against pretty much every government, at one time or another, but always on his own terms. He's even worked with us a few times. Didn't he and Uncle James once—?'

'Yes, he did,' said the Armourer. 'And we still don't talk about it. The point is, the Independent Agent has no loyalty to anyone other than himself. He's worked for every country, every cause, every organisation, and always strictly for cash. He's saved the world nine times, to our certain knowledge, and come close to destroying it twice.'

'I always thought he did it for the challenge,' said the Matriarch. To my surprise she was smiling, and her usually calm and cold voice had a touch of the wistful in it. 'To see if he could do it, when no one else could. Alexander has been the best spy in the world for almost seventy years now. He admits to being ninety-one years old, but could be even older. The point is, he became increasingly choosy about his missions, turning down most people. He said it was because there were no real challenges left any more; but age catches up with all of us, even the incredible Independent Agent. In fact, he's been quiet for so long most of us thought he'd retired.'

'He did contact us during the Hungry Gods War, to offer his services,' said the Armourer. 'But that was when Harry was running things, and he said no. I don't think he wanted to be overshadowed. Of course, that was before we realised how serious the whole affair was.'

'The point is,' said the Matriarch, glaring sternly at the Armourer until he sank back into his chair, 'Alexander King has contacted us. He says he's dying. And is therefore prepared to divulge a lifetime's hoarded knowledge and secrets to whichever present-day agent can demonstrate that they are worthy to take his place when he dies. To ascertain this, he is summoning the six most promising agents in the world to his home, deep in the Swiss Alps. And he says he wants you, Edwin.'

'What? Me?' I sat bolt upright, honestly shocked. 'Why would he want me?'

'He probably wants you because you took on the whole Drood family and won,' the Armourer said dryly. 'And just possibly because you led us to victory against the Hungry Gods, and saved all Humanity. Anyway, he was most firm. He wants you, for this competition of his.'

'You have to go,' said the Matriarch. 'For the pride of the family, and to make sure the Independent Agent's accumulated treasure of secret knowledge doesn't fall into the wrong hands. That *cannot* be allowed to happen, Edwin. Alexander King knows things no one else knows. The kind of suppressed truths that can bring down governments, start wars, and quite possibly set the whole world at each other's throats. Any individual or organisation with that kind of knowledge would be a real threat to the Droods – particularly in our current weakened state.'

'And, of course, because there's always the chance they might not use that knowledge in the world's best interests,' said the Armourer.

'Well yes, that too,' said the Matriarch. 'Only we can be trusted with information like that.'

'Some of these hypothetical people might do a better job than us,' I said.

'Don't be silly,' said the Matriarch. 'No one does it better than us.'

'Of course,' I said. 'What was I thinking?'

'King says he knows who our traitor is,' said the Armourer. 'You have to go, Eddie, and you have to win. For the sake of the family, and the world.'

'You will win, Edwin,' said the Matriarch. 'Whatever this competition turns out to be. We'll give you whatever support and assistance we can, but . . . in the end, you must win. By any means necessary.'

'I suppose so,' I said. I still had a whole shed load of reservations, about practically everything involved with this competition, but I wasn't going to waste my breath discussing them with the Matriarch. She was right about one thing: we had to find out who our traitor was, for the sake of the family and the world. Everything else . . . I'd have to think on my feet. As usual. I nodded slowly. 'Do we at least know who the other competitors are?'

'No,' said the Armourer. 'King is playing his cards very close to his chest, for the moment. Typical of the man. We've been making some discreet enquiries, but no one significant has dropped out of sight. You'll receive your instructions at King's private headquarters, some old ski lodge in the Swiss Alps. Very private, very well defended. It's called Place Gloria. You might remember it from a rather famous spy film they shot there in the sixties.'

I shook my head. 'I never watch spy films. I can't take them seriously.'

'You're expected to make your own way there,' said the Armourer. 'Part of proving your worth, I suppose. The Merlin Glass could drop you off right at his door—'

'But you can't take it with you,' the Matriarch said immediately. 'Far too important to the family to risk the enemy getting hold of it. On the other hand, Alexander King is supposed to have a quite magnificent collection of objects of power and influence in his own private museum. Spoils of the world's secret wars – some of which he stole from us. We'd quite like those back, if you can manage it.'

'Along with anything else you can get your hands on,' said the Armourer.

'I remember Alexander ...' said the Matriarch. Her voice was definitely wistful this time, and her eyes were far away. 'I had a bit of a fling with him, in the autumn of 1957. In East Berlin, right in the shadow of the wall. We used to meet at this perfectly awful little café, that smelt mostly of boiled cabbage and served its vodka after the Russian fashion, with a little black pepper sprinkled on top. The idea being that as the pepper grains sank to the bottom of the glass, they'd take the impurities in the vodka with them. You really could go blind, drinking that stuff in East Berlin in 1957. Awful vodka, awful food, but I still have fond memories of that little café, or at least of the room we used to rent above it. Ah yes – Alexander ... This was before I met and married your father, Jack, of course.'

'Of course, Mother.' The Armourer looked more than a little uncomfortable at the thought of his mother getting it on with the Independent Agent, so I moved in.

'What were the two of you doing in East Berlin, Grandmother?'

'Oh, some nonsense about a Persian djinn being buried under the Berlin Wall, to give it strength. We never did get to the bottom of it. But you might mention my name to Alexander, Edwin, just in case he remembers me. A most charming fellow. Don't trust him an inch.'

'Of course not,' I said. 'He isn't family.'

And that was the end of the Council meeting. I was going to the Swiss Alps, to meet a living legend who was dying, and take part in a competition I didn't understand, with people I didn't know, all for a prize I wasn't sure I believed in. And no, I didn't get a say in the matter. Business as usual, in the Drood family.

There was no way the Armourer was going to let me go off on a mission without the benefit of his very latest gadgets of mass distraction. So down to the Armoury we went. It was set deep in the bedrock under The Hall, so that when the place finally did blow itself up through an excess of imagination and optimism, there was at least some chance the family home would survive. As always, the huge stone chamber was jumping with activity, and lab assistants running this way and that, sometimes in pursuit of an escaping experiment, sometimes because their lab coats were on fire. It took nerves of steel to work in the Armoury, and a definite lack of the old self-preservation instinct. The Armourer strode through the chaos, entirely unmoved, while I stuck close behind him. If only to use him as a shield.

'How did the mellow bombs work out?' the Armourer tossed back over his shoulder, ducking slightly to avoid an eyeball with wings as it fluttered past.

'Oh, fine!' I said, stepping quickly to one side to avoid a lab assistant arguing fiercely with a plant in a cage. 'Though the effects did seem to fade pretty fast.'

'I'm working on it, I'm working on it!'

We passed a huge plastic bubble of clear water, inside which two over-enthusiastic lab techs were trying out their new gills and clawed hands, and going at each other like Japanese fighting fish. Up above, a rather fetching young lass with new batwing grafts was flapping along with a blissful smile on her face. Another technician appeared and disappeared and appeared, shouting, 'How do you turn this bloody thing off?'

In the shooting alley, half a dozen interns were trying out their new gun prototypes, and making a real mess of the alley in the process. Someone else had just finished showing off their new invention: a knife that fired its blade at your opponent while the hilt stayed in your hand. Afterwards, the blade would return to the hilt to be used again. Didn't seem to have gone too well. As the Armourer and I left the shooting alley behind us, the technician was being led away sobbing, while his friends tried to gather up his fingers.

A man-sized cocoon stood leaning against one wall, under a sign saying 'Do Not Disturb'. I didn't ask.

The Armoury has provided the family with many useful weapons, devices and gadgets of quite appalling nastiness down the years. The armour can't do everything. But when you have an unlimited budget, unlimited imagination and a complete lack of scruples, you're bound to wander into some fairly unusual areas ... We use the good stuff in the field, and accept the occasional explosion or unfortunate transformation as teething troubles. It is, after all, a dangerous and downright treacherous world, and the Droods need every advantage we can come up with, if we're to hold our own. Besides, I like new toys to play with as much as the next man. And there's always something new in the Armoury. Uncle Jack and his nasty-minded co-workers see to that.

Use the same tactics too often in the field, and your enemies will have an answer waiting.

The Armourer sat down at his work station, brushing aside piles of paper, half a dozen unfinished devices he was still tinkering with, and a small bottle marked 'Nitro-glycerine; handle with care dammit!' He gestured for me to sit down opposite him, and I did. Somewhat cautiously, because you can't even trust the chairs in the Armoury.

'We'll start with this,' the Armourer said confidently, handing over a simple golden signet ring with runes engraved along the inside. 'Slip it on your finger. No, the other finger. Now, to activate, press the fingers on either side against the ring, twice. *Don't do it now!* That is a Gemini Duplicator; gives you the option of bilocation. Don't, Eddie. I have already heard every possible variation of any joke you might have been about to make involving the word *bi*. In this case, it means being in more than one place at the same time. Great for establishing alibis. I'm told it's rather confusing, doing two different things at the same time in two different places, but it's really just multi-tasking raised to the next level. I'm sure you'll soon get the hang of it. But be warned: if one of your duplicates should happen to be killed, the psychic shock could finish off both of you.'

I considered the ring, being very careful not to squeeze it. 'What happens if I use the ring to make more than two of me?'

The Armourer frowned. 'The more of you there are, the harder it will be for you to keep track of yourselves and think clearly. Over-extend yourself, spread yourself too thinly ... and at best, all your selves will slam back into one. Which will hurt, big time.'

'And at worst?'

'You'd end up lost in the crowd. Unable to reintegrate yourself.'

'Got it,' I said. 'Stick to two. Could add a whole new dimension to a threesome, mind.'

The Armourer sighed heavily. 'Now, the new Colt Repeater. I've made a few improvements. Not only does the gun still aim itself, and have an infinite number of bullets to call on; now it can draw on wooden-, silver- and holy-water-tipped ammunition, as well. If one of those doesn't kill your opponent, you're probably better off running anyway.'

He handed over the heavy silver gun, and its standard-issue shoulder holster, and then looked away so he wouldn't have to watch me struggle to get the damn thing on.

'No reverse watch for you, this time. No one's been able to make the damn thing work since you burnt out the last one.' He sniffed loudly, but couldn't stay mad at me for long; not while he still had so many new toys to impress me with. He handed me a small black box, with a flourish. I accepted it, a bit gingerly, and opened the lid with great care. The box held two cuff-links.

'Very nice,' I said innocently. 'Solid silver, are they?'

'They are the Chameleon Codex,' the Armourer said sternly. 'Programmed to pick up trace DNA from anyone you happen to brush up against, and then store the information so that at a later date you can transform yourself into an exact duplicate of the original. Doesn't last long, admittedly, but the opportunities for spycraft, deceit and general mischief should be obvious.'

'Male and female?' I said, hopefully.

He glared at me. 'Can't keep your mind out of the gutter for one minute, can you? Yes, male and female. Thanks to some rather exhaustive testing by one of my lab techs ... Don't put the cuff-links on till you leave The Hall. Things are confused enough around here as it is. Finally, this is a skeleton key, made from human bone, and if you're wise you won't ask whose. Opens any physical lock. Almost as good as a Hand of Glory, and a damn sight less obvious.

Never liked the hands anyway; nasty smelly things. Try to get by with the skeleton key as we're running low on hands at the moment. We need to hang some more enemies . . .'

I made the box and the bone disappear into my pockets, and then looked thoughtfully at the Armourer. 'What do you know about the Independent Agent, Uncle Jack?'

He smiled coldly then, as though he'd been waiting for me to ask. 'Your Uncle James knew him better than I did, though we both worked with Alexander, on occasion. We were a bit over-awed at first, two young Droods out in the field for the first time, working with such a living legend. He was all that was grand and glamorous about spying, and we both learnt a Hell of a lot from him. James and I took all kinds of damn fool risks, trying to impress him, but in the end it was James that Alexander took under his wing. I was killingly jealous, for a time.

'Alexander trained James, encouraged him, taught him discipline and determination. Helped make James into a spying legend in his own right: the Grey Fox. Whether that was a good thing in the end I couldn't say. But if anyone made James the man he was – determined to win at any price, and to Hell with what or who it cost – it was Alexander King.'

The Armourer looked at me steadily. 'If you get the chance, Eddie, kill him. The whole world will rest easier for knowing that bloody-handed old sinner is dead, and finally paying for his many crimes.'

I went outside to retrieve the Merlin Glass from my Rover 25, and found my car just where it had been, but now crushed and compacted into a metal ball some six feet in diameter. I stood there, looking at it, and only slowly realised that the new Sarjeant-At-Arms was standing beside me, waiting for me to notice him.

'You were right, Eddie,' he said easily. 'I couldn't move your car. So I thought of something else to do to it. Here's your Merlin Glass. I made a point of removing it first. The Matriarch said you'd need it, on your mission.'

I took the Glass from him, and for once I couldn't think of a thing to say. The new Sarjeant-At-Arms leaned in close.

'I'm not my predecessor. I'm sneakier. Welcome home, Eddie.'

*

I have my own room in The Hall, even though I have a very nice little flat in Knightsbridge. The Merlin Glass allows me to commute back and forth. The centuries-old hand mirror can function as a doorway to anywhere. I made a point of studying my reflection carefully. William had spooked me more than a bit, with his suggestion there might be someone or something trapped inside the Glass. Watching and waiting. But everything seemed as it should be, so . . . I said the activating Words, concentrated on a destination, and the Glass leapt out of my hand, growing in size to become a doorway between The Hall and the place where Molly Metcalf lived.

The wood between the worlds.

Through the doorway I could see tall trees, and rich green vegetation, and long golden shafts of sunlight. The oldest wood, the first wood, blazing with the bright primary colours of spring. The trees seemed to stretch away for ever, and there were glades and waterfalls, rolling hills and rocky promontories. I'd spent a lot of time exploring the wood with Molly. The wild wood was her home, where she belonged; and the only place where she and I could be together and still have a little privacy. Apart from the local wildlife, of course, who seemed to find Molly and I endlessly fascinating.

The wood between the worlds is an ancient place, untouched by civilisation, and never an entirely comfortable place to be. I was only welcome there because Molly vouched for me. The animals were always easy in Molly's company, but they only accepted me because she did, and many remained cautious and watchful. This was where the really wild things ran free, including many species that had long since vanished from the Earth. There were huge boars, with great teeth and ragged tusks. There were dire wolves and black bears; and older, stranger, more mythical creatures too. Some I only knew as glowing eyes in the gloom between the trees. Molly treated them all with equal ease and affection, slapping them away if they crowded her. The first time she did that, with a twelve-foot bear, I nearly had a coronary. There were all kinds of birds, too, filling the scent-rich air with their songs, and whole clouds of multi-coloured butterflies.

There were other insects too, and lots of flies; but none of them ever bothered us. When I asked Molly why, she just said, 'They wouldn't dare.'

She came running to greet me as I stepped through the Merlin Glass and into her world. My Molly Metcalf, the wild witch, the laughter in the woods, glorious and free. A gorgeous, wonderful woman a few years younger than me, with pale skin and jet-black hair, like a delicate china doll with big bosoms. She had eyes deep enough to drown in, more dark eyeliner than a Panda on the pull, and a bright red rosebud mouth made for sin and laughter. She was wearing a long pastel green gown with a golden belt, and half a dozen flowers pushed haphazardly into her hair. She threw herself at me, almost knocking me off my feet, and I held her like I'd never let her go.

Love came to me late in life, and unexpected. The Droods believe in marriage, rather than love. Marriage binds you to the family; love just gets in the way. The family never wants anything in your life more important than your duty to the family. Everyone has to know their place. Molly, bless her contrary heart, has never known her place; and that's one of the reasons I love her so much.

She ground her breasts against my chest as we kissed. She knows I like that. Butterflies fluttered joyously about us as we ripped the clothes off each other.

Some time later, we lay side by side on a grassy bank, the sweat slowly drying on our cooling bodies, snuggled happily together. I'd brought Molly up to date on my latest mission, and now she was sulking a bit because she couldn't go with me.

'You know we work best as a team, Eddie. Who's going to watch your back, if I'm not there?'

'I did survive as a Drood field agent for years, before we became an item,' I said, amused.

'It's a constant wonder to me you lasted one year. You're far too trusting.'

'The invitation from the Independent Agent is for me alone,' I said patiently. 'It's his game, so he gets to set the rules.'

'Why choose you anyway? I mean, I'm sorry sweetie, no offence and that, but why you out of all the Droods? Why not someone with more experience, and closer to his generation? Like your Uncle Jack, perhaps?'

'Because I saved the world from the Hungry Gods, apparently. You do remember that, don't you? I mean, you were there. Helping.'

'Don't pout, Eddie. It doesn't become you. Of course you deserve this honour, but I can't help wondering if this is some kind of trick or trap. Not necessarily aimed at you. What if ... What if it's an opportunity to get the six best spies in the world together in one place, and then kill them off? One final coup for the Independent Agent, to prove he's still the best after all these years.'

'What a wonderfully suspicious mind you have,' I said fondly. 'You're quite right, of course. Wouldn't surprise me at all if this turned out to be some kind of devious plot, or scheme. But I still have to go. The price he's offering is worth the risk.'

'Is it?' Molly rose on one elbow to consider me, frowning worriedly. 'I mean, what information could this man have that the amazing Drood family doesn't already have? Secrets don't stay secrets long.'

'Some do,' I said. 'And Alexander King has been around. He might not have made history, but he certainly helped shape it from behind the scenes. There's no telling what a man like that might know. In the hidden world of spies, there are often secrets within secrets. If anyone might know what we don't, it would be Alexander King.'

'So you have to go.' Molly sat upright, hugging her knees to her bare chest, deliberately looking straight ahead so she wouldn't have to look at me. 'All right. I get it. Duty calls, in spite of what you've done for your family, and it's done to you. You always were far too loyal for your own good.' She turned abruptly to fix me with her huge dark eyes, and then reached out and tweaked my left nipple hard, to make sure she had my full attention. 'You stay sharp, Eddie, and do whatever you have to, to win this bloody game. Meanwhile I'll chat to some of my friends and allies. People who wouldn't talk to the infamous Droods. See what they have to say about Alexander bloody King.'

'Of course, Molly. You can let go of my nipple now. Please.'

She let go, and looked away again. 'I may be out of touch for a while. I have some family business to take care of.'

'It's not your Uncle Harvey again, is it?' I said. 'The one who thinks he's a giant rabbit?'

'No, it's my sister, Isabella. She says she has news. She says she might, just might, have a lead on why our parents were killed by your family. The real reason, not the rubbish they fobbed you off with.'

'I have been trying to get at the truth,' I said.

'I know you have, sweetie.'

'In a family business the size of the Droods, there's often a lot of stuff going on where the left hand doesn't know what the right hand is doing. Things are done because they need to be done, and only officially authorised afterwards. If at all. A lot of the records from that period are a mess, thanks to interference by the Zero Tolerance faction.'

'There's more,' said Molly. Her voice was very serious. She still didn't look at me. 'Isabella says the death of our parents is linked to the death of your parents. That they were killed for the same reason; because of something they both knew.'

I didn't know what to say. My parents were Drood field agents, killed in action in the Basque area. Largely due to insufficient advance planning and unreliable intelligence. Or that was what my family told me. But like so many other things where my family was concerned, that might or might not be true.

'You be careful,' I said to Molly. 'If my family finds out that you're digging into Drood history, into secrets so awful they're still hiding them from me ... You be really careful, Molly. You have no idea what my family is capable of, when it comes to protecting itself. What makes your sister so sure about this? Who's she been talking to?'

'I'm not going to tell you,' said Molly. 'You wouldn't approve.'

'Molly ...'

'Eddie, trust me: you don't want to know. Now leave this to me. You concentrate on the Independent Agent, and winning his stupid game. When it's over, come back here to me and I'll tell you what I've found out. And then we'll decide together what to do. To avenge the murder of our parents.'

'Yes,' I said. 'We will do that. The guilty will be punished. Whoever they turn out to be.'

We lay back down on the green grass, side by side. The birds were singing, and a pleasant cool breeze gusted across our naked bodies. The air was rich with the scents of grass and earth and living things. I stared up at the sky, and thought of many things.

'If, by some foul treachery, you don't win,' said Molly Metcalf. 'If you don't come back . . . I will kill Alexander King for you.'

'Yes,' I said. 'You do that.'

CHAPTER THREE

In the court of the cryptic king

Fog, fog, everywhere; and not a bit of it real.

When I stepped through the Merlin Glass the world disappeared, replaced by thick grey walls of slowly swirling mists. Endless shades of grey, cold and damp, diffusing the light and deadening all sounds. I glanced behind me, but the Glass had already shut itself down, back in The Hall. I was on my own.

I could feel a hard surface beneath my feet, and the bitter cold searing my bare skin. The air was thin but bracing, so it seemed I was probably in the right place at least, somewhere deep in the Swiss Alps. I couldn't see a damned thing. The fog churned around me, thick and deep, like being at the bottom of a great grey ocean, and I had a strong feeling there was something else there in the fog with me. It wasn't real fog; I could tell by the way it glowed. This was flux fog, the pearly shades that mark where the barriers of the world have grown thin.

I definitely wasn't alone. There were dim, dark shapes moving in the mists around me, circling unhurriedly, like sharks hoping for the taste of blood in the water. There were faraway voices, like the echoes of old friends and enemies talking in forgotten rooms, and a constant sense of something important about to happen. I stood my ground, refusing to be tempted or intimidated into unwise action, while slow heavy footsteps sounded around me and dark shapes drifted in and out of focus, as though struggling to become firm and fixed. In a flux fog, the harsh and solid places of the world become soft and malleable, and all kinds of things become possible. I stood my ground, holding my calm before me like a shield. Make a sudden move in a flux fog, and you could end up someone else before you knew it.

Besides, I still wasn't entirely sure where I'd arrived. I'd given the

Merlin Glass the exact coordinates for Alexander King's retreat at Place Gloria, but all I knew for certain was that it was somewhere in the Swiss mountains. There could be one Hell of a long drop in any direction hidden in the fog.

And then a wind blew up out of nowhere, a soundless blast of bitter cold air that blew the fog away in a moment, and just like that I was standing on a deserted helicopter landing pad on the top of an artificially levelled-off mountain. The pale yellow marking lines were faded and broken, and the slumping half-rotten control tower clearly hadn't been used in years. There were five other people on the landing pad with me, as far away as they could get and not actually fall off the mountain. None of them appeared immediately dangerous, so I struck a nonchalant pose and looked around me, taking in the view.

I was high enough up to take my breath away, in more ways than one. Place Gloria was set right in the heart of the Swiss Alps, and the long broken-backed range of mountain ridges stretched away in every direction. Snow-covered peaks lay below me to every side, each with their own collars of drifting clouds, under a sky so blue and pure it almost hurt to look at. The air was thin and bitter cold, burning in my lungs as I tried for deeper breaths.

I was standing on top of the world, a long way from anywhere.

The sound of approaching footsteps turned my head, and I growled deep in my throat as I recognised who it was. He must have seen the cold rage in my face, but he didn't slow his approach. The Blue Fairy might have been many things, but he never lacked for balls. He stopped a polite and safe distance away, and waited to see what I would do. He looked ... watchful, but not especially worried. I did consider killing him, right there, on general principles; but it seemed likely we were both here as guests of Alexander King, personally selected for his great game, and I couldn't afford to upset the legendary Independent Agent. Besides, it wouldn't look good to be seen to lose control so easily, so early on in the proceedings. There would be other times. I fixed the Blue Fairy with a cold stare, and bowed my head to him, very slightly.

'That's better,' said the Blue Fairy, in an infuriatingly calm and drawling voice. 'Let us play at being civilised, for the time being at least. No squabbling, no accusing, no fighting in the playground.

This contest is too important for us to risk being thrown out for bad behaviour.'

'You'd know all about bad behaviour,' I said, and there was something in my voice that made him flinch, and actually fall back a step. 'You betrayed my trust. Stole a torc. Spat in the face of my family. There will be a reckoning, Blue. But not yet. There will be time for many things, once I've kicked your nasty arse right out of the game.'

He tried to smile haughtily, but his heart wasn't in it. I stared at him. He looked a lot better than the last few times I'd seen him. He seemed healthier, even younger – or at least he carried his years more easily. He'd lost some weight, his back was straight, and there was a new confidence about him. He was dressed in the height of Elizabethan fashion: tights and padded jerkin and silk ruff, the ruff pulled low to show off the stolen torc around his throat. The new style presumably came from his time at the Fae Court. The elves still affected the fashions of old England, from when they'd last walked our Earth. Partly because they're stubborn, partly because they like to pretend Humanity hasn't changed since those days. Made it easier for them to look down on us. The Blue Fairy also wore a ceremonial breastplate of silver and brass, chased and pointed and curlicued to within an inch of its life, and no doubt crawling with defensive magics and protections. I had to smile. Blue might think he was protected, but his armour was no match for mine.

Still, he looked . . . proud, arrogant, aristocratic. Very . . . elven.

'Being a thief and a traitor seems to agree with you,' I said finally. 'You're looking well, Blue. I'm pleased. Really. After all, where's the fun in kicking the crap out of a sick old man?'

'How unkind,' said the Blue Fairy, fixing me with his best supercilious stare. 'And I'm not a man, not any more. I have put aside my humanity and embraced my elven heritage. It's taken me many years to realise, but I was never cut out to be a man. To be just a man. I feel much more . . . me, as an elf.'

'We took you in,' I said. 'Made you our guest in The Hall. Gave you a place among us, gave you a home and a purpose, respect and friends. And right in the middle of our war against the Hungry Gods, with the fate of the whole world in the balance, you stole a torc from us and ran away.'

'If you're going to be an elf,' the Blue Fairy said easily, 'go all the way. Or what's the point?' He raised his left hand, and ran the fingertips caressingly along the golden torc around his throat. 'You should have told me, Eddie. You should have told me how the torc can make you feel. I never felt so alive. Like there's nothing I can't do.'

'You always were a sucker for a new drug, a new addiction,' I said. 'Enjoy it while you can, Blue. I'll take it back when I'm ready.' I considered him thoughtfully for a long moment, and he stirred uncomfortably under my gaze. I smiled. 'What secrets did Alexander King offer you, to sucker you into his game? Something you could use to protect you from the fury of the Droods?'

'I'm not alone any more,' the Blue Fairy said defiantly. 'I don't need protecting. I have allies, support and backing you wouldn't believe.'

'Oh, please,' I said. 'You really think the Fae Court will stand up for a taboo half-breed like you if the Drood family says "It's him, or you"?'

Give him credit, he actually managed a smile. 'I'm not here to represent the Fae Court,' he said. 'My allies are older, and more powerful. I do not bend the knee to Titania and Oberon. I serve Queen Mab.'

I shuddered then, and it had nothing to do with the chill wind sweeping across the abandoned helicopter pad. Mab was an old name, and not a good one. If the long-exiled original Queen of Faerie was back, there would be fire and blood, death and destruction, and perhaps more than one world would be thrown down into horror and despair . . .

'You poor damned fool,' I said to the Blue Fairy, meaning it. 'You never could resist backing an outsider, could you?'

He sneered at me, his face cold and inhuman. 'Be afraid, Drood. Be very afraid. Now Queen Mab has taken back the Ivory Throne from Titania and Oberon, she will lead the elves to a new destiny. We're coming home, Eddie. All of us, all the elves that ever were, returning in power and glory to save the world from the savages who've ruined and spoiled it. We will trample Humanity underfoot, and stamp them back into the dirt they crawled out of.' He smiled suddenly, and it was not a human smile. 'And just maybe, when we come, we'll all be wearing torcs.'

This time, there was something in his voice that stopped me cold. But never let them know they've got you on the ropes. So I stared calmly back at him, and changed the subject.

'This is supposed to be a contest to find the greatest spy in the world,' I said. 'Featuring the six best field agents operating today. So, and don't take this the wrong way, Blue, what the Hell are you doing here?'

'The young always forget that the old were young once,' said the Blue Fairy. 'You only ever knew me as a broken old man, brought low by his own weaknesses, so you assumed I'd always been like that. But back when I was your age, Eddie, I was a name to be reckoned with. I worked for anyone, for any cause, took on the major players of the day with only my wits and a few craftily purloined weapons, and made them cry like babies.'

'So what happened?' I said.

'What always happens. I got old, and I got slow,' said the Blue Fairy. His voice was dispassionate; he might have been talking about someone else. 'I lost more cases than I won, I started leaning on the booze and the drugs, to keep me sharp, to make me feel like I used to feel. It's easy to fall off the edge, you know. All it takes is one really bad day, and a disaster so bad you can't lie to yourself any more.' He looked at me almost pityingly. 'I was like you Eddie. At the top of my game, convinced I had the world by the throat. It's a long way to fall, and you wouldn't believe how much it hurts when you hit the bottom. That's your future, Eddie. That's what you've got to look forward to.' He smiled suddenly. 'But I have been given a second chance. The torc has made me young and sharp and alive again. I'm the player I used to be, the greatest field agent of my time.

'And what use is your youthful confidence in the face of my years of experience? I'm back, Eddie, and I'm going to run circles around the lot of you.'

'That's the torc speaking,' I said. But I wasn't entirely sure.

We both turned sharply as one of the other figures came striding across the landing pad to join us. She stopped a cautious distance away, looked us both over, and smiled widely.

'Hi,' she said. 'I'm Honey Lake, CIA. Don't everyone cheer at once.'

She had presence, give her that. Honey Lake was tall, Amazonian, with a splendid figure, dark coffee skin and closely cropped hair. She wore a tight-fitting pure white jumpsuit under a long white fur coat, and thigh-high white leather boots. I was sensing a theme. She had strong pleasant features, with high cheekbones, a broad grin and merry eyes. Her sheer physical presence was almost overwhelming, like being caught in the headlights of an oncoming car. I'd have been impressed, if I believed in being impressed, which mostly I don't. The best agents go unnoticed, walking unseen through the world; standing out in a crowd only makes you a better target. I let my gaze drift over her, making it clear I wasn't dazzled, and happened to notice that she had enough heavy gold rings on the fingers of her left hand to double as a knuckle-duster. She also wore a silver charm hanging on a chain round her neck, bearing the sign of the Eye of the Pyramid. As I looked at the charm, the Eye winked at me.

Honey Lake was studying me just as openly, grinning like a child who's been given a new toy to play with.

'Wow,' she said. 'A Drood! Colour me impressed ... so that's what a torc looks like. I'd always thought it would be more ... impressive. Still, an actual Drood! Not often we get to meet one of you face to face.'

'We prefer to keep to the background,' I said. I stepped forward and offered her my hand, and she shook it briefly with a firm grasp. Up close, she smelled of musk and perfume and gunpowder. Not an unpleasant combination.

The Blue Fairy cleared his throat meaningfully. 'Hi. 'I'm—'

'Oh, I know who you are,' said Honey, not taking her eyes off me.

'I'm Eddie Drood,' I said. I was starting to feel a bit uncomfortable. Honey was doing everything but hit me over the head with her sexuality. Which was probably the point; it's an old trick, to keep a man off balance. 'So,' I said, as casually as I could manage, 'you're CIA? Might have known the Company would insist on a presence here.'

'Oh, I was chosen,' said Honey. 'Personally selected, by the Independent Agent himself. And I'm only sort of CIA.'

I had to raise an eyebrow at that. 'Only sort of?'

'You know how it is, Eddie. We're like an onion: no matter how many layers you peel away, there's always one more underneath.

I work for one of those departments within departments that don't officially exist. Our remit is to protect the United States from threats of an . . . unusual nature. By all means necessary.'

'Does that include the Droods?' I said.

'Of course! We don't trust anyone who isn't one hundred per cent American. Hell, we don't even trust most of the people who work for the CIA. On really bad days, I don't trust anyone but myself.' She smiled brightly. 'I love the smell of paranoia in the morning. It's so bracing.' She turned abruptly to look at the Blue Fairy, who was standing stiffly to one side, like the guest at a party no one wants to talk to. 'I didn't know the Droods had a half-breed elf lurking in their woodpile.'

'We don't,' I said. 'He stole that torc.'

Honey Lake raised an elegant eyebrow. 'And you let him live?'

'It's . . . complicated,' I said.

'Oh,' she said. 'It's like that, is it?'

'You tell me,' I said. 'You're CIA. You know everything.'

She laughed. 'If we did, we wouldn't need field agents. It really is fascinating to meet you, Eddie. In the flesh, so to speak. Normally we only get to see Droods in action, from a distance, wrapped up in your amazing armour. And then only if we're very lucky. You're the urban legends of the espionage field. Often talked about, rarely glimpsed, never sticking around to accept praise or answer questions. *Who was that masked man?* we cry, and never a response. The CIA has massive files on you Droods, but we don't trust anything that's in them. You wouldn't believe some of the stories we hear about you.'

'Believe them all,' I said solemnly. 'Especially the really weird ones.'

'I met the Grey Fox once,' said Honey. 'In a bombed-out bar in Beirut. Such a gentleman. Stole the courier I was escorting right out from under my nose.'

'Uncle James,' I said. 'He always was the best of us.'

'What happened to him?' said Honey. 'I heard he died, but—'

'He turned his back on the wrong woman,' I said. 'It's what he would have wanted.'

'Why don't you tell her who killed the Grey Fox?' said the Blue Fairy.

'Shut up, Blue,' I said, not looking round.

We all jumped a little as another figure joined us. He was suddenly standing there with us, though none of us had heard him approaching. And I'm really hard to surprise. He looked very much like the typical City gentleman, in his smart expensive suit, old school tie, bowler hat and rolled umbrella. He seemed entirely unprepared for the cold mountain air, but if it affected him he didn't show it. He was average height and weight, middle-aged but in good shape. Sharp, stylish and sophisticated, with a calm smile and cool watchful eyes. He nodded to each of us in turn, and actually tipped his bowler hat to Honey.

'Good afternoon,' he said. 'I'm Walker. From the Nightside.'

For a long moment, none of us said anything. It's not often I'm genuinely impressed, but we'd all heard of Walker. The Nightside is the hidden dark heart of London, where bad things live and worse things happen. Where it's always night because some things can only thrive in the dark. Where gods and monsters plot and war, and often frequent the same swingers' clubs. The Nightside has the best bars and clubs in the world, but the door charge can be your soul, and you'd better find what you're looking for before it finds you. By ancient treaty, the Droods stay out of the Nightside. We're not barred, as such; we choose not to get involved. An organisation known as the Authorities used to run the Nightside, in as much as anyone did or could, and Walker was their man on the spot. It was his job to keep the lid on; and no one ever messed with Walker. Even gods and monsters walked lightly when Walker was on the prowl. But now the Authorities were dead and gone, and Walker . . . was here. Which was interesting. He smiled easily around him, very polite, very courteous.

Like a crocodile in a Savile Row suit.

'This is a day of surprises,' said Honey Lake. 'I can honestly say I wasn't expecting to see anyone from the Nightside. You people don't tend to play well with others. In fact, there are those who say the fate of the whole world will be decided there, some day.'

'No,' said the Blue Fairy. 'You're thinking of Shadows Fall.'

'I try very hard not to,' said Honey, still not looking at him. 'The elephants' graveyard of the supernatural, where legends go to die when the world stops believing in them? That place gives me the creeps.'

'So,' I said to Walker, 'what brings you out of the dark, and into the light?'

'The imminent passing of a legend,' said Walker, leaning casually on his furled umbrella. 'Rumour has it the Independent Agent knows things that even the Nightside doesn't know. Knowledge and secrets lost and forgotten by the rest of the world. He offered me a place in his little game, and I really couldn't say no. I have been promised something, you see; something even the Nightside can't provide. And I want it.' He looked at me thoughtfully. 'I should have known there'd be a Drood here. It wouldn't be an honest competition without one.'

'Hold everything,' I said. 'You can see my torc too? Damn! What's the point in having a secret weapon if everyone knows about it?'

'Ah,' said Walker. 'But then, we're not just everyone, are we?'

I nodded, acknowledging the point. 'Still,' I said, 'why would Alexander King choose you, Walker? No offence, but you're not an agent, as such.'

'Perhaps not,' said Walker. 'But who knows more about the real secrets and mysteries of the world than I?'

We turned to face the next new figure as he strolled unhurriedly across the landing pad to join us. He came to a halt before us, nodded briefly and then stood his ground, letting us look him over. Truth be told, he didn't look like much. A vaguely handsome, even elegant young man in his early twenties, wearing a fashionably cut fashionable suit with ease and grace. Blond hair, blue eyes, in good shape but nothing to boast about. He had a reserved, bookish look, and a pale, essentially characterless face. In fact, the same kind of instantly forgettable face as mine – an agent's face. He didn't offer to shake hands with anyone, and if he felt the impact of Honey's sexuality, he kept it to himself.

'Peter King,' he said shortly. 'The Independent Agent is my grandfather. He insisted I take part in this last crooked game of his. Not that I expect him to cut me any slack. He never has before.'

'What part of the business are you in, Peter?' I asked.

'Corporate intelligence,' he said stiffly. 'Industrial espionage. Stealing or protecting secrets, or other privileged information. Arranging the defection and safe conduct of important personnel –

that sort of thing. Not as glamorous as what you do, perhaps, but there's always good money to be made in helping businesses screw each other over.'

'Can't say I've actually heard of you, Peter,' said Honey, not unkindly.

He smiled briefly. 'That's because I'm very good at what I do.'

And there was no arguing with that. The best agents leave no trace that they were ever there.

'Still, Alexander King's grandson,' Honey Lake said. 'The Company has no files on King ever having any family.'

'Grandfather never did believe in leaving hostages to fortune,' said Peter. 'If the world didn't know about his family, the world couldn't use them against him. The grand old man of secrets delighted in having secrets of his own. Don't ask me about my father, or my mother. Some things should stay secret.' He looked around the deserted landing pad. 'This is the first time I've ever been here. To the house at the top of the world, where Grandfather sits in his jealous little web of intrigue hoarding his secrets like the miser he is. My mother told me stories about this place. Even years later, she still had nightmares about her time here. And now here I am, the not-so-prodigal grandson come to compete for what should be my legacy.'

'Family histories are always so embarrassing,' said the Blue Fairy.

'Can't argue with that,' I said.

There was the sound of high heels clacking briskly across the concrete, as the final contestant in the game came forward to join us. I watched her approach, and she was worth the attention. I felt like whistling and applauding, just on general principles. Peter was grinning openly, the Blue Fairy was smiling almost despite himself, and Walker . . . looked calm and composed, as always. Honey Lake studied the final contestant with a cool, thoughtful gaze. She knew a threat to her position when she saw one. The delightfully stylish young lady swayed to a halt before us, struck an elegant and utterly bewitching pose, and bestowed her most charming smile upon us.

'Greetings and salutations, darlings,' she said, in a low purring voice, like a cat licking cream off a mouse. 'I am Lethal Harmony, agent for hire, out of Kathmandu. Please call me Katt. Everyone does.'

80

There was something feline about her. A sense of graceful style, casual cruelty, and vicious power concealed behind a hair trigger, ready to be unleashed on absolutely anyone at a moment's notice. Honey Lake made a Hell of a first impression, but she looked like an innocent corn-fed cheerleader next to Lethal Harmony of Kathmandu. Honey blazed, but Katt smouldered.

Katt was tall and slender, with delicate streamlined curves, and enough presence and poise to take any man's breath away. She wore a long black silk gown, tucked in tightly here and there to accentuate her figure, and as she turned this way and that to make sure we all got the benefit of her smile, I glimpsed an ornate oriental dragon embroidered the full length of the back of her gown. Katt had sweet oriental features under sharply-styled black hair, dark eastern eyes, and a happy smiling mouth with lips the colour of plums. Beautiful, graceful, and no doubt very deadly when required. Katt, indeed.

I still got the impression she practised that smile in front of the bathroom mirror, though. It was just too good.

She was playing a part, but it was a good part, and I appreciated the effort she'd put into it. If you can't be anonymous, like me, hide behind a cliché and they'll never see the real you. Until it's too late.

'Lethal Harmony,' said Honey Lake, her voice coldly amused. 'Dear little Kitty-Katt. I should have known you'd turn up. The espionage field's very own wannabe dragon lady.'

Katt glared at Honey, who glared right back at her. I half expected them to hiss and bare their claws at each other.

'Are we to take it you two know each other?' said the Blue Fairy, not bothering to hide his amusement.

'We've worked together,' Honey said shortly. 'When the job demanded it. Don't trust her, don't turn your back on her, and never go Dutch on anything.'

'How unkind,' said Katt, still smiling her perfect smile.

'I notice you're not denying any of it,' said Honey.

'Why should I?' said Katt. 'We're all agents here. We know how the game is played.' She leaned forward to look at me more closely. 'Ooh, a Drood! How thrilling!'

'Oh Hell,' I said, put out. 'Can everyone here see my torc?'

'Well, yes,' said Peter. 'We wouldn't be top field agents if we couldn't, would we? I'm more concerned with what the half-elf is doing with a torc. Elves are dangerous enough as it is, without giving them the nuclear option.'

'How very kind,' drawled the Blue Fairy. 'It's always nice to be appreciated.'

'So, Katt,' I said, ostentatiously changing the subject. 'Who do you work for?'

'Anybody, everybody,' Katt said lightly. 'Morals are all very well, but a girl has to eat, darling. It's a cold cash world these days.'

'Do you believe in anything?' said Honey Lake.

'I believe in being paid,' Katt said firmly. 'And you're a fine one to talk, little miss *I'm not really CIA, I just screw people over because I'm good at it*. No, sweeties; I am no man's slave, and no dogma's, either. I am the last of the great adventurers, darlings, and I love it!'

'Always good to have a fellow realist on board,' said the Blue Fairy. He extended a hand to Katt, and she looked down her nose at it as though she'd been offered a turd. Blue withdrew his hand, managing to look hurt but still dignified.

'Never trust an elf,' Katt said flatly. 'And even then, trust an elf before a half-breed.'

'Harsh words,' Blue said calmly, 'especially from such a notorious *femme fatale*, the espionage field's very own *belle dame sans merci*. How many men and women have died in your poisonous embrace, dear Katt? How many lovers have you seduced and betrayed? At least I had the basic decency to pay for most of mine ... Tell me, dear Katt: is it true you prefer your victims to die in bed, so you can suck their last dying breath into your no-doubt luscious mouth, and savour it?'

Katt drew herself up to her full height. 'You'll never know.'

'Such a relief,' said the Blue Fairy.

'Children, children,' murmured Walker. 'Play nice.'

'This is why I prefer industrial espionage,' said Peter. 'No personalities to get in the way.'

I looked around the empty landing pad. 'Is this it? Just us? No Russian or Chinese agents?'

'They're mostly concerned with internal problems these days,' said Honey.

'You'd know,' said Walker.

'Still,' I said, 'this isn't quite the gathering I'd expected. I mean, we're the six greatest agents operating in the field today? Us?'

'I think that says more about the current state of the world than I am comfortable knowing,' said Walker.

'Grandfather chose us,' said Peter. 'He must have his reasons.'

'And why the flux fog?' said the Blue Fairy. 'What was the point of that? We all know where we are.'

'Do we?' I said. 'Once we arrived and stepped into the flux fog, it could have taken us anywhere. This is supposed to be the Swiss Alps, but I couldn't prove it. One mountain chain looks much like another. It would seem Alexander King wants to keep the exact location of his private lair a mystery, right to the end.'

'And no one here to greet us,' said Peter. 'How typical of Grandfather. What are we supposed to do – stand around in the cold until he feels like talking to us?'

He'd barely finished speaking when the concrete rocked under our feet. There was a loud grinding noise, and puffs of dust flew up in long lines around us, forming a great square. The concrete seemed to drop out from under our feet, and suddenly we were descending a huge dark shaft, leaving the cold and the light behind. We moved to stand close together, forming our own square so we could look in every direction. The light above us disappeared, and for a long moment there was only the dark and a sense of movement as we descended towards some unknown fate. And then the concrete slab groaned to a halt, there was a sudden flare of light that made us wince and we realised we were standing in a vast entrance lobby.

The air was refreshingly warm, after the cold up above. I looked down, but the concrete slab fitted perfectly into the floor. The entire lobby was bare and empty. No sign of life anywhere. No sign that anyone had ever lived here. Just where had Alexander King brought us? His tomb? And then we winced again as a voice sounded inside our heads. That isn't supposed to be possible, when you wear the Drood torc; we're supposed to be protected from such invasions. But the Independent Agent always did play by his own rules.

Welcome to Place Gloria, said the voice. *Welcome to my home. Welcome to the greatest game of all.*

I waited, but that was all there was. I shook my head gingerly, half expecting something to leak out of my ears. That voice had been seriously loud. I looked at Peter.

'Can you identify that as your grandfather's voice?'

'No,' he said. 'I've never been here before, never met the old bastard, never talked to him on the phone. Not even a card on my birthday. If there were any letters, my mother kept them to herself. I got my invitation to this game through an ... intermediary.'

He broke off, as we all turned abruptly and looked in the same direction. There was new information in my head that I very definitely hadn't put there, telling me which way to go to meet Alexander King. It had the feel of a summons.

'It's a magical working,' the Blue Fairy said quietly. 'An influence. Sort of like a low key geas. I didn't know he could do that.'

'What do any of us really know about Alexander King?' said Katt. 'Come on, darlings. We came here to meet the man. Let's get this show on the road.'

We stepped smartly forward, not wanting to be left behind, and not ready to acknowledge any of the others as leader by letting them get ahead of the rest of us. We crossed the empty lobby, our footsteps echoing loudly in the quiet, and a door opened in the far wall before us. We walked through, into the very lap of luxury. The fittings and furnishings of Place Gloria were soft and plush, sensual and sybaritic. I was so fascinated by the riot of colours before me, I almost didn't hear the door closing itself behind us. The décor was basically very sixties and seventies. Lots of comfort and bright colours, artistic furniture and Day-Glo art, from the decades that taste forgot. The huge low-ceilinged room, with its concealed lighting and its rich scents of sandalwood and attar, boasted luxury and wealth wherever you looked, along with an almost complete lack of restraint. We moved slowly forward, tugged inexorably on by King's subtle influence.

There were niches in the walls, each with their own special lighting, to show off the Independent Agent's many spoils of war. There were treasures and wonders to every side, the loot and tribute of a lifetime's secret wars. I had to smile. Alexander King could almost have been a Drood. We stopped before a small statuette of a black bird.

'Oh come on, that couldn't be the real thing! Could it?' said the Blue Fairy, leaning in for a close look.

'I wouldn't touch,' I said quickly. 'It's bound to be protected.'

Blue straightened up and glared at me. 'I wasn't going to touch! I'm not an amateur! Credit me with a little sense.'

'I suppose it could be the real thing,' said Walker. 'If anyone has the original, it would be Alexander King.'

'Hell,' said Honey. 'For all we know, he could have the Holy Grail itself tucked away here somewhere.'

'No,' I said. 'That's the one thing he definitely doesn't have.'

They all looked at me. 'Don't say the Droods have got the Grail,' said Katt.

'No,' I said. 'But we know where it is, and we're very happy for it to stay there. The Sangreal is not for the likes of us. It ... judges you.'

'You mean we're not worthy?' said the Blue Fairy. 'How will I ever recover from the shame?'

'Of course we're not worthy,' said Honey. 'We're agents. You can't do what we have to do, and still be able to wash the blood off your hands.'

'Speak for yourself,' said Walker unexpectedly. 'I do my duty, and I sleep perfectly well at nights.'

'So do I,' said the Blue Fairy. 'With a little medicinal help, some-times.'

'It's not what you do,' I said. 'It's why you do it.'

'Typical high and mighty Drood,' sneered Blue. 'Always so sure you're better than everyone else.'

'Mostly, we are,' I said. 'Mostly.'

King's influence nagged at us and we moved on, only to stop again as we came face to face with the Mona Lisa.

'Supposedly that's the real thing,' said Peter. 'Stolen from the Louvre in the sixties. Grandfather never could resist a challenge.'

King also had on his walls two Pickmans, an unknown Shlacken, and the Painting That Devoured Paris. Which suggested, if nothing else, that the Independent Agent was more of a collector than an art critic. There were also a number of display cases, showing off items of unusual interest. The skull of an alien Grey peered blankly back at us, with holes and long grooves in the bone showing where bits of alien technology had been rudely extracted. Hopefully, after death. A bottle of unholy water from the original Hellfire Club, Tom Pearce's Old Grimoire, a stuffed Morlock, and a mummified monkey's paw nailed very firmly to its stand. And, finally, a human skeleton, wired together and standing upright inside a grandfather clock.

'That's my mother,' said Peter. We stared at him, but he only had eyes for the skeleton. 'After she died, Grandfather claimed the body and had it brought here. Stole it, in fact, from the undertaker I'd entrusted her to. Had the body smuggled out of the country before I knew what was happening. I got a solicitor's letter some time later informing me that Grandfather had used carpet beetles to consume the flesh, leaving only the bones, as they do in museums. And that Mother's skeleton would be on display at Grandfather's home, along with his other prized possessions. There was a photograph enclosed. Grandfather can be sentimental, but not in ways you'd expect. I was never allowed to visit Mother, until now. Remember this, if you remember nothing else: Grandfather never lets go of anything he owns.'

'Put it back,' I said sternly to the Blue Fairy.

'What?' he said, projecting injured innocence.

'That small black-lacquered puzzle box you picked up and pocketed from the occasional table when you thought no one was looking,' I said. 'Just because it isn't in a case, doesn't mean it's up for grabs.'

'Don't know what you're talking about,' the Blue Fairy said airily.

'I could pick you up, turn you upside down and shake you, and see what falls out,' I said.

Blue sniffed, and put the puzzle box back on the table. 'I only wanted a souvenir ...'

King's subtle influence pulled us on, into a long narrow hall whose walls were covered with photos of people and places from around the world, celebrating King's many famous missions and triumphs. Some so famous that all of us had at least heard of them. Roswell, Loch Ness, Tunguska. We pointed and whispered and nudged each other, like children in a museum.

'The Case of the Kidnapped Village,' said Peter, peering closely at a black and white photo of a crowd of people in 1950s clothing assembled in a village square. They were turned obediently towards the camera; but none of them had any faces.

Another photo simply showed a severed human hand, with the

index finger missing. 'The Case of the Cannibal Ghosts,' murmured Walker.

And a photo of Buchanan Castle, in Scotland. The sky was dark, almost night, and there were lights on in every window except one. A figure of a man stood silhouetted against a great light in the open doorway. There was something horribly wrong about the figure.

'The Case of the Recurring Ancestor,' I said. 'The Droods get told that story when we're young, to keep us from getting cocky.'

The influence urged us on, like an invisible dog leash, through room after room, past wonders and treasures beyond counting, until finally it brought us to a sealed door. Black stained oak, eight feet tall and almost as wide, studded with brass and silver, and several lines of deeply inscribed protective wards, in half a dozen languages that no sane human being had spoken in living memory. The influence snapped off, and I think we all sighed a little with relief. I was still debating whether to knock, or give the door a good kicking, when it swung suddenly open before us, smooth and steady despite its massive weight. Beyond the door was a huge baronial hall, with towering bare stone walls and great interlocking wooden beams for a ceiling. A fire blazed cheerfully in the huge open fireplace, but there was no sign of anyone to greet us. The sheer size and scale of the place rooted the others to the spot; but I grew up in Drood Hall, so I strode right in. The others hurried after me.

'I'm beginning to wonder if there's anyone here at all,' I said finally. My voice seemed very small in such a great hall, as though it had been designed and constructed for beings much larger than men. 'I mean, King couldn't run a place this size on his own, particularly if he's on his death bed, as he claims. Where are the servants, bodyguards, nurses? Could the Independent Agent have already died, before the game's even started?'

'Reports of my death ... are no doubt highly anticipated,' snapped a cold, authoritative voice; and an image of Alexander King appeared suddenly out of nowhere before us. 'I value my privacy, and I don't have the time or the strength left to waste on unnecessary interactions.'

The legendary Independent Agent sat on a huge wooden throne, his back straight, his legs casually crossed. You could tell it was just an image, projected from somewhere else in Place Gloria; although it was sharp and clear and had three dimensions, it lacked ... presence. The image of Alexander King looked frail and shrunken, but nonetheless vital. And nowhere near as old as he was supposed to be. Illness or age had dug deep furrows in his face, but he had a long mane of silver-grey hair, his mouth was firm and his gaze was sharp. He was still handsome, in a ravaged sort of way, and he sat on his throne as though he was king in fact as well as name. He wore a purple crushed velvet smoking jacket over checked tweed flares.

'I always felt most at home in the seventies,' he said calmly. 'Such a glorious time to be young and alive and have the world by the throat.'

'Is that really you, King?' said Honey Lake. 'Or have we come all this way to be greeted by a glorified recording?'

'Oh, I'm very definitely me,' said King, grinning nastily. 'Not gone yet, despite everything your pernicious Company has done to try and hurry me along. I am safe and secure, in my private vaults; and I plan to stay that way until my game has run its course.'

'Hello, Grandfather,' said Peter.

'Peter,' said Alexander. He didn't look or sound particularly pleased to see his only grandson. 'Such a disappointment to me. All the things you could have done, the people you could have been; and you settled for industrial espionage. Such a grey little world! Where's the glory, or the glamour, in grubbing through big business's waste bins?'

'It pays well,' said Peter. He studied his grandfather thoughtfully, absorbing every detail.

'It would have to,' said Alexander. 'Well, now at least you have a chance to prove yourself. But you'll get no help from me. No advice or special preference, just because you're family.'

'Wouldn't have it any other way, Grandfather,' said Peter.

From their cold, distracted voices, they might have been discussing the weather. They sounded a lot like each other.

'Why us?' I said, and Alexander's piercing gaze switched immediately to me. I stared right back at him. 'As I understand it, you wanted the six best field agents in the world today, to find the one best suited to take your place when you're gone. So why us? We're all names, I suppose, with good solid backgrounds of work; but I could give you a dozen other names off the top of my head, of agents more famous and more suited than any of us.'

Alexander King flashed me his nasty grin again. 'I know who you're talking about; and if any of them had been good enough, they'd have taken my place by now. No, I chose the six of you because you're young, and have potential. My game will bring out the best in you, or kill you. Either way, the winner will have proved themselves a worthy successor.

'Pay attention. This is the contest, and to the victor the spoils. You will go to five locations I have chosen, and there investigate five of the world's greatest mysteries. Discover the truth behind the legend. Then move on to the next, until the game is finished.'

'What if we can't solve any of these mysteries?' Honey Lake interrupted. 'What if it turns out there is no answer?'

'I found the truth,' said Alexander King. 'So will you, if you're worthy. Fail to uncover any one of these five truths, and you all fail. The game stops there. No secret knowledge for anyone. So don't fail.'

'Terrific,' murmured the Blue Fairy.

'To begin with, the six of you will have to learn to work together as a team,' said Alexander, his dark gaze sweeping over us dispassionately. 'But only one of you can return to claim my prize. So, in the grand old tradition of spycraft, as you progress you will have to secretly work against and betray each other. There can be only one.' He laughed briefly. 'Always did like that film. At least I don't require you to chop each other's heads off.'

We looked at each other. None of us seemed that surprised, or shocked.

'I'm not too keen on any of this,' I said. 'I don't jump through hoops for anyone. I'm a Drood.'

'You'll dance to my tune, Drood, if you want the identity of the traitor inside your family,' said Alexander King. 'My game, my rules.' He smiled coldly round at us. 'Concentrate on the prize. All the accumulated secrets of my extended lifetime. The greatest secrets of the secret world. Don't you want to know who JFK shot? What the Eye in the Pyramid really means? And who murdered the Great Dream of the Sixties? Of course you do! This isn't just about the particular little bits of information you came here for, it's about knowing why the world is the way it is. I have the answer to every question you ever had, and I'll give it to the winner, all wrapped up in a pretty bow.'

'Get thee behind me, Grandfather,' said Peter.

'Don't take too long,' said Alexander, ignoring his grandson. 'I don't have too much time left. A few months, maybe less. If I should die before you complete the game, Place Gloria will be blown to pieces and my secrets lost for ever. None of you will get anything. Now: five mysteries, five answers. That's the game. Starting with Loch Ness in Scotland, for its monster.'

'Any yetis?' I said hopefully. 'I always wanted to visit Tibet or Nepal, and track down an abominable snowman.'

Alexander glared at me. 'I once came face to face with a yeti, back in the fifties. Very old, very wise creature. Scared the crap out of me. You will leave the yetis alone, Drood, and pray fervently that they continue to leave us alone.'

'How are we supposed to investigate five separate locations if we only have a few months to work in?' said Katt.

Alexander King waved one hand negligently, though I sensed the effort the movement cost him. It was the only move he'd made since he appeared. We jumped a little as bulky metal bracelets appeared out of nowhere and clamped themselves around our left wrists. The Blue Fairy clawed at his, trying to prise it off, but it wouldn't budge. I looked at mine thoughtfully; my torc was supposed to protect me from things like this. The metal was a dull purple with strange lights pulsing deep inside. It felt cold; and it looked very like alien technology.

I had to wonder who the Independent Agent might have allied himself with down the years, to ensure his precious autonomy.

'The teleport bracelets stay until the end of the game,' said Alexander King. 'Coordinates for each location are pre-programmed. So none of you can leave, or drop out, now the game has started. If you try, the bracelet will kill you.'

Katt glared at him. 'That wasn't in the rules!'

'It is now,' said Alexander, grinning his nasty grin.

'Where did you get these bracelets?' said Honey. 'I know alien tech when I see it.'

'That's one of the secrets you'll be competing for,' Alexander said smugly. 'Oh, the things I know that you need to know.' He looked at each of us in turn, savouring the moment. 'You are the best I could find . . . But I can't say I'm impressed. How will the world survive, when I am gone? Well, let the game commence! Prove your worth, to me and to the world. And, just maybe, to yourselves.'

His image disappeared, and we were left alone in the huge and empty hall. We didn't have time to say anything, before very suddenly we weren't in the hall any more.

And I am here to tell you, if anything, Loch Ness was even colder than the Swiss Alps.

CHAPTER FOUR
Not Nessie

So there we were: the six best secret agents in the world, masters of the spying arts, standing around in the mud and the long grass and the freezing cold wind, wondering what the Hell to do next. We were trained to operate in dark city streets, in shadows and alleyways, where honest men and women knew better than to go. We plied our trade in smoke-filled rooms and concealed cellars, in abandoned offices and computer rooms at midnight. We were not equipped to deal with lochs. Without clues to follow, suspects to interrogate or things to steal, we were frankly at something of a loss. At least I had some experience of the great outdoors; the others gave every indication that they were experiencing the countryside for the very first time, and not enjoying it at all. Hell, sunlight was probably a new experience for some of them.

I looked unhurriedly about me. Grey looming hills rose up on either side of Loch Ness, tall and ragged, spotted here and there with clumps of spindly trees and splashes of thick tufty grass. The sky was also grey, the sun mostly hidden behind dark lowering clouds drifting in from the opposite end of the loch. The waters were a dark blue, still and serene, untroubled by any wildlife. It was a pleasant enough view, in a dour foreboding sort of way. It had the look of countryside that had been here long before man came along to trouble it; and would still be here long after we were gone. Loch Ness was more than old, it was ancient; and what mysteries it had it held close to its chest.

Walker surprised me by taking a deep lungful of the freezing cold air, and then smiling broadly. 'Now that's more like it. Fresh country air. Bracing! Makes you feel good to be alive.'

'You're as weird as everyone says you are,' snarled Peter King, hugging himself against the cold and looking thoroughly miserable and put-upon. 'It's cold, it's damp . . . and I appear to be standing in some sheep droppings.'

'Don't rub it off,' the Blue Fairy said. 'It's supposed to bring good luck.'

'It won't be lucky for the bloody sheep if I get my hands on it,' Peter said darkly, scraping the bottom of his shoe against the spiky grass with grim determination. 'These are expensive shoes. Hand-tooled by craftsmen to look good in expensive boardrooms, not assaulted by the unregulated filth of the countryside!'

'I didn't think it could get this cold outside the Arctic Circle,' said Honey Lake, shuddering inside her long white fur coat. 'I wouldn't be surprised to see a polar bear come swimming down those waters. Probably with a penguin tap-dancing on its back.'

'I like it here,' Katt decided. The cold didn't seem to be bothering her, despite her flimsy dress. She moved in beside me, and slipped a slender knowing arm through mine. She snuggled in close, and beamed happily up at me. 'It's very . . . scenic. Dramatic, even. I'd swear that wind's wuthering. Still, no place for a delicate flower of the city, like me.'

'You're about as delicate as a steam-hammer,' said the Blue Fairy. 'I've seen the state of some of your victims after you've finished with them.'

Katt pulled a face at him, and then smiled adoringly up at me, from where she was apparently welded to my side. 'You and I belong together, Eddie. We appreciate the true qualities of a place like this. We're both . . . free spirits, independent and unrestrained! We belong in the wild, far from the chains and restrictions of civilised behaviour.'

I had to smile at her. 'Before this goes any further, Katt, I feel I should point out that I am a Drood. We're trained to recognise a honey trap, and to know real bullshit when we hear it. So save the honeyed words and the ego massage for the civilians.'

Katt laughed easily, not offended in the least. 'Can't blame a girl for trying, darling. And you'd be surprised how many supposedly intelligent men will fall for the most blatant flattery, even in these so-called sophisticated days. Especially if I take a deep breath and push my bosoms out.'

I looked at her for a moment. 'How many, Katt? How many men have you seduced, betrayed and murdered, down the years?'

She shrugged prettily. 'I don't keep count, Eddie. It's just a job. Some men more than others. Some were quite sweet.'

'And you killed them all? Even the ones you were fond of?'

'Especially the ones I was fond of, darling. I've never allowed anyone to have a hold over me.'

'And you never loved any of them?'

'What a thing to ask, sweetie! I loved them all! In my own way.' She looked out over the loch, her beautiful oriental features untouched by any emotion I could recognise. 'I really don't know what I'm doing here. I mean, monster hunting is so not me. I have always been strictly espionage and problem-disposal, with the occasional side order of treachery and blackmail. Stick to what you're best at, that's what I say. The honey trap has always been part of the grand old tradition of spycraft. I am glamorous and decorative, not practical. I do not get my hands dirty. It's in my contract.'

'And I suppose you feel the need for a big strong man to look after you,' I said. 'To protect you from the nasty monster.'

'Exactly!' Katt snuggled in close again, and looked up at me from under heavily mascaraed eyelids. 'I don't do mysteries, I don't fight monsters, and I very definitely don't do roughing it. I mean, come on! What am I supposed to do if we should find a monster here? Chuck it under the chin, and beguile it with my famous charms?'

'If anyone could, you could,' I said generously.

Katt sighed. 'I don't know why Alexander ever thought to choose me for his precious contest.'

'I think the idea is we're supposed to learn to work as a group, calling on our various talents as required,' I said. 'All of us working together, for the greater good.'

'Until we have to betray each other,' said Katt.

I smiled at her. 'I'm sure you'll have no problem with that. Now, if I could have my arm back, please? I have no intention of getting close to you, in any sense of the word. I would quite like to die in bed, but preferably of old age. So do us both a favour, and go vamp somebody else.'

She smiled sunnily, let go of my arm and stepped away. 'Your loss, darling.'

She strode off, still somehow sure-footed and graceful even on the muddy bank of the loch. She was heading for Walker, and I mentally wished him the best of luck. I went to stand beside Honey, who was staring suspiciously out over the dark unmoving waters of the loch, as though she suspected them of planning something. She was standing straight and tall, her hands planted on her hips, looking very much like a general contemplating the field before a battle.

'We have to get organised,' she said, acknowledging my presence without looking round. 'We're on a deadline, and the clock is ticking. Alexander didn't look as bad as I'd been led to expect, but we have no way of knowing how accurate that vision was. He could go at any time and take his secrets with him, the selfish bastard. He has a duty to hand over his hoarded information to those best suited to make good use of it. Not make it the prize in a stupid game.'

'I don't think Alexander King has ever been very strong on duty,' I said.

She glanced at me, and smiled briefly. 'We'd better work together on this, Eddie. We're the only real professionals in this group.'

'There's Walker,' I said.

'Too much of an unknown quantity. Never trust anyone from the Nightside.'

'And the Blue Fairy might surprise us.'

'Never trust an elf.'

I had to smile. 'Come on, Honey. You're CIA. You don't trust anyone.'

She looked at me severely. 'You have to trust someone, or you'll never get anything done. The day of the independent operative is over, Eddie. The world's grown too big, too complicated, for the lone wolf following hunches and instincts. Only big organisations have the resources to deal with today's problems.'

'My family would agree with you,' I said. 'But I've always had problems with my family.'

'So I've heard,' said Honey. 'Why do you do it, Eddie? Why do the Droods feel they have the right to run roughshod over the whole world?'

'Because we've been doing it for hundreds of years,' I said. 'And we're very good at it.'

'Not always,' said Honey.

'Well,' I said. 'No one wants to be insufferable.'

She laughed. It was a free, easy sound, utterly at odds with her determined stance and coolly professional face.

'You give your whole life to this, don't you?' she said. 'All you Droods. You play the game till it kills you, or till you drop in your tracks. Why would you do that?'

'Someone has to,' I said.

'No, really. Why?'

'Really?' I considered the question. 'Duty. Responsibility. Or maybe because for all its treacheries and dangers, it's still the best game in the world. The only one worthy of our talents. Why do you do it?'

'Oh Hell, Eddie, it's a job. A way up the ladder, towards getting on and moving up. I'm going to be *somebody*, doing things that matter. Making the decisions that matter.' She glanced at me. 'You Droods don't care about politics. The rest of us don't have that luxury.' She looked out over the loch again, making it clear with her body language that the subject was closed. 'So, how do you find one monster in a lake this size?'

'Good question,' I said.

Out of the corner of my eye, I was watching Katt try out her charms on Walker. (It's a poor secret agent who can't think about two things at the same time.) Katt kept trying to slip her arm through Walker's, and he kept dodging her, without quite seeming to be aware that he was doing it. Finally he turned and looked at her, and she actually fell back a pace. Even at a distance, I could feel the chill in his gaze, colder than the Scottish air could ever be. He said something, and Katt reacted as though she'd been struck in the face. She gave Walker a quick professional smile, turned her back on him and stalked away with her nose in the air. Walker went back to studying the loch, his face calm and thoughtful and entirely untroubled. I decided I'd better keep a watchful eye on Walker. Anyone who could stare down Lethal Harmony of Kathmandu and send her running for cover was clearly a man to be reckoned with.

Katt stalked past the Blue Fairy without glancing in his direction, presumably because she knew her charms and skills would be wasted on the famously homosexual half-elf. She had nothing that would interest him. Except perhaps fashion tips. Honey was saying something useful but boring about the necessity for taking direct action, but I was still watching the Blue Fairy. We all of us looked out of place in this wild and savage setting, but he looked more than usually lost. He had his hands thrust deep into his belt, and his chin was buried in his wilting ruff as he glowered at the muddy ground before him. He looked tired and alone, and out of his depth. My first reaction was, Good. Serve him right.

But . . . I'd known Blue a long time, on and off. I liked him, trusted him, gave him a chance to be a hero in the Hungry Gods War. He turned his back on that, and on me, for a chance to ingratiate himself with his arrogant elf kindred. I should have known . . . and I should have known better. The Blue Fairy's whole history was one of broken words, cold-blooded betrayals and falling short. He liked to say he was somebody important, back in the day, but truth be told he wasn't, though he could have been if he hadn't thrown everything away indulging his many weaknesses. And he was half-elf. Never trust an elf. Everyone knows that. I really shouldn't take it personally, that he let me down in front of my whole family after I vouched for him. That he made me look bad.

That was what the Blue Fairy did.

He stole a torc from the Droods and got away with it. You had to admire him for that. No one else had ever managed it. Give the man credit for thinking big. And I of all people understood the demands of family; the need almost despite yourself to belong, to be accepted . . . and the stupid self-destructive things that it could drive a man to. So I left Honey talking authoritatively to herself, and strolled over to join the Blue Fairy. I didn't hurry. I wanted to give him time to move away. But he looked round as he sensed me approaching, raised one hand briefly to the golden torc at his throat, and then turned almost defiantly to face me. His head came up, his mouth firmed, and he stood his ground. He'd come a long way from the broken, defeated man I'd found more dead than alive in a poky little flat in Wimbledon. If nothing else, it seemed his time at the Fae Court had put some backbone into him.

I stopped a respectful distance away, and nodded briskly. 'Cold day,' I said. 'Don't suppose you've got a flask of something bracing about you?'

He smiled briefly, as though he wasn't used to it any more. His eyes were watchful. 'Sorry,' he said. 'I had to give all that up when I took my place at the Fae Court. They insisted. Elves take a very firm stand on personal weaknesses. Not merely frowned on; not allowed. When you're an elf, even your failings have to be on a grand scale. Anything less is beneath us. I do miss my old sins, my old indulgences . . . much in the way I miss my childhood, when I could make all the mistakes I wanted, secure in the knowledge it didn't really matter. But that was such a long time ago. I was a different person, then. I've finally grown up, Eddie, and I don't think I like it.' He met my gaze steadily. 'Are you really prepared to kill me, to get your precious torc back?'

'I don't know,' I said honestly. 'Probably.'

He nodded. 'You'd make a good elf.'

'Now you're just being nasty.'

We shared a smile. Perhaps it's only old friends and old enemies who can be really honest with each other. We stood side by side for a while, looking out over the loch. The grey skies were now definitely overcast, and the waters seemed darker. The wind was blowing steadily, the bitter cold sinking into my bones. I stamped my feet into the mud and spiky grass to keep the circulation going. If Blue felt the cold, he hid it well. He smiled suddenly, and drew my attention to further down the bank, where Katt was snuggling up to Peter King. It was like watching a cat stalk a mouse. But to my surprise, Peter didn't seem in the least intimidated by her practised glamour, or by the way she was expertly pressing her body against his. He politely disengaged his arm from hers, stepped back, and said something no doubt calm and civilised and utterly firm. Katt stared at him as though she couldn't believe it, and then dismissed him utterly with a turned back, kicking at the grass as she stomped away. I don't think she was used to being refused by so many men in one day.

'Didn't see that coming,' said the Blue Fairy. 'Thought for sure she'd eat young Peter alive.'

'A chip off the old block, I suppose,' I said. 'Alexander King was quite the ladykiller in his day. Sometimes literally. Oh, look – I think Peter's found some more sheep droppings.'

'How lucky can one man get?' Blue said solemnly. 'Have you

noticed? Walker seems quite at home in this primitive and entirely uncivilised place. Not what you'd expect from a man who spends his whole life walking the mean streets of the Nightside, where the sun never shines . . . It's as though nothing here can touch him.'

'Nothing here would dare,' I said. 'Everyone's heard of Walker. Hello! Now Honey's going to talk to him. I think perhaps we should wander over and do a little shameless eavesdropping. We can't afford to be left out of anything. Not in this group.'

'Hear all, see all, and keep our thoughts to ourselves,' said the Blue Fairy.

'You see?' I said. 'You'd make a good Drood.'

'Now who's being nasty?'

We laughed briefly, and then he looked at me with an expression on his face I couldn't read.

'It's all right that you never liked me,' he said finally. 'Not many do.'

'I liked you well enough,' I said. 'I just never approved.'

'I liked you,' he said. 'Admired you, even. For having the nerve to tell your family to go to Hell, and make it stick. For having the courage to live your own life, and go your own way, and to Hell with what anyone expected of you. When you brought me into your family, I really did mean to make you proud of me. But . . . you should never trust an elf, Eddie. And a desperate, lonely, stupid half-elf least of all.'

'Let's go and see what Honey and Walker are up to,' I said.

Why is it always the ones who aren't really your friends who insist on baring their soul to you?

As we joined Honey and Walker, she stuck her face right into his and demanded he use his legendary voice to summon the monster to the surface of the loch. Walker, not one bit intimidated, stood his ground and gave her back stare for stare. Peter and Katt hurried over, not wanting to be left out of anything.

'Voice?' said Peter breathlessly. 'What voice?'

'They say many things about Walker, in the Nightside,' I said. 'Most importantly, they say he has a voice no one can resist, that can compel anyone to say or do anything. A voice so powerful even the high and mighty gods and monsters of the Nightside must bow their arrogant heads and answer to it. There are even those who say Walker once made a corpse sit up on its mortuary slab and answer his questions.'

'It was just the once,' said Walker. 'I wish everyone would stop making such a big fuss about it.'

'Oh,' said Peter. 'That voice.'

'Would it work outside the Nightside?' said the Blue Fairy.

'I don't think it works at all,' I said, making a sudden connection. There was nothing in Walker's face or bearing to give the truth away, but suddenly I knew ... and a great many things made sense. 'You don't have your voice any more, do you, Walker? Because if you did, you would have used it on Alexander King to make him give up his secrets. You never jumped through hoops for anyone, before this. No, your voice was bestowed on you by the Authorities, when they first put you in charge of policing the Nightside. How else could one mortal man be expected to keep the peace in a place like that? But the Authorities are dead and gone now, and so is their gift. Right, Walker?'

He looked at me coolly, saying nothing; but sometimes silence is its own answer. I felt like jumping in the air and doing high fives with myself. I knew now what Alexander King had offered Walker to tempt him into this contest: a new voice. Honey made a short, exasperated sound, and moved abruptly away from Walker to stare out over the loch again.

'What do we know about this place?' she said. 'I mean, I know the story, the legend of Nessie, everyone does. But that's about it.'

'I can tell you that Aleister Crowley lived here once,' said Walker, unexpectedly. 'He had a house on the banks of the loch, to which he summoned his pathetic followers to teach them the ways of magick. And in that dark and feverish place, he and his circle danced and took drugs and had all kinds of sex, driving themselves to exhaustion and beyond; all in the service of one great unholy ritual.'

'Crowley,' said Katt. 'I sort of know the name, but—'

'Kids today,' said the Blue Fairy, shaking his head.

'The Great Beast,' Walker said patiently. 'Called by some, not least himself, the Wickedest Man in the World. In the thirties, his name was a curse on lips of the world, hated and feared and reviled, and he loved it. People would cross themselves when they saw him in the street. Perhaps he started to believe his own press; I don't know. But he came

100

here, and in that house, in that place, he and his followers tried to invoke and summon a great and primal power. But when he caught a glimpse of precisely what it was he was trying to bring through into our reality, he was so horrified he broke off the working and ran away screaming, along with his shattered followers. He ran all the way back to England, and many said he was never the same after that. The house is still here. It's said to be haunted, by bad dreams.'

'Was he really?' said Katt, after a pause. 'The wickedest man in the world, I mean?'

Walker smiled. 'No.'

'You'd know,' I said generously.

'Well, that was very interesting, I suppose,' said Honey, 'but when I asked if anyone knew anything, I meant anything *relevant*.'

'Legends about the monster of Loch Ness go back to the sixth century,' I said. 'Some saint was supposed to have come face to face with it while crossing the loch in a boat. He spoke gently to the creature, and it turned away and did him no harm. There were various stories after that, all for local consumption, but the first modern sighting was in 1933, which was when the world first learned about Nessie.'

'Why then?' said Peter. 'I mean, why 1933 precisely? What happened then?'

'They built a road alongside the loch,' I said. 'Up to that point, Loch Ness was way off the beaten track. But once the road was opened to regular traffic, linking two major cities, people started seeing things. There have been various sightings since the thirties, some photos and even a few short films, but never anything definite or definitive. Never any proof. Nessie is apparently a very shy beastie, and never pops her head above the surface for long.

'As for the loch itself: twenty-four miles long, averaging a mile or so in width, and reaches a depth of some seven hundred feet. If you'd care to consider the waters for a moment … Yes, they are pretty dark, aren't they? That's peat, stirred up from the bottom. Any disturbance in the water chums up even more peat, and soon enough you can't see a damned thing.'

'Teacher's pet,' said the Blue Fairy.

'How is it you know so much about our first mystery?' Katt said suspiciously.

'He's a Drood,' said Walker. 'They know everything.'

'Pretty much,' I said cheerfully.

'Anything else?' said Honey.

I shrugged. 'Not unless you want to argue over the merits of the various photographs and films. The exact nature of Nessie's identity is a much discussed and disputed matter. Some driven souls spend their whole lives here, perched on the edge of the loch hoping for a sighting. No one knows anything for sure. Not even the Droods.'

'That is why we're here, after all,' said the Blue Fairy.

'Oh, come on,' said Katt. 'We're supposed to solve a fifteen-hundred-year-old mystery, just like that, after everyone else has failed?'

'Why not?' said Walker, and smiled briefly. 'We are professionals.'

'Bloody freezing cold professionals,' said Peter, hugging himself and kicking miserably at the muddy ground. 'Where are we, exactly? And don't anyone say "Scotland" or there will be slaps for everyone.'

'A long way from anywhere civilised,' said the Blue Fairy.

Peter smirked. 'Like I said, Scotland.'

'If any locals should happen to wander by, I think I'd better do the talking,' said Walker.

'Hold everything,' I said. 'Where are the locals? I haven't seen anyone on or around the loch since we got here. There should be someone knocking about ... And where are the tourists? There should be boats going up and down the loch on a regular basis, as well as the more hardy souls out for an improving walk to see the scenery. Hell, there isn't even any wildlife about that I can spot. No birds on the water, or in the air. It's like we're the only living things here.'

'Perhaps the Independent Agent has kindly provided for us to have a little privacy while we work,' said Walker. 'Which would seem to indicate he still has connections with the outside world, for all his isolation.' And then he stopped, and looked thoughtfully at the darkening clouds filling the sky overhead. 'Can anyone tell me what time it is? My watch says mid morning, but I don't think I trust it. It feels much later than that.'

'I have a computer implant in my head,' said Honey, not at all self-consciously. 'And according to Langley's computers, it's exactly

15:17 here. We're missing some time. More than could be allowed for by different time zones.'

'So the bracelets' transportation isn't instantaneous,' said Walker.

'Or they're pre-programmed to deliver us to a particular point in space and time,' I said.

'Oh Hell,' said the Blue Fairy. 'I feel jet-lagged now.'

'A problem for another time,' I said. 'What are we going to do about Nessie? Shout, "Hey monster, we're very important people on a tight deadline, so would you please get your scaly arse up here and talk to us"?'

'Please do that,' said the Blue Fairy. 'I'd really like to watch you.'

'Don't be so negative,' said Honey. 'We're professionals. We can do this!'

Katt sniffed. 'You would say that. You're American. You can do anything.'

Honey smiled brightly at her. 'Exactly!' She looked decisively out over the still and placid waters of the loch. Her hands were back on her hips again. 'We could always lob in a few hand grenades, and see if anything comes up to complain about the noise.'

We all winced and the Blue Fairy hissed, 'Philistine! There have been creatures here for hundreds of years, and you want to risk killing what might be the last one?'

'Typical CIA,' said Peter. 'All brute force and ignorance.'

'Hey,' said Honey, entirely unaffected. 'Don't knock it if it works.'

'I still have contacts with the Army and the Navy,' said Walker. 'A few words in the right ears and I could have all manner of manpower and resources rushed up here, but that would take time, which we don't have. And I rather think it's part of Alexander King's game that we're supposed to do this on our own.'

'I have absolutely no problems with a little creative cheating,' said Peter. 'Especially if it means we can get out of this cold one moment sooner.'

'Quite right, darling,' said Katt. 'This is so not my professional venue. I flourish best in cities.'

'Yes,' said Honey. 'You do have the look of someone who should be walking the streets.'

'Girls, girls,' murmured Walker. The Blue Fairy sniggered openly.

Peter kicked at the ground again. 'I know I'm going to catch something. God, I'd kill for a Starbucks.'

I felt sorry for Peter. He was so clearly out of his element, and out of his depth. Probably only got his place in the contest because his grandfather saw one last chance to make Peter over into the kind of grandson the Independent Agent should have had.

'I could go fishing for the monster,' the Blue Fairy said abruptly. 'You have heard of my ability, to go fishing in other dimensions? One of the few useful talents I inherited from dear absent Daddy and his rampant elven genes. I've never gone after anything this big before, but . . .'

I considered the Blue Fairy. He didn't look like much, even with his new health and his somewhat damp Elizabethan finery, but I had seen him pull all kinds of amazing things out of a dimensional pool he could conjure up. He caught me looking at him, and smiled superciliously.

'I can handle anything I can sink my hook into, these days. I learnt a lot during my time at the Fae Court under Queen Mab.'

'I thought the elves killed half-breeds on sight?' said Katt spitefully. 'Breeding outside the species being their greatest taboo.'

'Not when you come bearing gifts,' said the Blue Fairy, one hand rising very briefly to the golden torc around his throat.

Everyone looked at me. I looked right back at them until they got the message and changed the subject.

'Could you really fish the monster out of the loch?' Walker said to the Blue Fairy.

'Maybe,' said Blue. 'But it would take time, and—'

Something stirred in the stunted shrubs nearby. We all spun round. Katt produced an impressively big gun from out of nowhere, and fired a single shot in the direction of the noise. The shrubs exploded and blood and fur flew on the air. The sound of the gun was shockingly loud in the quiet, echoing back from the surrounding hills. We waited, on guard, but nothing else moved in the tattered shrubs at the side of the loch. Honey looked at Katt with new respect.

'Can I ask where, precisely, did you produce that unnaturally large gun from?'

Katt smiled. 'Please, allow a girl her little secrets.'

'I once knew a girl who had teeth in her—' said the Blue Fairy, and then shut up when I looked at him.

Walker was already poking through the ruins of the smouldering shrubs with the tip of his umbrella. He bent over to inspect something and then sighed, straightened up, and looked at Katt.

'Congratulations, my dear. You have exploded an otter.'

She shrugged, and smiled prettily about her. 'Sorry, darlings. Instinct.'

'Otters are a protected species, aren't they?' said Peter.

'Not from me,' said Katt. Her gun had disappeared again. I had to wonder what else she might have hidden about her person. I wouldn't have thought there was room for anything under a dress that tight; not even underwear.

The Blue Fairy produced a fishing rod and reel. It looked battered and mended and much-used, but he handled it with professional ease. 'What do we think the monster is, anyway?' he said, without looking up.

'It's supposed to be some kind of dinosaur, isn't it?' said Honey. 'The last of its kind, preserved in a lake cut off from the rest of the natural world. The few photos I've seen show a long neck, and what might be the humps of an extended body.'

'I always hoped it would turn out to be a dragon,' said the Blue Fairy. 'Not those nasty things the elf lords ride; but the real thing from ages past, when there was still wild magic in the world.'

'You soppy old romantic, you,' I said.

'Maybe it's an alien!' said Katt. 'Descended from the crew of some crashed starship, long ago.'

'Could be some kind of elemental,' said Walker. 'Which would explain why it never seems to look the same twice.'

Peter sniffed loudly. 'More likely it's another tourist trap, making the most of an old legend to separate the gullible from their money.'

'If this contest wasn't so important, I think I'd be happy for Nessie to stay a mystery,' I said. 'After all, what would the rest of the world do, if presented with actual proof of Nessie's existence and nature? Trap it, or shoot it? Drag it out of the loch to be shown off at some aquatic zoo? It would certainly never know a moment's peace again. No, I think it's safer and better off as a legend.'

Walker stood at the very edge of the bank, staring down into the dark, still waters. 'What if there is no monster?' he said. 'No Nessie. What if that's the answer to the mystery: that there's nothing down there, really, and never was? How are we supposed to prove a negative? I mean, short of draining the whole loch—'

'Damn,' said Katt. 'You're actually considering it, aren't you?'

'Philistine,' said the Blue Fairy, deftly slipping a barbed hook on to the end of his fishing line.

Walker looked back at us, smiling. 'I doubt even the CIA could pull that one off, with all its resources. And certainly not without seriously upsetting the locals.'

'What we need,' Honey said firmly, 'Is a submersible.'

Her face became preoccupied, no doubt communing with her superiors at Langley via her computer implant. No way that was Earth technology. I was beginning to get a very good idea of which particular non-existent department Honey worked for. A few moments passed, and then a vast rent appeared in the sky above us, an actual tear in reality itself. Out of which dropped a large and very yellow and extremely futuristic-looking submersible. It was the size of an articulated lorry, and it fell almost lazily through the air, heading for the water right next to where we were standing.

'*Everybody back!*' yelled Walker.

He was already retreating at speed, and the rest of us were on his heels. The submersible hit the surface of the loch hard, and a great explosion of water jumped up into the air, raining down on where we'd been standing. Some of the icy waters still reached us, and Katt squeaked miserably as it splashed across her bare shoulders. Served her right for being so slow off the mark. Walker remained cool and calm under his opened umbrella. The rest of us glared at Honey, who pretended to be very interested in her newly acquired submersible, which had now steadied itself and was bobbing happily at the side of the loch. It was big and blocky, with wide fins, a blunt nose, and all kinds of bristling scientific protrusions. There was even a (hopefully reinforced) extra wide window at the front, backed up by glaring headlights. Which it was going to need down in the depths, when the submersible's passage alone would stir up enough peat to fill the water.

'Trust the CIA to show off,' said Peter.

'The CIA does big,' I said. 'Droods prefer subtle.'

Honey didn't look exactly inspired with what she'd been sent. 'Wonderful!' she said acidly. 'Someone who only thinks they have a sense of humour has sent me a yellow submarine. Probably programmed the ship's computers to sound like Ringo. Heads will roll when I get back, and other things too. I asked for a proper research vessel, not this . . . toy.'

'I'd mention Thunderbird Four,' said Walker. 'But it would only date me.'

'I think it's very pretty,' said Katt.

'How are we supposed to squeeze into something that size?' said the Blue Fairy.

'You aren't,' Honey said shortly. 'I've used that model before, and it's strictly a single-seater. And no, you don't get to draw straws over who goes. It's my submersible, so I get to drive.'

'Typical CIA,' said Katt. 'Never big on sharing.'

'We're supposed to let you go down there on your own?' said Walker.

'Unless one of you has gills, and can hang on to the outside,' said Honey.

'You might be able to locate Nessie with your wonderful new toy,' I said. 'But how are you going to get proof? I don't care what your new rubber duckie comes equipped with: you're not going to get a clear image underwater. It's been tried, and without a clear background to give you scale, any sonar image you get is worthless.'

'Why do I know you're about to suggest something clever?' said Honey.

'Because I'm a Drood,' I said. 'We always know best. It's in our job description. Look, this isn't exactly rocket science. First you find the creature, you bring it up to the surface and we photograph it next to your submersible. That gives us size and scale and a clear image. Right?'

'The submersible's cameras are only designed to operate underwater,' said Honey.

We looked at each other.

'I've got a really good camera built into my phone,' said Peter.

'Oh this is just so amateur night, darlings,' said Katt.

'It'll do,' Honey said shortly. 'I'm not begging and pleading with Langley for more equipment. This whole mission is drowning in paperwork and requisitions as it is, and they're sure to find some way to stick me with the overruns. I'll locate Nessie, goose her up to the surface, and Peter, you had better get some really good photos.'

'This is a state-of-the-art phone, with still shots and film,' Peter protested. 'I designed it myself.'

He started to spout off some detailed technobabble, only to shut up and sulk as it became clear none of us was listening. Honey stalked down to the edge of the loch, and we trailed after her. None of us was used to being left behind, while someone else went off to do the interesting fun stuff. Honey jumped lightly on to the side of the bright yellow submersible, grabbing one of the more sturdy protrusions to steady herself. The submersible hardly bobbed under her added weight. She hit the access panel with her fist, and a hatch swung slowly outwards. She wriggled in past it, and disappeared inside. This was followed by a certain amount of swearing as she couldn't find the light switch, and then the sound of powerful engines came on line, and the whole submersible seemed to shake itself like a hunting dog coming awake, ready for action. The access hatch opened itself a little wider, and we ducked and fell back as a package the size of a kitchen sink shot out over our heads and crash-landed on the bank behind us.

We turned to look, and then watched with interest as the package jumped up and down on the spot, turning itself rapidly over and around in mid air, shaking and shuddering as it unfolded in several different directions at once. It kept growing and growing in size, throwing out offshoots of itself, and finally sank several barbed steel legs into the ground to hold it securely in place. By the time it had finished showing off, the package had formed itself into a large and flashy remote communications centre, complete with radio, sonar, live television feeds, and a few things even I didn't recognise. Walker immediately strode across and commandeered the nearest keyboard, looked it over briskly, and then punched in a series of instructions that had the whole thing up and running in a few moments.

I wandered round the console, checking the data streams on the monitors, familiarising myself with the various comm systems, very careful not to touch anything. I was damned if I was leaving any fingerprints or DNA traces on the console's suspiciously gleaming surfaces for the CIA to study once the mission was over. After a while I moved in beside Walker, and casually indicated a few more things he could do to bring the console up to full power. The others crowded in beside us, peering over our shoulders.

'We have radio and video contact with the pilot,' said Walker. 'Direct feed from seven underwater cameras on those monitors there, and an ongoing display of whatever the submersible's long-range sensors are picking up. Almost as good as being there.'

'Can you hear me, Honey?' I said, leaning forward over the mike.

'Of course I can hear you! I can hear all of you.' Honey glared out at us from a small screen, strapped into a pilot's chair and surrounded very closely on all sides by enough instrumentation to take the submersible into near-earth orbit.

'Looks a bit snug,' I said.

'Snug? I've known spacier coffins. There isn't room in here to swing a flea. I've already severely bruised precious parts of my anatomy getting into the driving seat, and you don't want to know what I have to do to work the air conditioning. Still, all systems are go and we are ready to proceed.'

'We haven't decided how you're going to lure the famously shy Nessie out of hiding,' said Walker. 'You don't appear to have anything on board that will do the trick. Or at least nothing that hasn't been tried before.'

'Maybe I should try and attract the creature,' said Katt, half seriously. 'I do have an outstanding track record for attracting anyone and anything with a pulse . . .'

'Yeah,' said the Blue Fairy. 'That'll do it. Stand on the edge of the loch and show it your tits, Katt.'

'Crude little man,' Katt said frostily.

'Actually, you've given me an idea,' said Blue. 'Attraction – that's the key. We have to make Nessie want to come to the surface. And there are some things, some sounds, that will attract anything, luring them on against their will, pulling them in like a hook in the jaw. And I have just the thing in mind, something I've fished for before.'

We looked at him, standing tall and proud and only a bit be-draggled in his Elizabethan finery, his battered old fishing rod and reel at the ready. And perhaps I was the only one who saw how much he needed to be taken seriously.

'What did you have in mind?' I said.

'A mating call,' said the Blue Fairy, smiling at us, pleased at being the centre of attention. 'I once brought up from the dimensional depths, entirely by accident I have to admit, a kind of ... siren. A temptress, a seducer, whose call no mortal will could hope to withstand. Fortunately, this particular siren's call was only ever intended to work on those of a heterosexual persuasion, so I remained relatively unaffected and was able to throw the damned thing back.'

'Can you find it again?' said Walker.

'Well obviously,' said Blue, 'or I wouldn't have said anything. I'll find it, hook it and reel it in, and then we can use its call to bring Nessie to us.'

'Hold everything,' said Walker. 'Are you seriously proposing we call up another monster, and drop it into the loch? Isn't the situation here complicated enough as it is? Not to mention the problem we would be leaving behind for the future. What if the siren developed a taste for the locals? They could end up swarming here like so many lemmings.'

'I never suggested leaving the siren here,' the Blue Fairy said heavily, in a calm, patient and infuriatingly understanding voice. 'In fact, I think it would be downright dangerous to keep the thing around one moment longer than we absolutely have to. What I have in mind is much simpler, bordering on elegant. I bring the siren here, we record its call on this marvellous communications system and I throw it back again. We then broadcast the recording of the call into the loch's waters. Foolproof. Unless Nessie turns out to be gay as well, of course . . .'

'Let us very definitely not go there,' I said quickly. 'The recording sounds fine to me. Everyone? Right, do your thing, Blue. Catch us a siren.'

Of course, then he had to make a whole big thing out of finding the right spot along the bank of the loch. He walked us up and down through the mud and spiky grass, his face set in a rigid mask of concentration, which he had to spoil by occasionally glancing at us to see how we were taking it. He finally settled on one particular spot that looked exactly the same as all the others, and gestured grandly with his left hand. A glowing golden pool some six feet in diameter appeared before him, flat and featureless, not so much covering the ground as replacing it. The pool was a gateway to everywhere else, to all the dimensions that ever were or may be, and was painful to look at directly for more than a moment.

Blue's time with the elves had clearly helped him; I could remember when he needed to spill his own blood in sacrifice to summon the golden pool to him. And the pool looked a lot bigger than I remembered. A hole punched right through the walls of reality by sheer will power. Only the Blue Fairy was skilled enough and crazy enough to call it up so he could go fishing in it .

He worked his rod and reel expertly, and hook and line disappeared into the golden pool without in any way disturbing the glowing surface. Blue stood quietly, apparently calm and relaxed, and we stood and watched him. There's always something fascinating about watching someone do the one thing they're really good at. The sound of the line whining off the spinning reel was almost hypnotic as the line dived down and down, into depths we had no business fooling with. But that's an elf for you. And then the line snapped taut, jerking this way and that across the glowing pool, and the Blue Fairy's breath hissed between his clenched teeth as he worked the reel, putting a steady pressure on the line. Slowly, steadily, he began to haul his catch in.

I realised I was holding my breath. Blue didn't always get what he was after first time, and he had been known to haul some really nasty things up out of the depths. The line remained taut, rising very slowly, the reel clicking quietly. Whatever Blue had hooked, it didn't seem to be fighting him.

I glanced quickly around. We were standing far too close to the pool, and none of us had taken any precautions. I had my torc to protect me, but God alone knew what the others were relying on to save them from the siren's call. I started to say something; and then the golden pool exploded as the siren burst through into our reality.

It rose up and up, towering over us, too big to be contained by the pool through which it had found a foothold into our reality. It was huge and glorious, completely unearthly, unfolding and uncoiling in every direction at once. It was vast and wonderful, too beautiful to be borne, dark yellow flesh with rainbows exploding inside it. It sang; and I was lost. A glorious, wonderful, unbearable sound. I fell to my knees before it, and so did we all. Who knows what songs the sirens sang? Who knows what song Medusa sang for noble Perseus?

We knew, and I will hear that song in my nightmares for ever.

Because I was nothing, in the face of that song. Nothing that mattered.

The siren called, and we shuffled forward on our knees, gazing adoringly up at the living fountain of flesh towering over us. Even the Blue Fairy had dropped his rod and reel, caught up in a song that went for the soul. I could barely see my surroundings, feel the tough grass scuffing beneath my knees. The siren wanted us; and not for anything good. Death would be the kindest thing that would happen to us, once the siren had clasped us to its unforgiving bosom. I knew that, and I didn't care. I wanted to worship it for ever, worship it with my body until I died of it.

Except ... there was another voice in my head and in my heart, another face before my eyes. My Molly, my sweet Molly Metcalf, who had put her mark upon me long ago. As soon as I thought of her, I could feel the torc blazing coldly around my neck, trying to alert me to the threat ... and those two things together gave me the strength I needed to stop moving forward. I slowly turned my head to one side, looking away from the terrible, wonderful thing before me. It was all I'd ever wanted, right there waiting for me, and I fought it with every ounce of strength and will I had. I turned my head away, my whole body twitching and trembling with the effort, and saw another face looking at me.

The Blue Fairy had stopped moving too, and had turned his face away from the siren. Perhaps because of his nature, perhaps because he also wore the golden torc, perhaps because he was half-elf. Or maybe he was just stubborn, like me.

We looked at each other, and I slowly turned my gaze to the rod and reel lying abandoned before the Blue Fairy. He looked at it too, and with the last of his strength, he grabbed the reel and threw it into the golden pool, hook and line and all.

The line snapped taut again, dragging at the siren's fleshy orchid head, distracting its attention. I forced myself up on to my feet, turned my back on the siren, and lurched over to the communications centre. I had to record the siren's call, before it was sucked back down again. I subvocalised my activating Words, and my armour flowed over me in an instant, sealing me in and protecting me from the world. The golden strange matter encased me from head to toe, and just like that the siren's song was nothing more than noise. I hit the record button, and turned quickly to see what was happening.

The siren was no longer held to this world, but it didn't want to go. It had been defied, and it was angry. It had found an endless feeding ground, and it would not be denied. It towered high above us, flaring and pulsating; and even through the protecting filters of my golden mask, this extreme and awful creature was still the most beautiful thing I'd ever seen. The Blue Fairy was on his feet, but halfway transfixed again; and the others were very close to the siren now. So that just left me. Because that's a Drood's job: to be the last man standing, and stand between Humanity and all the threats from Outside.

I walked up to the siren and hit its glistening side as hard as I could with a spiked armoured hand. My fist slammed right through the pulsing, sliding substance, and my armoured arm sank deep into the shifting body, right up to my shoulder. The siren screamed, a terrible agonised sound that blew away its song's effects in a moment. The others scrambled back, away from the pool, away from what they'd been worshipping a moment before. I jerked my arm out, and drew back a fist to strike again. The siren plunged into the glowing golden pool, sounding for the dimensional depths where it belonged. Where prey knew its place.

I armoured down, the golden strange matter retreating into my torc. I wasn't ready for the others to see me in my armour, just yet. They'd look at me differently. I stood by the side of the loch, savouring the quiet. With the siren gone, I couldn't for the life of me remember what had been so entrancing about its song; and that was probably for the best. The others were back on their feet, their eyes still a little lost and dimmed, but they were recovering fast. They were professionals, after all.

Katt glared at the Blue Fairy. 'The next time you have a brilliant idea, feel free to keep it to yourself!'

'We have a recording of the call,' said Blue, giving her back glare for glare. 'Or at least as much of it as the console could handle.' He looked over the equipment, muttering to himself. 'We're missing most of the higher and lower frequencies, which is probably just as well, but what we have should do the job. More than enough to bring Nessie at the gallop, if only to see who's calling. Honey, I'm patching the recording through to you now. Are you getting it?'

'Got it. There's just under a minute of the call recorded, so I'll put it out as a repeating loop. Yeah, that should do it.'

'A thought,' Peter said suddenly. 'If what we're broadcasting is a mating call, won't everything in the loch with working glands come running? We could end up with every living thing in the loch trying to hump the submersible.'

'Thank you for that mental image,' said Katt. 'Which I know will haunt my nights for years to come.'

'I'll put the call through some filters,' said Honey. 'So only really large organisms should be affected.'

I leaned in close, so I could see her face on the tiny screen. 'Are you sure you can drive that thing?'

'Of course,' said Honey. 'I'm CIA. I can drive anything.'

'Want to bet she crashes the gears on her first try?' Peter murmured to Walker.

'I heard that!' said Honey. 'Okay ... Going down, people. See you in a while.'

We looked round, just in time to see air bubbles frothing around the yellow submersible as it drifted away from the bank, and then it sank slowly and with great dignity beneath the dark waters of Loch Ness. It was soon gone, not even a yellow glimmer in the water, with only the slowly widening ripples on the surface to mark its passing.

We crowded round the communications console, watching the data coming in and listening intently as Honey kept up a running commentary on her dive. Walker and I studied the data streams carefully, but there was no sign of anything out of the ordinary. Everything in the submersible seemed to be functioning as required. Honey sent it nosing carefully through the night-dark waters, broadcasting its looped siren call, watching and waiting.

Time passed, and after the first half dozen false alarms, we started to relax a bit. Two hours passed, then three. If anything, it got colder. A heavy wind blew the length of the loch, driving its chill through our clothes and into our bones. We ended up huddling together like sheep, to share our warmth. The sky was completely overcast now, the light fading, and it occurred to me we'd better scare up something while there was still enough light to photograph by.

The submersible prowled up and down the twenty-four miles of the loch, and most of what lived in the waters gave it a wide berth. The submersible's powerful lights hardly penetrated the underwater gloom, and while the sonar picked up shape after intriguing shape, Honey had to be almost on top of the object before she could identify it. So far, the most promising near misses had involved several hopefully shaped sunken treetrunks, half a dozen large shoals of fish, and a couple of quite surprisingly large eels. And that was it. Honey grew increasingly short and bad-tempered in response to our well-meaning suggestions, and ploughed more and more desperately up and down the loch. I think the overcrowded confines of the sub-mersible's cabin were getting to her. Her sonar did pick up a great many large cave mouths sunk deep into the sides of the underwater banks, some of which led into whole cave systems, further in than the sonar could follow.

'There could be miles and miles of caverns down there,' said the Blue Fairy. 'Maybe even rising above sea level, with breathable air. Maybe that's where the creature lives, when it's not in the loch itself. Maybe it only comes out to feed, or breed, and that's why it's so rarely seen.'

'The words "straws" and "clutching at" spring to mind,' said Katt. 'Can't we call this a day, and find a nice hotel somewhere? The monster will still be here tomorrow, if it's here at all. I hate this place! Beastly cold and ... grim! I've shivered so much I must have lost ten pounds through sheer exhaustion. Mind you, on me it looks good.'

'Heads up! I've got something!' Honey's voice crashed out of the console viewscreen, jolting those of us who were understandably half asleep on their feet.

'Oh, joy,' said Katt. 'Another suggestively shaped treetrunk? A stray duck with delusions of grandeur, perhaps?'

'I have a new contact on the sonar,' said Honey. 'It's big, it's moving, and it's heading right for me. Still too far off for the head-lights to reach it, but ... It's big. I mean seriously big. The computer estimates ... four hundred feet long, from end to end. Estimated weight ... No, wait a minute, that can't be right.'

Walker and I pressed our shoulders together as we leaned in over the data streams crossing the console screens. Whatever was heading for Honey and her little yellow submersible, the computer was estimating its weight as eighty-seven tons. No. Not possible; not in any living organism I understood.

'How close is it?' said Peter.

'It just changed direction,' said Honey, her voice calm and professional. 'It was coming at me head on, but now ... it seems to be circling the submersible, keeping its distance. Damn! These speed estimates can't be right either. Nothing that big and heavy could move so fast in these waters ...'

'Nothing we know,' said Walker. He was frowning. 'I think it's time for you to head for the surface, Honey. Let it follow the mating call—'

'Too late!' Honey's voice rose despite herself. 'It's here! Right here! It's huge ! It shot straight past the front window. I had it square in my headlights for a moment!'

'What is it?' said the Blue Fairy. 'What does it look like?'

'Ugly bastard,' said Honey. She sounded shaken, but her voice was under control again. 'It's gone back to circling the submersible. Moving more slowly now. I think it's curious. Oh! I just got a look at the face through the window. It came right up and looked at me. It's ... horrible. It's a monster. Not Nessie. Not Nessie at all. All right, that's it, I'm heading for the surface. I'm not staying down here with that ... thing one moment longer.'

'Slowly,' I said. 'Slowly and steadily and very carefully. Don't do anything that might upset or panic the beast.'

'Or frighten it off,' Peter said quickly. 'I can't film the thing till you get it up here on the surface.'

'Teach your grandmother to suck dick,' said Honey. 'Now shut up, and stop distracting me. I know what I'm doing. Damn, that thing is big! It dwarfs the submersible.'

'Does your craft have any defence systems?' said Walker. 'Guns, force shields, that kind of thing?'

'Not even a loudspeaker for me to shout harsh language through,' said Honey. 'Apparently this happy little yellow toy was never meant for anything but short-range reconnaissance. Which is not what I asked for ... I shall have words with certain people, once I get back to Langley. I'm still rising, very slowly. I'm not far from you. I should end up surfacing within a few yards. The beast is following, and sticking pretty close. Just the wash of its passage is enough to rock me from side to side.'

'Can you identify it yet?' said Katt. 'I can't make head nor tail of what your sensors are sending us. Is it a dinosaur, do you think? A brontosaurus, or a plesiosaurus, something like that?'

'Beats the Hell out of me,' said Honey. 'Big and ugly, that's all I can tell you. Just the glimpses I've seen in the headlights were enough to make my skin crawl. Whatever this is, it doesn't belong in our world.'

'Get to the surface,' I said. 'We can't do anything to help you while you're down there.'

'I know that,' said Honey. 'Still rising. Still heading in your direction. Should be with you soon.'

I looked out over the loch, searching the dark waters with my eyes, but I couldn't make out a damned thing. The overcast sky had turned the waters dark as night. The surface was disturbed by the gusting wind, but that was all.

'Shit! Shit!'

Honey's voice sounded more angry than alarmed. I looked quickly back at the console. On the screen, her dark face was shaken, but determined.

'What is it, Honey?' said Walker, his voice steady and reassuring.

'My engines have shut down.' Honey's voice was reasonably calm, but her distraction showed in the way her hands flew across the controls, hammering at the keyboard with unnecessary force, to no effect. 'Engines are off line, sensors have shut down. It's all I can do to keep this link open . . . Shit. There went life support. Not good, people. I'm dead in the water, power levels dropping, and . . . I'm sinking again.'

'Is the mating call still going out?' said the Blue Fairy.

'No. At least the hull is secure— Oh!'

We heard the heavy muffled thud as something hit the submersible from outside, shaking Honey violently back and forth in her chair. Only the restraining straps held her in place. Something hit the submersible again, even harder. Alarms and flashing lights filled the cramped cabin. Honey was thrown back and forth in her chair like a rag doll.

'Hull . . . is intact!' she managed finally. 'But I don't know how many more knocks this stupid piece of shit can take. It wasn't designed for this ... Oh Hell.'

'Now what?' said Peter.

'The mating call's still going out! It shouldn't be, but it is.'

'Turn it off!' I said. 'Maybe then the monster will lose interest and go away.'

'I can't!' Honey's voice was rising sharply now. 'I'm shut out of the computers. There's no way this is coincidence. Someone sabotaged my submersible.'

We looked at each other, and I knew we were trying to remember which of us might have had enough time alone with the communications console to rewrite the submersible's programming. Could have been any one of us.

'The air's stopped circulating,' said Honey. 'And the lights are going out.'

Something hit the submersible again, driving it sideways. The alarms in the cabin sounded shrill and raucous.

'You're almost here, Honey,' said Walker. 'Only a few hundred yards. Can't you coax a little more out of your engines? Any last emergency power reserves?'

'Hull breach!' said Honey. 'I've got water coming in ... half the electricals I've got left are shorting out. I'm sinking, people. There's no way I can reach you. Oh God ... It's getting cold in here. Cold. And dark. I never wanted to go out like this ...'

I armoured up, and the others fell back from me, crying out in shock. It's one thing to know about the inhuman power of the armoured Droods; quite another to see the transformation happen in front of you Not many do, and live to tell of it. I left the communications console and sprinted for the side of the loch. My golden feet sank deep into the ground as my armoured legs drove me on at supernatural speed. I hit the edge of the bank running, and dived headfirst into the dark waters.

I never felt the water or the cold as I swam strongly down into the depths of the loch. The armour protected me, and fed me the air I needed. I could walk on the Moon in this armour, and legend has it some of our family have. I still couldn't see far into the dark waters, for all the augmented vision my mask provided, but once I was underwater I could hear the looped mating call broadcasting from the dying submersible. It had only a shadow of its former power, but I would know that terrible sound anywhere. I headed for it, my armoured arms and legs ploughing me through the waters at incredible speed. I was running blind, the sound growing steadily louder, until suddenly I was on top of the submersible.

It loomed up before me, bright yellow in the gloom, and I grabbed a heavy-looking projection on its side, crunching the metal in my golden hand to make sure I wouldn't lose my hold. I knocked twice on the side, to let Honey know I was there, and then peered quickly about me. I couldn't see the monster anywhere, but in these peat-filled waters the bloody thing could have been right on top of me and I wouldn't have known. Not a comfortable thought. And then something shot past me, moving impossibly quickly, and the shock of its passing wave slammed me against the side of the submersible with enough force to kill an ordinary man. I felt as much as heard the hull creak and crack beneath me, and I knew I didn't have long to save Honey.

I pulled myself along the side of the submersible, from projection to projection, until I was round the front and peering in through the wide window. I think Honey would have jumped out of her chair at the sight of me, if the straps hadn't held her down. I gestured reassuringly at her, while I thought fast. The only way to get her out would be to rip the submersible open, and then carry her to the surface. Except I didn't know if she had any breathing equipment on board, the cold of the waters would probably kill her anyway, and I couldn't be sure of protecting her if the monster attacked on the way up. No; for the moment, she was safer where she was.

So I gave Honey another reassuring wave, swam down beneath the slowly sinking submersible, found its centre, and put my golden shoulder against it. And then, with slow careful movements, I took the weight of the submersible upon my armour and swam back up to the surface, pushing the damned thing above and ahead of me.

Sometimes my armour surprises even me.

All the way up, I could sense something huge and malevolent, circling the submersible and me from a distance, but I never saw anything.

I felt the change when the submersible broke the surface of the loch, and I slipped out from underneath it. Its own natural buoyancy would hold it up for a while. I hauled myself up the side of the craft, water streaming from my armour. Honey had already cracked the escape hatch, and smoke was pouring out. I ripped the hatch off, threw it aside and peered in. Honey had freed herself from her chair, and was staggering towards me through the smoke and flashing lights. The alarms were very loud.

The submersible was sinking again. Water was already spilling over the edge of the hatch. I grabbed Honey by the arm, ignoring her pained yelp, hauled her out of the hatch, tucked her under my arm and jumped for the shore. We soared through the air, my feet hit the ground hard, and I moved us quickly away from the edge. Honey was already struggling to be free, coughing harshly from smoke inhalation. I let her go, and looked back at the loch just in time to see the submersible disappear beneath the dark disturbed waters.

And then the monster came surging up out of the loch, and none of us had eyes for anything else.

It reared out of the water, rising and rising impossibly far, huge and dark and glistening, a vast pulsating pillar of grey-green flesh. It was overwhelmingly large, and its shape made no sense at all. Somehow it offended my eyes, my mind, as though this was something that had no business existing in my orderly, sane and logical world. The monster was long and scaled, and there were things that might have been limbs protruding from its heaving sides, thrashing the disturbed waters into an angry foam. It had a head like a flowering tapeworm, wide and fleshy, with thrusting horns and a great circular mouth packed full of teeth, and inhuman unblinking eyes set on the end of long wavering stalks, like a snail. This was an old thing, an ancient thing, from before history; some terrible survivor from the days when nature and evolution were still experimenting with shapes.

It made a sound, a flat, rasping alien sound that held unnerving echoes of the siren's song. The sound grated on my mind like fingernails down a blackboard, as long-buried atavistic instincts told me to run and run and never stop. It was the roar of the beast, and there was no emotion in it that I could recognise, or hope to understand. It was a monster, in every sense of the word. An abomination from the distant past, with no place in our human world.

Not Nessie. Not Nessie at all.

The great head came slamming down like a hammer, and everyone scattered. The head hit the communications console dead on and smashed it into a thousand pieces. Shrapnel flew murderously fast through the air. The head rose up again, soaring into the sky, roaring its terrible cry. More and more of its body was rising out of the water, in defiance of weight and mass and gravity. The Blue Fairy chanted something in old elvish, spitting the words out in his haste, and a faerie weapon appeared in his hands. I recognised it from books in the Drood Library. It was Airgedlamh, the legendary silver arm of Nuada. It shone supernaturally bright, too potent for human eyes to look on directly. Blue pulled it on over his left arm like silver armour, and then he ran lightly forward to face the monster.

Walker pulled a very large gun out of thin air, took careful aim, cool and collected as always, and shot the monster repeatedly in the head; to no obvious effect. Peter had his camera phone out, and was filming the monster's every movement with single-minded intensity. Honey had got her breath and her poise back, and she aimed a shimmering crystal weapon at the monster. Strange energies crackled from the weapon and exploded across the monster's head; but still it took no hurt. It was too ancient, too strong, too big; a survivor of centuries because there was nothing left in this world that could hurt it.

The Blue Fairy stood at the edge of the loch, shouting fiercely at the monster and brandishing Airgedlamh. It shone like the sun in the twilight air. The monster's head seemed to hesitate for a moment, hanging impossibly far above the Blue Fairy, as though perhaps it recognised and remembered the ancient weapon of the Tuatha De Danann. And then the head came driving down, whistling through the air, a great unstoppable bludgeon of flesh. The Blue Fairy stood his ground, waited until the very last moment, and then jumped neatly to one side and punched the monster in the head with his glowing silver hand. Chunks of grey-green flesh flew on the air as the whole head snapped aside. The monster roared deafeningly, and then the head came surging back with unfeasible, unstoppable speed, and Blue had to throw himself face down on the ground to avoid it.

I ran forward, my armoured legs driving me on. The monster's head was still only a few feet above the ground, and I jumped on top of it, grabbing one of the spiky horns to steady myself. The monster reared up immediately, rising and rising on its vast length of neck, carrying me up into the sky. One of the eyes swung round on its long stalk to look at me, and for a moment our gazes met. If there was any intelligence behind that unblinking gaze, it was nothing I could hope to recognise or understand. So I grabbed the stalk beneath the eye with one golden hand, and ripped it off the monster's head.

The fleshy stalk tore apart, spouting black blood, and the eye and its stalk wriggled fiercely in my hand until I threw them away. The vast head lurched sickly under my feet as it roared again, deafeningly loud. I steadied myself, raised my armoured right hand and concentrated, and the strange matter extended itself into a long golden sword blade. I slammed it into the monster's head with all my strength behind it, sinking the blade down until my knuckles slammed against the scaly hide. The head lurched under the impact, almost throwing me off. I pulled the blade back out, and watched the wound I'd made heal itself almost immediately. The head was simply too big. I hadn't even reached the skull, never mind the brain.

Assuming the monster had such things.

One of the other eyestalks drifted in temptingly close, and I cut it in half with my golden blade. The monster drove its head down towards the dark waters of the loch. I jumped off at the last moment, my armoured legs easily absorbing the impact of the landing. I stood on the edge of the loch, and watched the monster disappear into the concealing waters. The whole huge unnatural shape was gone in a moment, leaving only spreading ripples on the surface to mark its passing. I pulled the golden blade back into my hand, and armoured down. The monster was gone, and I doubted it would be back.

We hurt it; and it probably hadn't been hurt in centuries.

Just as well it was gone. I didn't want to be famous in history as the man who killed the Loch Ness monster.

I turned my back on the loch. Honey was sifting through the scattered remains of her communications console. Walker was looking at the gun in his hand as though he wasn't accustomed to using such things; and for all I knew, he wasn't. He made the gun disappear with a casual, elegant gesture, and moved over to where Peter was staring intently at his camera phone. The Blue Fairy was gazing at the silver arm of Nuada, covering his arm from shoulder to fingertips. He pulled a face, and sent the ancient weapon back where it came from. He looked at me, and I smiled as kindly as I could.

'It takes more than armour, Blue. Why call on Airgedlamh? Why didn't you use your torc?'

'Because it scares me,' said the Blue Fairy. 'I don't think I can use it, and still be me.'

He marched over to join Peter and Walker. 'Tell me you got the bloody thing on film!' he said loudly. 'Don't you dare say you screwed up, Peter King, or I will throw you into the loch to drag the monster up here again!'

'I got it! I got the whole fight on film!' said Peter, grinning from ear to ear. 'Proof – proof positive!'

Honey and I joined the group, and we studied the film on the phone's tiny screen. It looked good. Probably look a whole lot better blown up on a decent-sized screen, but like the man said: proof positive.

'Where's Katt?' Walker said abruptly. We looked around, but there was no sign of her.

We found her body eventually, under the main wreckage of the communications console. She'd avoided the main impact of the monster's head, but her neck was broken. With her marvellous vitality gone, she looked very small and delicate. Like a thrown-away flower, or a broken doll. Peter knelt beside her, and closed her staring eyes.

'Probably never even knew what hit her,' said Walker. 'Poor little thing.'

'Wish now I'd taken the time to get to know her better,' said Peter. 'I think she would have been . . . fun.'

'Oh, please!' said the Blue Fairy. 'She would have killed you first chance she got.'

'Like I said – fun.' Peter rose to his feet, and looked away.

'That's the spying game for you,' said Honey. 'Here today, gone tomorrow. I was going to blame her for sabotaging my submersible. No real proof; just a feeling. Now . . . I don't suppose it matters. We have the proof of the monster's existence. Time to move on to the next part of the game.'

'Just like that?' said Peter.

'Yes,' I said. 'That's the spying game for you.'

In the end, we dropped Lethal Harmony of Kathmandu's body into the loch. As good a resting place as any. Honey watched the ripples slowly settle on the dark surface.

'Scratch one submersible,' she said finally, 'and several billion dollars, probably. I know they'll find a way to stick me with the bill.'

CHAPTER FIVE

Hide and seek

In the forests of the night, there are many worse things than tygers.

The teleport bracelets dropped us into the heart of dense forest, with night falling fast. Trees stood tall and slender around us, draped with patchy greenery and hanging vines. The ground beneath my feet was hard and dry, the rough brown dirt cracked and broken. The vegetation grew thicker off to one side, leading down to a slow-moving river with treetrunks rising out of the muddy waters. The air was blisteringly hot and humid, harsh and heavy in my lungs after the bitter chill of Loch Ness. Sweat sprang out all over me. Off in the distance, beyond the treeline, the sun was going down in shades of orange and crimson. In less than an hour it would be dark, and this far from civilisation it would be very dark indeed. From all around came the sounds of bird and beast and the persistent buzz of insects.

'Wonderful,' the Blue Fairy said bitterly. 'An environment even more unpleasant than the last one, though I would have sworn on a stack of grimoires such a thing was impossible. Bloody place is like a blast furnace ... I can actually feel myself tanning. Are those mosquitoes?'

'Probably,' I said.

'Shit.' The Blue Fairy looked up at the darkening sky. 'Why me, Lord, why me? Was I really so bad in my last incarnation? What did I do – stamp on puppies?'

'You'd find something to complain about in Paradise,' I said, amused.

He sniffed loudly. 'They wouldn't let me into that place on a bet.' He glared around. 'Well, joy – another location I am not equipped to deal with. I am not an outdoors person; if I'd wanted to rough it, I'd have paid someone else to do it for me. Does anyone have any idea where the Hell we are now?'

'While you've been whining and wittering, I've been talking to Langley,' said Honey. 'They tasked a spy satellite to zero in on my implant, and apparently we're somewhere in the wilds of Arkansas, not far from the border with Texas and miles and miles from anywhere civilised.'

'Shoot me now and get it over with,' said the Blue Fairy.

'Don't tempt me,' I said.

'How many miles, exactly, to civilisation?' said Walker, practical as ever.

'Thirty, forty miles to the nearest small town,' said Honey. 'Hard to be sure. There aren't any accurate maps of this region.'

'Let me guess,' said Peter. 'Because no one ever comes here, right?'

'Maybe a few trappers, hunters,' said Honey. 'Backwoods hermits, who like to keep themselves to themselves.'

'Can you hear banjo music?' said the Blue Fairy.

'Shut up,' I said.

Honey set off through the trees, and since she looked like she knew where she was going the rest of us trailed after her, for want of anything better to do. She stripped off her heavy fur coat, dropped it carelessly on the ground and walked away from it. The rest of us stepped carefully over and around it. Honey was an agent; there was no telling what kind of dirty tricks she might have left behind with her coat. The Blue Fairy sighed appreciatively.

'Now that's style, that is. Drop off a few hundred thousand dollars of coat, and keep on walking.' He ripped off his wilting ruff, and threw it into the trees with a dramatic gesture.

'I should lose the breastplate while you're at it,' I said. 'It must weigh half a ton, and it'll only get worse in this heat. You don't need it, now you've got a torc to protect you.'

He looked down at the brass and silver breastplate, scored with protective runes, and shook his head stiffly. 'No. I don't think so. In the things that matter, it's always best to stick with what you can trust.'

I glanced back, to see how the others were doing. Peter King was wandering along, stumbling over the occasional raised root in the ground, because his attention was clearly elsewhere. If anything, he looked more out of place in the woods of the American South than

126

he had in the Scottish Highlands. He'd taken off his expensive jacket, slung it over one shoulder and rolled up his sleeves, and his pale bare arms had excited the surrounding insects into a feeding frenzy. Walker hadn't even made that much of a concession to the heat; he still wore his smart city suit like a knight's armour, though he had loosened his old school tie a little. He strolled along amiably, smiling about him and enjoying the scenery as though taking a tour of someone's private estate.

The vegetation and the trees fell suddenly away as we came to the river bank. Almost wide enough to qualify as a lake, the muddy waters ran calmly past us, swirling around the mottled trunks of gnarled and knotted trees. Small dark shadows shot this way and that through the waters; beavers, maybe? I'm not really up on wildlife. And I can't think of beavers without remembering the talking ones in Narnia. I'd make a lousy trapper. We all stood close together on the river bank, for mutual comfort and support in such alien surroundings, and looked up and down the river. Just more of the same, from one horizon to the next. It was getting darker. The Blue Fairy studied the crap brown waters with a sort of disgusted fascination.

'Do you suppose they have alligators here?'

'Almost certainly,' I said.

'Oh God . . .'

'I can deal with alligators,' Honey said cheerfully. 'I could use a new pair of shoes. Or even luggage.'

Shadows were lengthening, filling the gaps between the trees. The light was going out of the day, and the sky was the dull red of drying blood. Cries from surrounding wildlife were becoming louder, more urgent. Already the gloom was creeping in around us, and I couldn't see nearly as far as I could when we arrived. I had a strong feeling . . . of being watched.

'Did anyone else see that film, *The Blair Witch Project*?' said Peter.

'I liked it,' said Walker, unexpectedly.

'I saw it at the multiplex,' said Honey. 'Those jerky camera movements made me seasick.'

'I always thought they should have given James Cameron the sequel,' said the Blue Fairy. 'Let him do another *Aliens*. Send a whole company of heavily armed marines into the Blair woods, and have them blow away everything that moved. Like to see the Blair Witch deal with that . . .'

'Oh, tell me we're not here looking for the Blair Witch,' I said. 'That was fiction from beginning to end, and to Hell with what it said on the Net.'

'No,' said Peter. 'Sasquatch, maybe; you know, Bigfoot? Half man, half ape, maybe even the missing link. Often glimpsed, never properly identified.'

'Actually,' Walker murmured, 'Sasquatch was a Native American name for a particularly reclusive tribe called "The Shy People". The name "Bigfoot" is more recent, from tracks found in various locations.'

'I've seen some photos, and a couple of amateur films,' I said. 'But nothing even remotely convincing. And there's hardly anything about Bigfoot in the Drood Library. Mostly because we were never that interested in them. If they wanted to stay hidden and keep themselves to themselves, that was fine with us.'

'I saw a film on television, when I was a kid,' Honey said slowly. 'About a creature in Arkansas . . . Spooked the Hell out of me. The creature lurked around this small town, and even terrorised some people, but it was never identified. Maybe that's what we're here for.'

'Could be,' said Peter. 'Maybe Grandfather saw that film too.'

The insects were swarming around us now, clouds of them sweeping in from off the river. We flapped our hands around, trying to swat the damned things, but we might as well have been holding up signs saying 'Fresh meat! All the blood you can drink!' Since mosquitoes are known to breed around rivers, for the express purpose of passing on malaria to people, I was actually considering armouring up in self-protection when the Blue Fairy spat out half a dozen words in Old Elvish. And every single insect dropped out of the air, stone cold dead. The world seemed to pause, considering, and then the other insects boiling up off the river decided to go somewhere else. We looked at the Blue Fairy with new respect. He smiled happily.

'Works even better with pests at parties. Look, it's going to be night very soon now, and not even a Bates Motel to take us in. What was Alexander King thinking of, dropping us in the middle of nowhere? I mean, how are we supposed to find one bloody Sasquatch in God knows how many square miles of wild forest? It could be anywhere, and you can bet good money that if it wants to avoid us it's perfectly capable of hiding itself so completely we could walk right past it and not even know it was there! I am not tramping through this Godforsaken wilderness dressed like an extra from *Shakespeare In Love*, just in the hope we bump into the damned thing!'

'Easy, Blue,' I said. 'You're hyperventilating.'

'I'm entitled! Do any of us *look* like hearty outdoors tracker types?'

'I hate to break this to you,' said Honey. 'But our situation is even worse than that. According to Langley, these woods cover hundreds if not thousands of square miles, most of them completely unmapped, except for a single notation: "Here Be Deadly Wildlife That Will Bite Your Ass Off If You Don't Pay Attention".'

'I want to go home,' Blue said miserably.

'What – kind of deadly wildlife?' said Peter, looking quickly around him.

'Alligators, bears, wolves, wild pig, snakes, you name it,' Honey said cheerfully. 'Great hunting grounds. My uncles used to take me hunting, when I was younger. Though that seemed to consist mainly of drinking beer, wandering in circles, and telling stories that were entirely unsuitable for my young ears. Either way, I could bring down a full-grown buck with one shot, skin it and dress it out, before I was twelve.'

'How wonderfully primitive,' said the Blue Fairy.

'At least in Scotland we had a loch to look in,' said Walker, sensing things were about to get nasty. 'Where are we supposed to start here?'

Everyone looked at me.

'Don't,' I said. 'There are lots of stories about the Sasquatch, mostly of personal one-on-one encounters, but it's all very vague. There have been some edgy confrontations, but there's no recorded incident of a Sasquatch ever killing or even attacking a man. Mostly, they're supposed to be shy and diffident creatures.'

'Shy and diffident – great,' said the Blue Fairy. 'Shy and diffident I can live with.'

'And no Drood has ever bothered to track down the truth?' said Walker.

I gave him a hard look. 'We have a whole world to watch over and protect, often from the likes of you.'

If Walker was bothered by my look, he hid it well. 'I'm surprised no one's ever tried to catch or trap a Sasquatch,' he said thoughtfully. 'Especially given the locals are undoubtedly experienced hunting and trapping types. Why would they allow a dangerous and potentially exploitable creature to roam around their backyard unchecked?'

'If I'm remembering what I saw on the television right,' said Honey. 'They tried tracking it with dogs once. Pedigree hunting hounds, from all over the county. But the moment the dogs got a scent of what they were after, they tucked their tails between their legs, backed away and tried to hide behind each other. They didn't want anything to do with what they were smelling. Their owners took a lesson from that, and maybe we should too.'

'But it's never killed anyone,' I said. 'So why is everyone so scared of it?'

'Maybe it's a Neanderthal,' Peter said suddenly. 'Cut off from the world in one of the last great wildernesses on earth, the last of its kind—'

'Maybe,' I said. 'But Alexander King warned us off from disturbing the Yeti, so why is it okay for us to go bother the Sasquatch?'

'Clearly he knows something we don't,' said the Blue Fairy.

'I think you can count on that,' said Peter.

'Hold everything,' said Honey. 'Langley's told me something very interesting. These teleport bracelets we're wearing were pre-programmed to bring us here, to a particular location, at an exact moment in time. Well, the bracelets brought us to Arkansas safely, but Langley says we're missing a whole day. They say it's been twenty-six hours since they were last able to locate me.'

We looked at each other, and then at the alien mechanisms clamped immovably about our wrists.

'Alexander must have expected us to take somewhat longer with Nessie,' I said finally.

'But why drop us here and now?' said the Blue Fairy plaintively. 'It's almost night! It's so dark I can barely see my hand in front of my face. How are we supposed to find anything in this? Has anyone even got a flashlight?'

'I should sit down, put your head between your knees and breathe steadily for a while,' Walker said kindly.

'If these bracelets were pre-programmed to bring us right here, right now, Alexander must have had a reason,' I said. 'Maybe this is Sasquatch territory. This is where one of the creatures is to be found. In which case all we have to do is sit tight and wait for one to come along.'

'We must make a fire,' Honey said. 'Before it gets really dark. Perhaps the light will attract the Sasquatch.'

'Katt was right,' growled the Blue Fairy. 'This is so amateur night. Sit around and hope one of the rarest creatures in the world will happen to wander by. I know, I know, go with the flow, don't make waves. Does anyone actually know how to make a fire? I think it involves rubbing two boy scouts together.'

'In your dreams,' I said.

'I was a scout,' said Walker. We turned to him, but that was all he had to say on the subject.

'I'll bet he had some weird badges,' muttered the Blue Fairy.

In the end, we moved a comfortable distance away from the river, gathered some wood and some moss, and Honey made us a fire with brisk efficiency, and the use of a CIA monogrammed cigarette lighter. By then it really was night, and the dark was full and heavy. The light from the fire didn't travel far. The air was still uncomfortably humid, but the temperature was dropping fast. We sat in a circle round the fire, staring into the leaping flames. Gnarled twigs and branches stirred as the flames consumed them. Up above, the sky seemed to fall away for ever, full of stars, but with only a bare sliver of a new moon. From all around came the sound of various beasts going about their brutal business, though none of them entered the circle of firelight.

It turned out that despite his moaning, the Blue Fairy was the best provided of all of us. His padded jerkin had faerie pockets, subspace larders from which he produced drinking cups, bottled water, tea bags, milk and sugar, and even a small pot to boil the water in. The pot had pretty blue flowers on it, and the legend 'A Present From Lyonesse'. The essentials, Blue said smugly, for any journey. The only food he had was elf bread, which the rest of us politely declined. That stuff would give an elephant the runs, and it would stop for months afterwards to remember. Honey asked Blue if he had any coffee, and he took a certain amount of pleasure in telling her no.

We sat around the fire drinking tea from an assortment of ill-matched cups. Mine bore the legend 'World's Best Motherfucker'. While the water was boiling to make us a second cup, Honey produced a large knife from somewhere and slipped off into the darkness. Her white cat-suited figure glimmered briefly here and there in the darkness, like a ghost that couldn't make up its mind whether or not to materialise. There was a certain amount of crashing about, followed by some loud splashing, and then Honey returned triumphantly with a large beaver she'd caught and killed on the river bank. She skinned and prepared the thing with expert skill, and soon enough there was meat roasting on pointed sticks over the fire. It actually smelled pretty good. One beaver doesn't go that far between five people, and the taste was ... interesting, but we were hungry and no one turned up their nose. Walker ate his with great enthusiasm, and actually licked the grease from his fingers when he'd finished. The Blue Fairy started to smirk.

'Don't,' Honey said sternly. 'I have already worked out every possible permutation of any joke involving the words "eat", and "beaver". Also, I have a gun, and I will shoot you.'

'Listen to the noise out in the woods,' I said, tactfully changing the subject. 'It's like every living thing is killing, eating and humping each other. Not necessarily in that order. And possibly simultaneously.'

'This is what the wild sounds like, city boy,' said Honey.

'You should hear what the Nightside sounds like,' said Walker. 'Where the really wild things go, to screw each other over. We have the best night clubs and the greatest shows, the music never stops, you can dance till your feet bleed and Cinderella never gets to go home.'

'You know, Walker,' said the Blue Fairy. 'You disturb the shit out of me.'

'Thank you,' said Walker.

We sat around the fire, and the night passed slowly. If anything it got even darker. The heat of the day slipped away, and we ended up crowding as close to the flames as we could. The dancing firelight painted our faces with ever-changing shadows, sometimes suggesting unexpected revelations of character. Every now and again we'd hear something large and heavy crashing through the woods, but nothing entered our circle of firelight. To begin with we jumped at every sound, but it never came to anything, and after a while we stopped bothering. It was cold, we were tired, and you can only drink so much tea. Peter kept almost nodding off, and then jerking up his head with a start. Finally, the Blue Fairy stirred uncomfortably.

'I need to go to the toilet,' he said.

'Thank you for sharing that with us,' I said. 'Go do it in the river. That's what it's for.'

'But it's dark out there! There are . . . things. Hungry-sounding things, hiding in the dark. I don't want to go on my own.'

'Well I'm not going to hold your hand,' said Peter. 'Or anything else, for that matter.'

'Be brave, little soldier,' said Honey.

'What have you got to be scared of?' I said. 'You're wearing a torc, remember?'

He gave me a look, then lurched to his feet and shuffled off into the darkness. We could follow his progress from the muffled curses and the occasional banging into trees that didn't get out of his way fast enough. Finally, there came a distant splashing.

'I think he's found the river,' Walker said.

'Oh, good,' said Honey.

'If the Sasquatch was going to be attracted by the firelight, I think he would have turned up by now,' I said.

'Patience,' said Honey. 'Hunting is all about patience. And blowing something's head off with a very big gun, naturally.'

'No wonder you ended up in the CIA,' said Peter.

Walker winced. 'Perhaps we should decide in advance what we're going to do with the Sasquatch when it finally does deign to put in an appearance. Capture it on Peter's phone camera?'

'I'd like to shoot it,' said Honey. 'Have it stuffed and mounted. I've got just the place for it in my apartment. Or maybe a throw rug.'

'That might be all right if it is some kind of unknown ape,' I said. 'But what if it does turn out to be a Neanderthal, or a missing link? Maybe even the last of its kind?'

'What would you do with it, if it did turn out to be half human?' said Walker. 'Put it in a zoo, or give it the vote? No, Eddie, you had the right idea with Nessie. It would be a sin to make such a creature extinct, but at the same time it's far better off left alone. It doesn't need to be made a target, for hunters or conservationists. We'll take its photo and then leave it to its own devices, safe in the wilderness.'

'Right,' I said. 'This is its home. We're the intruders here.'

'You soppy sentimental thing,' said Honey. 'How did someone as soft-hearted as you end up a Drood field agent?'

I glared at her. 'I failed the compassion test for the CIA. They found I had some.'

'Children, children,' murmured Walker. 'We shouldn't take the possible threat posed to us by the creature too lightly. There have been accounts of violent behaviour. It might not want to stand still and pose for the camera. A certain amount of caution is advisable.'

I thought about the Colt Repeater holstered under my jacket. The gun that never missed, and never ran out of bullets. Whatever the Sasquatch might turn out to be, I was pretty sure I could put it down with the Colt, if I had to. To protect myself, or the others. But I really didn't want to kill it. We were supposed to be here for information, not trophies. So I didn't tell the others about my gun.

We heard the Blue Fairy returning from the river, scrambling through the woods with more determination than skill. He burst into the circle of firelight, took a moment to get his breath back, and then sank heavily down beside me and stretched out his slightly shaking hands to the flames.

'I hope you remembered to wash them afterwards,' I said.

He smiled briefly. 'You would not believe how many animals there are out there who have absolutely no idea of the concept of privacy. I could see their eyes, gleaming all around me. And I've never been able to go if there's anybody watching.'

'Shouldn't have drunk so much tea,' said Honey.

'Still, while I had ... time on my hands, I was able to do some thinking,' said the Blue Fairy, ostentatiously ignoring Honey. 'And I think I may be able to track and locate the Sasquatch.'

We sat up straight and looked at him, and he smiled triumphantly, happy to be the centre of attention.

'Its part of elf nature,' he said, 'to be aware of out-of-the-ordinary things. To sense the magical, unnatural creatures in this boringly material world. Their nature calls out to ours, like one nearly extinct species to another. My range is somewhat limited, since I'm only half elf, but still: if the Sasquatch should come anywhere near us, I should know almost immediately.'

'That's a lot of shoulds,' said Peter. 'I don't like the idea of just sitting around, waiting for something to happen. We've already lost twenty-six hours. Grandfather could be dead by now, for all we know.'

'Do you have a better idea?' said Walker. His voice was calm and steady, but it had the impact of a slap in the face. 'No? Neither do I. So we sit, and we wait.'

Time passed, very slowly. No one felt much like talking, and I couldn't have drunk another cup of tea if you'd put a gun to my head. So we sat, and waited, and listened to the night. In the wild, in the dark, time seems to crawl. I know about patience. I've sat my share of stakeouts. But in the city there's always something to look at, to hold your attention, and the cheerful amber glare of overhead lamps pushing back the night. Here there was only the fire, and the dark, and five people not talking to each other. I fed branches to the fire every now and again, just for something to do, but the light never seemed to press any further. There was a definite chill to the air that the fire did little to keep out.

This heavy oppressive dark, full of strange sounds and unknown dangers, was getting on my nerves. It felt like there could be anything out there, anything at all.

We kept glancing hopefully at the Blue Fairy, who grew increasingly twitchy and finally scrambled to his feet and yelled at us:

'Stop looking at me! I'll tell you the moment I feel anything. All right?'

After a moment he sat down again, staring sulkily into the flames.

'I've had a thought,' said Peter suddenly.

'Good for you,' said the Blue Fairy. 'Had to happen eventually.'

'No, listen! When I filmed Nessie on my state-of-the-art camera, the submersible was still broadcasting its siren mating call. It should be audible on the recording. If I was to play it back now, perhaps the song would bring the Sasquatch to us!'

We considered the idea, but in the end Walker shook his head.

'The mating call was filtered through the communications console so it would only attract really large creatures, remember? So unless you want to be humped to death by an over-sized alligator . . .'

'Ah,' said Peter. 'Yes.'

'Nice try, though,' I said. I reached for another branch to throw on the fire, and found there weren't any. 'Damn.'

'We'll have to go into the woods and get some more firewood,' said Honey.

'What's this *we* bullshit, kemo sabe?' said the Blue Fairy.

'I'll go.' Honey stood up and looked at me. 'How about it, sailor? Care to keep a girl company?'

'Your father wasted his money on that finishing school, didn't he?' I got to my feet. 'Let's do it.'

'Sure,' said Honey. 'And afterwards, we can gather some wood.'

'Hormones are a terrible thing,' said the Blue Fairy.

I followed Honey out of the firelight, as she headed for the river. She strode off into the darkness as though it was no big thing. And maybe, for her, it wasn't. Away from the fire, my eyes adjusted to the gloom, but not by much. I could sense as much as see the trees, and managed to avoid most of them. As soon as we were out of earshot of the others, Honey stopped and turned to face me. I wasn't surprised. She couldn't have made it more obvious she wanted to speak privately with me if she'd announced it through a loudhailer. Honey clicked her CIA lighter, and a heavy wavering flame shot up some six inches, providing enough glow to illuminate our features.

'Thanks for taking the hint,' she said, her voice professionally low and discreet. 'I wanted to thank you, properly, for saving my life back at Loch Ness. I thought the game was over when my systems crashed and the water started flooding in. And I would have hated to die in that bright yellow coffin. So tacky.'

'No problem,' I said. 'You would have done the same for me.'

She smiled briefly. 'No, I probably wouldn't. This is supposed to be a contest, remember? I'm here to win this game, whatever it takes.'

'Of course,' I said. 'You're CIA.'

We shared a smile. Since you spend most of your time in the spy game getting lied to by all and sundry, these occasional moments of real honesty between allies or enemies are always something to be treasured. And it's not often you can talk freely, with someone who understands. Molly tries, bless her, but she's never been an agent. A free spirit, a rogue operative and a spiritual anarchist, yes; but never an agent. She didn't have the experience to comprehend the compromised ethics and dubious deals even a Drood field agent has to make sometimes, to get the job done. We protect Humanity, but it's best they never learn how. They wouldn't approve of some of our methods.

God knows I don't, sometimes. I do try to be a good person; but now and again the job just won't let you.

'That armour of yours was even more impressive than I'd imagined,' said Honey. 'Is there anything it can't do?'

'Like I'd tell you,' I said cheerfully.

Honey gazed at me. 'Shame about what happened to poor Katt.'

'Yes,' I said. 'That was a shame. Such an unfortunate accident.'

'Yes,' said Honey. 'Did you kill her, Eddie?'

'No,' I said. 'I was busy with the monster, remember? I take it you don't think it was an accident?'

Honey gave a bitter laugh. 'Hardly. Six experienced field agents in one place, competing for the biggest prize in the world, and one of them suddenly turns up dead? She could have died of a heart attack while being hit by a meteorite, and I'd still have suspected foul play. I was planning on killing her myself, at some point. I was convinced she'd sabotaged my submersible. But now ... I'm not so sure. And to kill her off this early in the game, when we could still have made good use of her talents? That's cold. Someone in this group is playing hardball, and for once it isn't me. You understand why I immediately thought it might be you?'

'Of course,' I said. 'I'm a Drood. Still, I suppose it's almost a compliment, from a CIA operative. How did you get into the spy business?'

'Oh, I'm third-generation spook,' she said easily. 'Both my grandfathers worked for the OSS during the war, and most of my uncles ended up in the CIA. A couple of aunties as well. My family has been destabilising countries and executing bad guys for generations. And doing a little good along the way, when we could.'

'So, are you people really responsible for all the evil in the world?' I said.

'Not entirely. We try, but we don't have the manpower. We protect our own interests, like every other spy organisation, by undertaking the dirty, necessary, unpleasant tasks that the people, bless their timid little hearts, don't need to know about. The spying game is not for the faint of heart, Drood. You know that.'

'My family doesn't deal in politics,' I said carefully. 'Or at least, we try very hard not to. We defend everyone, whether we approve of them or not. And usually from the kind of threats you Company types are too busy, or ill equipped, to handle. Don't ever think we're the same, Honey. We might be in the same game, but we're playing for different reasons.'

'There's nothing I've done that you haven't,' said Honey. 'There's probably more blood on your armoured hands than on mine.'

'It's not what you do,' I said. 'It's why you do it.'

'I do it for America.'

'I do it for all Humanity.'

'Oh, please! Isn't that what terrorists say? Our terrible methods are justified by our glorious intentions?' Honey looked as though she was about to spit. 'Who put you Droods in charge? Who do you answer to? Is there anyone in this world with the power to say. 'Stop, too far, too much'? You get to decide what's best for us, and we don't get any say in the matter. You're everything the Company exists to fight, everything America was founded to overcome.'

'You see?' I said. 'It always comes down to politics with you. Droods have to take a larger view. And we're harsher on ourselves than anyone else could ever be.'

'Don't make your inability to choose a side some kind of moral high ground!' Honey said fiercely. 'Everyone has to choose a side, and fight for what they believe in! Think what your people and mine could accomplish, working together, with your armour. With a weapon like that at our disposal, we could sweep this world clean of everyone who threatens our way of life.'

'You'd use it against anyone who didn't think like you,' I said. 'Or anyone who didn't want the things you wanted. That's why the Droods stay separate. We protect you all, and we try very hard not to judge. We're shepherds, not policemen.'

'Your only loyalty is to your family,' said Honey. 'Everyone knows that. Some of us have greater loyalties. I have sworn to fight and if need be die in defence of my country. And I meant it.' She grinned suddenly. 'Which is why I'll probably have to kill you at some point, Drood. Access to the Independent Agent's treasure trove of information might finally make us your equal.'

'Honey,' I said. 'You couldn't kill me on the best day you ever had.'

'I do so love a challenge,' she said, and we both laughed.

'You're everything I hoped a Drood would be,' she said finally. 'You get disappointed so often in this game ... but you're the real deal, Eddie. I'll enjoy working with you – for as long as it lasts.'

I liked Honey. So sure of herself, and her motivations. I hadn't been sure of anything, since I found out my family's history was based on a lie. I didn't think Honey would appreciate being told that the only reason my family doesn't rule the world is because it can't be bothered. We have more important things to worry about, like the Hungry Gods. I fight the good fight against the many enemies of Humanity, because that's what I was brought up to do. Trained from the earliest age to be loyal only to the family, because only the family stands between Humanity and the forces of evil. I still believe that. Mostly.

My Molly didn't have much time for the Droods, even after fighting alongside us during the Hungry Gods War. 'Power corrupts,' she was prone to say darkly, 'and your family has become so very powerful, Eddie.' I think perhaps that's why I didn't fight to stay on as leader of the family. I didn't like what it was doing to me.

'We don't appear to have gathered much wood,' I said. 'They'll be wondering what we're doing out here.'

'Of course they will,' said Honey. 'They're agents.'

We gathered as much firewood as we could carry, and headed back towards the light of the fire.

We dumped our armfuls of wood on the ground so everyone could see them, but it didn't fool anyone. They knew we'd been talking. I sat down by the fire and looked round the group with my best authoritative stare.

'We need to talk,' I said. 'All of us. We're still mostly strangers to each other, and strangers can't function as a team. I think everyone here should tell a story. Something meaningful, and significant from your life. Could be your weirdest adventure, your greatest triumph, or failure. Anything, as long as it matters to you. Something to help us know you.'

'What brought this on?' said the Blue Fairy. 'I don't do therapy groups.'

'We were talking about who might have killed poor Lethal Harmony from Kathmandu,' said Honey, settling herself comfortably down by the fire. 'Eddie seems to think he can prevent future deaths by having us bare our souls to each other.'

'How quaint,' said the Blue Fairy. 'You always were the sentimental sort, Eddie.'

'Agents don't have souls,' said Peter. 'Everyone knows that.'

'Have you got anything better to do while we wait for the Sasquatch to show up?' I said.

'Good point,' said Walker. 'One more cup of this inferior tea and I'll piss tannin. So who goes first?'

We looked at each other, and then Honey shrugged easily. 'Oh Hell, I might as well get the ball rolling. Don't we all love a good spooky story by firelight?

'I was sent to Cuba, a few years back. And please, no jokes about making Castro's beard fall out. We've given up on that. I was there, extremely unofficially, to investigate some rather unsavoury rumours that had drifted into Miami concerning the working practices at a new and suspiciously productive factory set up in the hills of Cuba far away from anywhere civilised. Never mind how I got on to the island; that's still classified. I could tell you, but then I'd have to kill you all and firebomb the whole area, just in case. Anyway. Rumour had it that the reason these factories were so productive was because the managers were using zombie labour for their workforce. The idea had a lot going for it: the raised dead could work twenty-four hours a day till they wore out, and you could always make more.

'The factory turned out to be surrounded with all kinds of security protections, scientific and magical. Far more than you'd expect for any business operation. Ugly place: rough stone walls, electrified fences and more floating curses than you could shake a gris-gris at. I slipped in easily enough, and made my way to the factory floor.

Sometimes I think that's the best part of this job – skulking around in the shadows, being places you're not supposed to be and watching people who don't even suspect they're being observed. I should have been a voyeur, like Momma wanted.

'Turned out the rumours were almost right. The entire workforce were dead, but they weren't zombies. They were patchwork men. Frankenstein creatures, pieces stitched together to make new forms, and all of them with clear lobotomy scars on their foreheads. A workforce that could easily be controlled, would never tire, and didn't need paying.

'I found an office, and ransacked their records. The various body parts had come from executed prisoners and dissidents, the political opposition, artists, homosexuals. The usual. Anyone the current regime didn't approve of. Executed secretly, and then brought back to life to labour for the State for ever. I wasn't going to put up with that. So I crashed their computers, planted some explosives where they'd do the most good, and burned the whole place down. I waited outside, and shot everyone who escaped the flames. Neatness always counts. I suppose I should have interrogated a few people, got the details on how they did it, but the sight of those poor bastards on the factory floor, alive and not alive, suffering for ever ... No. Not on my watch.'

'A nice story,' I said, after it was clear she'd finished. 'But with a few gaps in it. If you're going to tell a story, Honey, you really should tell all of it.'

'Really?' said Honey. Her voice was light, but her eyes were cold. 'I wasn't aware the Droods even knew about this mission.'

'We didn't,' I said. 'But it doesn't take a rocket scientist to work out why you were sent to Cuba. Zombie slave labour is nothing new. Some countries have been using zombies for centuries. But the raised dead wear out quickly and fall apart, no matter how many preservatives you pump into them, and they need a lot of overseeing. But patchwork men – that's new. Cutting-edge science, especially if you add computer implants to the subjugated brains. I can think of a whole bunch of American industrialists who would love to get their hands on a process like that. No more unions, no more relying on illegal aliens ... and no more back talk. Your orders must have been pretty clear; find out if the rumours were true, and if so how it was done. Then steal the details and bring them back. Only you couldn't bring yourself to do that, could you, Honey? Not after you'd seen the suffering involved. So you disobeyed orders, and did the right thing. You soppy sentimental idealist, you.'

Honey smiled dazzlingly. 'Don't tell my superiors. They think the Cubans blew up the factory rather than have its secrets stolen.'

'You can trust us,' said the Blue Fairy.

'It would never have worked anyway,' said Peter. 'Too much public resistance to the idea.'

'Not if no one ever finds out,' said Walker. 'I've seen worse practices, in the Nightside.'

We waited, but he had nothing more to say. So Peter told his story next.

'Most of my work in industrial espionage is actually pretty boring and every day. Watching and listening, spending hours in front of a computer searching for patterns and trends, trying to second-guess your opponents even as they're second-guessing you; and always looking to spot someone useful on the other side who might be persuaded to jump ship with the right amount of encouragement. In the old days it was all bribes, honey traps and blackmail, but everything has to be legal and above board now. Boring; but I have seen a few . . . unusual cases. Perhaps because of my family name. I've always tried to play down my connections to the legendary Independent Agent, partly because I needed to prove to everyone that I could make it on my own, but mostly because I can't stand the old bastard. But, people will talk.'

'I was hired to investigate a new firm that had just entered the tricky field of GM foods. There's been a lot of public resistance to genetically modified crops and animals, especially since the tabloids dubbed it "Frankenfood". A very hard public sell, but lots and lots of money waiting for the first company to crack the market. This new company didn't seem to be working on anything particularly new or outrageous, but rumours were spreading of some quite extraordinary advances in certain areas where every other company had failed. So I was sent in, extremely undercover, to have a little look around.

'Took me almost a month to weasel my way into the right people's confidence, but people who've achieved something really big are always desperate to talk to *someone* – and who better than their new best friend? It turned out the genetic manipulation hadn't been confined to the food; it had been extended to the workforce as well. They were manufactured, grown, right there in the sub-levels under the factory. You can see why Honey's story reminded me of this one ... Accelerated human clones, with added X-factor. Alien genetic material, to be exact, bought on the black market. You can buy anything these days if you know where to look.

'These human/alien hybrids looked pretty normal to the casual glance, but mentally they were sharper, faster, and they could convince you of anything. Anything at all. Something about the voices, or maybe pheromones or telepathy. I never did get the details. But these people really could sell freezers to Eskimos, or morals to a politician. They could make you change your mind, your sexuality or your religion, just like that. They were gearing up for a truly massive sales campaign, to shift their new product, a cheap and tasty snack packed with trace alien DNA. And since you are what you eat, eventually ...

'Who knows what's really in our food these days?

'Like our delightful little friend from the CIA, I disapproved; so I blew up the factory and killed everyone involved. Very definitely including my new best friends, who were far too blasé about what they were planning. A shame, but you can't make an omelette without bashing in the heads of a whole bunch of eggs. I made it look like an accident, from which I barely escaped with my life – and with just enough computer files to convince my superiors that there was nothing worth following up. Shame. I was in for a really big bonus, if I'd brought home the goods.'

'Would I be right in assuming that not everyone who worked in that factory knew what was going on?' said the Blue Fairy. 'That there were in fact quite a few innocent and entirely human workers there when you blew it up?'

Peter shrugged. 'I try not to think about that too much. This is a human world, and I intend for it to stay that way.'

'Well,' said the Blue Fairy, after a pause. 'It seems there's no doubt you really are Alexander King's grandson. My turn now, I think.'

*

'Nothing so everyday as factories or big business, or unnatural working practices. You think so small, people. The world is a bigger place than you imagine; bigger than you *can* imagine. It contains wonders and marvels, monsters and terrors. Back in the day, when I was young and virile and a major player in my own right, I was … well, hired isn't quite the right word. More properly, I was press-ganged by the Droods into cleaning up a particularly awkward problem that they preferred to handle at a safe and very deniable distance. In case it went horribly wrong.

'You've seen the stories in the news, about the occasional whale who becomes confused, gets lost and ends up swimming up the River Thames, right into the heart of London? Of course you have. Well, something much larger and decidedly less kiddie-friendly was making a nuisance of itself in the Thames. To be exact, a kraken had risen from the depths, taken a wrong turn, and was now threatening to block the Thames with its massive bulk and disturbingly long tentacles. Big things, kraken. Also very dim, and even harder to argue with. Especially when you're trying to hide the bloody thing from public gaze.

'There wasn't a hope in Hell of persuading it to turn around and go back, and there wasn't time to come up with an elegant or even particularly nice solution. So I used the Hiring Hall to call together every ghoul operating in and around London, provided them with knives and forks and told them to get stuck in. All the sushi you can eat, provided you swallow every last bit of it.

'And they did. Ghouls will eat anything.'

'I may never eat calamari again,' said Walker. He didn't look especially disturbed, but then he never did. 'My turn, I believe. A tale of the Nightside, then, where it's always dark. Always three o'clock in the morning, and the hour that tries men's souls. Except … someone wanted to change all that. There's always someone planning to smuggle sunlight into the Nightside, usually one of the more extreme do-gooder religious groups who believe evil can only flourish in the dark. Idiots. There's nothing darker than the deepest recesses of the human heart.

'Apparently this particular group believed that if only bright healthy sunshine can be hauled into the Nightside, by brute force if necessary, then suddenly everyone there would have an abrupt change of heart and start playing nicely together. Save me from well-meaning idealists; they do more harm than all the monsters.

'Anyway, my illustrious lords and masters the Authorities very definitely preferred the Nightside the way it was, turning out a regular profit for them. So I was instructed to put a stop to this nefarious scheme, by any and all means necessary. Didn't take me long to track down the man funding the operation. People are always ready to tell me things, when I ask in the right tone of voice. The instigator of this illuminating scheme turned out to be a failed businessman, failed politician, failed . . . well, everything, really. But still convinced that he had a destiny, and a right to change the world for the better, according to his beliefs.

'He had found religion in jail, and once he was out he attracted a whole bunch of followers, as his kind usually does. Somehow he got his hands on a grimoire, *Quite Appallingly Powerful Spells For Dummies*, and somehow, again, managed to smuggle it into the Nightside. Which is not unlike a terrorist smuggling a backpack nuke into an armoury. Actually, I think I would have preferred a backpack nuke. I know how to deal with those.

'I found the man and his nasty little book easily enough, because that's what I do. Or, rather, that's what I've trained my people to do for me. I've always believed in delegating the hard work and then strolling on stage at the end to take the bows. I confronted the trouble-maker, in what he thought was his secret lair, and did my very best to explain to him why what he was planning was in fact a Very Bad Thing, and wouldn't achieve what he wanted anyway; but he wouldn't listen. People who hear strong inner voices telling them to Do Good very rarely listen to anyone else. Because if their inner voices could be argued with, and proved wrong, well they wouldn't be special any more, would they? "You'll have to kill me to stop me," he said, froth at the corners of his mouth. "And I don't think you've got it in you to kill a good man in cold blood; a man who's only doing what is right."

'He was wrong, of course. I know my duty. I did what was necessary, and he died with a rather surprised look on his face. He should have known better. You don't get to lay down the law in a place like the Nightside, unless you're prepared to be even colder and more focused than anyone else in that corrupt place.'

We looked at Walker, and he gazed calmly back. It's always the quiet ones you have to watch out for.

'Well,' I said, and everyone looked at me. 'My turn. A tale of the Droods. And the messes we have to clean up.

'A few years back, I was called in to investigate a strange collection of murders, in one of the most quiet and law-abiding suburbs of London. Strange, in that although the same person was identified as the killer in each of the seven cases, that individual always had an unbreakable alibi for each and every killing. At the exact time the victims were dying horribly, the woman identified by dozens of witnesses as the killer was out in public somewhere else, surrounded by friends, and caught very clearly on surveillance cameras. Even though there was all kinds of forensic evidence linking the woman to the murders, there was no way in Hell she could have done it. Unless she was twins. Which she wasn't. First thing I checked.

'The police couldn't do a thing. So I took over.

'I learned all there was to know: read the files, checked the evidence, ruled out clones ... And then watched the woman from a safe distance, steeping myself in her boring, suburban, everyday life. A quiet, reserved lady of a certain age, with a nice house and a nice life, and not an enemy in the world. One ex-husband, with whom she got on fine. No children. A boring but worthy job, and no hidden life at all. No dark secrets, and certainly no reason to savagely kill and dismember seven people. The only odd thing in her file, so mild it hardly qualified as odd, was that for a short period earlier that year, she'd attended meditation classes.

'When I looked into that, I finally turned up something interesting which wasn't in the files. She'd left the meditation group because it wasn't doing anything for her, but she moved on from one group to another, searching for ... something. And ended up as part of a very quiet, very under-the-radar, really quite extreme group that specialised in exploring the deepest, darkest recesses of the human mind. Extreme beliefs, extreme practices, and just occasionally ... extreme results. God alone knows how such a quiet little soul ended up in that group. Maybe someone thought it was funny.

'If so, the joke was on them, because my timid little miss took to these new disciplines like a duck to water. At first, it was hard to get

146

anyone in the group to talk to me, but it's amazing how persuasive I can be when I've someone by the balls with an armoured hand. Turned out the group threw her out, because they were scared of her. Scared of what she was achieving. She'd gone deeper into her mind than any of the others had managed. And when she came back ... she brought something with her.

'Do I need to tell you that the murder victims had been members of the group?

'I confronted the woman, in her nice little house. Showed her my armour, calmed her down, and explained who and what I was. Told her that I was there to help her, if I could. But she had to be honest with me. She burst into tears then, but they were tears of relief. It might have been my reassuring manner or my impressive armour, but I think she'd been desperate to tell someone. Someone who'd believe her.

'The group she'd worked with had been about identifying and confronting one's own inner demons, so they could be controlled or exorcised. But something went wrong. She went deep into her mind, into the dark places most of us don't even want to admit exist, and came face to face with all the foul, selfish impulses of the id, the monsters of the mind. She brought them up into the light, and expelled them from her, horrified that someone as ... nice as her could have such terrible things within her. But once freed from the confines of her mind, the expelled darkness took on shape and form in the material world.

'Her shape and form.

'It's called a tulpa. A spirit made flesh, a doppelganger that embraces the impulses we normally control. And this tulpa went out into the city to do all the appalling things the woman had ever dreamed of, but would never have admitted even to herself. Avenging every slight, every perceived fault, indulging its endless appetite for blood and slaughter.

'I called in a few favours, mastered a few new tricks, and tracked the tulpa half across London and back. It ran before me, spitting and cursing, lashing out at anyone who got in its way. But I was always right there on its trail, closing in, preventing it from doing any real damage or horror, and finally it did the only thing it could. It went home. I crashed through the front door of the nice little house only minutes behind it, and found the woman standing over the tulpa's unconscious body. She'd hit it over the head with a vase of flowers.

'They really did look exactly the same. The woman came to me, and nestled into my arms, sobbing like a small child, desperate for me to tell her that the horror was finally over. Except it couldn't be, as long as the tulpa existed. It had to die. The woman didn't protest. But . . . she couldn't do it herself. Not to something that looked so like her. She begged me to do it for her.

'She really was very good. She would have fooled anyone else. But you can't work in this business for as long as I have, and not be able to tell the difference between a human being and a spirit form. The woman was unconscious on the floor; the thing with the tear-stained face looking up at me so beseechingly was the tulpa. Begging me to kill its original so it could run free at last.

'I killed the woman. Because I knew the one thing the tulpa didn't. Once freed, there was no way of putting a tulpa back into its host. It would go on killing and killing for ever until it was stopped – in the only way a tulpa can be stopped. By destroying the host that birthed it.

'I killed the woman quickly and efficiently. She never woke up. And the tulpa faded away into nothing, screaming its rage to the last. I like to think of myself as an agent, not an assassin. But sometimes that's the job.'

'Well, Eddie,' said the Blue Fairy after a pause. 'That was pretty hardcore. Didn't know you had it in you.'

'Of course he does,' said Walker. 'He's a Drood.'

'You did what you had to,' said Honey. 'Like you said, it's the job.'

'Sometimes,' I said.

'Stories like that are why I decided to specialise in industrial espionage,' said Peter.

We sat around the campfire, staring into the flames rather than look at each other. The storytelling hadn't gone as well as I'd hoped, and I wasn't sure what I'd learned from them. That we were hard, focused professionals, quite capable of making harsh decisions when we had to? That we were killers? That any one of us was capable of stabbing any other in the back, to be sure of getting Alexander King's prize? I already knew that. I was a little relieved that the stories had demonstrated a certain amount of moral responsibility. Or at least an awareness of it.

Least of all Peter's, surprisingly enough. Though maybe that was just big business for you.

'You know,' the Blue Fairy said suddenly, 'even though we all work, or have worked, for different masters ... we operate in the same greater, magical world. Maybe that's why Alexander King chose us, rather than better known names. It's not even as though we're complete strangers to each other. I know you, Eddie, and I worked with Walker once, on that Heir To The Throne business.'

'Which you took a very solemn oath not to discuss with anyone,' Walker said coldly.

'I'm not discussing it! I'm just mentioning it, to make a point! Do you know anyone here, Walker?'

'I know Honey Lake,' he said.

'What was the CIA doing in the Nightside?' I said.

'Meddling,' said Walker.

'Nothing that need concern the Droods,' Honey said quickly.

I looked at Peter, but he just shrugged. 'I've heard of the CIA, and the Droods, and the Nightside, but that's about it. I never needed or wanted to be part of your greater, magical world, Blue. I wanted a life as far from Grandfather's as possible. But ... he was a spy and I'm a spy. Maybe it is in the blood.' He looked around the fire, studying us. 'Why did you become spies? Or agents, if you prefer?'

'For me, it was the family business,' I said. 'I was filled full of duty and responsibility from my school days on. Indoctrination starts early in the Droods. I was raised to fight the good fight, to be a soldier in a war with no end. There were many ways you could choose to serve Humanity, but doing anything outside the family was never an option. I found a way to leave The Hall and be a fairly independent field agent, but I never left the family. I am a Drood, for all my many sins, and always will be. We exist to protect Humanity, and once you find out how many things it needs protecting from that the rest of you couldn't hope to cope with, it's hard to turn your back on it.'

'Yes,' said Walker. 'Duty, and responsibility. Stern task-masters, but not without their rewards. Someone has to stand their ground against the forces that would drag the world down. Someone has to crack the whip, and keep the lid on things. And I've always been good at that.'

'I wouldn't know duty and responsibility if I fell over them in the gutter,' said the Blue Fairy. 'I play the game for thrills and money, and any pretty young things I might encounter along the way. I am an agent for the sheer damned glamour of it. Once you discover how big and marvellous and strange the world really is, how could you not want to wade in it, up to your hips?'

'For me, it has always been about serving my country,' Honey said firmly. 'Doing the dirty, necessary jobs because someone has to.'

'Money,' Peter said flatly. 'For me it's always been show me the money. I take a certain pride in my successes, in a job well done, but if I could find anything that paid better I'd change occupations so fast it would make your head spin. There's no glamour in industrial espionage, no good guys or bad guys. Just varying amounts of greed, deceit and betrayal.'

There didn't seem much to say about that, so I turned to the Blue Fairy. 'When you were a major player, who did you work for, apart from my family?'

He shrugged. 'Anyone who could meet my price, or had an intriguing case. I always was a sucker for a pretty face with a sob story. I was a regular at the Hiring Hall for many years. Had my own stall, for a while. Go anywhere, do anyone ... But nothing lasts, particularly not in this business. Soon enough they want to be rescued by a younger agent, with less mileage on the clock, someone whose glamour isn't quite so—'

And then he broke off and sat up straight. He cocked his head slightly to one side, as though listening to something only he could hear.

'It's out there,' the Blue Fairy said quietly. 'In the dark. Watching us.'

We glanced around us, trying not to be too obvious about it, but the dark held its secrets to itself. But gradually, bit by bit, the shrieking and shouting from the local wildlife died away, birds and beasts going to ground in the presence of something more dangerous than themselves. The night seemed suddenly larger and more threatening. A tense brittle silence, as though everything in the world was holding its breath to see what would happen next. The only sound left was the quiet crackling of the fire. Almost without realising it, the five of us stood up and formed a circle round the fire, standing shoulder to shoulder staring out into the night, so nothing could come at us undetected. The Blue Fairy stood to my left, almost quivering with eagerness.

'Are you sure about this?' said Peter. 'I can't see a damned thing.'

'Oh, sure,' said Honey. 'The whole forest has fallen quiet because it can't wait to hear your next story.'

'It's out there,' said Blue. 'I can feel its presence, like a weight on the world, a disturbance in the night. But I can't tell what it is. It's natural and unnatural, both at the same time. Strange . . .'

'Is it human or animal?' said Walker, practical as ever.

'It has elements of both,' said Blue. 'But if I was pressed, I think I'd say neither . . .'

'Is it dangerous?' said Honey.

'Oh, yes,' said Blue. 'I can smell fresh blood on it.'

'As long as it doesn't turn out to be some kind of ape, or missing link,' said Peter, his voice too loud and carrying for my liking. 'Probably end up throwing its poop at us.'

'It's not an ape!' Blue snapped, not looking round. 'Nothing so ordinary . . . Something about this creature puts my teeth on edge. Just making mental contact with it makes me want to wash my soul out with soap.'

'But the descriptions of Sasquatch agree on a large, hairy, man-like figure,' said Honey. 'If not actually an ape, at least some kind of proto-human.'

'No,' the Blue Fairy said flatly. 'Not an ape. Not human. Nothing like that. In fact, I'm beginning to wonder if this is a Sasquatch at all. Perhaps it is something else, something different . . . and that's why Alexander King sent us here instead of to the more usual Bigfoot locations.'

'Okay,' I said. 'No one make any sudden moves. We don't want to frighten it off, after waiting so long for it to put in an appearance. If it retreats into the dark, we might never find it again.'

'Quite,' said Walker. 'Last thing we want is to go rushing off into the dark after it. Only too easy to split us up, and pick us off one at a time.'

'Are you worried about the Sasquatch, or one of us?' said Peter.

'Come on, Blue,' I said. 'We need information. What can you tell us about this creature?'

'It's not natural,' the Blue Fairy said doggedly. 'I can feel the wrongness in it, like teeth gnawing on my instincts. There's a— an instability ... Yes! That's it! The damn thing's a shapeshifter. Sometimes one thing, sometimes another. Sometimes human, some-times something else.'

'You mean it's a werewolf?' said Walker.

'Damn,' said Honey. 'And me without my silver bullets. Did any of you wonder why the Lone Ranger only ever used silver bullets? I always felt Tonto knew more than he was telling ...'

'If we could stick to the point, please,' said Walker.

'It's not a werewolf,' said Blue. 'I know what they feel like. This isn't any kind of were.'

'If it is a shapeshifter,' Walker said thoughtfully, 'that might explain why it's never been successfully tracked or identified. At the end of its ... hunt, it would turn back into a man again and disappear into its community with no one the wiser.'

'No ... no!' said the Blue Fairy, practically talking over Walker in his excitement. 'I've had this feeling before! I know what this is. That thing out there is a Hyde! Not some poor sad bastard bitten or cursed to be were, but a man chemically changed, transformed into something more and less than a man. I can almost smell the chemicals in him, this close.'

'Rather you than me,' said Peter.

'I shall slap you in a minute,' said Walker. 'And it will hurt. Pay attention!'

'What's so impressive about a Hyde?' I said. 'I've seen dozens of them working as bodyguards, or thugs for hire. Over-sized muscle freaks usually, and drama queens to a man.'

'The diluted serums that Harry Fabulous and his kind hawk around the Wolfshead Club aren't a patch on the real thing,' said Blue. 'The effects from those potions are as much psychological as physical. No one's ever been able to duplicate Henry Jeckyll's original formula, the one to let loose the evil in a man. Some mysterious impurity in the original salts.'

'Yes,' said Walker. 'Even Jeckyll couldn't recreate his original dose. That was why he lost control over the change, and Hyde kept re-emerging even without the formula. Perhaps there's some plant or flower or vegetable growing naturally here that contains the original impurity. Local people would eat it, unknowing, and then succumb to its effects. Then either the affected ones go off into the woods on their own, to make sure they won't hurt anyone . . . Or more likely the community recognises the signs and drives the afflicted one out into the wilderness until it's safe for them to return.'

'That's why Grandfather sent us here,' said Peter. 'The mystery of this creature solved: not a Bigfoot but a Hyde. Of course, we've still got to catch the thing on camera, as proof—'

Something was there, out in the dark. It was circling us, slowly and unhurriedly, making no effort to conceal its movements. It wanted us to know it was there. It moved around us in a complete circle, always careful to stay just out of the firelight, as though it had already taken our measure and decided we were no threat to it. And then it stopped, and the heavy silence of the night returned. What could be so scary, that every single beast and bird in the wood was afraid to draw its attention?

'It's in front of me,' the Blue Fairy said quietly. 'Watching me.'

I strained my ears against the quiet, and gradually I made out a low, harsh breathing, more beast than man.

'This can't be a Hyde,' I said. 'Not the real thing. Jeckyll was quite clear in his diaries. Edward Hyde was all the evil in a man, made physically manifest. Driven by instinct, ruled by his id, unconcerned with consequences or conscience. A thing of wants and needs and no self-control. A man with the mark of the beast upon him. Nothing but rage and lust and hate, and the need to kill.'

'Like your tulpa?' said Peter.

'Worse,' said Blue. 'Much worse.'

'Eddie has a point,' said Walker. 'If this is a Hyde, why hasn't he attacked us?'

'Let him try,' said Honey. 'I'll kick his nasty ass for him.'

'You're missing the point,' I said. 'Sasquatches don't kill. There's never been a recorded incident of a Sasquatch killing a man. Not here, not anywhere.'

'But this far out in the woods, what chance would he get to kill people?' said Walker. 'If he did make his way back to his home town, the people there would shoot him on sight. Hydes may be brutal, but they're not stupid. He'd know he was safe out here in the wilds, satisfying his violence on the wildlife.'

'Then why hasn't he attacked us?' said Honey.

'Because he's enjoying this,' said Blue.

'We've got to lure him forward, into the light,' I said quietly. 'We need to see exactly what we're dealing with.'

The Blue Fairy looked at me for the first time. 'You want to get up close and personal with a full-blown Hyde? Pure evil in human form? Well, you know best, I'm sure. You're a Drood, you know everything. You go right ahead. I'll be several miles away, running for the horizon at speed.'

'Where's your pride?' I said.

'Where's your common sense?' said the Blue Fairy.

'We wear the torc,' I said patiently. 'Nothing can harm us.'

'You keep believing that,' said the Blue Fairy. 'I'll put my faith in a good pair of running shoes.'

'Unfortunately, I have to side with the Drood on this,' said Peter. 'We have to supply proof of what this creature is, and while I have my state-of-the-art phone camera at the ready, to get a good picture I need the thing to step forward into the light. In fact, I'd really like to get some before and after shots, and maybe even some film of the actual transformation.'

I hated to agree with the annoying little twerp, but he had a point. 'I could armour up, drag him in, and hold him down,' I said. 'Hydes may be big and brutal, but they're still just flesh and blood. My armour should be able to handle him.'

'You armour up and he'll run,' said the Blue Fairy. 'And you'll never catch him in the dark.'

'I'm still not too happy about letting that thing get too close,' said Walker. 'Hydes live to kill.'

'I know an industrial spy we can hide behind,' said Honey.

A sound came to us from out of the dark. It might have been a growl, or a chuckle. Something about the sound made my hairs stand on end. No man ever made a sound like that, nor any kind of beast. There was a touch of Hell itself in that sound; and the Hyde knew it, and gloried in it.

'Well,' said Walker. 'I was hoping to save the last vestiges of my voice for a real emergency, but ...' He stepped forward, and addressed the dark directly in front of the Blue Fairy. *'You. Come. Here.'*

I shuddered at the sound of his voice. I think we all did. It was Walker's legendary voice that could not be argued with or disobeyed. Some say it contained vestiges of the original voice, the one that said, 'Let there be light'. I didn't like to believe that. It would have opened too many questions as to just where Walker got his voice from ... The dark itself seemed to hesitate, as though struggling; and then the Hyde came lurching forward into the firelight. Drawn forth against his will, like a dog on a leash or a fish on a hook. He lurched forward another step, fighting every inch of the way, hating us, but still he came, and stood before us.

He was clearly a man, but just as clearly something more and less. He was taller than any of us, but seemed shorter because he was so stooped over. His great over-muscled back rose up into a hump, and his square bony head thrust out at the level of his chest. He glared at us with blood-shot eyes from under heavy protruding brows. Long ragged jet-black hair hung down around a fierce, ugly face full of every sin man ever contemplated. His clothes were rags, torn and tattered and soaked with blood not his own. His huge hands were thickly crusted with dried blood, like scarlet gloves reaching up to his elbows. Elsewhere his skin was flushed, stretched taut, full of pulsing blood. His eyes were deep-set, watchful, crafty; and he smiled a cold happy smile, full of all the evil in the world.

To look at him was enough to make you want to kill him. The very sight of him filled me with disgust, hatred, loathing: a basic primordial need to attack and destroy something that shouldn't exist in this world. Something too horrid to be borne, an abomination on the earth. Standing before us, he was all the forbidden needs and impulses of man, made flesh and blood and bone and let loose in the world. All the worst actions that a man could conceive of, without conscience or compassion or any fear of consequences. All the most

155

evil men in the world, and there have been so very many of them, were just glimpses of the Hyde within.

I could feel my torc burning coldly round my throat, as though trying to protect me from the contamination of the creature's presence.

Almost instinctively, the five of us had moved to form a circle round the Hyde, like hunters with a prey too dangerous to be allowed to escape. Though none of us wanted to get too close. I could see the same confused expressions of fear and loathing in the faces of the others, see their hands clenched into fists, twitching and jerking, wanting to reach for weapons. Or maybe just to kill the awful thing with their bare hands. I knew what they were feeling, because I felt the same.

The Hyde stood very still, half crouching like an animal, his eyes darting back and forth though his head never moved, searching out which of us was the weakest and most vulnerable. The one it would be most fun to torment. His crafty eyes finally settled on Honey, the only woman in our company, and her dark-coffee face went stiff and taut under the impact of his loathsome gaze.

'Pretty pretty,' said the Hyde, in a voice smooth as silk, sweet as cyanide. 'So good of you to come and visit me in my backyard kingdom. I like you. You look good enough to eat.'

'Shut your filthy mouth,' said Honey. Her voice wasn't as firm as usual. She couldn't hide the revulsion she felt.

'Change back,' Walker said to the Hyde. 'Become human again.'

But though his words cracked on the night with all the authority of a man used to being obeyed, it wasn't enough. They were only words. He'd used up his voice. The Hyde laughed soundlessly at him.

'What's your name?' I said. He looked at me, and the force of his gaze was like a backhand across the face.

'Names,' he said. 'Why, sir, does plague have a name? Does rape or torture, cancer or senility have a name or identity? I am what I am, and I glory in it. I'll trample you beneath my feet, rip the flesh from your bones and stick my dick in the holes I make.'

'Your name,' I said. 'Tell me your name.'

'You mean, who I was, good sir? Forget him. He doesn't matter. He never did. But I matter. I will do terrible things until the world

156

sickens from my very presence. I will wade in blood and offal and sing happy songs, and I will make children from every woman I meet, because I am a very potent nightmare. I will people this land with Hydes, remake this rotten world in my awful image, and love every minute of it. My name? Edward Hyde, at your service, sir; and this is Hell nor am I out of it. The old jokes are always the best, are they not?'

His smile was very broad now, and I hated him more than I had ever hated anyone.

'How does it feel?' said Peter, fighting to keep his voice steady. 'How does it feel, to be Hyde?'

The Hyde studied him curiously, and Peter actually flinched. 'I am this thunder, this lightning,' said the Hyde. 'I teach you this: man is something to be overcome. I am the tumour in the brain, the wind that uproots trees and the thing that hides under your bed at night. And I love it! It is a glorious thing, to be free of fear, to be the thing that everyone else fears. Oh, my dear sirs and madam, you have no idea how *good* this feels ... to throw away the constraints of man and the chains society binds us with. To be free at last, because the only real freedom is the freedom to do *anything* ...' He laughed soundlessly again. 'I am everything you've ever wanted to be, but didn't dare admit to yourself. I will do what I will do, and none of you can stop me. And when they finally find what's left of your bodies – and see what I've done to them – they'll cry and puke and scream their minds away.'

He broke off, because Honey's shimmering crystal weapon was suddenly in her hands. Her lips had pulled back in a deadly smile like a death's-head grin. The Hyde giggled suddenly, a harsh, high-pitched, soul-destroying sound. And then he surged forward impossibly quickly, a blur in the firelight. He slapped the weapon contemptuously out of Honey's hand and threw her to the ground with a single vicious backhand slap. Blood from her mouth and nose flew on the air. She hit the ground hard.

Walker was pulling an aboriginal pointing bone from his waistcoat pocket. Peter was drawing a large handgun from a concealed holster. The Blue Fairy was chanting a curse at the Hyde, old elf magic, but his voice was a deep slow crawl. Because I had armoured up the moment the Hyde started moving, my golden armour sealed me in and insulated me from the almost subliminal effects of the Hyde's presence. I could think clearly now, no longer blinded by the impact of his foul nature.

I still hated him just as much.

I surged forward to meet the Hyde, my armour moving me so fast the world slowed to a crawl. Even so, he sensed me coming, and turned away from Honey to face me. Which was what I wanted. I fell upon him, my fists slamming into him like golden hammers. Blood flew from the Hyde's face as I turned it into pulp. I felt as much as heard bones in his face and skull break and splinter. The Hyde didn't give an inch. He struck at me with fists like mauls, but the force of his blows merely smashed his hands against my unyielding armour. He had the strength of his terrible condition, and the conviction to fight without restraint; but in the end he was still mostly a man, and the armour made me so much more than that.

He was a Hyde; but I was a Drood.

I beat him to death with my spiked golden fists. I killed him – for what he was, what he'd done and what he intended to do. He went down still fighting, and he died cursing me. I broke his arms and legs, smashed in his ribs, drove my fist deep into his skull. And when it was done, and I stood over his body breathing harshly, blood dripping from my spiked hands, I didn't feel anything. Anything at all. I looked slowly around me. Honey was back on her feet, pressing a handkerchief to her bloody mouth and nose. Her eyes were very wide. For a moment, I didn't recognise the expression on her face. She was looking at me the same way she'd looked at the Hyde. As though one monster . . . had been replaced by another.

I looked down at the dead Hyde. I'd half expected him to turn back into his original, human form; but he hadn't. Only the potion, or the plant, or whatever he'd taken, could do that.

I armoured down, and looked at the others with my naked, human face. I was shaking. Walker looked at me thoughtfully. Peter's face was blank, empty, as though he didn't know what to think. Honey came slowly forward to stand before me. Her mouth was swollen, and already dark bruises were rising on her coffee skin.

'It's all right, Eddie,' she said. 'We understand.'

'Do you?' I said. 'Maybe you can explain it to me. I never lost it like that before. Never lost control so completely. You can't afford to lose control when you wear the golden armour. I never knew I had that much rage and anger within me.'

'We all have a Hyde within us,' said Walker. 'Perhaps his presence awoke some of that.'

Peter moved around the Hyde with his phone camera, filming the dead body from every angle. When he was finished, he put the phone away. 'So,' he said. 'What do we do with the body?'

'Drop it in the river,' said Honey. 'Let the alligators take care of it. Nobody would want to claim it, looking like . . . that.'

'Wait a minute,' I said. 'Where's Blue? Where's the Blue Fairy?'

We found his body on the other side of the fire, almost hidden in the darkness at the edge of the firelight. His neck was broken, the head lolling to one side. His eyes were open and staring, and a small trickle of blood had run down from his slack mouth. He looked . . . confused, as though he couldn't understand how such a thing could have happened to him. I knelt down beside him and closed his eyes.

'Damn,' said Honey, standing behind me. 'The Hyde got him.'

'No,' I said. 'I don't think so.'

'He was never strong,' said Walker. 'One blow from the Hyde would have been enough.'

'It's not as if he's such a great loss,' said Peter. 'Never trust an elf.'

'Shut up,' I said, and something in my voice made him obey immediately. 'Leave me alone with him,' I said. 'Blue and I have private business.'

Walker escorted Peter back to the fire. Honey hovered behind me for a while, but when I wouldn't look round, she went away too. Let the others think what they liked; the Hyde didn't do this. He hit Honey, and then I was upon him. He never had a chance to get to anyone else. Someone in the group killed Blue while the others watched me beat the Hyde to death.

Two members of our group gone, both dead of a broken neck. Both sacrificed to a prize that might not even be worth it. But someone thought so; someone in our little group was playing for all the marbles. I let my fingertips drift over Blue's copper and brass breastplate. The elven protections had been stripped away. Not an easy thing to do. But even so, the torc should have protected him.

All he had to do was activate it . . . Unless he really was too scared to use it.

I brought him out of his retirement. I brought him to Drood Hall, found a place for him in the family, in our army. Tempted him with the prospect of a Drood torc, and then was surprised when he couldn't wait and stole one for himself. He was a friend of sorts of many years.

'Sorry, Blue,' I said quietly. 'But you have something that doesn't belong to you.'

I touched a fingertip to the golden circle around Blue's throat and the strange matter of the torc flowed up my hand and my arm and was immediately absorbed by the torc around my neck. Blue's body would have to go back to his people, to the Fae Court; but he couldn't be allowed to take the torc with him. Even though it was the only real achievement of his life.

And then I stopped, and listened, as the Blue Fairy's voice came to me, clear but faint, as though it had to travel a long way to reach me.

'Hello, Shaman. If you're hearing this, I'm dead, and you've taken the torc back . . . Ah well! Easy come, easy go. I'm leaving this message for you in the torc, just in case. Hope you don't mind me calling you Shaman. I always knew Shaman Bond better than Eddie Drood. I liked Shaman. He was my friend; I was never sure about Eddie. It must be complicated, having to be two people and live two lives. Perhaps only a half-elf could understand.

'I just wanted to say that whatever happens, however I die – and I'm assuming I've been killed – it's not your fault. I went into this game with my eyes wide open. Would I have killed you, at the end, to be sure of gaining Alexander King's prize for the Fae Court and Queen Mab? I don't know. Shaman Bond was my friend, but I think I could have killed Eddie Drood. You don't know what the Droods did to me, Shaman. What they made me do.

'So, Shaman, hail and farewell. Win the game, whatever it takes. None of the others can be trusted with the prize. And I hate to be a poor loser, but if you do find out who killed me . . . rip their head off and piss down their neck.'

His laugh faded away, and was gone.

I reactivated one of the spells on his breastplate, and used it to send his body home to the Fae Court. I couldn't leave him here, in the dark, alone. He always hated the countryside. I went to join the others by the fire, and for a long time we just sat and looked at each other, and none of us had anything to say.

CHAPTER SIX
Out of time

The Norsemen believed that Hel was a place of endless ice and freezing weather; a terrible cold to sear the soul for ever and ever. There are places on this earth that explain why.

This time there were only four of us for the teleport bracelets to throw across the world. Myself, Honey Lake, Peter King and Walker. Two missions down, and already two of us were dead. After we solved this new mystery, would there be only three of us left to travel on? Alexander King said 'There can be only one'; and it looked like someone in our group was taking that very seriously.

The hot and sweaty woods of Arkansas disappeared, and the next moment we were standing in the middle of a large frozen forest. The fierce cold hit us like a hammer, and we cried out involuntarily at the shock of it. Harsh dead ground underfoot, tall dark trees with leafless branches all around, and a bitter wind that cut to the bone. I had thought Loch Ness was cold, but it was nothing compared to this. Everywhere I looked, I saw nothing but dead trees in a dead land under a harsh grey sky. The sun shone brightly directly overhead, but its warmth couldn't reach us. The air burned in my lungs with every breath, and my bare face and hands ached horribly. I shuddered helplessly, and hugged myself as tightly as I could to hold in some warmth.

The four of us stumbled over to each other, feet dragging on the uneven and unforgiving frozen ground. We huddled together in a circle to share our warmth, driven by the same brute instinct for survival that makes sheep pack together on the moors. Our teeth were chattering loudly and uncontrollably, and our breath steamed thickly on the bitter air. Honey made a soft pained sound with every breath she let out. She didn't even know she was doing it. Peter made low moaning sounds, and, while Walker was wearing his best stiff upper lip, he was shaking and shivering as badly as the rest of us. We huddled in close, shoulder to shoulder and face to face, heads bowed against the fierce chill of the gusting wind. And for a while that was all we did. The cold was simply overwhelming, freezing our thoughts as well as our bodies.

Eventually, I forced my head up and looked around. We had to find shelter soon, or cold like this would kill us. But there was only the widely spaced trees and the harsh stony ground, stretching away to the horizon in all directions. Miles and miles of nothing but forest. My face and hands were already numb, and I could see hoarfrost forming on the others' faces, flecks of grey ice across blue-grey skin. Ice forming on my eyelashes made my eyes heavy.

'Where the Hell has your grandfather dumped us this time?' said Honey, forcing the words past numb lips as she beat her hands together to keep the circulation going.

'Don't ask me,' said Peter. 'You're the one with a computer in your head.'

'No wonder you put Area Fifty-two in the Antarctic,' said Walker. 'Safest place to store all that alien technology you've accumulated down the years, and still don't know how to operate.'

'First things first,' I said quickly. 'We need to find some kind of shelter. Anyone know how to build an igloo?'

'I think you need snow for that, don't you?' said Peter.

'Contact Langley,' Walker said to Honey. 'Have them find out where we are, and then drop us some survival gear.'

'I've been trying!' Honey said, through teeth gritted together to stop them chattering. 'They're not answering. I'm not picking up any comm traffic. The best my diagnostics can suggest is that something is blocking the carrier signal. That would take a Hell of a lot of power, so the source must be somewhere nearby.'

'Good,' said Peter. 'Let's go there right now, and get warm. Before things I'm rather fond of start falling off me.'

'Look around,' I said. 'There isn't anything but trees. We're on our own out here.'

'What?' Peter glared wildly about him. 'There has to be some-where!'

'Try not to panic quite so loudly,' murmured Walker. 'It's bad enough being frozen to one's marrow without being deafened in one ear.'

'Screw you!' said Peter. 'I can't feel my balls any more!'

'If you're looking for help there, you're on your own,' said Honey.

'I think you're supposed to rub snow on them, to prevent frost-bite,' I said.

'Rub some on yours!' said Peter ungraciously. 'Mine are cold enough as it is!'

'You just can't help some people,' said Walker.

'Let me try something,' I said.

I forced myself away from the relative warmth of the group, subvocalised the activating Words, and armoured up. The golden strange matter slid over me in a moment, covering me from crown to toe, and it was like slipping into a well-heated pool. I gasped out loud as the armour insulated me from the cold and the wind, and already I could feel sensation flowing back into my numbed extrem-ities. I gritted my teeth against the pins and needles of returning circulation, and through my featureless golden mask I looked slowly around me. The mask boosted my vision, until I could see clearly for miles and miles, my eyes seeming to dart and soar over the dead and frozen ground. And still there was nothing, until I raised my Sight as well; and then at last I detected faint emanations rising in the distance. An energy source of such size and scale practically promised a good-sized city. But it was seven, maybe eight miles away, on foot, through cold dead wilderness.

Under normal conditions, an easy stroll. Here possibly a death sentence for some of us.

I armoured down, gasping as the shock and pain of the awful cold hit me again. I gestured north-west with a shaking hand.

'There's a city ... that way. I think. Can't say what kind of welcome we'll get, but it's our best bet. Hell, it's our only bet.'

'How far?' said Walker.

'Seven miles,' I said. 'Maybe less.'

We looked at each other. No one said anything. No one had to We knew what that meant.

'Let's go,' I said. 'Sooner we're there, sooner we can lounge around in front of a great big fire with hot toddies and a steaming fondue.'

'Fondue,' Peter muttered disparagingly as we set off. 'So bloody up itself. It's only bread and cheese, when you get down to it.'

*

I led the way through the trees, and the others stumbled after me. We couldn't huddle together for warmth any more; the uneven ground kept shaking us apart. So for a long time we struggled along in silence, heads bowed to keep our vulnerable faces out of the cutting wind, conserving our energy as best we could. The unyielding ground made every step an effort, like walking along the bottom of the sea with chains round our ankles. There wasn't a sound to be heard anywhere in the forest. No birds singing, not the slightest sound from any animal. As though we four were the only living things left in this dead deserted land. My feet grew so numb I had to crash them against the dead ground to feel the impact, and then my legs grew so tired I couldn't even manage that any more. I kept going. Complaints wouldn't help, and would only take up energy I couldn't spare. Besides, I was damned if I'd be the first one to stop and call for a rest.

Not least because if we did stop, I wasn't sure all of us would be able to find the strength to start again. Real cold is constant and unforgiving, and it kills by inches when you aren't looking.

After a while, I realised Honey had moved forward to trudge along beside me. I raised my head, to look at her. Honey's coffee skin had gone grey from the cold, and her eyes had a flat, exhausted, hurting look.

'Why aren't you wearing your armour?' she said abruptly. 'Then you wouldn't feel the cold.'

'I chose not to,' I said. My mouth was so numb I had to concentrate on carefully forming each word. 'Because ... we need to work as a team. Working together, striving together. As equals, respecting each other. Because if we're a team maybe we'll stop killing each other.'

'You didn't believe Katt and Blue's deaths were accidents for one minute, did you?' said Honey.

'No. You?'

'Of course not. I'm CIA. We're trained to see the worst aspect of any situation, and plan accordingly. And you heard the Independent Agent. Only one of us can return to claim the prize. Killing each other off was inevitable, at some point.'

'Killing is never inevitable,' I said roughly. 'I'm an agent, not an assassin.'

Honey shot me a heavy glance from under iced-up eyelashes. 'You really think you can keep this group from each other's throats?'

'Of course,' I said. 'I'm a Drood. I can do anything. I have it in writing, somewhere.'

'You could put on your armour,' said Honey. 'Run ahead to the city, and send back help.'

'No telling how long that would take,' I said. 'Or how many of you would still be alive when I got back.'

'You can't worry about us.'

'Watch me.'

She chuckled briefly. 'You're a good man, Eddie Drood. How you ever got to be a field agent is beyond me.'

'I bribed the examiner.'

We strode on, fighting for every step and every breath, forcing our slowly dying bodies through the dead forest. I lost track of time. The sun seemed always overhead, the shadows never moved, and every part of the forest looked like every other part. No landmarks, nothing to aim for, nothing to mark distance passed. We were all close to failing, the last of our hoarded strength draining away, only will power and brute stubbornness keeping us going. No one complained, or cursed, or asked for help. We were, after all, professionals.

I could have armoured up. Gone on, and left them behind. But I couldn't do that. Someone had to lead this group by example, and unfortunately it looked like it was down to me. Considering how much trouble I always have with authority figures, it's amazing how often I end up being one. Sometimes I think this whole universe runs on irony.

And then, long after I'd reached the point where I couldn't take any more, and couldn't go on, and did anyway, the trees fell back and I stumbled to a halt at the top of a long gentle slope leading down to a city in the middle of a wide open plain. There wasn't much to see: just high stone walls surrounding blunt and functional buildings. Not much bigger than a decent-sized town, really, with only the one road leading in and out. Could have been any place, anywhere. No traffic on the road, no obvious signs of life. Could we have come all this way across a dead land, just to reach a dead city?

It didn't matter. It was shelter. And the mood I was in, I'd burn the whole place down to build a fire.

The others crowded in beside me, looking down at the city on the plain, too cold and numb and exhausted to ask even the most obvious questions. I started down the gentle slope. No point in arguing anyway. There was nowhere else to go.

We followed the only road to the main gate, set deep into the towering wall. The brickwork was seriously weather-blasted, but it still stood firm and strong, which was more than could be said for the massive main gate. Something had torn it off its hinges and left it lying on the cold featureless ground outside the boundary wall. It could have happened yesterday, or years ago. There was no way of telling. Inside the towering walls, the city lay still and open and utterly silent. The streets were deserted, with no signs of life in any of the buildings, and not a sound anywhere, of men or machines. A brief Cyrillic inscription had been carved deep into the stone above the gateway.

'Cyrillic!' said Walker. 'We're in Russia! Anybody read Cyrillic, by any chance?'

'I do,' said Honey.

'Of course you do,' I said. 'Know thy enemy. Well; what does it say?'

'Probably "Abandon all hope, ye who enter here",' grumbled Peter.

'No,' said Honey, trying to frown with her frozen forehead. 'It's just one letter and two numbers. X three seven.'

'*Oh shit.*' I said.

'Somehow it always sounds so much worse when he says it,' said Walker. 'What's wrong, Eddie? Are we to take it you know of this place?'

'If there was anywhere else to go, I'd go there,' I said. 'Running. I know this city's reputation. I know what it is, and what it was for; and we shouldn't be here.'

'I want to go home,' Peter said miserably.

'Russia,' Honey said. 'I have contacts here, if I can find a working comm system ... What's so bad about this place, Eddie?'

'Who cares?' said Peter. 'It looks warm.'

'This is one of the old secret Soviet science cities,' I said. 'Abandoned years ago. X thirty-seven means we're in Tunguska territory, in northern Siberia.'

'Wait a minute,' said Peter. 'As in the Tunguska Event of 1908? That must be what we're here for!'

'I hope so,' I said. 'There's a mystery in X thirty-seven too, but I really don't think I want to know what it is. X thirty-seven was a bad place where bad things happened, and maybe they still are.'

'It offers shelter, and the possibility of warm clothes and food,' said Walker. 'First things first.'

And so we became the first people to enter X thirty-seven for many years, lambs to the slaughter, walking its empty streets looking for a suitable store to break into. To keep our minds off the cold, and to keep the others from asking too many questions about X thirty-seven just yet, I did my usual Drood font-of-all-knowledge bit, and filled them in on what I knew of the great Tunguska Event.

In 1908, at 7:17 a.m. on 30 June, something hit northern Siberia with enough force to shake the world. There was a huge explosion in the remote and largely uninhabited territory of Tunguska, since estimated to be between ten and twenty megatons – more powerful than any nuclear bomb ever exploded. The force of the explosion felled some eighty million trees, uprooting them and knocking them flat, over a range of eight hundred and thirty square miles. The light generated by this impact was so bright and lasting that men in London were able to read a newspaper in the street at midnight.

But the event wasn't properly investigated until some twenty years later. The First World War and the Russian Revolution got in the way, and the Soviet authorities consistently refused offers of outside scientific help. In 1928, a team of Russian scientists made the long and difficult journey into the frozen heart of northern Siberia to investigate; and that's when the mystery began. Because what the scientists found there made no sense at all.

Everyone's first thought was that a really big meteor had made its way through the atmosphere and struck us a killing blow; but there wasn't any crater. Nothing. Not even a dent in the ground. So it couldn't have been a meteor. Next thought: a comet. Since comets are mostly composed of ice and gas, it was possible that a huge comet had exploded at ground level. Such things had been known to happen on a much smaller scale. But in every such case, the exploding comet had driven certain identifying chemicals and elements into the ground; and there weren't any at Tunguska. So, not a comet.

Then someone came up with the idea of a volcanic explosion from underground, caused by accumulated pressure. Except that would have left a crater too. There have been more theories down the years: a crashing alien spacecraft, a miniature black hole passing through, even an escape attempt from Hell. But my family would have known about those. A century after the Tunguska Event, the scientists are still arguing, and getting nowhere.

'That's all very well and groovy,' said Peter. 'But that's there, and we are here. What is this place? Why doesn't it have a proper name? And, most importantly, why the "Oh shit"?'

'Those old science cities had bad reputations,' I said. 'But X thirty-seven was in a class of its own. And it may be coincidence or it may not, but we're not that far from one of the great Drood secrets. Some miles from here, something very old and unspeakably powerful lies sleeping, buried deep under the permafrost. We need to be extremely careful while we're here that we don't do anything that might waken it.'

'Just for the sake of argument,' said Walker, 'what would happen if we did?'

'The end of everything,' I said. 'The destruction of the world, and Humanity as we know it. Hell on Earth, for ever and ever.'

'Ah,' said Walker. 'Let's not do that, then.'

'Best not,' I said.

'You can be such a drama queen sometimes, Eddie,' said Honey. She looked at me suspiciously. 'How is it you Droods know so much about this godforsaken area, anyway?'

I smiled as much as my frozen mouth would allow. 'Wouldn't you like to know.'

We trudged on, through the deserted city. Still no sign of anyone. The only sound in the streets was the tramp of our unsteady feet, echoing back from blank, unresponsive walls. We were all deathly tired now, inside and out, every movement an effort. I felt like shouting out, to challenge the quiet, to see if anyone might answer; but I didn't. If anyone was still alive in this abandoned place, I was pretty sure they wouldn't be the kind of people I'd want to meet. And even beyond that this city was too still, too quiet. Like a crouching cat, ready to jump on its prey. It felt like we were being watched. From everywhere.

The street lamps were out, and there wasn't a single light burning in any of the windows. No sign of power in any part of the city. Now and again we'd come across an old-fashioned boxy car with its doors open and its windows and windshield shattered, great rusty holes in the metalwork as though it was rotting away. The buildings were typical old Soviet architecture: massive concrete blocks and brutal stone edifices with all the character and appeal of a slap around the face. No sign of occupation, anywhere.

We finally found a clothing store. Behind the smeared glass there were heavy coats and hats on display. We gathered before the display like starving children confronted with an all-you-can-eat buffet. Walker tried the door, but it was locked.

'Let me beat some feeling back into my hands, and I'll have that lock picked in under a minute,' said Honey.

I armoured up and kicked the door in. My golden foot slammed the heavy door off its hinges and sent it flying back several feet into the store. I armoured down. The others were looking at me. They still weren't used to seeing me in my armour, and all the things it could do. Good. Keep them respectful, and off balance, and maybe they'd think twice about killing each other. Honey looked almost envious, that I should have such a useful thing and she didn't. Certainly beat the Hell out of her yellow submersible. Walker appeared thoughtful. Peter kept his distance, and tried to pretend he wasn't staring at the torc around my throat.

Inside the store, we grabbed the heaviest overcoats we could find from the display dummies and wrapped ourselves up in them, almost moaning with pleasure. We then spent some time just walking up and down, hugging ourselves with furry arms as warmth slowly returned to our frozen bodies. We swore and grimaced as feeling bit back into our numbed extremities, and when we could feel our hands again we clapped on lumpy hats, heavy leather gloves and boots, and long woollen scarves. We were out of the bitter wind at last, but our breath still steamed on the damp store air. Walker suggested breaking up the furnishings to make a fire, but I had to say no. I didn't want us doing anything that might get us noticed. Not yet. Peter had all but buried himself under the biggest coat he could find, together with an over-sized fur hat and half a dozen scarves. The colour had come back into his face, and the ice in his eyelashes had melted. He noticed me watching him, and scowled.

'I'm still cold,' he said, his voice muffled behind a pulled-up scarf. 'And very hungry.'

'And utterly unfashionable,' said Honey. Incredibly, she'd managed to find another long white fur coat to replace the one she'd left in Arkansas. And a white pillbox hat, white gloves and white leather boots. Somewhere, a nude polar bear was shivering in his cave and cursing mankind.

Walker looked smart but casual, which was no mean feat when wrapped in old-fashioned Soviet tailoring, which went in more for bulk than quantity. He looked at the mechanical till on the counter, with its dusty brass keys, and frowned.

'Do you suppose we ought to leave something? As payment? Feels a bit like stealing, otherwise.'

'Leave it to who?' said Honey. 'Everyone's gone.'

'Odd, that,' said Peter, from deep inside his huge fur coat. 'It's like everyone just got up and went. Maybe they left some canned food behind. You got a can opener in that armour of yours, Drood?'

'How can you be hungry already?' said Walker. 'You had some perfectly nice charred beaver only a few hours ago.'

'I am trying very hard to forget that,' said Peter. 'Look, I am so hungry right now that if we should happen to come across a monster in this city, I am going to kill, skin and eat the whole thing. Not necessarily in that order. In fact, someone had better find me a monster pretty damned soon, because you guys are starting to look increasingly edible.'

Strength returned with warmth, and we went back out into the street. One direction seemed as good as any other. I was still wondering what we were supposed to be looking for; which particular mystery Alexander King had sent us here to solve.

'What are we after, exactly?' said Walker.

I shrugged, though my heavy coat muffled most of the movement. 'If we are where I think we are, we're a long way from the impact site of the Tunguska Event. So I assume we're here to find out what happened to this city, to X thirty-seven. On the whole, I think I'd rather stick my dick in a light socket.'

'You still haven't properly explained what the problem is with this city,' said Walker. 'Why was it built all the way out here, in the middle of a wilderness? I thought the Soviets only used Siberia for forced labour camps. What happened here, Eddie? Where is everyone?'

'Well,' I said, reluctantly, 'X thirty-seven was one of a whole series of secret science cities, all of them without any official name, just a designation. None of them officially existed, except on very secret maps in very secret offices. The building programme began in the fifties, at the height of the Cold War. Scientists on both sides were soldiers then, their discoveries ammunition for the war. The science cities were built using forced labour from the camps, deliberately set miles from anywhere civilised. Partly for security, partly because some of the experiments being run were so extreme that even the Soviet people wouldn't have stood for them – but mostly so that if anything did go severely wrong, no one else would be affected. Especially if the whole city had to be shut down, or bombed into rubble to cover up what had happened. Which did occur more than once, to my certain knowledge.'

'So only scientists lived here?' said Peter.

'Scientists and their families, and enough people and infra-structure to support them,' I said. 'And a military presence, to keep an eye on everyone. Most of the people who lived here probably never knew what horrors were being perpetrated in the strictly off-limits laboratories. Curiosity was not an encouraged trait in Soviet Russia.'

'What kind of experiments are we talking about, exactly?' said Walker.

'Nasty ones, from the few files I've seen,' said Honey. 'Early organ transplant technology, using criminals and dissidents as subjects. I once saw some disturbing black and white film of a man with two heads, both of them very much alive and aware. Other subjects were exposed to radiation, at varying doses, just to see what it would do to them. They were a long way from any kind of protection or cure, in those days. They needed data to work with.'

'Then there was chemical warfare,' I said. 'Biological, psychic and supernatural, all the officially forbidden weapons of war. The Geneva Convention didn't reach out here. But as the years passed, and the pressure of the Cold War intensified, the research in these completely deniable cities took stranger and more dangerous turns. City X seventeen was tasked with trying to open gateways into other dimensions. They must have had some success, because the whole city vanished in 1966. That did leave a crater. X thirty-five specialised in making superhumans out of ordinary people, using drugs, radiation, tissue grafts and implanted alien technology. All they got for their trouble was a series of very expensive monsters. Who broke loose, in the end. The military hit the whole area with a thermonuke in 1985. No one got out.

'X forty-eight produced cloned duplicates of important personages, with organic bombs hidden in their bellies. The ultimate suicide bombers, and the very best unsuspected assassins. My Uncle James terminated that programme, with extreme prejudice, in 1973. But X thirty-seven was the worst of all, by far.'

'Did your family shut this city down?' Honey said suddenly. 'Did you do this?'

'No,' I said. 'The Soviets hid what they were doing very successfully, until it was too late. By the time we got a whisper of what they were trying to do, it had already blown up in their faces. All we could do was send in a couple of agents to watch from a safe distance and stand ready to contain it, if necessary. It wasn't. X thirty-seven ate its own guts out.'

'What the Hell did they do here that was so terrible?' said Peter.

'Yeah,' said Honey. 'I'd like to know that myself, before I take one step further.'

'X thirty-seven specialised in genetic research and manipulation,' I said. 'Ripping human DNA apart to see what made it tick. Cutting-edge stuff, in the early 1980s. They were looking for secrets, for marvels and wonders, and they found them. Poor bastards.'

The others waited, but that was all I was prepared to say, for the moment.

'If I remember correctly, most of these science cities were shut down or abandoned in the nineties,' said Honey. 'Too expensive to run, in the more austere days of the new order, with the economy crashing around everyone's ears. A lot of scientists weren't being paid, so they voted with their feet and walked out. The soldiers didn't try and stop them, because they hadn't been paid in months either. A few cities survived for a while by switching over to commercial research, with corporate or mafiosa backing, but by the turn of the century all these backwater places were deserted and abandoned. Expensive leftovers from the Cold War, pretty much forgotten in the new corridors of power. No one cared. No one even remembered what most of them had been working on.'

She stopped, and looked at me. So did Peter and Walker. I sighed, and reluctantly continued.

'X thirty-seven. Genetic research and manipulation. And not the kind you stumbled across, Peter. No frankenfood, no goldfish that glow in the dark, no mice with human ears growing out of their backs. And no alien intruders going skinny-dipping in our gene pool, either. No ... the scientists here were exclusively interested in uncovering the secrets of human DNA. It makes us who and what we are, but we still don't know what most of it does. What it's for, what it was intended to do. The Soviet scientists approached the problem in their usual blunt and pragmatic way. They experimented on people. Criminals and dissidents, Jews and homosexuals, anyone who spoke out or wouldn't be missed. There was never any shortage of unpeople in the bad old days of Soviet Russia. No one knows exactly how many people suffered and died in the secret laboratories of X thirty-seven. Hundreds, thousands, hundreds of thousands? No one knows.'

'Why didn't your family do something about it?' said Walker.

'Most of what we know, we only found out afterwards,' I said. 'When it went bad and the Soviet military tried to shut the place down, and failed. It's a big world, and even the Droods can't be everywhere at once. Though I understand we're working on that ...

'The scientists here were struggling to identify, stimulate, and just plain poke with sticks every part of human DNA they didn't understand. All this information, coded into each and every one of us on the most basic level. If they could access and learn to control even a part of it, maybe they could produce something more than human. So ... here they were, working blindly in the dark, pushing buttons pretty much at random. Like walking into a room full of gas and striking a match to see where the leak is.'

'What happened?' Peter said impatiently.

'We don't know, exactly,' I said. 'The first clue the Soviets had that something had gone terribly wrong was when X thirty-seven suddenly went quiet. No comm traffic at all. No answers to increasingly urgent inquiries. The Russian authorities followed their usual procedure, and sent in the military. And not just soldiers, either; these were spetznaz, their equivalent of the SAS. Hardened veterans of hard fighting on the Afghanistan front. They were ordered to go in, restore order at any cost, and ask pointed questions until someone provided answers.

'But even they couldn't deal with what was running loose in X thirty-seven.

'Five hundred heavily armed men went in; nineteen came out. Broken, hysterical, traumatised. Screaming about ... monsters. The Kremlin was preparing to nuke the city, but by then we'd picked up on what was happening and we stepped in to stop them. It hadn't been that long since Chernobyl, and there was no way the world would have stood for another travelling radioactive death cloud. World War Three was a lot closer than most people realised, in those days. We were run ragged, stamping out bush fires and making people play nice. Anyway, we sent in two of our local agents to look the place over, from a safe distance, but the city was, to all intents and purposes, quite dead. So we declared the area off limits to everyone, on pains of us getting really peeved at them, and let sleeping dogs lie.

'And now here we are: breaking every rule there is just by being here. If we had any sense we'd get the Hell out while we still can.'

'And go where?' said Honey. 'There is nowhere else.'

'And the teleport bracelets won't move us on till we've solved the mystery,' said Peter.

'I don't like this city,' said Walker. 'It's unsettling.'

We all looked at him. 'Oh come on,' I said. 'You police the Nightside! One of the most dangerous and distressing locations in this or any other universe. And you're ... unsettled?'

'Something bad happened here,' said Walker. 'I can feel it. I feel ... vulnerable. Not something I'm used to feeling. It's invigorating, I think. Yes ... Been a long time since I faced a real challenge, with no backup, no voice, just me. The fate of the whole world could be resting on our shoulders, depending on what we do next. Isn't it marvellous?'

'You're weird,' said Peter.

'No,' Honey said immediately. 'That's Eddie.'

'I am not weird!' I said. 'I'm just differently normal.'

No one had much to say after that, so we moved on, pressing further towards the centre. Like most Soviet-designed cities, the streets were set out in a simple grid, each of which was just wide enough to let a tank through, in case of insurrection. No signs of life anywhere, past or present. But after a while we began seeing evidence of fighting, of armed struggle and mass destruction. Doors kicked in, or out. Windows with little or no glass left in them. Fire damage, smoke-blackened walls, burnt-out homes. Whole buildings blown apart, reduced to single walls and piles of rubble. Some gave indications of being blown out from the inside. And there were lots and lots of bullet holes.

'There was a major firefight here,' said Walker. 'Guns, all kinds of calibre. Grenades and incendiaries, too. So why aren't we seeing any bodies?'

'The few soldiers who staggered out of this place spoke of monsters,' I said. 'Those who were so traumatised they never spoke again. So who, or what, were they firing at? There must have been bodies at some point, soldiers and civilians. So who moved them?'

None of us had any answers, so we kept walking. We passed one building so weakened and precarious that just the rhythm of our footsteps was enough to bring it down. It slumped forward quite slowly, almost apologetically, giving us plenty of time to get clear. The walls simply folded up and fell apart, and the whole thing slammed down into the street. A great cloud flew up, as much dust as smoke, but the sound of the collapse was strangely muffled, and the echoes didn't last. The silence quickly returned, as though it resented being disturbed.

Honey had her shimmering crystal weapon in her hand, glaring around her, ready for an attack or a target, but nothing showed itself. Part of a wall crumbled forward unexpectedly, and Honey whirled around and shot it. The vivid energy blast blew the brickwork apart, sending fragments flying through the air. We ducked, then straightened up and looked at Honey accusingly. She gave us her best I *meant to do that* look, and made the crystal weapon disappear.

'Well done,' said Walker heavily. 'That wall will never jump out at anyone ever again. And if there are any survivors here, they now know for certain that they have visitors. Visitors with guns and a complete willingness to use them. Perhaps you'd like to shoot one of us in the foot, while you're at it?'

'Don't tempt me,' said Honey.

'In dangerous situations, self-control is a virtue,' said Walker.

'Don't you patronise me, you stuck-up Brit,' said Honey. 'Sometimes you just have to shoot something.'

'Typical CIA,' said Peter.

We headed deeper into the city, and the evidence of hard fighting became more extreme. Whole buildings blown apart, leaving gaps in street terraces like teeth pulled from a jaw. Those left standing had been gutted by fires left to burn until they died down naturally. We checked inside a few of the safer-looking ruins. Still no bodies. There were long straight cracks in the walls, almost like claw-marks, and gaping holes like jagged wounds. There was something ... off about it all. I've seen my share of fighting and the damage it causes, but this was different. The pieces of what had happened here wouldn't fit together, no matter how I arranged them.

And then we came to a street covered and caked in dried blood. More black than red, the great stain ran the whole length of the street, rising in long tidal splashes along the sides of buildings. As though a great raging river of blood had swept from one end of the street to the other.

'So much blood!' Honey whispered. 'How many people died here?'

'And who killed them?' said Peter, looking quickly about him.

'Still no bodies,' observed Walker, leaning casually on his umbrella and studying the scene with professional interest.

'Maybe something ate the bodies,' I said. 'Monsters, remember? Something's still here. I can feel it. Watching us.'

'Hope it's not rats,' Peter said abruptly. 'Can't stand rats. Not too keen on mice, either.'

'Oh, mice are no bother,' I said. 'When I was a youngster, part of my duties at Drood Hall was to go round before breakfast and check the mousetraps. Then I'd take the filled traps to the toilets, and give the little bodies a burial at sea. Used to make quite a ceremony out of it, when I was in the mood.'

'You see?' said Honey. 'Weird.' And then she broke off, looking at me thoughtfully. 'Eddie, you said earlier there was something very powerful not far from here, sleeping deep under the permafrost. Could it have anything to do with what's happened here?'

'No,' I said immediately. 'First, we buried him over a hundred miles away. And second, if he had even stirred in his sleep, we'd have known about it long before this. If he'd been involved with what happened here, it would have been much worse.'

'How much worse?' said Walker, professionally curious.

'Apocalyptically worse,' I said.

Walker shrugged. 'Been there, done that.'

I didn't challenge him. He probably had. I did once think about visiting the Nightside; and then had a nice lie down with a cold compress on my head till the idea went away.

'Could this ... thing, person, whatever, have had anything to do with the Tunguska Event?' said Peter.

'No,' I said. 'My family planted him centuries before that.'

'Something or someone that dangerous,' Honey said accusingly. 'And you never told anyone?'

I met her gaze steadily. 'It was Drood business. No one else's. It wasn't like there was anything you could have done. Then, or now. There's a lot we don't tell anyone else. Because if you knew, you'd never sleep well again. Droods guard Humanity, in all senses of the word.'

Honey looked like she wanted to argue the point, but she could tell this wasn't the time. She settled for giving me her best hard look, and then ostentatiously turned her back on me and glared at the bloodstained street.

'So,' she said, 'What were the scientists of X thirty-seven trying to achieve? Something to do with unlocking the hidden secrets and the potential of human DNA. Potential ... perhaps that's the key word. Could they have been trying to produce psychic gifts, to order? During the Cold War both sides put a lot of time and money into psychic research, hoping to produce people they could use as weapons.'

'Yeah,' said Peter, sniggering. 'I saw that documentary. Trying to produce soldiers who could make goats fall over, just by staring at them. Then there was that general of yours who was convinced he could learn to walk through walls if he could only concentrate right. And let us not forget the whole Remote Viewing fiasco.'

'We were getting good results with that, towards the end,' said Honey, still not looking round.

'Yeah,' I said. 'I heard. Problem was, you couldn't keep them out of Pamela Anderson's bedroom. Or George Michael's bathroom.'

Honey's stiff back positively fumed, while Peter and Walker and I exchanged smiles. I didn't have the heart to tell Honey that the Droods sabotage all such government programmes as a matter of course. We have the best farseers and psychics in the world, and we're determined to keep it that way. We didn't interfere with the fainting goats thing, though. Didn't need to.

'This city covers a lot of ground,' said Walker. 'We could spend whole days walking up and down in it. And we don't have days.'

'And I'm still cold and I'm still hungry,' said Peter. We looked at him. He sniffed loudly. 'Well, I am.'

'We should have left you in the car,' said Honey.

'There has to be some way we can cut to the chase,' said Walker. And he stared at me. So did Peter. Honey turned round, so she could join in.

I sighed, and armoured up. The golden armour slipped over me in a moment, immediately I felt sharper, stronger, better able to cope. I hadn't realised how much the city was affecting me until my armour protected me from its malign influence. Interestingly enough, the armour still fit me like a second skin, with no sign of the bulky fur coat beneath. Interesting, but a thought for another day. I looked around me, focusing my Sight through my featureless golden mask.

At once, the street was full of ghosts. Men and women and children running and screaming and dying from no obvious cause, all of them trapped in repeating loops of time. Images, echoes, from the Past. People, terrified, howling like animals, dying ... Images imprinted on to the surroundings, repeating over and over again.

Even with the Sight, I couldn't see what it was that scared them, what was killing them. Just glimpses of something, at the corner of my mental eye. Quick impressions of something unbearably awful, hanging over the city like a storm, running wild in its streets, close and threatening and utterly unstoppable. Inside my armour, my skin was crawling.

As though the Devil himself had come to X thirty-seven, and was standing behind me.

I sent my Sight soaring up into the harsh grey sky, and looked out over the woods, miles and miles away; to where the terrible old thing lay buried, deep and deep under the permafrost. I could feel his presence, like a wound in the world; but he was still sleeping soundly, hopefully till Judgement Day itself. I looked down at the city spread out below me, and my Sight immediately picked up strange emanations blasting up into the sky from one untouched research building, only a dozen or so streets away from where we'd stopped. A shuddering, staccato glare of unnatural energies stabbed into the sky like a stuttering searchlight. Pure psychic energy, spiking from a single location, as though to say *Here I Am!* for anyone with the Sight to see it. So there was at least one survivor left in X thirty-seven, after all.

I dropped back into my head, shut down my Sight and sent my armour into my torc. The cold oppressive gloom of the city weighed down on me again. It was actually harder to think clearly. I told the others what I'd seen, pointed out the direction, and we set off immediately, glad to leave the street of blood behind us.

The atmosphere of the city seemed to change subtly as we closed in on its secret heart. There were shadows everywhere I looked, dark and deep and threatening. The light seemed to be fading, even though the painfully bright sun was still directly overhead. The streets became narrower, closing in on us, and the buildings leaned inwards, as though the brick and stone walls might bulge forward and engulf us at any moment. There was something in this city that didn't want to be found. I increased the pace, striding down the increasingly narrow streets with a confidence I wasn't sure I felt. I've always been happiest with menaces I could hit. The sooner we got to the heart of this mess and did something about it, the better.

'What's the hurry?' Peter complained. 'Whatever happened here, it's over and we missed it.'

'No,' I said. 'It isn't over. It's still happening. The beast is waiting for us to come to it. I think it wants to show us things.'

'Beast?' said Honey. 'No one said anything to me about a beast.'

'Oh,' I said, 'there's always a beast. Come along, Peter, don't lag behind. That's a good way to get picked off. Besides, the exercise will do you good.'

'Oh God,' said Peter. 'Someone shoot me now, and put me out of my misery.'

'Don't tempt me,' said Honey and Walker, pretty much in unison.

I looked at Honey, and she caught my eye and inclined her head slightly. I fell back to walk beside her, letting Walker take the lead. Peter trudged along, head down. Honey started talking without looking at me directly.

'I always knew there were places like this. Hidden places, secret cities, where the Soviets did terrible, unspeakable things to their own people, in the name of patriotism and the all-powerful State. It never occurred to me, until now, to wonder if there might have been secret cities in other countries. If everyone had them, including America. I never heard a whisper that there were, but we all did terrible things in the Cold War in the name of security. Not only my people, the Company; there was a whole alphabet soup of secret departments in those days. Very covert, very specialised agencies, doing necessary unspeakable things that were always strictly Need To Know. Officially they were shut down after we won the Cold War. But in these days of terrorist atrocities and rogue nations, who's to say someone hasn't set up an X thirty-seven in America? What monsters might we be producing right now, just so we can feel a little bit safer?

'Eddie, if there were such places, cities like this, on American soil . . . You'd know, wouldn't you? You'd tell me, if there were?'

'I don't know,' I said carefully. 'Not my territory. For years I was a field agent based in London. Hardly ever left the city, never even went abroad till the Hungry Gods War. Field agents are only told what they need to know, when they need to know it. It's your country, Honey. What do you think?'

'I don't know, Eddie. It seems to me the more I learn from solving these mysteries, the less sure I am of anything.'

181

She leaned in against me, and I put an arm around her. Our heavy furs rather muffled the gesture, but she cuddled up against me anyway. For warmth, or comfort. Or perhaps something else entirely.

We came at last to the building blasting psychic fire into the heavens. The street seemed very dark, the shadows deep and furtive. We stood close together, alert and ready for a covert attack that never quite seemed to materialise. From the outside, the building we'd come so far to find didn't look very different from the others in the street. Stark and brutal, smoke-blackened and bullet-holed, but the front door was still in place and the windows were unbroken. There were no signs anywhere to tell us what went on inside.

Presumably because either you already knew, or you had no business asking.

'Are you sure this is it?' said Honey. At some point in the journey she'd pushed herself away from me and made a point of walking alone. Whatever moment of humanity or weakness or affection had moved her, she was over it now.

'Something bad happened here,' said Walker. 'I can feel it so strongly I can almost smell it. What were they doing in this place?'

'Beats me,' I said. 'But it left a Hell of a strong impression on its surroundings. Bad things linger; really bad things sink in. And they can take a lot of shifting.'

I moved forward, for a closer look at the ordinary, everyday door that was the only entrance to the building. A big block of badly stained wood, with a surprisingly complicated electronic lock.

'Primitive stuff,' sniffed Honey. 'I can crack that, easy.'

I armoured up and kicked the door in. Honey glared at me as I armoured down.

'Will you stop doing that, Eddie! The rest of us do like to contribute something, now and again!'

'Sorry,' I said.

'Men like kicking things in,' Peter explained. 'It's a guy thing.'

It took us a while to find the main laboratory on the top floor. The lobby was a mess, with overturned furniture and scattered papers everywhere. None of them in any condition to be deciphered. There were no signs on the wall, no arrows pointing out various departments. Again, either you worked here and knew where your place was, or it was none of your business. The first surprise was that the building's heating system was working, and the place was warm enough for us to undo our coats. The second surprise came when the lights snapped on, without anyone even touching a switch. The lobby immediately looked a lot less gloomy and threatening.

'First time I've felt human since I arrived in this godforsaken wilderness,' said Peter. 'This ugly pile must have its own generators in the basement, though I'm surprised the activation sensors are still working after all these years.'

'Russians built things to last,' Walker murmured, peering about him in an absent-minded sort of way. 'I wonder what else has survived here.'

I armoured up, and looked around through my golden mask. The others backed away a little.

'Eddie?' Honey said carefully. 'What are you doing?'

'Checking for things that might have survived,' I said. 'Radiation, hot spots, chemical or bacterial spills ... But I don't see anything. Until I use my Sight, and then ... The whole building's a repository of past events, ghosts and echoes and memories. Just memories, though: no living presence I can detect. Just a lot of bad feelings. Pain and horror and death. And something very like despair.'

I armoured down. The others made a point of being very interested in something else, to show they weren't impressed by my transformation any more.

'The generators worry me,' Honey said abruptly. 'They shouldn't still be working, after being down for so many years. Soviet technology, for the most part, was never that efficient or reliable. If the city's designers spent serious money, on top of the line machinery, what the scientists were doing here must have been really important.'

'The psychic energy source is very definitely upstairs,' I said. 'It's so strong it's blasting out through the roof. So let's pop upstairs, people, and see if we can scare up a few ghosts.'

'I never know when he's joking,' said Peter.

We found the laboratory on the top floor easily enough, by following the heaviest electrical cables along the walls. Extra cables had clearly been added later, and somewhat clumsily too, as though the work had been done in a hurry. The whole place seemed strangely clean.

No dust, no cobwebs, nothing to mark the passing of so many years' neglect.

The laboratory itself turned out to be a great open room, cut in two by a huge one-way mirror. So someone could observe the scientists. Without being seen themselves. And there you had Soviet Cold War thinking in a nutshell. They even spied on each other. We stayed in the observation room, looking through the one-way glass. I had a really bad feeling about the other room, and the others were so jittery by now they were quite happy to accept that.

The laboratory was packed with bulky, old-fashioned computer equipment, powerful enough in a brutal sort of way. Old and new models were crowded together, and sometimes even connected to each other. A single skylight let in a dim glow from outside. And directly under this natural spotlight was set something very like a dentist's chair: all cold steel and black leather, complete with heavy arm and leg restraints. The chair was bolted to the floor. It didn't look like the kind of chair anyone would sit down in by choice.

The room we were in was mostly full of recording equipment. Old-fashioned reel-to-reel and bulky video tape recorders, and a single large television set to play them back on. It looked very neat and organised, as though nothing had been disturbed for years. And again: not a speck of dust anywhere. Someone, or something, was preserving this room just as it had been, before ... whatever had happened here happened. Honey bent over a pile of video tapes, her lips moving slowly as she worked her way through the handwritten Cyrillic labels.

'Anything?' I said, trying hard to sound calm and casual.

'Mostly just dates, and names. Nothing to indicate what they were up to.'

'That chair does not inspire confidence,' said Peter. 'What did they do there that they needed bullet-proof one-way glass to protect the observers from what they were observing?'

We all looked at him. 'How did you know it was bullet-proof glass, Peter?' said Walker.

'I just ... felt it,' he said, frowning. 'Ever since I came in here, it's been like ... remembering someone else's memories. Creepy ...'

In the end, we took a video from the pile at random and stuck it in the nearest machine. The old television set took a while to warm up, and when the picture finally arrived it was only black and white. The recording showed exactly what the scientists had been doing in the other room: experimenting on unwilling human subjects, and testing them to destruction. We watched as the subjects yelled and screamed and shouted obscenities, straining desperately against the heavy restraining straps, while blank-faced men and women in grubby lab coats stuck them with needles, or exposed them to radiation, or simply cut them open, to see what was happening inside.

It was bad enough in black and white. In colour, it would have been unbearable.

We ran quickly through the tapes, checking a few minutes from each. A few minutes was as much as we could stand. They were all pretty much the same. Cold-blooded glimpses of Hell.

One man's head exploded, quite suddenly, blood and brains showering wetly over the attending scientists. Another man melted right out of the chair, his body losing shape and cohesion, his flesh running through the restraining straps like thick mud. He screamed as long as he could, until his vocal chords fell apart, and his jaw dropped away from his face. He ended up a frothing mess on the floor. One of the scientists stepped in it by accident, had hysterics, and had to be led away.

A middle-aged woman sat on the floor, wearing nothing but a stained over-sized nappy. She had a huge bulging forehead, held together with heavy black stitches and crude metal staples. She was assembling a strange machine, whose shape and function made no sense at all. When the scientists expressed displeasure at what she'd built, and gestured at the chair, the woman calmly picked up a sharp piece of metal and stuck it repeatedly into her left eye, until she died.

And one man, with a Y-shaped autopsy scar still vivid on his chest, and rows of steel nozzles protruding from his abdomen from implanted technology, burst the straps holding him to the chair and killed three scientists and seven of the soldiers sent in to restrain him, before one of them got close enough to shoot him repeatedly in the head.

We watched as much of it as we could bear, and then I told Honey to check the dates and find us the tape from the last experiment.

The thing the scientists were working on before it all went wrong.

'Whatever happened here,' said Walker, 'they deserved it. This isn't a scientific laboratory; it's a torture chamber.'

'What did they think they were doing?' said Peter. 'What were they trying to achieve?'

'I think they were quite mad,' said Honey. 'If they weren't when they started out, what they did here drove them mad.'

'No,' I said. 'I don't think they had that excuse. I think they did what they were told. Perhaps because if they didn't, they'd end up in the chair themselves.'

'We should burn this city to the ground,' said Walker. 'And seed the earth with salt.'

'Play the tape,' said Peter. 'The sooner we're out of here the better.'

We stood before the television screen, standing shoulder to shoulder for mutual comfort and support. For a long time there was just static, as though an attempt had been made to wipe the tape, and then the picture cleared to show a man sitting in the chair. He was naked, the leather straps cutting deeply into his flesh. He sat stiffly upright, unable to move a muscle. He looked tired, and hard used, and severely under-nourished, but there was nothing visibly unusual about him. Except for what they'd done to his head.

Two scientists, a middle-aged man and a somewhat younger woman, watched the man in the chair from a safe distance. They looked tired too, and from the way they kept glancing at the one-way mirror, I sensed they were under pressure to get results. The woman had a clipboard and a pen, and ugly heavy-framed glasses. The man was smoking a cigarette in quick, nervous puffs, and dictating something to the woman. He didn't even look at the man in the chair. They had a job to do, and they were getting on with it. The man in the chair was of no importance to them, except as the subject of their current experiment.

I wondered who he was, what he did, what his life had been like before they brought him here and took away his name in favour of an experiment number. I wondered if they tattooed the number on his forearm.

The man's head had been shaved, and there were signs of recent surgical scars. Holes had been drilled through his skull at regular intervals, so electrical cables could be plugged directly into his brain. Recently clotted blood showed darkly around the holes. The cables trailed away to a bunch of machines on the far side of the room. I didn't recognise any of them.

Without quite knowing how or why, I began to understand what was happening. I just . . . seemed to know. The scientists were sweating, nervous, under intense pressure to produce results to justify the money that had been spent so far. Practical results, that the military overseers could present to the Party, to ensure further funding and preserve their own precious skins. So certain short cuts had been taken.

X thirty-seven's scientists had been studying the mysteries of human DNA for eleven years now, and had nothing useful to show for it. Just a Hell of a lot of dead ends, and almost as many dead experimental subjects. Not that that mattered; they could always get more. Still, everyone was getting a bit desperate. This particular experiment involved exposing selected genetic material to certain radioactive elements, and then grafting the new material directly onto the brain of the test subject. So far, so good. The subject had survived the operation. Now the scientists were electrically stimulating certain areas of the brain, to see if they could make something happen.

The two scientists, the man and the woman, talked nervously together, sometimes clearly, for the record, and sometimes talking across each other as they studied the monitor displays and argued over what was happening. I seemed to understand what they were saying, even though I knew only a handful of words in Russian.

(What was going on? Where was this information coming from? Was the past sunk so deeply into its surroundings that playing the tape was enough to evoke it again, in all its details? Was the laboratory . . . waking up?)

The male scientists spoke of those parts of human DNA that resisted explanation. Whole areas, whose purpose and function remained a mystery. Both scientists were convinced hidden talents lay buried in human DNA, just waiting to be forced to the surface. Old talents, long forgotten by civilised man. The male scientist's name was Sergei. He spoke of old DNA, ancient genetic material from before man was really human, about the earliest civilisations where men talked directly with their gods. They saw this as an ordinary, everyday thing, quite commonplace and not remarkable at all. Gods and devils, monsters and angels walked openly among mankind, their conversations described in great detail in the oldest written records. Gods walked and talked with men. No big deal: just the way things were back then. If you believed the written records, said the female scientist, whose name was Ludmilla. If these records were accurate, said Sergei, as accurate as everything else they described, who or what were these early humans talking to? Not gods, obviously; both scientists were good Party members and did not believe in such things. But something powerful, certainly. Could it be that these gods and devils still walked among us, but we had lost the ability to see them?

I thought about that. They were talking about the Sight, the ability of specially trained people to See the whole of the world, not the limited part most people live in. (Just as well, really. If most people knew who and what they were sharing their world with, they'd shit themselves.) But though the Sight had shown me many strange and wonderful and dangerous things, it had never once shown me anything like a god.

I said some of this to the others, and Walker nodded.

'There are things very like gods in the Nightside. They have a whole street set aside for them, so they can show off for the tourists. But I am here to tell you that most of them are only supernatural creatures with delusions of grandeur, and not worth the breath it takes to damn them. Godly pretenders and wannabes are one of the oldest con tricks Humanity has had to endure.'

'I talked with the Wizard of Northampton once,' Peter said diffidently. 'He said gods and demons are artificial constructs of the deeper recesses of the human mind. We create these sub-personalities so the conscious mind can communicate more easily with the sub-conscious. Or maybe ... so an individual could make contact with the human mass-mind, Jung's collective unconscious. The wizard said gods and demons were two sides of the same superluminal coin.'

'Yeah, well, writing comic books for twenty years will do that to you,' growled Walker.

'I'm picking up all kinds of information from this room,' Honey said abruptly. 'I know things I have no way of knowing. It's like suddenly remembering a book I read long ago that I know for a fact I never read. My head hurts.'

'It's the psychic imprinting,' I said. 'What happened here was so powerful, so traumatic, it literally soaked into its surroundings. Genius loci, and all that. A stone tape. And now we've started the tape playing again. I know things too. The man in the chair is mentally ill. His name is Grigor, and he hears voices in his head. Almost certainly paranoid schizophrenic, though no one's bothered to accurately diagnose him. Apparently Sergei and Ludmilla there believed that people who hear voices and speak to people who aren't actually there are being dominated by ancient DNA that's been accidentally reactivated. So they've been experimenting exclusively on the mentally ill, to try and locate and control that particular part of human DNA in case they are seeing gods and devils.'

'That's crazy,' said Peter.

'Bastards,' Walker said succinctly.

'Bad idea either way,' said Honey, staring fascinated at the flickering black and white images on the television screen. 'If the old gods and monsters really are projections from the sub-conscious, they might not take kindly to being forced out into the light. We keep things locked away in our heads for a reason.'

'Let sleeping gods lie,' said Peter.

'Well, quite,' said Walker.

'This conversation is getting seriously strange,' I said. 'What does any of it have to do with what happened out in the city?'

'It's something to do with the man in the chair,' Honey said flatly. 'With Grigor. I can feel it. Can't you?'

'Could we be talking about Jungian archetypes here?' said Walker. 'They were all the rage, in my young days. Ideas and concepts given shape and form, and even identities. Dark dreams from the depths of the human mass-mind, driving people in directions they would never have chosen otherwise ... Fads and fancies, politics and religions. Things are in the saddle, and ride mankind. Pardon me. I'm rambling, I know. But we are on very dangerous ground here, and I think it behoves us to tread carefully. Remember that film *Forbidden Planet*? Monsters from the id? Unbeatable and unstoppable, rage and horror and all our most unspeakable lusts given form and let loose on the world? Like the Hyde, only more so. Is that what happened here, in X thirty-seven?'

'You're right, Walker,' said Honey. 'You are rambling.'

I was still studying the man in the chair, and the two scientists. Grigor and Sergei and Ludmilla. Whatever information I was picking up, it wasn't coming from the video recording. It was coming from the other room. Haunted, stained, by what these people had done in it. The scientists had wanted to access the old DNA, so they could learn to talk with gods again, and bend them to the State's will.

Children playing with nuclear weapons.

Grigor suddenly convulsed, his scrawny naked body fighting the leather straps that held him in place. The chair creaked and groaned, but the straps held. (I was right there with them now. I could hear and see everything. Smell Grigor's sweat, feel the static charge building on the air.) Sergei checked the readings on his instruments, and Ludmilla scribbled frantic notes on her clipboard. The cameras recorded everything. Grigor's face writhed, his eyes bulged, his breathing grew faster and faster. The cables leading from his shaven head lashed back and forth.

And then he stopped moving. He held himself unnaturally still, as though afraid of drawing something's attention. Sweat ran down skin flushed from exertion. Grigor was barely breathing now, his expression set and fixed. He was Seeing something, I could sense it; something not present or evident to normal human senses. He Saw it, and I think it Saw him. His face twisted with horror and revulsion, racked by a terror beyond bearing. He screamed like a small child, like a wounded animal, like a soul newly damned to Hell.

I knew what was happening, even though I couldn't see it. Information was pouring into my head, forcing its way in despite everything I could do to keep it out.

The scientists had done it. The old DNA was awake again, on line and up and running. Grigor's eyes were full of the Sight. But he hadn't looked outwards, as intended, beyond the fields we know into other worlds and dimensions, or the many overlapping layers of our complicated reality. Instead, his Sight had turned away from the world that had hurt him so very much, turned away and turned inwards. He looked deep into himself, into Humanity, into the hidden secrets of our DNA. And he found something there, something buried deep in the genetic material of us all; something so awful in its significance that he couldn't stand it.

His mind broke, leaping up and out, his artificially augmented thoughts tapping into the human mass-mind, the shared unconscious that linked all the people of X thirty-seven. He drew upon the power he found there, took it and shaped it and sent it out to destroy every living thing in the city. So that the vile experiments would finally stop, and the awful knowledge Grigor had stumbled across would die with him.

Let them die, he said *They're all guilty. They knew what was happening.*

Grigor called up nightmares, all the things we're really afraid of. Monstrous shapes, terrible archetypes, the private and personal horrors that have power over us in the dark, in the early hours of the morning, when we dream awful dreams, of things we can only escape from by waking up and leaving them behind. Grigor summoned them up from the mass-mind, gave them material shape and form, and turned them loose on the people of X thirty-seven.

And the city screamed.

The scientists realised something had gone terribly wrong with their experiment. Grigor wasn't crying out or straining against his straps any more. He sat perfectly still. Sergei and Ludmilla approached him cautiously. He slowly turned his tortured head to look at them. Blood ran in endless tears from his unblinking eyes. Having finally Seen the truth, he could not look away, even though it was killing him. But he still managed a smile for his tormentors.

They're coming, he said. *They're coming for you. Every single one of them; and they all want a piece . . .*

He sounded like a dead man. A man who can speak unbearable truths, because he has nothing left to lose. Sergei backed away, calling hysterically for help. Ludmilla threw her clipboard aside, ran to the control board, and hit the abort button. It should have killed Grigor instantly, frying him with a massive electrical charge; but he wasn't ready to let go just yet. Huge sparks spat and sputtered on the air, discharging into the surrounding equipment. Ludmilla grabbed a fire axe from the wall, and chopped at Grigor in his chair with hysterical strength. The heavy steel blade bit into his flesh again and again; but he didn't cry out, and he wouldn't die.

Sergei tried to escape, but the door wouldn't open. Security guards were pounding on it from the other side, but it wouldn't budge. Ludmilla backed away from the bloody mess in the chair, that was still smiling at her, and she laughed shrilly past the dishevelled hair falling into her stark white face. The axe head trailed a bloody path across the floor, as though it had grown too heavy for her to hold up.

They came through the walls, and up through the floor, and down from the ceiling. Real and solid, not alive, still bearing the wounds that had killed them. All the subjects who'd been experimented on, who'd suffered and died in the chair, screaming for help and mercy and simple compassion that never came. Sergei and Ludmilla died slowly and died screaming at the hands of those they'd wronged. And when the dead were finally finished with them, they left the bloody messes behind on the floor and went out of the room and into the city, to do even worse things.

The tape stopped. I looked round, startled. I'd forgotten who and when I was. The room, what had happened in it, had filled my head. I took a deep breath, and wiped sweat from my mouth with the back of my hand. Honey had shut the tape machine down. She was breathing hard. I wondered if she'd seen the things I had. Walker was looking at the floor. Peter had his back to us. I looked through the one-way mirror into the next room. It was empty, and so was the chair.

'How much of it did you pick up?' I said, after a while. It didn't sound like my voice. It sounded ... shocked, uncertain. Lost.

'Enough,' said Walker. 'Monsters from the id. The city's id.'

'He killed a whole city with their own nightmares,' said Honey. 'A whole city ...'

'The one thing no one can face,' said Peter. He turned around, but looked past us to stare into the other room.

'Good thing the crazy bastard's dead and gone, then,' said Honey, trying for a brisk, professional tone and not quite managing it. 'No telling how much damage he might have done otherwise. No wonder the Soviets couldn't cope.'

'They wanted a weapon,' said Walker. 'They got one.'

'I think he's dead,' I said. 'No one could See what he did, and survive. But I don't think he's gone. What he did was so powerful, the psychic energies stamped themselves into the physical surroundings. Ready to emerge again, at any time. Why isn't Grigor's body in the chair? Why aren't the scientists' bodies on the floor – or at least what was left of them? Why didn't we discover a single corpse in the whole damned city? Because the nightmares are still here. Still active. Still hungry.'

'I can feel it,' said Walker. 'Like the tension in the air before a storm breaks. Like the pause before the axe falls—'

'Will you shut up?' said Honey. 'All of you, pull yourselves together! We're professionals; we can handle this.'

'Are you crazy?' Peter's voice was shrill, almost hysterical, and the colour had gone from his face. It was the first time I'd seen him really scared. 'We have to get out of here! The city's coming alive, and the nightmares are returning. All the bad dreams you ever had. There are things in dreams no man can face!'

'Get a hold of yourself, Peter,' said Walker, but his voice lacked its usual authority and conviction.

'Hush,' said Honey, and something in her voice stopped us dead. 'I think . . . it's here.'

The video recorder turned itself back on. The television screen came to life again. We turned unwillingly to look. Grigor was sitting in his chair, hacked apart but alive. The two bloody messes that had been Sergei and Ludmilla were spread out on the floor before him, like sacrifices to an unforgiving god. From outside the room, from the surrounding streets, came terrible sounds. Screaming and shouting and the roaring of what might have been maddened animals. Grigor turned his bloody head and looked through the one-way mirror at us. He smiled, and there was little of humanity in that smile, and less of compassion. It was the smile of a man who had looked beyond the gates of Hell, and seen what they did there; what was waiting for him.

You have to die, he said. *You all have to die.*

'Why?' I said. 'We never hurt you.'

Of course, he couldn't hear me. Grigor was dead, long dead. This was a recording, of his last message to mankind.

We're not who we think we are, he said. *We never were. You have to die. Because no one must ever know the truth.*

'What truth?' said Honey.

'Why nightmares?' said Walker. 'Why kill the people of this city in such a terrible way?'

Because we deserve it.

The tape snapped to a halt, and the television screen went dead again.

'Well,' I said, putting a lot of effort into sounding calm and casual. 'That was ... worrying. And more than a bit spooky.'

'What did he See in our DNA?' said Honey.

'Probably best we don't know,' I said.

'Could Grigor still be alive somewhere, do you think?' said Walker. 'Hiding, perhaps, transmitting these images, to us?'

'No,' I said. 'If there was anyone else alive in this whole damned city, I'd know. Nothing's lived here for years. Even the animals have enough sense not to come. I don't think anyone could live here for long, not after what happened. This is a city of memories. Stored memories, gone feral.'

It was getting colder, and darker. The room on the other side of the one-way mirror was almost gone now, consumed by shadows. The lights in our room were dimming, as though the power was being sucked out of them. Our breath began to steam on the air, and we buttoned up our coats again. There was a growing atmosphere of imminence; of something about to happen. The four of us moved together, and then moved away again, driven by a need to be able to look in all directions at once. From outside the building there came noises. Voices ... almost human. First as scattered individuals, then in growing numbers, until finally it was the voice of the crowd and the mob, driven mad by horror and bloody slaughter.

The sound of an entire city maddened and murdered by its fears.

'What is that?' said Honey, clapping her hands uselessly to her ears. 'What's making that noise? There's no one here; this city is empty! It is! There can't be anybody out there!'

'The dead don't always stay dead,' said Walker. He looked confused, as though someone had just hit him.

'No,' I said quickly. 'There's no one there. Not as such. It's the memory of nightmares. When the people here died, when the city died, when all the men and women and children trapped in this place fell victim to their own nightmares, that outpouring of emotion and trauma completed what Grigor started. Everything they experienced was psychically imprinted into the stone and brick and cement of X thirty-seven. The whole place is one gigantic stone tape. And by entering the city, we've started it up again.'

'So, it's not real?' said Peter.

'Real enough,' I said. 'Real enough to kill us, if we let it.'

'But where's the energy coming from, to fuel that kind of manifestation?' said Walker. 'What's powering the playback?'

'We are,' I said. 'Whatever happened here is still happening, and always will. Grigor started this by drawing on the power of the human mass-mind, and we're part of the mass-mind. Just by being here, we've reactivated the recording, and powered it at the same time. X thirty-seven is a trap, Grigor's revenge on a world that would allow such awful things to be done to him.'

'We've got to get out of here!' Peter was shouting now, his voice strident and ugly.

'Where can we go?' said Walker. 'There is nothing out there – just the woods, the cold, and certain death. So suck it in, and be a man.'

'Something's in the building with us,' said Honey. 'I can hear it, coming up the stairs. It doesn't sound . . . human.'

'We'll all start hearing things soon,' I said. 'Whatever scares us.'

'There must be something we can do!' said Peter. 'You're a Drood! Do something!'

'I think Grigor's still here, in this building, in some form,' I said. 'He's the origin and the focus, for the stone tape. We have to find what's left of him, and shut him down.'

'How?' said Walker.

'I'm open to suggestions,' I said. 'I'm just jumping from one educated guess to another.'

'You've got the Sight,' said Honey. 'And the armour. Find him for us, Eddie. Before our nightmares find us.'

'It's not that simple,' I said.

'I knew he was going to say that,' said Peter. 'Didn't you two know he was going to say that?'

'Shut up, Peter,' said Walker. 'What's the problem, Eddie?'

'The stone tape recorded what Grigor originally Saw,' I said carefully. 'If I go looking for Grigor, I might See it too. If that should happen, kill me.'

'No problem,' said Honey.

I armoured up, and the golden strange matter flowed out and around me in a moment, insulating me from the city's psychic assault. I hadn't realised how close to the edge I'd come, until the armour brought me back. Everything in the city was now dedicated solely to the destruction of the human mind and soul. I took a deep breath to steady myself, and then looked out over the city through my featureless golden mask, my Sight sending my mind soaring over the broken city streets, searching for a single pattern: the last remaining traces of the man called Grigor. There were other patterns, strange and awful, surging through the streets and closing in on the building where I and my associates were hiding; but I couldn't look at those too closely. Man was not meant to stare upon the Medusa.

Something tugged at my mind, half a warning and half a summons, and I turned my Sight in that direction. Grigor looked back at me, nailed to a cross made of intertwined technology. The computer leads trailing from his head had wrapped themselves round his brow in a crown of thorns. He smiled at me, a cold and pitiless smile. His face was full of something more than insanity, as though he'd gone through madness and found something else on the other side.

Don't fight me, he said.

'I must,' I said.

You need to See. To know, to understand why this is necessary. Why you have to die, for your own and Humanity's sake. When you know what I know, what I was made to know, you'll want to die.

I couldn't tell exactly who or what I was talking with. It wasn't just the stone tape, a recording of past events. Something of Grigor himself had been stamped into the stone and concrete of X thirty-seven. I could feel his presence; the ghost in the machine. It took every bit of will power I had to turn my head away and shut down my Sight. I didn't dare See what Grigor had Seen. A madman in Drood armour would be more dangerous to the world than any nightmare currently running through the streets of X thirty-seven. Grigor's presence receded into the distance, still trying to latch on to me, as I fell back into my head and shut down my armour. I was breathing hard, as though I'd just run a race and come scarily close to losing. My knees buckled, and I think I would have fallen if Walker hadn't got a chair under me. Honey leaned in close, pushing her face right into mine, holding my eyes with hers.

'What is it?' she said. 'What did you See, Eddie?'

'Grigor is quite definitely dead,' I said. 'But unfortunately not entirely departed. He's the key to this. Stop him, and we stop the nightmares, the city, everything.'

'All right. What do we do?' said Peter.

'Only thing we can do,' I said. 'Grigor's part of the stone tape, which exists through the city. So the whole city has to be destroyed. Reduced to ashes, and less than ashes. A physical and a psychic strike, to destroy Grigor and X thirty-seven on all the levels they currently inhabit. This entire city has become spiritually corrupt, a real and present danger to the whole of Humanity. Body and soul.'

'How the Hell are we supposed to take out an entire city?' said Honey.

'He's lost it,' said Peter. 'He's raving.'

'No,' said Walker. 'He's right. Destroy the city, and seed the ground with salt.'

'Wonderful!' said Peter. 'Anyone got an exorcist on speed dial? Preferably one with side interests in nuclear devastation?'

'Shut up, Peter,' said Walker. 'You're becoming hysterical.'

'Even if I could contact Langley, which I can't,' said Honey, 'and call in a dozen long-range bombers armed with city busters, Langley would never authorise it. An unprovoked attack on Russian soil? We're talking World War Three, and *Halleluiah! The missles are flying!*'

'If we could contact the Russian authorities and explain,' said Walker.

'We can't,' said Honey. 'And anyway, what makes you think they'd believe a CIA agent, a Drood and someone from the Nightside?'

'Good point,' said Walker.

'Bombs wouldn't be enough anyway,' I said. 'Not even thermo-nukes. You could reduce the whole city to one big crater that glowed in the dark, and the imprinting would still remain, bound to this specific location. Genius loci. Grigor's revenge has been stamped on space itself.'

'So what do we do?' said Honey. 'Could your family help?'

'That's what I've been considering,' I said slowly. 'A psychic strike that would wipe the area clean. But you'd need an incredible amount of power for that: enough energy to burn out any human mind, or combination of minds. Even if I could call home, which I can't, no one there could help me with this. But there is a power source nearby that I might be able to draw on. More than enough to do the job. But it means disturbing what lies sleeping under the permafrost. I think I can tap into his power without waking him. But if I'm wrong ... if he wakes up we could end up worse off than we are now.'

'Worse?' said Peter, waving his arms around. 'The whole city's come alive and wants to kill us horribly with our own nightmares! What could be worse?'

'It's time for the truth, Eddie,' said Walker. 'We need to know. Who, or what, did your family bury here all those years ago?'

'One of us,' I said. 'He's family. A Drood, put to sleep like a dog that's gone bad, buried so deep he's already halfway to the Hell he belongs in. Bound with iron chains, wrapped in potent spells and curses, left to sleep till Judgement Day and maybe even longer. Our greatest shame, our greatest failure. The Drood who tried to eat the world.

'Our torcs and our armour make us powerful beyond anything you've ever imagined, but for one of us, one Gerard Drood of the eleventh century, that wasn't enough. He explored the possibilities of the torc, studied its nature more deeply than any of us had ever done before. He upgraded his torc, using certain forbidden techniques and ancient machines, and used it to absorb the torcs of others. Hundreds of them, men, women and children. He became unspeakably powerful. An eater of souls. A living god.

'Having defeated and subjugated the family, he set out to subdue all Humanity to his will, and remake the world in his own image. He very nearly succeeded. Whole countries fell beneath his influence; millions of people bent the knee and bowed the head and praised his unholy name. He carved his features into the surface of the Moon, so that the whole world could look up and see him smiling down on them.

'But there have always been more Droods than are officially acknowledged, field agents and the like. The Matriarch called them in, all the Droods who still held out against the traitor's will. She bound them into a Drood mass-mind, hundreds of torcs working together against Gerard's stolen ones. And in the end, even that wasn't enough to defeat him. All that power, and all they could do was put him to sleep, bind him tight, and bury him deep.

'Gerard Drood. Grendel Rex. The Unforgiven God.'

'I've heard of him!' said Peter. 'He's buried under Silbury Hill, in the south west of England.'

'Actually, no,' I said. 'We let that rumour get out, as a distraction. Silbury Hill is a burial mound from Celtic times, with so many legends wrapped around it that one more slipped in easily enough. No, we brought him here, to what in the eleventh century was the ends of the earth. A harsh and bitter place where no one with any sense would want to live. Where nobody would disturb him.'

'If he isn't buried under Silbury Hill,' said Walker, 'who is?'

I managed a small smile. 'You can't expect me tell you all my family's secrets.'

'Why let the rumour out anyway?' said Peter.

'Because Grendel Rex had followers,' I said patiently. 'His kind always does. They can dig their tunnels into Silbury Hill for ever and a day, and never find anything.'

Honey was frowning. 'I never heard of Grendel Rex before this. And I certainly never read about any such takeover in the history books.'

'We wiped every trace of him from history,' I said. 'Destroyed every account, burned every book and manuscript, shut up everyone who tried to talk. We could do that, in those days. Only myth and legend remained; and we could live with that. Scrubbing the Moon clean was a bit more difficult, but we managed.

'Do you understand now why I'm so reluctant to do something that might reawaken the Unforgiven God, and let him loose on the world again?'

'Hell,' said Peter, 'if the Tunguska Event didn't wake him ...' He paused. 'Or was it supposed to, and failed?'

'A lot of my family wondered about that,' I said. 'But he slept on. Our ancestors did good work. That's what gives me the confidence to try this. But if I accidentally break the bonds that hold him, he will rise up. And perhaps this time, not even the efforts of the Droods and our allies and our weapons would be enough to put him down again.'

'Oh come on!' said Honey. 'Get over yourself, Drood! The world's come a long way since the eleventh century. We have access to weapons and resources unheard of in those days. I speak for the CIA; we've put down living gods before, in our time.'

Walker looked at her and then at me. 'Eddie, what is the worst that could happen if he did rise again?'

'He'd finish what he started,' I said. 'Subjugate all Humanity, reshape the continents according to his whim, absorb the souls of every living thing into himself, and leave us just enough of our minds to love and worship him. Hell on Earth, for ever and ever and ever. That's what could happen, if I get this wrong.'

'Well,' said Walker. 'Try not to do that, then.'

The bedlam in the street outside was growing louder. Screams and howls that had as much of the beast in them as anything human. They came from all sides, surrounding the building. We were under siege, by the reawakened ghosts of old horrors. The room seemed colder than ever, a spiritual cold, a bleakness of the soul. The shadows were very dark, like holes that could swallow you up, or down which you could fall for ever. They moved sometimes, when you weren't looking at them directly. The room was changing, in small subtle ways. Growing larger or smaller or deeper, while the corners seemed to have too many angles.

I could feel my breathing coming fast and hard. I could feel my pulse racing, and a vein throbbing almost painfully in my temple. I've been scared before; being a Drood doesn't make you immune to pain or death or failure ... but this was different. A different kind of fear; primal, almost pure. We were surrounded by nightmares, crossed over into the waking world and closing in. Despite myself I remembered running from things in dreams; unspeakable, unbearable, implacable things, that I could only escape from by waking up. And I couldn't wake from this.

Anything can happen in dreams; in bad dreams. The dead can walk again, and say unforgivable things. Physical shapes lose their integrity, become uncertain, their edges loose and slippery, no longer tied down to shapes you can cope with. I could feel a whimper building in the back of my throat. Honey had a hand at her mouth, gnawing on a knuckle. Walker had his back against a wall, lashing his umbrella before him like a sword. Peter's bulging eyes were darting this way and that, anticipating something awful that always seemed to be coming from somewhere else.

Soon we'd start to see each other as nightmares. Maybe even attack each other, because you couldn't trust anything or anyone in a dream. Shadows were rising up everywhere, taking on unnerving shapes, rich with terrible personal significance. The floor beneath my feet was soft and spongy, and the walls were leaning inwards, slumping forward like tired old men. Cracks in the walls took on the shape of human faces, smiling at what was to come.

Heavy hands slammed against the closed laboratory door. It shook in its frame, the wood bulging unnaturally under the force of the blows. Dreadful voices from outside cried, 'Let us in! Let us in!' I armoured up; but it didn't help. Even that couldn't protect me from the unleashed power of my own nightmares. I grabbed the nearest piece of heavy equipment, and hauled it over to the door to make a barricade, but the solid metal turned soft and putrid and fell apart in my armoured hands. I couldn't depend on anything any more.

That's the real horror of nightmares.

Lethal Harmony of Kathmandu and the Blue Fairy walked through the closed door as though it wasn't there. I backed away. They looked at me accusingly, heads lolling limply on their broken necks. Honey saw them too. She opened fire with her shimmering crystal weapon. The energy blast shot right through the figures and blew up the door behind them. And then the weapon wilted and twisted in Honey's hands, curling and coiling slowly and deliberately like a snake. Honey threw it away from her in horror.

Katt and Blue turned into my mother and father, and advanced slowly on me. They didn't look like zombies, or the living dead; or two people who'd been in their graves for most of my life. They looked the way they always did when I thought of them: in the last photograph taken, before they went off on the mission that killed them. Except they weren't smiling now. I backed away, and they came after me. They didn't say anything. They didn't have to. They looked accusing, disappointed, damning.

'*No!*' I yelled, so loudly it hurt my throat. 'My parents wouldn't think that of me! They know better! They wouldn't do this! *You're not them*!'

And in the face of my certainty, they faded softly and silently away.

Honey grabbed my golden arm with a shaking hand. 'How did you do that?' she said shrilly.

'I have worse things than that on my conscience,' I said.

'Then do something!' shouted Walker. 'Before the worse things show up!'

Peter was spinning round and round now, convinced there was something sneaking up on him from behind, no matter which way he looked. Walker began to shrink, in sudden jerks and shudders, until he was a child again, swamped in a man's suit. He tried to say something, but couldn't get the words out, and began to cry helplessly. Honey dropped down abruptly, sinking into a floor that had taken on the consistency of quicksand, sucking her down in slow, purposeful gulps. I grabbed her arm and tried to haul her out, but the pull of the quicksand was too great. I pulled harder, and Honey screamed in agony.

'Let go, Eddie! You'll pull my shoulder out of its socket before it'll let me go! You have to risk waking your sleeping god! Nothing could be worse than this. At least he's real!'

And so I let her go. Turned my back on them, drew on the power of my torc and my armour and made contact with Grendel Rex, the Unforgiven God. The devil in his cold dark Hel, deep and deep under the permafrost.

Finding him was easier than I expected. My mind shot across the miles separating us in a moment, my Sight drawn like a magnet by the bond we shared. Of family. My vision sank down into the frozen earth, and immediately I was hit by the impact of his ancient presence, huge and forbidding and still impossibly powerful. I felt like a scuba diver, swimming through the cold night of the ocean, and coming unexpectedly upon a blue whale or a giant squid. I felt so small, overwhelmed by the sheer size and scale of him. A mote in his eye.

I carefully reached out and touched his power; it was like sticking a drinking straw into an ocean, or dipping a bucket into a bottomless well. The power surged into me, rich and raging, all I needed and more. And one great eye slowly opened in the dark, and looked at me.

Well, now. Who disturbs me at this time?

I stopped where I was, absolutely frozen by fear. 'I'm Edwin Drood,' I said finally. 'Doing my job. Trying to save Humanity from destruction.'

So the sheep still have their shepherds. Why come to me, the old pariah, for help?

'Because what I'm doing is important, and necessary. Because I've nowhere else to go. And because . . . I'm family.'

Ah, yes. Of course. Anything for the family. What is this threat you fear so much, that you're prepared to make a deal with the devil?

I started to explain, but he pushed effortlessly past my defences and took what he needed from my mind.

Yes. I see. Very well, little Drood. Take what you need.

I should have taken the energy and left, but I had to know.

'What did Grigor see in the depths of our DNA? What could he have seen, to terrify him so completely? Do you know?'

Perhaps. Here is the truth, for those that have the strength to hear it. We can all be gods, or devils. We can shine like the stars. We were never meant to stay human. We're just the chrysalis, from which something greater can emerge. I think perhaps your Grigor caught a glimpse of what we really are, and could be; and he couldn't cope. There is so much more to reality than man and woman, gods and devils. So much more.

The great eye slowly closed, like an eclipse moving across the face of the sun. *I'm tired. It's not time to wake up yet. Tell the family . . . I'll be seeing them.*

I ran, holding myself together through sheer force of will. The power I'd taken burned inside me, demanding release. Already it was consuming me from within; if I didn't let it loose soon, it would overwhelm me. I left the permafrost behind, my mind streaking over the frozen forest, and the city loomed up before me like a bug on a windshield. The streets were full of unspeakable things. Buildings rose and fell, or melted into each other. A tidal wave of screaming faces swept down a street, like so many possessed and terrified masks.

The sun was a giant face, screaming with rage. Grigor's face.

I called up the power I'd taken, and bent it to my will. I held it in one hand, spitting and fizzing like a million lightning bolts, and then I threw it at the city. A great cry went up from the milling streets, of rage and defiance and soul deep horror, but I was riding the lightning with my mind. I slammed it down into the dark heart of X thirty-seven, and drove the nightmares out; up and out into the sun with Grigor's face. For a moment I held all the writhing horror of X thirty-seven in one place, every last bit of Grigor's revenge . . . and then I sent it away. Threw it in the one direction it could never return from.

Into the Past.

I watched with godlike eyes as the compressed psychic energy shot back through time, screaming and howling all the way, until finally it couldn't hold itself together any longer and it exploded into nothingness over the empty plain of Tunguska, at 7:17 a.m., 30 June 1908.

I woke up back inside my own head, lying on the laboratory floor. The power was gone, and I didn't feel like a god any more. I was exhausted, I hurt all over, and my eyes felt like they'd been sand-papered. I sat up slowly, wincing. I wasn't wearing my armour. I looked around me. The floor was hard and certain beneath me, the walls were just walls, and the building and the street outside were silent. X thirty-seven was no longer haunted by the ghosts of its own atrocities.

The floor had spat Honey out. She was sitting on a chair, shaken and trembling, but already bringing herself back under control. Walker was himself again, calm and collected and giving his full attention to adjusting his cuffs. Peter was trying very hard to look as though nothing had happened. I rose slowly to my feet, and they all turned to look at me.

I told them what had happened, and what I'd done. I didn't tell them what Grendel Rex had said concerning human DNA. He was a devil, and devils always lie. Except when the truth can hurt you more.

'So, *you're* the cause of what happened, in 1908?' said Peter. 'You're responsible for the Tunguska Event?'

'A Drood did it,' said Honey. 'I should have known.'

'Proving it to my grandfather is going to be a tad difficult, though,' said Peter.

'Are you kidding?' I said. 'You can't hide something like this! Psychics and telepaths across the world will have been deafened by what I just did. You won't be able to stop them talking about it, though my family will undoubtedly try. Luckily only the four of us know the details, and I think it's better we keep it that way.'

'Or the Droods will come and make us forget, like they did over Grendel Rex?' said Honey.

'Yes,' I said.

'Another reason why we don't let you people operate in the Nightside,' murmured Walker. 'Only I am allowed to be that arbitrary.'

'Can we please go out and find a food store now?' said Peter. 'There must be some canned goods here somewhere. If I was any hungrier, my stomach would leap up my throat and eat my head.'

'You know, I think I'd pay good money to see that,' said Honey.

We left the laboratory, and the building, and set off through the deserted streets. I hung back a bit, considering the others while they were still relatively open and vulnerable. Peter interested me the most. I'd never seen him really scared before. In fact, for all his youth and inexperience with the greater world, he'd taken the Loch Ness monster and the Hyde pretty much in his stride. He was interested, even impressed; but when the time came for action he didn't hesitate, just got stuck in with the rest of us. Rather more than you'd expect, from a man who's only experience of spycraft was in industrial espionage.

So; he was Alexander King's grandson, after all.

But it was useful to know he had his limits. The nightmares had shattered his self-control, reduced him to hysterics. Perhaps because they were so clearly outside of his control. In fact ... when it came to fighting the Loch Ness monster and the Hyde, he'd taken the first opportunity to fall back and let the rest of us do the hard work while he filmed it with his precious camera phone.

Whatever happened, I had to get my hands on that phone.

Walker fell back to walk with me, and we talked quietly together.

He deliberately slowed our pace, allowing some distance to develop between us and Honey and Peter.

'While you were gone,' he said, quietly and entirely matter of fact, 'someone tried to kill me. Even in the midst of all that was happening. With so much madness running loose it's hard to be sure, but someone quite definitely tried to remove my head from my shoulders, from behind. Would have succeeded, with anyone else; but fortunately my years in the Nightside have made me very hard to kill.'

'Even with the Authorities gone?' I said.

'Especially now they're gone. I'm protected in ways you can't imagine. But the point is we now know who killed Lethal Harmony and the Blue Fairy. It has to be either Honey or Peter.'

'Always assuming,' I said, 'that you're telling the truth.'

'Ah,' said Walker. 'There is that, yes.'

'None of us can be trusted,' I said. 'We're all agents.'

CHAPTER SEVEN
All at sea

There was sun and light and warmth, the tang of sea salt in the air, and after the bitter cold of Tunguska and X thirty-seven it felt like very heaven itself. All four of us cried out in relief, as the teleport bracelets delivered us to our new destination in the sun. And the first thing we did was tear off our heavy fur coats and drop them in a pile on the ground before us. Hats and gloves and everything else that reminded us of X thirty-seven followed as fast as we could rip them off, and when the pile was complete we gave it a good kicking, just on general principles. And only then did we take the time to look around and see where we were.

We'd been dropped off in a neat little side street looking out over the docks of some major city. Ships everywhere, mostly Navy, but some commercial, some tourist, and some fishing boats. American Navy: big, impressive ships, longer than some roads, equipped with the very latest technology and the very biggest guns. Crewmen swarmed over the huge decks like ants serving their queen. Not, therefore, a good place for four strangers strolling around asking questions. I moved down to the end of the side street, and looked out over the sea. Blue-green waters without a trace of a swell under a pale blue sky with not a cloud to be seen. The sun was high in the sky, fat and friendly and deliciously warm. Seagulls rode the thermals, their distant voices raucous and mocking.

'I'm back in contact with Langley,' Honey announced, one hand pressed to the side of her head. Though how that helped with a brain implant, I wouldn't know. She frowned, almost wincing. 'There's a lot of shouting going on. Apparently they took it pretty damned personally when I fell off the edge of the planet, and they couldn't locate me any more. They've had three different spy satellites tasked to do nothing but look for me ever since. They were concerned. Which I'd think was very sweet of them, if they'd just stop shouting at me . . . Ah! It seems we are currently in Philadelphia, Pennsylvania.'

'How long have we been off their radar?' I said.

'Three days, seven hours,' said Honey. 'I'm being asked a lot of questions.'

'Who cares?' said Peter. 'I smell food!'

'What kind?' said Walker.

'I don't care, I'm going to eat it.' Peter glared about him, sniffing the air like a bloodhound on a trail. He plunged forward into the main street, following his nose, and all we could do was hurry after him.

'I will admit to feeling a bit peckish myself,' said Walker, striding along with a military gait. 'Are there any noted restaurants in Phila-delphia?'

'Oh, bound to be,' I said cheerfully. 'Sailors like their food. And booze, and tattoo parlours and—'

'Langley is demanding to know exactly where we were, and what we've been doing,' said Honey, striding along beside me like a tall dark goddess in her blazing white jumpsuit. 'They were under the impression there wasn't anywhere they couldn't follow me with their brand-new toys, the poor babies.'

'Don't tell them anything,' Walker said immediately. 'Not just yet. There might come a time when we need confidential information to bargain with.'

'Why would I wish to bargain with my own superiors?' said Honey coldly.

'I meant, bargain with Alexander King,' Walker said patiently. 'It's well known the Independent Agent has contacts everywhere, in every organisation. Except possibly the Droods. Either way, I think we need to hold our secrets close to our chest until the game's over.'

'He's right,' I said. 'Secrets only have power and value as long as they remain secrets.'

'So what do I tell Langley?' said Honey. 'I've got to tell them something, if only so they'll stop shouting inside my head.'

'Tell them about X thirty-seven,' I said. 'But not what we did there. They'll be so excited about the confirmed location of an old Soviet science city, they won't worry about us and what we did.'

'What *you* did,' said Walker. 'I'm still a trifle uneasy over that.'

'That's a good way to feel about Droods,' I said. 'Helps keep you properly respectful.'

'Blow it out your ear,' said Walker.

Honey's face went vague, as she presumably filled in her CIA handlers with information about X thirty-seven, hopefully being a bit discreet about the whole Tunguska thing. Of course, she could have been telling them absolutely anything. Or everything. I had no way of knowing. It was important to remember that she was an experienced field agent, and I couldn't afford to trust her. Or Walker. Or Peter.

Katt was dead. And the Blue Fairy. And . . . I never saw a thing. I couldn't help feeling that if I'd been more on the ball, a bit more observant, I might have seen something. Done something. Katt was a rival, and I hardly knew her. And after what Blue did, to me and my family, we were enemies to the death. But even so, I liked Katt. And Blue was my friend.

This is why I prefer to work alone in the field. There's nothing like people to complicate a mission.

Peter took us straight to the eatery he'd sniffed out. By that time we'd got the scent, and were practically treading on his heels. I hadn't realised how hungry I was. A little beaver doesn't satisfy you for long. Peter barged through the front door, without even glancing at the bright shiny posters on the windows, but Walker took one look and balked.

'But . . . this is a burger bar!' he said plaintively. 'I wanted food. Real food!'

'Don't be such a snob,' said Honey. 'This is America, home of the brave and incredibly fast food.'

'And even faster indigestion,' Walker grumbled. 'Any country that has to advertise laxatives on television at prime time is in serious trouble.'

'Oh shut up and get in there,' I said. 'I can smell dead animals burning, and my taste buds are kicking the crap out of each other.'

'If anyone even attempts to serve me something in a bucket, there will be trouble,' Walker said ominously.

Honey and I pushed him through the front door, and joined Peter at the table he'd commandeered. He'd already attracted the attention of a pretty young waitress in a seriously ugly pink uniform, and was giving her his order. He was only halfway down the card, and already she'd filled up most of her pad. As burger bars went, this was perhaps a little better than most. Clean enough, not too crowded, and the piped muzak had been selected by someone who'd at least heard of tunes. There were big glossy posters everywhere, with marvellous illustrations of the wonderful things you could order. Presumably there so that if you couldn't read the menu, you could still point at things. I have a soft spot for the big happy posters, even though what they're showing you usually bears only a passing resemblance to what you actually end up with. I keep hoping that one day I'll actually get what I order; a triumph of optimism over experience.

'What do you fancy, Eddie?' said Honey, running her eyes down the laminated menu.

'Anything,' I said. 'Everything. Just kill a cow and bring it to me. I am seriously hungry. I may eat you if the service takes too long.'

'That's a nice thought, Eddie,' said Honey. 'But maybe later, okay?' And she fluttered her eyelashes at me.

'Mostly I prefer Burger King,' I said, tactfully changing the subject. 'At least there you get what you ask for, and nothing else. I mean, if I order a bacon double cheeseburger, as I have been known to do on St Cholesterol's Day, that's what I want. Double beef, cheese, bacon, in a bap. *Nothing else.* No bloody lettuce, no bloody gerkin. If I'd wanted a side salad, I'd have asked for one.'

'Fussy, fussy,' said Honey, not taking her eyes off the day's specials.

In the end, between us we ordered the entire menu. I took a look around as the waitress laboriously wrote it all down. The big clock on the wall said 2:25 in the afternoon, which helped to explain why the place wasn't too crowded. I drew Honey's attention to the clock, and she nodded.

'God alone knows where my body clock is at,' she said, stretching slowly and languorously, like a cat. 'I hate teleportation; it always gives me jet lag. And your luggage usually ends up in another dimension.'

We'd persuaded Walker to order some of the more straight-forward choices, but he was still fussing over the drinks list. He sighed, shook his head, and finally looked up at the waiting waitress.

'A tea, please, my dear. Do you have Earl Grey?'

'Don't embarrass me,' Honey said firmly. 'You'll have coffee and like it.'

'American coffee,' said Walker. 'I am in Hell. Just bring me a cup of water, my dear.'

'You don't want to drink the water round here, honey,' said the waitress. She'd rather taken a shine to Walker, or at least his accent. 'Even the bottled stuff is suspect. Tell you what – I'll bring you a nice Dr Pepper. How about that?'

Walker smiled at her. The waitress was a tall healthy-looking girl, whose prominent bosom put an unfair strain on the front of her ugly pink uniform.

'Thank you. That would be lovely, my dear.'

The waitress flashed her perfect teeth at him, and tottered off with her pad full of orders.

'What's a Dr Pepper?' said Walker.

'It's like the docks,' Honey said kindly. 'Close to water.'

The food finally arrived, and we gave our attention to pounding it down. Nothing like real hunger to make everything taste good. To my relief, my burgers arrived entirely uncontaminated with lettuce or pickle, and neither had they been skimpy with the cheese. None of us felt like talking; we just sat and chewed and swallowed, along with the occasional grunting noise of satisfaction. Walker wolfed his stuff down too, and even ended up trying bits from everyone else's plate. Though no doubt he'd go to confession later and admit that his stomach had gone slumming.

It wasn't as though we had much to say to each other, even after all we'd been through together. Perhaps because of what we'd been through. A lot of what happened at X thirty-seven, the things we experienced ... were too private, too personal to discuss. We were hurting, on a spiritual as well as a physical level. I remembered seeing my parents. Or something that looked very like my parents. Nothing ever has a hold on you like unfinished emotional business. When this was over, and Alexander King had his information, and the Drood family had his precious secrets locked safely away from the rest of the world ... it was time, and well past time, that I finally got to the truth about what happened to my parents. Who really killed them, and why. And Molly's parents too, perhaps. Was there really a connection? Molly always was ready to see the worst in the Droods. Still, I'd waited long enough for the truth. Once this game was over, I would make time for something that really mattered.

I'd allowed my family to distract me for far too long.

We finally reached the point where even brute will power couldn't force another morsel past our lips, and we sat back from the table, favouring our distended stomachs, and looked at each other to see who felt like talking first. And since none of us felt like talking about X thirty-seven, we talked about Philadelphia and why we'd been sent there.

'Has to be the Philadelphia Experiment,' I said.

'Has to be,' said Honey, nodding emphatically.

'Didn't they make a film about that?' said Walker.

'I've seen it,' said Peter. 'Started badly, ran out of steam, and then really went downhill. Sequel wasn't bad, though.'

'If all you know is the movie, then you don't know anything,' I said. 'The film was about time travel, while the experiment wasn't.'

'I always thought the Philadelphia Experiment was just another urban legend,' said Walker. 'The Case of the Vanishing Ship. I've never seen any official files on it – and I've seen files on most things that matter. Remind me to tell you about the Unholy Grail some time.'

'I wouldn't touch a straight line like that for all the tea in China,' I said firmly. 'The experiment—'

'You're about to lecture us again, aren't you?' said Honey, not unkindly. 'Droods know everything. Right?'

'Right!' I said. 'You're catching on! Now hush while I tell you a nice story. The legend first. There are many variations, but the gist is that on October the twenty-eighth 1943, the USS *Eldridge* was used as the setting for a very advanced scientific experiment, to see if a Navy ship could be made invisible to enemy radar. This was also known as Project Rainbow. But something went very wrong with the experiment.

'The *Eldridge* set off from the docks, reached open waters, and set their brand-new machines working. Other ships in the area were standing by, to observe any changes that might happen. They weren't prepared to see the *Eldridge* completely disappear, become actually invisible. All they could see was a deep depression in the water where the ship had been. And then the gap in the ocean suddenly filled up as the *Eldridge* vanished. Thrown out of our reality entirely by the power of its new machinery.

'The ship reappeared a few moments later, at Norfolk, Virgina. It was observed, and identified, and then it disappeared again, returning to Philadelphia's waters. The scientists on shore radioed the *Eldridge* again and again, demanding to know what had happened. But got no reply. There was a lot of dithering among the scientists and the Navy brass over possible radiation leaks and the like, but in the end the Navy had no choice but to send ships out to make contact with the *Eldridge*, sitting still and silent on the water.

'When the team of volunteers got on board to investigate, they found blood and death and horror. Most of the crew were dead. Many were insane. Quite a few were missing. There was extensive damage to the ship, as though it had taken part in a major firefight, but no clue as to who or what they'd been fighting. Worst of all, something had gone terribly wrong when the *Eldridge* teleported. Some of the crew had re-materialised inside steel walls and doors. Flesh and metal, fused together on the molecular level, but still horribly alive and begging to be put out of their misery. Luckily, they didn't last long.

'The whole thing was hushed up by Naval Intelligence, denied all the way up the line. And while a success has many fathers, a clusterfuck has no friends. The ship was broken up for scrap, after the burnt-out machines had been removed, and another ship was given the *Eldridge*'s name. The surviving crew . . . disappeared. It was wartime, after all. I like to think they were taken care of properly; the US Navy has a long tradition of looking after its own.

'And that is the legend of the Philadelphia Experiment. The US Navy still denies any of these things ever happened.'

'Right!' said Peter. 'If you look up *Philadelphia Experiment* on the Net, the first site it offers you is run by the US Navy, presenting their answers to the most Frequently Asked Questions, denying everything. Backed up by loads and loads of official-looking records.'

We looked at him.

'I was curious,' said Peter. 'After the film . . .'

'Be that as it may,' said Walker, 'that is the legend. What do we know about the facts?'

'Not a Hell of a lot,' I said cheerfully. 'Various Droods have looked into it down the years; we're fascinated by mysteries, and we don't like not knowing something that might turn out to be important. But American Naval Intelligence has gone to great lengths to deny, hide and destroy any evidence of what really went down on that day in October 1943. And short of launching a major offensive on US soil, we had no way of progressing. So we didn't. We didn't care that much.'

Our waitress had been busy removing empty plates for some time, coming and going so often that we'd forgotten she was there, and talked openly in front of her. That's why servants and service staff make such great sources of information. They're around so much they're practically invisible. And big people do so love to pretend that little people don't really exist.

'You folks here about the *Eldridge*?' she said cheerfully, and we jumped, suddenly aware of her presence. 'We get a lot of tourists, 'cause of that. We got whole shops dedicated to selling nothing but. They can fix you up with books and posters and DVDs and God knows what else. All junk, of course. Don't waste your money. They make most of it up, over drinks in the back rooms of bars. Tourists do love a good tall tale, God bless them. You know, my granddaddy worked right here in the docks, during the war. What he always called The Big One. He said people back then used to call that ship the *Eldritch*, cause of the weird stuff that went on around it.'

'What kind of weird things?' said Honey, as casually as she could.

'Oh, shoot. Bright lights, strange noises, lots of coming and going. And tons and tons of brand-new equipment. Granddaddy always said the ship would have had to be bigger on the inside than it was on the outside to fit it all in!'

'And the legend?' said Walker. 'The tall tales ... was your grandfather here when that happened?'

'Bless you, no, honey!' said the waitress. 'Never saw any such thing! It's just stories to bring in the suckers. Sorry, tourists. Got to work that tourist dollar!' She smiled at Walker. 'You know, if you want, I could get you a cup of tea from the cook's private stock. Real tea bags!'

214

'We're not stopping,' Honey said firmly. 'Could we have the check, please?'

The waitress bestowed another gleaming smile on Walker, and swayed off on her high heels.

'She likes you,' I said.

'Shut up,' said Walker.

'She likes you. She's your special waitress friend.'

'I am old enough to be her father,' said Walker, with great dignity.

'What's that got to do with anything?' said Peter. 'This is America. Most men here wouldn't be seen dead with a woman old enough to be their wife. This is the only country that thinks zimmer frames are sexy.'

Honey slapped him round the back of the head.

'Stop that!' said Peter, edging his chair back out of her reach.

'Then stop being you,' said Honey.

'Well,' I said quickly, 'I think it's safe to assume we were sent here to investigate the mystery of the Philadelphia Experiment.'

'Seems like our best bet,' said Honey.

'You could ask your people at Langley to lean on Naval Intelligence,' said Walker. 'Get them to open some of these secret files they claim not to have.'

'Take too long,' said Honey. 'Our Intelligence agencies have a really bad track record when it comes to cooperating with each other. Partly politics, partly jurisdiction, partly because each agency has its own secret agenda; but mostly it's just a pissing contest. The Company has more clout than most, but even so—'

'We don't have the time,' I said. 'Especially since we lost three days at Tunguska.'

'Right,' said Peter. 'Grandfather could be dead by now, or getting close.'

'I have to say,' said Walker, 'that you don't sound too concerned.'

'Well, that's probably because I'm not,' said Peter. 'Except that the old goat could turn up his toes at any time, and then all this would have been for nothing. Are any of you going to try and pretend you care?'

'I don't know the man,' said Honey. 'All I know is the legend of the Independent Agent.'

'It's always sad when a legend passes,' I said. 'One less wonder in the world.'

'Like your Uncle James?' said Walker. 'The famous, or perhaps more properly infamous, Grey Fox?'

'Yes,' I said. 'Like that.'

'How did the Grey Fox die, exactly?' said Honey. 'We never did get the details.'

'And you never will,' I said. 'That's family business. We will now change the subject.'

'What if we don't want to?' said Peter.

I looked at him, and he stirred uneasily in his chair. 'Don't push your luck, Peter,' I said.

'Now, children,' said Walker. 'Play nice.'

'We need to go back to the docks,' I said. 'I can use my Sight, boost it through the armour, if necessary. Perhaps pick up some ghost images of the experiment itself, back in 1943.'

'You think they'll still be here?' said Honey.

'Of course,' I said. 'Bad things sink in, remember?'

'Have we got time for some dessert?' said Peter. 'Stop hitting me, woman!'

'How are we going to split the bill?' said Walker.

'Hell with that,' I said. 'Honey can pay. CIA's got the deepest pockets of anyone at this table.'

Honey scowled as she reached for her credit card. 'Hate doing my expenses,' she growled. 'They challenge everything, these days. Whole damn Company is run by bean-counters.'

Before we left, Walker made a point of leaving a generous tip for the waitress.

We headed to the docks, strolling along with the portly, unhurried steps of the well-fed. There were tourists all around, in brightly coloured shirts like mating birds of paradise. Mostly they seemed interested in architecture, historical points of interest, and shops selling over-priced tat. We were the only ones standing on the edge of the docks, staring out at the ships and the sea. No one paid us any special attention. I checked. The sea was calm and peaceful, the sky was untroubled by cloud or plane, and the sun was pleasantly warm. Just enough of a breeze blowing in off the sea to be refreshing.

I raised my Sight, and looked at the sea again. To my surprise, I couldn't make out a thing. So much psychic energy had been released in the vicinity that the aether was jammed solid with an overlapping mess of signals. As though so many strange and wonderful things had happened here that the atmosphere had become super-saturated with information. It was a fog of events, magical and scientific, piled on top of each other like a thousand voices shouting at once, desperate to be heard. I subvocalised my activating Words, and clad myself in golden armour. Honey moved in close beside me.

'Is that wise?' she hissed. 'We're supposed to be undercover agents, remember? Aren't you in the least concerned that the tourists will see you in your armour and run screaming for their lives? Or an exorcist? All it needs is one quick-thinking onlooker to catch you on his phone camera and we will be the local news, on every channel!'

'Try not to panic,' I said, still looking out over the sea through my golden mask. 'It's very unbecoming in an agent. My torc broadcasts a signal that prevents anyone from seeing the armour. Unless I decide otherwise.'

'We can see it,' said Peter.

'Only because I let you,' I said.

'Hold everything,' said Walker. 'Are you saying your torc has influence, even control, over our thoughts?'

'Pretty much,' I said. 'Don't worry about it. I am a Drood, and therefore by definition far too nice and good and noble to even think of abusing such a privilege.'

'Typical Drood arrogance!' said Honey. 'You never thought to mention this before, because . . .'

'I thought you knew,' I said. 'You're CIA. You know everything.'

'Don't hit him,' Walker said to Honey. 'You'd only hurt your hand. Wait till he's armoured down, then do him over.'

'My turn to say "Hold everything",' I said. 'I See something.'

Focused through my mask, my Sight forced its way through the mass of information to show me ghost images of the final voyage of the USS *Eldridge*. The long ship came out of the docks on a grey afternoon in 1943, not knowing it was sailing out of history and into legend. The *Eldridge* was travelling severely low in the water, as though carrying far more weight than it was designed for. Every square inch of the open decks was covered with bulky equipment, trailing wires and cables, all fussed over by uniformed sailors dashing frantically back and forth. Tall spiky antennae thrust up at regular intervals the whole length of the ship, and long traceries of vivid electricity crawled up and down them, spitting and crackling. Strange energies pulsed and seethed, building an increasingly powerful aura around the ship.

Up till then, it was just a weirder than usual scientific experiment; but that changed abruptly with the arrival of the green fog. It appeared out of nowhere; no warning, no clue, just thick green mists boiling up around the ship and enveloping it from stem to stern. A green fog, thick with otherworldly magic, merging with and then suffusing the *Eldridge*'s energy field. Magic and science combining, producing an effect neither could achieve on their own.

I could hear the sailors screaming faintly. The green fog rose up, swallowing the ship, and then both fog and ship were gone in a moment, and nothing remained. No invisible ship, no depression in the water. Just . . . gone. Snatched away. The other ships sent out to observe the effects of the experiment sailed back and forth across the empty waters, to no avail. Back on shore, scientists and Navy brass shouted hysterically at each other.

And then the fog returned, thick and pulsating, glowing with its own sick bottle-green light. The colour and the texture of the fog was subtly different now; it looked . . . rotten, corrupt, poisonous. The *Eldridge* burst out of the green mists, as though forcing its way out, and headed jerkily for the shore. The green mists faded away, almost reluctantly, revealing a ship that had been to war. The antennae were gone, nothing left but jagged trunks and snapped cables, as though they had been torn away by some gigantic hand. The ship's hull had been breached in several places, fore and aft. It was a wonder she was still afloat. There were great blackened burn marks and fire damage all over the superstructure, smashed glass, stove-in bulkheads and blast damage. And dead crewmen, scattered the length of the ship, many torn to pieces.

Blood everywhere.

I concentrated, focusing my Sight still further, closing in on the ghost image of the ship to get a better look at what had happened. Because I had a horrid feeling I knew where the *Eldridge* had been, and who and what had done this to her and her crew. And it had nothing to do with invisibility or teleportation.

The green fog had been the first clue, and the unearthly lights that burned within it. I had Seen the colours of magic, interfering and then combining with the ship's science, heard the great sound of a door opening between dimensions. The *Eldridge*'s brand-new machines had inadvertently opened a portal to outside, and something had reached into our world and taken the ship and its crew as casually as a hand removes a goldfish from its bowl.

Up close, it was clear the *Eldridge* had fought a major battle. Hours or even days had passed for the ship in those few moments it had been away. Solid steel bulkheads had split like paper, compartments were crushed, and the crew ... Torn and broken, crushed, ripped apart, the pieces scattered over the blood-soaked deck. And yes, some caught up in the misfiring energies of teleportation had merged horribly with steel walls and doors, were trapped in bulkheads, had re-materialised inside metal, flesh fading seamlessly into steel. Screaming for help that would never come. This crew had fought one Hell of a battle, and only some of them had come home to tell of it.

I shut down my Sight, put away my armour, and looked at the others. 'Bad news, people. I'm pretty sure I know what happened to the *Eldridge*, and it has nothing to do with Project Rainbow, or any other of the myths and stories of the Philadelphia Experiment. I don't know what that technology they put on board was supposed to do, but something about it interfered with a soft spot, a weak place in reality, and opened up a long dormant portal to another place. Somewhere ... outside our reality. And something in that Other place reached out and dragged the *Eldridge* through the gateway.

'Something bad happened in that place, and the *Eldridge* had to fight her way out. She got home again, but her crew paid a terrible price. Hundreds dead, and worse than dead. No wonder the Navy hushed this up. No wonder they never experimented with that equipment again. They couldn't risk reopening the portal. Something might come through, from the Other side.'

The others looked at me for a long moment. They all wanted to ask questions, but something in my face and in my voice stopped them.

In the end, it was the old soldier Walker who nerved himself to ask the obvious question.

'Do you know where the *Eldridge* went?' he said. 'Do you know who took them?'

'Yes,' I said. 'They went to the Land Beneath The Hill. To the Sundered Lands. The Faerie Kingdoms. To the place the elves went, when they walked sideways from the sun and left this world behind them. The elves did this.'

Honey pursed her mouth, as though she wanted to spit. 'I'm supposed to tell my superiors at Langley that the *Eldridge* was abducted by fairies?'

'I've never known what the big deal was with elves,' said Peter. 'Elves aren't scary. Pointy-eared losers in period costumes, playing stupid jokes on mere mortals . . . Elves aren't hard. Wouldn't be even if they wore black leather and drank cider. I mean, look at the Blue Fairy.'

'Blue was only half-elf,' I said. 'And he could still have taken you with one hand, on the best day you ever had.'

'Oh come on . . .'

I glared at him till he stopped talking. 'The only ones you ever see in this world are the broken-spirited ones. The ones who stayed behind, or got left behind because they weren't good enough. The beachcombers of Faerie, wasting their remaining energies in screwing over humans, because that's all they've got. The real thing . . . is so much more. Monsters. Inhuman, soulless, immortal – or at least so long-lived it makes no difference. They breathe magic and sweat sorcery. They can bend the rules of reality just by thinking about it.

'We stole this world from them. Not by defeating them, or bettering them, but by out-breeding them. Do you wonder they still hate us, after all this time? In the Faerie Kingdoms, they are powerful and potent. They can do things we can't even dream of, with magics and technologies beyond our comprehension. They were here first, and they dream of returning and delivering a terrible revenge upon us. And we're going to have to go there, to the Elven Lands, to the Unseeli Court, to get the truth about what happened to the *Eldridge* and her crew.'

'I don't think I want to know that badly,' said Walker. 'I've had ... experience with elves in the Nightside. The real thing. They're always bad news.'

'Is it true they don't have souls?' said Honey. 'And that's why they're immortal?'

'Not as such,' I said. 'Not souls, as we understand the term. The elves are an ancient breed, far older than Humanity, born of a time when the very nature of this world was different. Our rules and restraints don't apply to them; but then they don't have our certainties, either. Like Life and Death, Good and Evil, Heaven and Hell.'

'I don't see why we have to go there,' glowered Peter. 'You say you Saw them take the *Eldridge*. What more do we need?'

'You really think your grandfather will settle for my word?' I said. 'I wouldn't. He'll want facts, details, evidence. No one will win the prize unless they can tell the whole story. Besides the *Eldridge*'s technology opened a door between Philadelphia and the Land Beneath The Hill, and I think it's still there. A soft spot in the world, a potential door waiting to be pushed open by one side or the Other. A vulnerable back door through which the Fae might one day invade. We have to check it out.'

'What do you mean, "*we*", paleface?' Peter said immediately.

'Are you sure it was the Fae, Eddie?' said Honey, ignoring Peter. 'You have to be sure about this before we risk disturbing them.'

'The *Eldridge* disappeared into a green fog,' I said steadily. 'Nothing to do with electromagnetic radiation or radar invisibility. The green mists are one of the traditional ways the Fae use to disguise an opening between their world and ours. That fog was thick with magic; and I know eleven magic when I See it.'

'The Land Beneath The Hill,' muttered Peter. 'The Elven Lands. The Faerie Kingdoms. How many names does this place have, anyway?'

'As many as it needs,' said Walker. 'In old magic, to know the true naming of a thing was to have power over it; so the Fae like to confuse things. It appeals to their ... mercurial nature. They're not fixed and certain, like us. They're many things, all at once. More than us, and less. Greater than us, but still childlike in many ways. The only human qualities they have are the ones they've copied from us, because it amuses them.'

He turned and looked at me. 'Even if we can close this door, there are others. Other ways of accessing the Faerie Kingdoms. The Street of Gods in the Nightside. A doorway in Shadows Fall. A deep tunnel beneath a small town in the south-west of England. There are openings and soft places all over the world, fortunately forgotten or overlooked by most people.'

'But if this is an unknown, unsuspected entrance, we have to shut it down,' I said steadily. 'Or persuade the Fae to close it from their side, at least long enough for us to set up the usual defences and observers.'

'I still don't see what the Fae would want with a US Navy ship anyway,' said Honey.

'We'll have to ask them,' I said. 'When we get there. This is a mystery that needs solving, not just for us, but for the sake of Humanity. We can't have the elves thinking they can reach out and grab us whenever they feel like it. I think I shall have to speak quite sternly to them about that. Are you with me?'

'Not if you're going to be rude to elves,' Honey said immediately. 'They don't like it. And I like my organs on the inside, where they belong.'

'I shall be polite and diplomatic at all times,' I said. 'Right up to the point where I decide not to be, and administer a good slapping. Don't worry – I'll give you plenty of warning so you can duck. Walker?'

'We have to go,' said Walker. 'Duty is a harsh mistress, but she never asks more of us than is necessary.'

'Always knew you were kinky, Walker,' said Honey. 'Langley's gone very quiet. I've brought them up to date and asked for instructions, and they're passing the buck back and forth so fast they're wearing it out. So let's get going before someone tells me not to. No one takes a US ship and its crew and gets away with it on my watch.'

We all looked at Peter, who shrugged. 'You're right. Grandfather isn't going to cough up his precious prize for an incomplete story. I'm in.'

'How much do you know about elves, Eddie?' said Honey. 'I know enough to be seriously worried about this.'

'Right,' said Peter. 'The best way to win a fight with an elf is to run like fun before it even knows you're there.'

'I thought you weren't afraid of elves,' I said. 'And when did you come in contact with the Fae, in your time in industrial espionage?'

He shrugged angrily. 'I get around. I hear things. Even in my business, Grandfather's reputation follows me. Anything with even a trace of weird attached to it ends up on my plate. One of the reasons I've worked so hard to maintain a good distance between my world and his. All I ever wanted was a sane, sensible, normal life. It's safer.

'I've heard about elves. But I don't believe half of it.'

'Well, you're about to get a crash course, the hard way,' said Honey. 'Try not to cry.'

Peter sniffed loudly. 'I think I liked it better when you were hitting me.'

'The Blue Fairy was a guest at the Fae Court before he joined up with us,' I said. 'According to him, there'd been some major upheavals there. He said Queen Mab is back, after centuries of exile, and sitting on the Ivory Throne. Which begs the question, what's happened to Oberon and Titania? Has there been civil war in the Elven Lands? Who's in, who's out, who's been horribly maimed and disfigured? Could make a big difference to how much we can reasonably hope to achieve. I mean, Oberon and Titania might have been flitty psychopaths with a really unpleasant sense of humour, but at least they were a known quantity. My family have been able to make deals with them, in the past. Mab is an unknown quantity.'

'Why was she exiled?' said Honey.

'No one knows,' said Walker. 'The elves have never talked about it. I had heard Mab was back; we had an elf turn up in the Nightside, begging for sanctuary. Not that we could do much for him. Someone had turned the poor bastard inside out all down one side. We killed him, eventually. As a kindness.'

'You really think we can get answers, maybe even concessions, out of the elves?' said Honey. 'They never miss a chance to do us down! Pride's all they've got left.'

'No,' Walker said immediately. 'It's more complicated than that. Elves are always passing through the Nightside on some errand or other, and I've had my share of dealings with them. Can't say I've ever got to know one; they're just too different. They are honourable in their way, but it's not an even remotely human way. They admire courage, and boldness, and outright insanity. You really think you can make the elves do anything they don't want to, Eddie?'

'Of course,' I said. 'I'm a Drood.'

'This is going to end in tears,' said Peter.

'Shut up, Peter,' said Honey.

'Queen Mab was still away in 1943,' I said. 'So whatever happened to the *Eldridge* was down to Oberon and Titania. Maybe we can use that. The real question is: if the elves did take the ship, why did they let her go? The *Eldridge* looked like she'd been through a real fight, but even so their weapons wouldn't have been enough to hold off elves.'

'No,' said Honey, looking out over the sea. 'The real question is: is the soft spot out there? Is the doorway still there? And if it is, can you open it, Eddie?'

'That's three questions,' said Peter. 'Ow! Damn it, Walker, that hurt!'

'Good,' said Walker. 'It was meant to.'

'It's like working with bloody kids,' I said, glaring about me. 'Can we please stick to the subject? All we need is a boat to get us out there, and I can do the rest. But I'm not taking any of you anywhere until I'm sure you're taking this seriously. There is a really good chance the elves will kill us on sight. They've been given good reason to respect the Droods, but they have very recent reasons to hate my guts.'

'Oh, wonderful,' said Peter. 'This gets better all the time. What did you do, pee in their wishing well?'

'I killed a whole bunch of elven lords and ladies,' I said.

Honey and Walker looked at me sharply, with what I liked to think was respect. Even Peter looked at me in a new way.

'I think I'll get Langley to express order us some really big guns,' said Honey.

'Nice thought,' I said. 'But they wouldn't help.'

'How are you intending to force your way into the Sundered Lands?' said Walker. 'I wasn't sure such a thing was possible, even for the legendary Droods. Even if it is a soft spot—'

'Blue had a torc, stolen from the Droods,' I said. 'Though he never did learn how to operate it, or he'd still be alive. Anyway, after he died I used a spell built into his elven breastplate to send him home. My armour remembers the spell; and I can use it to force open the soft spot.'

'I didn't know your armour could do that,' said Walker.

'There's lots of things it can do that people don't know about,' I said airily.

But that wasn't one of them. My armour is strange matter, not magic. Whole different thing. I had a different plan to get us through. When Blue stole his torc from us, he took it to the Fae Courts and they put their mark upon it. When I absorbed Blue's torc into my armour, those changes became a part of my strange matter too. Changes I could follow right back to their origin. I could break into the Elven Lands any time I chose.

So why did I lie to my companions? To mislead them, and keep them off balance. To keep something to myself. In the spy game, you take your advantages where you can find them.

Honey used her CIA contacts to hire us a boat. It wasn't much of a boat, just something to run tourists around in, but it was close at hand and we were in a hurry. And it wasn't as if I was paying for it. The *Hope Street* was little more than a long paint-peeling cabin set over an antiquated motor, but it looked sound enough. Honey found a discarded captain's hat, clapped it on her head and took over the steering wheel as though she'd been born to it. Walker stepped gingerly aboard, poking things with the tip of his umbrella and then shaking his head sadly. Peter dithered on the dockside, reluctant to step aboard.

'You have got to be kidding,' he said unhappily. 'Surely we can do better than this piece of shit?'

'It's a perfectly seaworthy piece of shit,' Honey said firmly. 'And that's all that matters. We're not even going out of sight of land, technically speaking. It is also the very best boat available at such short notice.'

'You're CIA,' said Peter, not unreasonably. 'Couldn't you have commandeered something more reliable, on the grounds of National Security?'

'We are supposed to be keeping our heads down,' said Honey. 'I start throwing phrases like that around, and the local authorities will be all over us. Now get on board, or I'll have you keel-hauled or something equally nautical and distressing.'

'Should never have given them the vote,' muttered Peter, slouching on board.

I looked over Honey's shoulder, and studied the instrument panels set out before her. They looked surprisingly up to date, and mostly functional.

'You sure you can run this thing?' I said, trying hard not to sound too dubious.

'What's the matter?' said Honey, grinning broadly. 'Is there something here the high and mighty Drood field agent can't operate?'

'I can drive anything modern,' I said defensively. 'But have you seen this tub's engines? Wouldn't surprise me to find they ran on coal. Or clockwork.'

'I could pilot this tub through the Bermuda Triangle and out the other side,' said Honey. 'She's sound. Nothing to it. Easy peasy.'

Walker sank into a battered old leather chair, which creaked noisily with his every movement. 'Then let us get underway, Captain.'

'I'm still waiting for Peter. Peter! Where are you?'

'I'm here, I'm here!' He slouched into the cabin and peered about him miserably. 'I hate boats and I hate the sea. In particular, I hate the way boats go up and down when they travel across the sea. I know I'm going to be unwell. I really enjoyed my meal, and I was hoping not to see it again any time soon.'

'The sea is perfectly calm,' Honey said patiently. 'And there's not a cloud in the sky. If the surface was any flatter you could roller derby on it.'

'It just looks that way,' Peter said darkly. 'But it's planning something. I can tell.'

'Don't worry,' said Walker. 'I know an infallible cure for seasickness.'

'Really?' said Peter.

'Of course. Sit under a tree.' He chuckled at the look on Peter's face. 'Ah, the old jokes are always the best.'

We left the Philadelphia docks and headed out to sea. The *Hope Street* chugged along cheerfully, the engines reassuringly loud and steady. Peter clung grimly to the arms of his chair, but the sea remained calm. Honey stood happily at the wheel, whistling a sea shanty, her captain's hat pushed back on her head. I did my best to give her a proper heading, but really all I could do was point her in the direction where I'd seen the *Eldridge* disappear into the green mists, back in 1943. It was entirely possible the soft spot had drifted since then. Still, Honey aimed the *Hope Street* in the right direction, and we all mentally crossed our fingers.

We hadn't been on the water long when dark clouds appeared in the sky out of nowhere. The wind whipped up, and the waters became distinctly choppy. Honey glared at the instruments before her.

'Weather reports didn't say anything about a storm. Supposed to be calm and sunny all day. Well, that's weather for you. Brace yourselves, everyone. We're in for a bumpy ride.'

'Told you,' said Peter.

'It's you, Peter,' Walker said calmly from his chair. 'All your fault. You're a jinx. Or maybe a Jonah. If I see a whale, you're going overboard.'

I used my Sight, without my armour. This close, I didn't need it. The soft spot was hanging on the air, dead ahead, strange magical forces churning around it like a vortex. Something in our approach had activated it; perhaps my torc. Or the changes Blue had added. The doorway was forming, becoming more solid, sucking us in. Just its presence in our world was enough to disrupt the weather patterns. The closer we got, the more I could See and the less I liked. This wasn't merely a soft spot, or a natural opening; someone had fashioned a proper door here and wedged it open a crack, against all the powers of this world to heal itself. Someone intended this door to be used.

A growing tension filled the *Hope Street*'s cabin as we drew steadily closer. We could all feel it: a basic wrongness in the warp and weft of the world that raised ancient atavistic instincts and grated on our souls. The tension grew worse, like an axe hanging over our heads, like a danger we could point at but not identify. It felt like walking the last mile to our own execution. Give Honey credit, she never flinched, never changed course, never even slowed our approach.

I could See the gateway hanging on the air ahead, waiting for us, drawing us in with bad intent. A convoluted spectrum of forces, as though someone had taken hold of space and time with a giant hand and ... twisted them. And the closer I got, the more I realised it wasn't an actual door, as such; more a *potential* door. That's why my family had never suspected its existence. It wasn't ... *certain* enough to set off our alarms and defences. As though the elves had set this up and then gone away, waiting for the right person to come along and activate it ... and walk into their trap.

Had to be a trap. It's always a trap, with the elves.

Wisps of green mist appeared around the *Hope Street*, materialising out of nowhere, long green streamers twisting and turning on the air as the boat rose and fell on increasingly violent swells. The mists thickened steadily: elf magic, summoned into being by our proximity to the doorway. The thick green fog was cutting us off from our world, bending the rules of our reality to make easier the transition to the Land Beneath The Hill. Walker and Peter scrambled out of their chairs and hurried over to join Honey and me at the wheel. We felt the need for simple human contact.

The boat was heaving and pitching on the water, as the fog surrounded us. Honey struggled to hold the *Hope Street* on course. It felt like leaving all certainty behind us, losing everything we'd learned to depend on. As though the ship itself might fall apart, and disappear into the green mists ...

'We're almost there,' said Walker. 'I can feel the doorway right ahead. It's like staring down a gun barrel.'

'I don't feel anything,' said Honey. 'Except that it's really cold in here, all of a sudden. And my skin's prickling, like the feeling you get before a lightning strike. And I'm not sure I'm steering this boat any more. The wheel's stopped fighting me, but it's not answering me either. I think this boat knows where it needs to go.' She took her hands off the wheel, and nothing happened. The *Hope Street* was still on course.

'The storm's getting worse!' yelled Peter, above the howl of the rising winds outside. 'Listen to it!'

'I don't think that's the storm,' I said. 'The door is opening.'

'So we'll be safe once we're through the door?'

'Well,' I said. 'I wouldn't go that far—'

'I want to go home,' Peter said.

The green fog was boiling all around us now, thick bottle-green mists that isolated and insulated us from the outside world. Strange lights flared and sputtered inside the cabin. They smarted where they touched my bare skin, making it crawl with revulsion. There was something basically unclean about the green fog. It smelt of sulphur and blood and strange animal musks. It was getting hard to see anything, even inside the cabin. The *Hope Street* pressed on, not bucking or heaving nearly so much now, but travelling faster and faster, like a runaway train.

'One problem,' I said.

'Only one?' Honey said immediately. 'I can think of hundreds!'

'Getting through the door isn't going to be a problem,' I said. 'I think it recognises my torc. But getting back again might prove a little tricky.'

'Terrific,' said Peter. 'Why don't we just throw ourselves overboard, and swim back?'

'I wouldn't,' said Walker. 'I'm pretty sure we're no longer in our world, as such. No sea, no sky; just green mists. We're in the soft place now, the inbetween place. And it smells really bad.'

'Throw yourself overboard here,' I said, 'And there's no saying where you might end up.'

'I may cry a little, if that wouldn't upset anyone,' said Peter.

'Stand tall, that man,' said Walker. 'You show weakness in front of the elves, and you'll be carrying your inner organs home in a goody bag.'

'You're really not helping,' said Peter.

'It's not as if we're going in there alone,' said Honey. 'I'm CIA, remember? I can call on serious backup and resources, and dirty tricks even elves have never thought of.'

'They won't care,' said Walker. 'I speak for the Nightside. I have powerful friends, and enemies, who'll come if I call, or would avenge my death. But the elves will still kill us if they have reason to – or even if they don't. They are creatures of whim and malice, and have no care for consequences.'

Honey looked at me. 'But you're a Drood, Eddie. You even ran your family, for a while. They wouldn't dare touch you.'

'Elves dare,' I said. 'It's what they do. My family would certainly avenge my death, might even do terrible things to the Sundered

Lands, but still the elves will do what they will do, and no one can predict or punish them. And, as I said, the elves do have good reason to want me dead. Or worse.'

'Maybe we should have left you behind,' said Walker.

'You'd never get in without me,' I said.

'You say that like it's a bad thing,' said Peter.

'So,' said Honey. 'No backup, and no threats we can use to enforce our position. Not really what I wanted to hear.'

'Have the CIA ever had any direct dealings with elves?' said Peter. 'Not because I particularly care, you understand; I'd just like people to keep talking, to distract me from thinking about the terrible things still to come.'

'Quite understandable,' said Honey. She gave the wheel a good turn, and then watched it sway back and forth, not affecting the *Hope Street* in the least. 'If the Company ever did have direct dealings with elves, which is possible, on the grounds that the Company has had dealings with far worse in its time when necessary, and no I'm not going to go into details . . . It would have taken place on a much higher level than mine. I'm only ever told what I need to know, when I need to know it.'

'Trust me,' I said. 'Elves are powerful creatures, yes; but at heart they're just another bunch of aristocratic snobs who think they're better than anyone else. And I've been talking rings around creeps like that my whole life. I'll get us in, and I'll get us back again; and I might get us the keys to the city and a big box of chocolates to take home with us while I'm at it.'

'That's it,' said Peter. 'He's delirious.'

'Trust a Drood?' said Honey. 'Things aren't that desperate. Not yet, anyway.'

'Getting damned close,' muttered Peter.

'Shut up, Peter,' said Walker, not unkindly.

The green fog filled the cabin, thick and unrelenting. I couldn't see the cabin. Couldn't see anything except Honey and Walker and Peter. We linked arms and held hands, to make sure we wouldn't be separated. We were all breathing hard, as though there was less and less air in the fog. It smelt like the crushed petals of flowers from other worlds, like the breeze off unknown alien seas, like the stench of piled-up bodies of creatures that could never have thrived in our world. It smelt of elves. The stench raised the hackles on the back of my neck, tugging at my deepest fears. As though my very DNA remembered elves, and cringed at the thought of encountering them again.

All perfectly normal and sensible. Any sane man would be afraid of elves. But I had been here before, walked in the Fae Courts before, and I knew how to handle them. If I could stay alive long enough.

The *Hope Street* dropped suddenly, as though the ocean had been snatched out from under her, and we fell sprawling, crying out to each other as we were forcibly separated. The green mists rushed away in all directions, revealing the gateway hanging open and beckoning before us. I couldn't look at it directly; it hurt my eyes, and my mind. It wasn't real, as we understand real things. It was an insult to everything humans understand about how our universe works. Elf magic; elf thinking.

I subvocalised my activating Words, and the golden armour slipped around me in a moment, hugging me tight like a friend, or a lover, determined to stand between me and danger. I picked myself up and made myself look at the doorway directly, through my golden mask. It still hurt like Hell, but I could stand it; perhaps because the torc's strange matter was as unnatural as the elves' construct.

We weren't moving. The boat was hovering, held where she was on the edge of the event horizon, as though the door was waiting for ... something. I reached out with a golden hand, and thrust it into the energies pulsing before me. I took a firm hold, and then pulled with all my armoured strength. The boat surged forward, and we were on our way.

The doorway unfolded before me, over and over again, like some great alien flower blossoming in endless iterations, until finally it swallowed us up and we passed through, leaving the world behind.

And so we came to the Sundered Land, the Land Beneath The Hill. The world the elves made for themselves when they left the Earth behind. No one's really sure why. The elves certainly didn't leave for the good of Humanity, or because they recognised any human authority over our world. Some say we outnumbered them, crowding them off their land because we bred so much faster than the long-lived elves; and their pride would not allow them to take second place. Some say the elves fought a war, against someone or something they still won't talk about. They fought a war and they lost, so they ran away to somewhere safer ... And some say the Droods found that safe haven for the elves; which is why they still respect and hate us.

They say a lot of things about the elves. Believe what you will, or whatever makes you feel most comfortable. The elves don't care.

The *Hope Street* was sailing a whole new sea now, beneath a pale pink sky with three huge moons hanging low and a sun too bright to look at directly. Long slow ripples spread out from the boat as we chugged steadily towards the simple docks straight ahead of us. The water was thick and viscous, almost syrupy, with half a dozen vivid colours swirling in it, like a painter's palette. Far, far below, huge dark shadows swam in great slow circles around the *Hope Street*, escorting us to shore.

We passed between massive elven ships, standing tall and graceful in the multi-coloured waters. Old-fashioned three-masters with billowing sails, and delicate metal hulls, thin as foil, dainty as petals, strong as eternity. The sails were made from tanned hides, their rigging as intricate as the most delicate lace or cobweb. No one stood on the decks, or at the wheels, but none of the ships moved despite the gusting wind. We slid between these sleeping giants like small children creeping through an adult's world.

'They're more like works of art than working vessels,' said Walker. 'Like the dream of a ship in the designer's mind ...'

'They're real enough,' I said. 'Their sails are made from the stretched skins of vanquished enemies.'

'Including humans?' said Peter.

'Most definitely,' I said.

We stood very close in the cabin, watching the docks approach. A simple construction made up of thousands of bones, neatly fitted and locked together. On either side of the docks stood two huge elven statues, carved from a dark, green-veined marble. They towered above us, sixty feet tall and more, like the legendary Colossus of Rhodes. At least, I thought they were statues; until they slowly turned their heads to follow our progress.

Beyond the docks lay vast stretches of green land. Not exactly grass or moss, but close enough to pass, of a shade so sharp and vivid it almost glowed. And striding across these peaceful greenlands, their feet slamming down in perfect lockstep, came the elves. Thousands of them. They finally crashed to a halt at the very edge of the land around the docks, standing straight and tall in perfectly set out ranks. Thousands of elves, standing impossibly still, watching the arrival of the *Hope Street* with cold glowing golden eyes.

They were tall and noble, and far more dangerous than the broken-spirited elves I was used to seeing, on Earth.

The *Hope Street* slid expertly in beside one of the docks, and we jumped as the engine shut down without us telling it to. We looked at each other, and then we left the cabin and went out on deck. None of us made any move to step out on to the dock. Having a whole army of elves studying you, silently and implacably, is enough to give anyone pause. I could have armoured up to show them who I was and who I represented, but I didn't. Encasing myself in protective armour might have been taken as a sign of fear, or even weakness. And no man can afford to be thought weak when dealing with elves. Up close they looked almost painfully beautiful. Some have sought to dismiss this as mere glamour, protective illusion, but that's not strictly true. The elves can be, or seem to be, anything they choose. Especially here, in the world they made for themselves.

'What is that they're wearing?' said Walker, very quietly. 'Some kind of armour?'

'Made out of china, or porcelain maybe?' said Honey, just as quietly. 'Though how it hangs together ... the pieces seem to be moving independently.'

'They're shells,' I said. 'Up close, you can hear them rasping against each other as they move. The creatures inside those shells are still alive, stitched together, constantly suffering. That's the elven way.'

'How do you know this?' said Peter.

'Because I've been here before,' I said. 'Let's go ashore and say hi. Can't have them thinking we're afraid of them.'

I led the way forward, across the bony dock. The ridges were soft and polished under my feet, worn down by long use. The elves made no move as we approached, standing impossibly still, and utterly silent. They looked more alien than ever now, almost unbearably glamorous, burning with an intensity no human could ever match.

The sheer passion of their presence beat in the air like a fast drumroll I could feel down in my soul. I could feel the weight of their massed gaze; and there was nothing of surprise in it. They were here because they'd known we'd be here. Elves don't have the same relationship with time as everyone else. They treat it like a pet, and make it do tricks for them, for their amusement.

'What can you tell me about this place?' Honey said, murmuring the words into my ear.

'It's dangerous,' I said. 'This is the world the elves made, and we have no place in it. Have you noticed, there are no birds flying in the sky? Not even any insects? When the elves first came to this place they killed everything that lived here, right down to the last of every kind and the smallest of species. The only things that live here now are the elves and the creatures they brought with them. Or made. They always did like tinkering.'

'The light hurts my eyes,' said Peter. 'It's too bright.'

'It was never intended for human eyes,' I said. 'Look down – we don't even have any shadows here.'

'Now that is disturbing,' said Walker. We came to a halt at the end of the docks, and he looked out over the massed ranks of assembled elves, his gaze impressively cool and calm. 'Which one is Queen Mab?'

'She wouldn't come here to meet us,' I said. 'She's the Queen of all the Elves; we're nobody. So we go to her.'

'How?' said Honey. 'They're blocking the way.'

'They'll make a way for us,' I said. 'When they're ready. They're great ones for protocol. And intimidation.'

Honey sniffed. 'I'm American. We don't bow our heads to foreign royalty.'

'You do if you're a diplomat,' I said patiently. 'Our only hope for surviving this is if we're perceived as representatives of greater powers. And . . . I think we've stood around here far too long already. We have to put on a good show, or they'll never respect us. So follow me, and whatever happens . . . *don't let it get to you*. The elves love to see us afraid.'

I strode forward off the docks, heading for the nearest rank of elves. They stood firm before me, an implacable wall. I still didn't armour up, but I did lift my chin a little so they could clearly see the torc around my neck. At the very last moment, the elves stepped gracefully to one side, leaving a narrow gauntlet for me to walk through. I kept my face carefully calm and composed, as though I'd expected nothing else. I could hear the others hurrying behind me, and hoped they were putting on a good show. There were limits to how much I could hope to protect them in this world.

I could feel the steady pressure of the elves' regard as I walked through their massed ranks. It's not easy walking through a crowd of people any of whom might kill you in a moment, for any reason, or none. The skin on my back crawled, in anticipation of an attack that never came. I could sense as much as feel my companions all but treading on my heels, close behind me.

And then the ranks of elves fell away abruptly, revealing a great and wondrous city. I led the way through the massive gateway, carved from the skull of a dragon. A single skull, bigger than a house. The teeth had been yanked out of its long jaws, and the empty eye sockets were crammed with strange alien flowers. They writhed and hissed at me as I passed by them and went into the city.

The streets were wide, and wandering. The towering buildings to every side were all different, individual, diseased; like the dreams of a mad mind. Their shapes were basically organic, sick and harsh and even distressing. They looked like they might have been grown as much as constructed. Most of the shapes made no sense to my human eyes and aesthetics. And they moved, all of them, subtly changing; only ever still when looked at directly. Only fully real when actively perceived. I thought about quantum states and observer's intent, and then tried hard not to think about it at all.

In a small open square we passed by an elf who had been made into a statue and forced to function as a fountain. Water gushed from his open eyes and mouth, but I could make out enough of his face to know he was still alive, and aware, and suffering. Later we passed by a pile of severed pale hands, a pile as tall as a man. The fingers were still twitching. The ground became sticky beneath our feet, making every step an effort. The impact of the overbright sun beat down on my head, and my bare skin tingled and smarted from the light, as though exposed to alien radiations.

A dragon flew by overhead, plunging us into darkness with its shadow. Not the ugly wyrms the elves ride when they come to earth, but the real thing, vast and glorious, bigger than a jumbo jet, with wings so huge and wide they hardly flapped as it flew past. Very beautiful, and very deadly. Half a dozen dragons could take out any major city. Fortunately, there are barely half a dozen of them left now.

We stopped abruptly to let a huge beast go by – a great unnatural creature with skin stretched so tight you could see the organs pulsing within. It strode on long stilt-like legs, and elves rode on its back. They beat at its pulpy head with long barbed sticks, and laughed musically as it moaned. Small scuttling things stuck to the shadows of side streets, trying not to be noticed. And now and again the walls I passed would have pulsing veins, or eyes that opened, or would slowly melt away. I kept looking straight ahead. It helps if you have an aim, a destination to concentrate on. The human mind isn't equipped to deal with a world where there are no certainties or constraints; nothing on which you can depend.

Honey moved forward to walk beside me. Behind me, I could hear Walker murmuring comfortingly to Peter. Of course the elf world wouldn't bother Walker; he was used to the Nightside.

'You've been here before, Eddie,' said Honey. Her voice sounded steady, but strained. 'What are the protocols for meeting the Queen?'

'Damned if I know,' I said. 'It's always different here. The city didn't look anything like this the last time I was here. The sea and the sky weren't those colours. The Elven Lands are always changing. They like it that way. I suppose when you're immortal, you can get tired of things pretty quickly.'

'I thought you said they weren't immortal,' said Honey. 'Not literally.'

'They're not, but they might as well be. Either way, don't tell them they're not immortal. They tend to take it rather badly.'

'What were you doing here before? I thought you were a field agent for your family, based in London?'

'I was,' I said. 'But you go where you're needed, where the family needs you. A few years back, an elf called Peaseblossom came to London and misbehaved himself on a rather grander scale than usual. He started out by abducting small children and carrying them away – easy enough with his glamour. I was sent after him to get the children back, but by the time I tracked down his lair he'd already eaten three of them.' I could still remember the cold rage, the bitter helplessness. 'I was ready to kill him on sight, but there are ancient pacts, agreements, between the Droods and the Fae. The best I could do was send him back to the Fae Courts for punishment.

'But then things got complicated. I was able to rescue the surviving children from the elf's squalid little den in the subterranean levels deep under London, but Peaseblossom was already gone. He hadn't come to London for children. They were merely appetisers. He was on his way to the Old Soul Market, in Crouch End Town. The fool.

'Elves don't have souls. Not as such. Or at least nothing we'd recognise as a soul. Peaseblossom wanted to buy one for himself. Not as difficult as you'd think, and not actually a problem in itself; but word soon got to me that the damned fool elf didn't know what he was getting himself into. The Old Soul Market is almost as ancient as the elves, and the proprietors didn't take kindly to discovering that Peaseblossom thought he could just waltz in, demand their very best merchandise and expect to pay on credit. So they mugged and rolled him, locked him in a cage and made arrangements to sell his stuffed and mounted corpse to the Collector. (Apparently he was a collector's item because he'd been namechecked in Shakespeare's *A Midsummer Night's Dream*.) I was ordered to get the elf out, and take him home before he started a war. I retrieved Peaseblossom, through my usual mixture of reasonableness, calculated diplomacy and applied mayhem. Was he grateful? What do you think? So I beat the crap out of him on general principles, and took him home to the Fae Courts.'

'You do get around, don't you?' said Honey. 'So the elves are beholden to you? They owe you for your help?'

'Not necessarily,' I said. 'It's more complicated than that. It always is, with the elves.'

'It always is with you,' said Walker, appearing suddenly on my other side. 'What did you do to get the elves angry with you, Eddie?'

'I killed a whole bunch of elf lords and ladies, while I was rogue,' I said. 'To be fair, they were trying to kill me at the time. But still, there are many here who would love to watch me die slowly and horribly. Except they can't kill me, because then they'd never be able to pay back the favour they owe me.'

'But if they tried to kill you before . . .' said Honey.

'I was rogue then,' I said. 'Disowned by my family. Fair game. Now I'm a Drood again, in good standing with my family, they can't touch me. Unless they can find a way to justify it to themselves. Elf honour is really complicated. Remember, once we get to the Fae Court, don't eat or drink anything they offer you, don't speak unless you're spoken to directly, and don't start anything. Leave that to me. And above all don't try to have sex with them, or you'll be carrying your genitals home in a bag.'

'Was that last bit really necessary?' said Walker.

'You'd be surprised,' I said. 'Okay, everyone, look sharp and cool and very confident. We're here.'

We had come at last to Caer Dhu, the last great Castle of Faerie, brought here in its entirety from our world long and long ago. Caer Dhu; home to the Unseeli Court, and the rulers of Faerie. Once, and for many many years, that had been King Oberon and Queen Titania; but if Queen Mab really was back . . . then maybe the returned Queen had had new thoughts about the old pacts that bound the Droods and the Fae.

From the outside, Caer Dhu looked like a huge golden crown, with a massive raised dome surrounded by hundreds of golden spikes reaching up into the sky. And on those spikes, transfixed and impaled, were hundreds of elves. Still alive, still suffering, their golden blood streaming endlessly down the long spikes, collecting in the guttering and gushing from the mouths of screaming gargoyle faces. Elves are very hard to kill, but that's not always a good thing. Above the entrance, a dozen lesser spikes were surmounted by severed elf heads. The faces were alive and aware, and their mouths moved when they saw us approach, as though trying to warn or curse us.

That's civil war for you. There are always fallen heroes, leaders of the losing side who must be publicly punished as an example to others. And the elves know all there is to know about punishment.

I held my head up high, and strode into the Unseeli Court as though I had every right to be there and an engraved invitation that promised free drinks. Honey and Walker and even Peter took their cues from me, and strode along beside me with their noses in the air. Inside Caer Dhu, it was dark. The only dark place in the Elven Lands. The Fae Court was huge and empty, barely visible through the gloom.

A single shaft of light slammed down like a spotlight, illuminating the two Ivory Thrones standing on a raised dais at the back of the court. A huge dark form sat on the left-hand throne, but the other was empty.

I strode across the great empty space, heading for the thrones, and the others hurried along with me. Despite the open space, our footsteps didn't echo at all. The further into the court I went, the bigger it seemed to get. Crossing the open space seemed to last for ever, but finally I came to a halt at the base of the dais and looked defiantly up at the huge dark figure on its throne. Before I could say anything, I heard a faint sound behind me, and looked back. The open space of the court was now crammed from wall to wall with rank upon rank of silently watching elves. Thousands of them. I swallowed hard, and looked back at the throne. No Oberon, no Titania, not even a sign of the Puck, the only elf who was not perfect. Instead, Queen Mab sat on the Ivory Throne, wreathed in shadows, so much larger than life and a thousand times more dreadful.

Four elves appeared suddenly out from behind the second, empty, throne. They draped themselves insolently at Mab's feet, and smiled at me. Mab's current favourites. I knew their names, from my previous visit. Peaseblossom, looking as arrogant as ever. His child and lover, Mustardseed. And Cobweb and Moth, two lowly enforcers sent out occasionally into the human world to do necessary dirty work. I wouldn't have chosen any of them as my favourites; but no doubt they had their uses.

Peaseblossom remembered me. He scowled fiercely and started to say something, but I ignored him, ostentatiously giving my attention to the Elven Queen while I tried to figure out what was wrong with the Fae Court. It felt too big, too large, stretched thin like old skin, like something forced to serve a purpose long after it should have been retired and replaced.

After all this time, were the elves really getting old?

'I am Eddie Drood,' I said loudly. My voice seemed such a small thing in that large place. 'I am here to speak with the Queen of the Fae.'

'We know who you are,' said Cobweb.

'We hate you,' said Peaseblossom.

'You're expected,' said Moth.

'Hate you for ever and ever,' said Mustardseed.

'Queen Mab will have words with you,' said Cobweb.

'Won't that be nice?' said Moth.

Their voices all sounded the same: like evil or insane children pretending to be polite, knowing that something really nasty is planned, and held in reserve.

'How could they be expecting us?' said Honey. 'We didn't know we were coming here until a few hours ago.'

'They know, because they're elves,' I said.

'Is this bad?' said Peter.

'It's not good,' I said. 'But then, I never thought it would be.'

And then Queen Mab leaned forward on her throne. The darkness fell away from her like a discarded cloak, and the sheer impact of her appearance was like a slap in the face. Mab was huge, greater in size and scale than any other elf. Ten feet tall, supernaturally slender and glamorous, naked save for blue-daubed magical signs and sigils, glowing fiercely on her iridescent pearly skin. She was beautiful beyond bearing, radiating power and authority. I couldn't have looked away if I'd wanted to. Her eyes were pure gold, with no pupil. Her mouth was a deep crimson, the red of heart's blood, red as sin itself. Queen Mab was a first-generation elf, and it showed. There are records at Drood Hall, in the Extremely Restricted section of the Old Library, that suggest she might be older than the Nightside, older then Humanity itself. Perhaps, even older than our world ... But then, you can't trust anything you read when it comes to elves.

No one knows how or why Mab was removed from power, and replaced by Oberon and Titania. It's dangerous even to ask.

Queen Mab looked down on me, and my companions, like an artist considering early sketches and wondering whether they should be erased. Meeting her gaze was like staring into a searchlight. One wrong word and she'd kill me and my companions with a gesture. But I'm a Drood; and we don't take shit from anyone.

'So, Mab, how's it going?' I said pleasantly. 'Getting much?'

There was a subtle but still audible stirring among the massed ranks of elves behind me, and angry hissings from the four favourites grouped at Mab's feet. They actually started to rise up, flexing their clawed hands, only to stop abruptly at some unheard command from their Queen. They sank back reluctantly, curling round her pale feet like sulky pets. The Queen did not move, did not look away, didn't even seem to be breathing. But another elf stepped out from behind her throne, and came forward to the edge of the dais to look down on me. He was tall, long-limbed, clad in diaphanous silks, his skin so pale as to be almost translucent. Long-stemmed roses plunged in and out of his flesh, the heavy-thorned stems skewering his body. They wrapped around his limbs and plunged through his torso, and the points of the thorns rose and fell, rose and fell, breaking his skin over and over again. Golden blood ran and dripped, endlessly. And one white rose blossomed from his left eye socket, completely replacing the eye. As I watched, the tips of thorns pressed up against the underside of his face, threatening and then retreating, biding their time.

I couldn't even imagine the kind of agony he must be in, but his step was sure and certain as he descended from the dais to face me, and when he spoke, his voice never wavered once.

'I am the Herald,' he said, fixing me with his one golden eye. 'Queen Mab's Herald. I speak for her, to lesser things. And yes, I am being punished, for sins beyond your comprehension. Or appreciation. Still, it is good to have you here, Drood. It's been so long since we had anything human to torment.'

I armoured up and took him out with one punch to the head. His skull cracked and broke audibly under the impact of my golden fist, and he sat suddenly down, as though someone had pulled the floor out from under him. Start as you mean to go on, I always say. The massed ranks of elves stirred again, and the four favourites hissed with rage, but Queen Mab raised one perfect hand and immediately they were still and silent again. The Herald rose slowly to his feet, the bones of his head creaking and cracking as they slowly moved back into place. Golden blood ran down the side of his head and dripped steadily off the lobe of his pointed ear. The blow would almost certainly have killed anyone else, but elves are hard to kill. You couldn't even slow an elf down with a wrecking ball. Not in their own world.

'I am Edwin Drood,' I said flatly to Queen Mab, ignoring the Herald. 'The Droods are bound to the Fae, and the Fae to the Droods, by ancient pact and treaty. Or have the elves forsaken honour?'

'The elves are honour,' said Queen Mab, in a slow heavy voice like poisoned honey, as though she was still half dreaming. 'More than can ever be said for humankind. But be you welcome to our lands, Edwin Drood, and your companions. Do keep them under control. If they make a mess we will have them disciplined.'

'They're with me,' I said. 'And therefore protected by the Drood protocols.'

'Speak,' said Queen Mab, neither agreeing nor disagreeing for the moment.

'You did not inform us of your return, Your Majesty,' I said carefully. 'We would have sent envoys to welcome you home.'

'We have returned,' said Queen Mab. 'Let all the worlds tremble, and all that are, beware.'

'Well, yes,' I said. 'Quite. So, what's happened to Oberon and Titania?'

'Is that what you came here to ask, Drood?'

'No, just making conversation.'

'They are gone. Mention them not in our presence.'

'All right,' I said. 'Where have you been, Your Majesty? You've been gone a long time.'

'Oberon sent us away.' Her dark red mouth widened slowly, in a terrible smile. She had the look of the Devil contemplating a new sin. 'He really should have had us killed, but he always was too sentimental for his own good. It took us a long time to claw our way back and take our long-anticipated revenges on those who betrayed us.'

'Where did he send you?' I said, honestly interested. 'Where could he send someone of your undoubted power?'

'Where all the bad things go, little Drood. He sent us to Hell. Damned us to the Pit, to the eternal Inferno.' She was still smiling her awful smile, her golden eyes fixed on me. And even inside my impenetrable armour, I could feel beads of sweat popping out on my forehead. 'While we were in Hell, little Drood, during our long sojourn in the Houses of Pain, we met your precious witch, Molly Metcalf. Such a sweet thing. Shall we inform you of the deals she made? Of the awful things she agreed to, in return for power?'

'Let us make a deal, Your Majesty,' I said. 'I will not talk of Oberon and Titania, and you will not talk of my Molly. Yes?'

'Speak, little Drood,' said Queen Mab. 'Tell us what brings you

242

here, to our magnificent court, to our noble presence. Tell us what brings you here, with the blood of so many of our noble cousins still wet and dripping on your armoured hands.'

'Ah,' I said. 'I wondered when we'd get round to that. They attacked me, Your Majesty. They really should have known better. I might have been rogue at the time, but I was still a Drood and they were just elves. Even if they had been armed with strange matter by a traitor within my family.'

Peaseblossom hissed loudly, and started to rise up again. Queen Mab shot him a glance, and he flinched and fell back as though he'd been hit.

'Keep your pets on a leash, Your Majesty,' I said. 'Or I might find it necessary to discipline them.'

The Queen considered me silently for an uncomfortably long moment. There was no sound in the Unseeli Court, apart from the heavy breathing of my companions. I should have been able to hear the massed breathing of the thousands of watching elves, but there was nothing. I didn't look back, but I knew they were blocking the only way out; and it was highly unlikely they'd step aside for me again, without Mab's command. I had to win the argument with the Queen, get the information I needed and strike some kind of deal that would get me and my companions out of here with our organs still on the inside. The odds were not good, but I'm a Drood; and when you wear the golden armour the odds do what they're told, if they know what's good for them. In the end Queen Mab nodded, very slightly, and I felt a great weight rise off me. She was ready to listen, at least.

'I've come about the USS *Eldridge*,' I said. 'An American naval vessel that found its way here in 1943. You weren't on the Ivory Throne at the time, Your Majesty, but I'll bet the Herald was around back then. I need to know what happened to this ship, how it was able to come here and what happened to it while it was here.'

Queen Mab turned her head slowly to look at the Herald, who bowed low in return.

'I do indeed remember the occasion, Your Majesty. Would it please you to have me tell of it?'

'Show them,' said Queen Mab.

The Herald clenched his left hand into a fist. Razor-sharp thorns burst out of the back of his hand. Golden blood splashed on to the floor before him, quickly spreading out to form a golden scrying pool. And in that pool appeared images from the past, showing all that had befallen the unfortunate USS *Eldridge*.

'Your world was at war,' whispered the Herald, his golden eyes fixed on the images forming in the scrying pool. 'Its very boundaries weakened by the sheer extent of the savagery and slaughter. So when one of your ships came knocking at our door, we were tempted and let it in. Such cunning machines in that ship – primitive, but effective. They pushed open a doorway we had long forgotten, and all we had to do was help them through. I wonder where they thought they were going. It was a warship, yes, but small and pitiful compared to our glorious vessels. They came right to us, not knowing where they were and the danger they were in.

'We played with them for ages, teasing and tormenting as the impulse took us, delighting in their pain and horror. They cried so prettily. And then it occurred to us what a fine jest it might be to alter the ship and its crew in subtle, deadly ways, and send them home again. To corrupt them, body and soul, and send them back to your world as a spiritual plague ship. We debated for hours, searching for something especially sweet and cruel and amusing . . . but that delay gave the crew of the ship time to recover. The *Eldridge*'s captain took control again, roused his crew and had them reactivate their cunning machines. They opened the door and fled our shores in search of it. See what happened next . . .'

The images were clear and sharp in the scrying pool. The USS *Eldridge* was heading out to sea. The decks were slick and running with blood and shit and other things, but the sailors ran frantically back and forth, leaping over dead and mutilated bodies where necessary, while the captain screamed orders from the bridge. There were enough of the crew left alive to do the work, though their faces were racked with memories of pain and rage and horror. On the bridge, the captain stared straight ahead, with sunken dark eyes like cinders coughed up out of Hell.

Strange energies began to glow and crackle around the *Eldridge*, as the powerful machinery packed into the compartments below began to operate. And that was when the elves attacked.

The huge three-masted sailing ships surged out after the *Eldridge* and soon overtook it, though there was scarcely wind enough to stir the massive sails. They circled lazily round the *Eldridge*, taunting the ship and its crew until the sailors manned the deck guns and opened fire. The cold iron of their ammunition punched through the sliver-thin hulls, and made ragged messes of the spread sails. Elves danced and shimmered on their decks, moving too fast to be hit, but unable to stay still long enough to operate their weapons. The *Eldridge* kept up a steady fire, blowing the elven ships apart, inch by inch.

The elven vessels fell back, raging and frustrated, and the *Eldridge* sailed on.

Elf lords and ladies laughed merrily, high in the sky, mounted on the back of a dragon. Impossibly large, it hovered over the *Eldridge* like an eagle over its prey. The ship's guns fired, but could not touch it. The dragon opened its great mouth, and breathed fire. Raging streams of liquid fire washed over the decks of the *Eldridge*, consuming sailors, blowing up guns and ammunition, and scorching the metalwork. The elves on the dragon's back unlimbered strange unearthly weapons that blew huge holes in the *Eldridge*'s super-structure. Sailors died in their hundreds, but still some manned the deck guns, or fired up at the dragon with rifles or handguns.

The captain kept his ship going, into the heat of the attack, even as his bridge disintegrated about him, heading doggedly towards the door he knew had to be there, the door that would take his ship and his remaining crew home. A door out of the Hell he had brought them to. Even as his ship fell apart around him, and his deck burned with dragonfire, as his skin blistered and blackened, he battled on.

Until the green mists rose, and he headed the *Eldridge* into them; and the ship disappeared. Safe from elven rage and spite. My heart went out to the captain. He had no way of knowing that getting home would not be enough. That his ship's marvellous new equipment had been damaged, or perhaps even sabotaged. That he would return home not in triumph, but only to more horror. Because the *Eldridge* had been through Hell; and it had left its mark upon them all.

The last images faded from the scrying pool, and it was just golden blood upon the floor.

'We let them go, in the end,' said the Herald. 'Their machineries were . . . interesting, but they could never have left our lands without our help and consent.'

'Why?' said Honey. Her voice was strained, hoarse. 'After everything you did to them, and planned to do, why?'

'They fought well,' said the Herald. 'We admire courage. And by letting them pass through the gateway again, their science and our magic combined to do what neither could do alone: force it all the way open. An unsuspected back door into your world. We thought it might come in useful.'

'You bastards,' said Honey.

'Easy,' murmured Walker.

'No!' said Honey. 'Those were good men, doing their duty in a righteous war, and you—'

'Hush,' I said. 'Hush.'

'We have given you what you required, little Drood,' said Queen Mab, entirely unaffected by Honey's outburst. 'Now you must give us what we require: the Blue Fairy's torc. It was not on his body when he returned to us, and it is ours by right.'

'He stole that torc from its rightful owner, nearly killing him in the process,' I said.

'What is that, to us?' said Queen Mab.

'Torcs belong to Droods, and no one else,' I said. 'That was true before you were sent away, and it's still true now.'

'Such a childish attitude,' said Queen Mab, smiling lazily. 'To have such pretty toys, and to refuse to share them. Well, those who will not play nicely with others must be punished, for their own good. Do you really think you can defy me, little Drood?'

'Thought I'd give it a bloody good try,' I said.

'We have you,' said Queen Mab. 'And so we have your torc, as well as his. You can either present them to us of your own free will, and know our gratitude; or we will take them from your broken body. And from these torcs we shall learn to make more. Enough to equip an army of elves. And then we shall lead our people home, through the unsuspected door, and take back what was ours from the treacherous little creatures that currently infest it. There shall be blood and horror and killing beyond your capacity to imagine, little Drood. And all because of you – because you came here and brought us what we need—'

She broke off as I laughed at her. 'Not going to happen,' I said cheerfully. 'The source that powers our torcs and our armour resides with the Droods, and answers only to us. It likes us. It would never work for such as you. It has much better taste than that.'

'Merely a suggestion,' murmured Walker. 'Let's not antagonise the incredibly powerful and psychotic Queen of all the Elves.'

'Hell with that,' I said, glaring up at the Queen. 'Listen to me, Mab. No one threatens Humanity and gets away with it as long as the Droods still stand. And we still stand, despite the years you've been away. Now you can apologise to me, or I can drag you off that throne and make you kneel to me. Your choice.'

'You underestimate us, little Drood,' Queen Mab said calmly. 'Your small and limited kind always did. There is nothing our sciences and magics cannot duplicate, given time. And we have nothing but time. Whatever your source is, we shall bind it to our will and make it ours. Still, it was good of you to confirm the existence of this source, separate and distinct from the dreaded Droods. We had reason to suspect its nature, but no proof until now. Makes our planning so much easier. For if we have this source, what do we need the Droods for?'

'Any weapon is only as good as the one who wields it,' I said. 'It's not the armour, but who's inside it.'

'Well, you would say that, wouldn't you?' said Queen Mab. 'Now inform us of the true nature and extent of this source.'

'I don't think so. That's Drood business.'

'Then we shall take first the truth and then the torcs from your screaming shell,' said Queen Mab. 'We shall have such fun, tearing the secrets from you and breaking your spirit, bit by bit.'

'You proceed from a false assumption, Your Majesty,' said Honey. I was so caught up in the moment I'd actually forgotten she and the others were with me, and it made me feel a little better to know I wasn't alone in this.

'You tell her, Honey,' I said, hoping she could buy me time to think of something. Anything.

'You would not like the Earth as it is these days, Your Majesty,' Honey said smoothly. 'You wouldn't recognise the old place, after all we've done to it. It's very ... normal, now. Very sane and reasonable. All science, with magic forced into the shadows and the nooks and crannies. The Earth has changed and evolved, like Humanity. Whereas you and your people, Your Majesty, haven't. There's no place for you in our world any more. You're better off here. Really.'

'Speak again, little thing, and we will change you into something amusing,' said Queen Mab. 'We speak only to the Drood, and only then because his family is bound to us, and us to them.'

'And because you're still afraid of my family,' I said. 'That hasn't changed. Stay here, Mab. Where you're safe.'

She leaned suddenly forward, a movement as unexpected as a statue bending in two. Her great head came down to glare at me, and it was all I could do to keep from falling back. Up close, her golden eyes blazed like the sun.

'You killed my Blue,' she said, in a voice soft and implacable as death. 'He wasn't much. A half-breed, born of taboo. But he had courage, and we liked his style. The only elf ever to trick his way into the stronghold of the Droods, win their trust and steal a torc. Not for himself, but for us. That we might return in glory again. We would have raised him high in our regard, forgetting the taint in his blood, but he insisted on going back alone to your world to play one last game. We couldn't say no. It meant so much to him, to prove his worth in your world as well as ours. And you killed him for it.'

'I didn't kill him,' I said. 'I was his friend. A real friend; not like you. I valued him for who he was, not for what he could bring to the table. I sent you his body as a sign of respect. To him, as well as to you.'

'Not good enough, elf-killer. There are many other elf lords and ladies in good standing with this court dead by your hand, lost to your unnatural Drood weapons. Did you even bother to learn the names of those you killed? They had noble names and mighty lineages, their lives and deeds and accomplishments were the things of legend. And you murdered them. Their spilled blood calls out for revenge, and we are minded to have it.'

I deliberately turned my back on her and looked over the ranks of elves lined up in the Unseeli court. They all had some kind of weapon in their hands and every single one of them was smiling, anticipating suffering and slaughter – food and drink to elven kind. An old story, where elves and humans were concerned; but unfortunately for them, I wasn't playing by the old rules. Honey stepped away, to give herself room to work. The shimmering crystal weapon was in her hands. Walker leaned casually on his umbrella, beaming happily about him, apparently completely unconcerned, as though he knew something no one else did. And perhaps he did; this was Walker, after all. And Peter King ... was looking at me. He didn't seem especially concerned or scared, just interested to see what I was going to do.

I turned back to Queen Mab. 'You've been gone so long you've forgotten the first rule of the universe. Don't mess with the Droods.'

I concentrated, and my armour glowed and glared like an angry golden flame. Razor-sharp blades rose out of my armoured arms and legs, thick spikes protruding from my knuckles. My featureless face mask became a savage demonic visage, topped with curling horns. Strange exotic weapons burst out of my back on long golden streamers, covering the elves in their ranks, and rose up over my shoulders to threaten Queen Mab on her Ivory Throne. This was the battleform the Deathstalker had taught me to make from the malleable strange armour of my new torc. I hadn't had time to perfect it before the War with the Hungry Gods was over, but I'd spent a lot of time working on it since.

The elves stood very still. This was a new thing; and the elves have always been cautious of change. They don't know how to react to new things.

'Meet the new boss, even more of a bastard than the old boss,' I said to Queen Mab, my voice amplified to a deafening roar, filling the whole vast chamber. Honey and the others actually flinched away from me, and Queen Mab sat back on her throne.

'You dare to threaten us, in our own court, in our own land?' she said. But she didn't sound nearly as certain as she had before.

'Why not?' I said. 'Who are you?'

'What are you?' whispered the Herald. 'What have the Droods become?'

'Shamans,' I said. 'Protectors of the tribes of Man. Threaten Humanity, and you threaten us. Threaten one of us, and the whole family stands ready to go to war. Is that what you want, Queen Mab? War in the Sundered Lands between your people and mine? To throw away your word and your honour and everything you've recovered here, in a quest for torcs you couldn't use and a world you couldn't live in? Is that what you want?'

'No,' said Queen Mab, slowly and reluctantly. 'But speak not to us of honour, Drood. Your family is corrupt, rotten from within, riddled with traitors. We have heard this, even here.'

'We're cleaning house,' I said. 'And then let the worlds tremble, and all that lives beware.'

I allowed my armour to return to its usual smooth and gleaming human form, blades and spikes and weapons sinking smoothly into the golden surface. My devil's face had become a featureless mask again. Maintaining the battleform took a Hell of a lot out of me, so much that I'd never been able to use it in training for more than a few minutes; but of course Queen Mab didn't know that.

'We're leaving now,' I said. 'We've learned what we needed to know. Open the door for us, assist our departure, and then close the door and seal it shut behind us. My people will check, at regular intervals, to make sure it stays closed.'

'Why should we assist you, in even the smallest of ways?' said Queen Mab. It was meant to be a threat, but it sounded more like the sullen sulky tones of a disappointed child.

'Well, put it this way,' I said. 'You wouldn't want us to stick around and spoil the rest of your day, would you?'

'Go,' said Queen Mab.

We sailed the *Hope Street* through the green mists, back through the gateway to our own world, and no one tried to stop us. We cheered as the green mists fell away, dissipating rapidly to reveal a reassuringly normal sea and sky. We took great lungfuls of sharp fresh salt sea air, and laughed, and clapped each other on the back. Honey jumped up and down at the wheel, and then poured on the speed, putting as much space as possible between us and the gateway; just in case.

'I don't believe it!' she said. 'You stared down Queen Mab! You went eyeball to eyeball with the Queen Bitch Psycho herself, and she blinked first!'

'I have to say I'm impressed,' said Walker, reclining comfortably in his leather chair. 'To see elves back down, confronted by nothing more than words and nerve, is unprecedented. Were you bluffing, Eddie?'

'I'll never tell,' I said, letting the sea breeze flow soothingly over my unarmoured face. It felt good, natural . . . everything the Sundered Lands were not.

'But no, really: how did you get away with it?' said Honey.

I sighed, suddenly tired. 'Because the elves are not what they were. They're finally getting old. Couldn't you feel it? In the air, in the land, in the ships and in the buildings? Time is finally catching up with them.'

'But they're . . . if not immortal, then near as damnit,' said Walker.

'Did you see any children there?' I said. 'Any signs of children? The elves are proud of their rare offspring, and never miss a chance to show them off. And we didn't see a single child anywhere, in the whole city. I can't prove it, but I can feel it in my bones: the elves we saw today are all the elves there are, now. I think they stopped breeding completely when they left our world. That's why they're so desperate to return. Because they're dying out, in their splendid sterile new land. And it's a shame.'

'A shame?' said Honey, actually turning round from the steering wheel to look at me.

'Yes,' I said. 'Because then there would be one less wonder in the universe.'

Walker nodded slowly. 'They are very beautiful. And you can't have the rose without the thorns.' He stopped suddenly, and looked around. 'Where's Peter?'

We searched the boat from stem to stern, but he wasn't on it. I couldn't believe I hadn't noticed it before, but Peter had not returned with the rest of us. We reconvened in the cabin, and studied each other soberly as the *Hope Street* drew steadily closer to the Philadelphia docks.

'Did we leave him behind?' said Honey. 'We couldn't have left him behind in the Elven Lands! We would have noticed!'

'Would we?' I said. 'When did you last see him? Did you see him get on board before we left? I thought he was with us, but I had my mind on other things – like a last-minute attack from a spiteful elven Queen.'

'Maybe Mab kept him,' said Walker. 'As punishment, for your insolence to her.' His mouth compressed, and he stood very straight.

'Turn this boat around. We have to go back. We can't leave him there.'

'We can't go back,' I said. 'The elves sealed the doorway behind us, remember? That was the deal.'

'We don't know he's there,' said Honey. 'He could have disappeared anywhere.'

'And he has his teleport bracelet,' I said. 'He could simply turn up at the next location.'

'If it works in the Sundered Lands,' said Walker. 'We have to go back! There are other ways, other entrances! We can't leave him in their hands!'

'No!' I said, with such force that both of them looked at me sharply. I made myself sound calm and reasonable. 'If they've got Peter – and that's *if*, we don't know – they'll be waiting for us. He'll be the bait in a trap. We'd have to force our way in past strongly defended doorways, and that would take all the resources and most of the manpower of the Drood family. It would mean war between the Fae and the Droods, with the fate of Humanity hanging in the balance. I won't risk that on an "if".'

'What else could have happened to Peter?' said Honey.

I looked at her steadily. 'You could have killed him. Or Walker. While my attention was distracted. Stuck a knife between his ribs and tipped him over the side. In the thick green mists, no one would have seen or suspected anything.'

'How can you say that?' said Honey.

'Someone killed Katt and Blue,' I said, 'and may have tried to kill Walker in Tunguska. If he's to be believed.'

'You could have killed the others,' said Walker. He sounded quite reasonable, not at all accusing. 'You could have killed Peter. You're a Drood. That's what Droods do.'

'Any one of us could be the killer,' I said. 'There can be only one to return for the prize, remember? And we all want that prize so very badly.'

For a long while, no one said anything. The Philadelphia docks were looming up before us. Walker stirred suddenly.

'What are we going to tell his grandfather?'

'Alexander King set the rules for his precious game,' said Honey.

'And he was the one who pushed his grandson into the game in the first place.'

'I shall miss Peter,' said Walker. 'Or at any rate, I shall miss his exceedingly useful phone camera. I mean, without it we have no direct proof of what happened to the USS *Eldridge*.'

'Then it's as well I had the foresight to pick Peter's pocket on our way to the boat,' I said, holding up the phone camera.

CHAPTER EIGHT
Blood and horror

It all went bad so quickly.

We arrived at our last destination in a blaze of bright sunshine, to the sound of happy laughter. We were standing in the middle of a crowded main street, surrounded by people strolling back and forth chatting pleasantly to each other and paying the three of us no attention at all. Which was . . . odd. The air was hot and dry, and the people passing by stirred up low clouds of dust from the sidewalks. But everyone seemed in a good mood, and well under the influence of the holiday spirit. Walker and Honey and I waited for a while, to see if Peter might teleport in to join us; but he didn't.

'Very well,' Walker said finally. 'Where are we this time?'

Honey indicated a large sign on the other side of the street, and we studied it in silence. Underneath a bright and cheerful cartoon of a Grey alien leaning out of the top of a flying saucer was the oversized greeting 'Welcome to Roswell! The UFO town!'

'Oh, no,' said Walker.

'The first person to use phrases like "Out of this world" or "Far out!" gets a severe slapping,' said Honey.

'Oh, come on,' I said. 'This is it? Really? The climax and finale of the great game? Bloody *Roswell*? It's a joke! There's no mystery here, and never was; just a tall tale that got out of control. My family has been monitoring alien visitors to this world for hundreds of years. If anything had actually happened here, I'd know about it.'

'There must be something worth investigating, or Alexander King wouldn't have sent us,' said Honey.

'Interesting,' murmured Walker. 'We appeared here out of nowhere, right in the middle of a busy shopping centre, but so far no one has batted an eye. In fact, no one is paying us any attention,

254

except to walk around us. So either this particular crowd has a lot on its mind, or—'

'Or what?' said Honey.

'Damned if I know,' said Walker. 'If I didn't know better, I'd say someone was running an avoidance field.'

'No one knew we were coming here,' said Honey.

'Alexander King knew,' I said. 'Maybe he's trying to help.'

'He never helped before,' said Walker. 'What could there be in Roswell that the Independent Agent thought we might finally need assistance?'

'Roswell,' I said disgustedly. 'When my family finds out I was here, they'll laugh themselves sick.'

'I take it everyone knows the basis of the legend?' said Honey. 'On July eighth 1947, outside the small town of Roswell, New Mexico, a farmer found strange metallic objects scattered across his field. He couldn't identify them, so he brought them into town. The Air Force base informed the local newspaper that they were the remains of a crashed flying saucer. The local radio station wasted no time in spreading the news to an excited world . . . at which point the Air Force slammed on the brakes and went into reverse. Swore blind it was the remains of a crashed weather balloon. End of story.'

'Except,' I said, not to be left out, 'thirty years later, people started saying it was a cover-up. The Air Force admitted the weather balloon stuff was a lie, but the explanations they've come up with since have proved equally flawed. All of which has probably nothing to do with flying saucers and a Hell of a lot more to do with the fact that the 509th Bomb Group was stationed outside Roswell, the only bombing command authorised to carry nuclear bombs at that time. Hardly surprising they didn't want the world's attention anywhere near them. Especially if they were carrying out missions the public weren't supposed to know about.'

'It is interesting how the legend has continued to change and mutate down the years,' said Walker. 'Everything from crashed UFOs with alien bodies scattered over the mesa, to alien autopsy films, to a really screwed up First Contact. The last version I heard talked about the direct downloading of an alien consciousness from a higher dimension. Absurd.'

'Oh, sure,' I said. 'Utterly absurd.'

'I watched that alien autopsy film,' said Honey. 'Never saw anything so obviously fake-looking in my life.'

'Right,' I said. 'Alien autopsies don't look anything like that.'

Walker and Honey looked at me for a long moment.

'Moving forward,' said Walker, turning to Honey. 'You'd know, if anyone, what's going on here, so . . . what's going on here?'

'Not a damned thing, as far as I know,' said Honey. 'Though admittedly, if it was anything really important, it would be discussed on a much higher level than I have access to. I know what I need to know, but I don't need to know everything. On the other hand . . . you're right, Eddie. People like us – if there was anything to the legend, we'd have heard *something*.'

'So why are we here?' I said. 'What mystery are we supposed to investigate?'

'Beats the Hell out of me,' said Honey.

'Why don't you use that frankly rather disturbing computer implant in your head, and phone home?' said Walker. 'Ask your higher echelons at Langley if anything of interest has happened here recently.'

Honey's face went blank for a moment, and then she scowled heavily. 'The signal's jammed. Again. I can't get through . . . Eddie?'

I reached out to my family through my torc . . . and there was nobody there.

'You too?' said Honey. 'Cut off *again*? That shouldn't be possible.'

'Can't be a coincidence,' I said. 'Someone here doesn't want us talking with anyone outside Roswell. Someone . . . or something.'

'Maybe something's due to happen here,' said Honey. 'Something important, or significant, and somebody doesn't want to risk us calling in reinforcements.'

'The nearest Drood field agent is in Texas,' I said. 'Do your people have anyone useful closer than that?'

'Not that I know of. Besides, this would be FBI business and the Company has never get on well with the Bureau.'

'Why don't you try Peter's mobile phone?' Walker said reasonably. 'See if it's just the two of you who've been jammed, or whether it's more general.'

I tried Peter's phone. Couldn't get a signal. We walked down the street till we found a public pay phone, and tried that. Nothing but dead air; not even a hiss of static. I put the phone back, and we looked at one another.

'I would be willing to wager good money that the whole town is like this,' said Walker. 'Someone (or something, yes, Eddie), has gone to great lengths to isolate Roswell from the outside world. So why hasn't anyone else here noticed? Why has no one raised a fuss?'

'Look around you,' said Honey. 'Roswell is a tourist town. Most of these people are tourists. Probably haven't a clue anything unusual is going on.'

'And the local people?' said Walker.

'That's what makes this interesting,' I said. 'They might be keeping quiet so as not to scare off the tourists, or— Actually, I don't have an *or*. Something's definitely happening here, and we need to investigate.'

'I don't know.' Honey looked around her, her face cold and thoughtful. 'What if this is just a distraction? The Independent Agent sent us here to solve the mystery of Roswell. We go back without that specific information, we could forfeit the prize. And I have come too far, and been through too much, to miss out on that now.'

'She has a point,' Walker said to me. 'We're here for a specific purpose, and nothing can be allowed to interfere with that. Alexander King's hoarded secrets are of vital importance to the world. They must not be allowed to fall into the wrong hands.'

'He chose the time and place of our arrival,' I said. 'So what's happening here, or about to happen, must be significant.' And then I stopped dead, as I suddenly made a connection. 'They're all significant! All five locations we've been to! Remember the photos and trophies we saw at Place Gloria? Scenes of the Independent Agent's most important cases? We've been following in his footprints. He's been here before us!'

Honey and Walker both nodded. 'So,' said Walker, 'are we reliving his past triumphs or making up for his greatest failures? Is that the point of the game? That only the agent who could get to the truth, where he failed, would be worthy to replace him, and have access to his treasure?'

'Let's take a look around,' said Honey. 'Get the lay of the land. See what's really going on here.'

'Okay,' I said. 'Hey! Let's follow that gaudily painted mini van with the four kids and the over-sized dog. They look like they'd know a mystery when they saw it.'

'You really do get on my tits sometimes, Eddie,' said Honey.

Roswell, not surprisingly, was something of a tourist trap. Far too many of the shops and stores we passed were dedicated to offloading over-priced UFO junk on gullible tourists, all of it linked to one or other of the many prevailing Roswell myths. And the happy families swarming through the packed streets ate it up with spoons. One man sold three-foot-tall balloons shaped like cartoonish Grey aliens. A man and a woman in reptiloid costumes handed out leaflets headed 'Impeach David Icke!' Plugging their new book, apparently. A towering statue of a Grey alien bestowed a fatuous smile on passersby, and blessed them with a peace sign. (Boy, had they got that one wrong. I wouldn't turn my back on a Grey unless I had my armour on.) Someone had graffitied the base of the statue: 'ET was a fink!'

A lot of the tourists were wearing Star Trek costumes, original and Next Generation. I couldn't help but feel there should be a strict weight limit enforced on people who wear skin-tight costumes. Lycra isn't meant to stretch that far.

We passed by an entire restaurant in the shape of a flying saucer. Outside the front door a full-sized replica of Robby the Robot recited the day's specials in his roboty voice. A DVD shop had a poster in its window proudly proclaiming the imminent arrival of a new big-budget remake of *The Starlost*, directed by Harlan Ellison, starring Laurence Fishburne and Paris Hilton. Even more distressing was that many stores were given over to that crystal-channelling, angel-worshipping, flower-aromatherapy New Age bullshit, all of it priced through the ceiling. I sometimes feel people should be required to sit a mandatory IQ test before they're allowed into places like that.

I vented some of this to Walker, who nodded and said 'Angels!' in a rather grim tone of voice. I didn't press him. I didn't think I wanted to know.

We finally stopped beneath a large sign from the Roswell Chamber of Commerce, bearing the invitation: 'Hey Space People! Come On Down And Be Friendly! You're Sure Of A Welcome Here!' Stephen Spielberg's got a lot to answer for. Never met an alien yet that was prepared to share the secrets of the universe with us. Mostly they see our world as real estate – once they've got rid of the inconvenient species currently inhabiting it. And don't even get me started on the ones who come here on sex trade cruises.

A television crew was doing a vox populi, stopping passersby and asking them fatuous questions for the local news channel. The interviewer's hair had been teased and sprayed to within an inch of its life, and her teeth were blindingly bright. It was the usual fluff, with lots of bad puns and jokes about illegal aliens. I did consider asking them if they'd seen or heard anything unusual, but none of them looked like they'd know a real news story if they fell over it.

The three of us gave the camera crew a wide berth, and wandered on through the town. People had finally started to notice us, but in a weird kind of way. They'd glance at us, then look away, and then stare openly when they thought we weren't looking; as though they thought they recognised us, but couldn't quite place us. They didn't seem startled or disturbed . . . just intrigued. Honey started to get a bit irritated.

'I am a CIA agent!' she said huffily, in a voice that was perhaps a little too loud and carrying. 'I am not supposed to be noticed!'

'Maybe they think you're a supermodel,' Walker said generously.

'It's the Elven Lands,' I explained. 'Some of their glamour rubbed off on us. Don't worry – it won't last long.'

'I've always wanted to be glamorous,' said Walker a bit wistfully.

'I don't like being so visible,' muttered Honey.

'Relax,' I said. 'They're not seeing us, only the glamour. Probably think we're film stars or local celebrities, or someone they've seen on a reality show. If anyone comes up and asks for an autograph, glare haughtily at them and brush them aside, and they'll go away quite happy.'

'Why did you steal Peter's phone?' Walker said abruptly.

I'd been considering that myself. 'I don't know,' I admitted. 'It was an impulse, done as soon as thought. I can't help wondering if some outside influence nudged my thoughts, for good or mischief. Can't say I regret it, though. I don't trust Peter. Too quiet, too watchful. Always hanging back and doing his best never to get directly involved. And he does seem to know rather more about our weird world than someone of his supposed background should.

'You think he's a ringer,' said Honey. 'Planted on us to report to his grandfather. The spy within.'

'Let's just say . . . I wasn't comfortable with Peter having the only hard evidence of all we've discovered,' I said.

'And now he's gone,' said Walker. 'I always knew you Droods could be ruthless on occasion.'

'Have you checked the phone's camera files,' said Honey, 'to make sure it really does hold the proof Peter said it did?'

'Not yet,' I said. 'And I have to wonder whether he'd gathered any evidence of our trip to the Sundered Lands. I'm not even sure our technology would work in a place like that.'

'The boat worked,' said Honey.

'True.' I looked at Honey, and then at Walker. 'Did either of you see Peter use his camera in the Fae Court?'

'Can't say I did,' said Honey. 'But we were somewhat preoccupied at the time.'

'So we might not have any evidence of the elves' involvement with the USS *Eldridge*?' said Walker.

I weighed the phone in my hand. 'Not necessarily. And . . . I'm reluctant to try and access any files on this without checking it over thoroughly first. Peter was the Independent Agent's grandson. No knowing what kind of booby traps he built in to protect his data.'

'We could always go back to the Elven Lands and ask them to pose for photos,' said Honey.

'Let's not,' said Walker. 'I'm more concerned about what Alexander King might say if we don't have any hard evidence to back up our stories.'

'What's this *we* stuff, paleface?' said Honey. 'There can be only one, remember? The CIA didn't send me on this mission to share the spoils with anyone else.'

'We started out with six, and now we are three,' I said. 'Wouldn't take a lot now, to whittle us down to one. Treachery and back-stabbing have always been a recognised part of the spy's trade.'

'Sometimes literally,' said Honey. 'Where were you, Eddie, when Katt and Blue died? Or when my submersible was sabotaged, and I nearly died?'

'I saved your life,' I said.

'Good misdirection,' said Honey. 'How better to make me trust you?'

'We could still be four,' said Walker. 'Peter might turn up.'

'Perhaps,' said Honey. She looked at me for a long moment. 'Keep a close watch on that phone, Eddie. I'd hate for it to go ... missing.'

'Right,' said Walker. 'A tourist trap like this is bound to be lousy with pickpockets.'

Honey sniffed loudly. 'If I find someone else's hand in my pockets, I'll tie their fingers in a knot.'

I smiled, perhaps a little complacently. 'No one steals from a Drood and lives to boast of it.'

'The Blue Fairy stole a torc from you,' said Walker. 'Is that why you killed him?'

I turned to face him, slowly and deliberately, but to his credit, he didn't flinch.

'Is that an accusation?'

'Not yet,' said Walker.

'You're sure someone killed them?' said Honey. 'No way it could have been chance?'

'I don't believe in chance,' said Walker. 'Not where professionals like us are concerned. And especially considering someone tried to kill me in Tunguska.'

'So you say,' I said.

'Well, quite,' said Walker.

'We have business to attend to,' Honey said firmly. 'Starting with working out exactly what that business is. Everything else can wait.'

'Yes,' I said. 'It can wait.'

'For now,' said Walker.

'Men ...' said Honey. 'Why don't you just get them out and wave them at each other?'

We walked on through the town, taking in the sights, hoping for a glimpse of something significant. The sun blazed fiercely in a clear blue sky, not a hint of a cloud in sight and not a whisper of a breeze to take the edge off the increasingly uncomfortable hot dry air. And, still, tourists everywhere: large, red-faced happy souls in colourful outfits with not a care in the world … or any sense of danger, apparently.

'I may be wrong about this,' Walker said quietly, 'but I rather think we're being followed.'

We stopped, looked into a shop window full of cute little stuffed aliens, and then casually turned and looked about us, as though wondering where to go next. I let my gaze drift easily back and forth, but with so many people milling about it was hard to spot anything unusual.

'I don't see anyone,' I said. 'And I'm pretty good at identifying tails.'

'I run the Nightside,' said Walker. 'You don't last long in the Nightside without developing especially good survival instincts. There's someone out there; and they've been following us for at least five, maybe ten, minutes.'

'I don't see anyone,' said Honey. 'But I do feel … something.'

We walked back the way we'd come, darting in and out of shops, using front and rear entrances, doubling back and forth and using shop windows as mirrors … all the usual tactics for surprising a tail into betraying himself. And not a glimpse of anyone anywhere doing anything they shouldn't. But now I was definitely getting that prickly feeling at the back of my neck, of being watched by unseen eyes. Someone was out there, shadowing our every move; someone really good at what they were doing.

A professional; like us.

'Who knows we're here?' Honey said finally. 'Who knows who we are? Hell, even we didn't know we were coming till we were here!'

'Alexander King knew,' I said. 'He could have arranged for word to get out, for any number of reasons. And we have been making waves. We were bound to attract attention sooner or later from any number of groups or organisations, or even certain powerful individuals. Damn, this is creepy. I spy on people; I don't get spied on.'

'Use the Sight,' said Walker.

'No,' I said immediately. 'If he's as good as I think he is, and he must be really bloody good if he can hide himself from me, he'll detect it the moment I raise my Sight. And then he'll know for sure he's been spotted.'

'He must know that now, the way we've been acting,' said Honey.

'No,' I said. 'He may suspect, but he doesn't know. And as long as he's still not sure, we've got the upper hand.'

'Perhaps,' said Walker. 'Whoever they are, they must represent whoever it is that's responsible for whatever's happening here ... or what's scheduled to happen. God, I hate sentences like that. But consider this: if you were setting up a major operation in a small town, and all of a sudden you happened to notice a Drood, a CIA agent and the man who runs the Nightside wandering around taking an interest in things ... You'd want to know more about them, wouldn't you?'

'Let him watch,' I said. 'Let him follow. He can't do anything without revealing himself, and if he's stupid enough to do that, I will then quite happily bounce the bugger off the nearest wall and ask him pointed questions.'

'Sounds like a plan to me,' said Honey.

Our attention was attracted by a small group of tourists gathered in front of a shop window. They seemed more than usually excited. We strolled over to join them, and found they were watching a news programme on a television set in the window. The local news anchor, a small man in a large suit, with a deep voice and an obvious toupee, was getting quite excited over the story that was coming in through his teleprompter.

'We've heard about cattle mutilations,' he said, his voice only slightly muffled by the shop window, 'cattle found dead of no obvious cause, with bits missing and numerous incisions made with almost surgical skill. Various people (and others) have been blamed for these: aliens, mad scientists, government agencies backed by their ubiquitous black helicopters, even Devil worshippers and extreme vegetarians. But events right here at Roswell have now taken a new and disturbing turn.'

I looked at Honey. 'Black helicopters?'

'Nothing to do with me,' she said. 'Cattle mutilations are *so* beneath us. We'd never be involved in anything that messy and obvious.'

She broke off as several people in the crowd shushed her, and we turned our attention back to the news anchor.

'Early this morning, seven dead and mutilated cattle were discovered on the ranch of well-known local businessman Jim Thomerson, some twenty miles outside of Roswell,' he said. 'In each case, major organs were missing, removed from the carcasses with professional skill. Strange burn marks were noted on the ground near the dead cattle ... but no other signs to show how the attackers came and went, according to local law enforcement officials. Disturbing enough, you might think, but the breaking news is that Jim Thomerson himself has been found dead and mutilated, not far from his cattle. His body has been brought into town, to the new morgue, for forensic examination.'

The news anchor forced a smile for the camera. 'Have our little Grey friends finally gone too far? We hope to be able to show you actual photos from the crime scene later this evening. We must warn you that these photos are likely to be of a graphic nature. Viewer discretion is advised.'

'Translation: everyone gather round the set, this is going to be good!' said Honey. 'Yes, I know; shush.'

And then the television screen went blank. The four other sets in the window, that had been showing other channels with the sound turned down, also went dead. The crowd stirred nervously, broke up into couples and families, and drifted away, chattering animatedly. Walker and Honey and I looked at each other.

'This is weird,' said Honey. '*All* the local stations going off the air at the same time? If it was a technical thing, the screens would be showing the usual variations on *Normal service will be resumed as soon as possible*, accompanied by lots of be-happy-don't-worry-music. No, those broadcasts are being jammed, like ours. Which, if nothing else, must take a Hell of a lot of power. Someone doesn't want this news getting out of Roswell.'

'So it's not only our comms that have been targeted,' I said. 'The whole town's been cut off from the outside world. Isolated. So whatever's coming, or maybe even already started, no one from outside will know till it's over and too late to do anything.'

'But even so, cattle mutilations?' said Walker. 'They're just rural myths, aren't they?'

'Not when it starts happening to people,' I said. 'I think we have to assume this is the mystery we were sent here to investigate.'

'King knew in advance this was going to happen?' said Walker.

'Who better?' said Honey. 'The man was and is seriously connected.'

'That farmer's body should have got here by now,' said Walker. 'I think it behoves us to visit this new morgue and take a look for ourselves.'

'I love it when you use words like "behove",' I said. 'Oh please, Walker, teach me to talk proper like you, so I can sound like a real agent.'

'Shut up, Eddie,' said Walker.

'We can go take a look,' said Honey. 'And then you can make the poor guy sit up on his slab and tell us what happened. Right, Walker?'

'*It was just the one time!*' said Walker. 'I do wish everyone would stop going on about it!'

'Any idea where the local morgue might be?' I said. 'It's not the kind of thing you can go up and ask complete strangers. They tend to look at you funny.'

'Maybe we should find someone in local law enforcement,' said Walker.

'And maybe you two should try living in the twenty-first century with the rest of us,' Honey said scathingly. 'We passed a cyber café a few blocks back.'

It didn't take long to log in on the town site, call up a map and locate the new morgue. It wasn't that far from where we were. Walker and I carefully didn't look at each other. Honey looked decidedly smug as she led us out of the cyber café.

'What's the matter, Walker? Don't you have computers in the Nightside?'

'Of course,' he said stiffly. 'Some of my best friends are artificial.'

'Somehow that doesn't surprise me,' said Honey.

The morgue was a calm and civilised structure, very modern and stylish and not at all threatening. Honey bluffed her way in with fake Homeland Security ID that she just happened to have about her person, while Walker and I did our best to look properly mean and hard and American. No one gave us any trouble. The locals were only too happy to have someone experienced on hand to come in and take over. A deputy carrying too much weight, topped off with a hat far too small for his head, led us through the outer offices to the morgue at the back of the building. People watched us pass with wide eyes, and spooked, scared expressions. It was one thing to make your living exploiting alien visitations, and quite another to have them turn up in your back yard with chainsaws and scalpels, intent on playing doctor. The deputy became more nervous the closer he got to the morgue. He was sweating profusely, despite the arctic air conditioning, and jumped at every sudden sound.

'All communications systems are down,' he said abruptly. 'Can't get a word in or out. You folks know anything about that?'

'Sorry,' said Honey, in her best brisk and professional voice. 'Information only on a need-to-know-basis. You understand how it is.'

'Oh sure, sure.' The deputy actually relaxed a little in the presence of such obvious authority and competence. 'Good to have some-one here who knows what they're doing. We're mostly part-timers. Sheriff's off sick with his allergies, and Doc Stern's busy with a car wreck on the other side of town. This is . . . a Hell of a sight more than I signed on for.' He looked at Honey sharply. 'Did your people know this was going to happen? Is that why you're here?'

'It's our job to know about things like this,' said Honey. 'Has there been any panic in the town? Any rush to get out of Roswell?'

'Well, no,' said the deputy, frowning heavily. 'Everyone here was expecting the tourists to get in their cars and head for the hills, once the news got out, with the townsfolk right behind them, but every-one's being real calm about it. Doesn't make a blind bit of sense . . . I'd leave, if I had anyone halfway competent to put in charge, but it doesn't seem right to go off and leave old Jim Thomerson lying there in the morgue. Not . . . respectful. Here, this is it.'

He showed us a large reinforced steel door with a keypad lock. More security than I'd expected. We waited impatiently while the deputy keyed in the six-digit number with great concentration.

'I don't normally get back here much,' he said. 'Only the sheriff and the doc ever come in here. Doc'll be back as soon as he can. You want me to stick around?'

'No,' said Honey. 'Return to your post, Deputy. We'll handle it from here. And, Deputy: no one comes here till we're done, and no one says anything to anyone. Got it?'

'Yes, ma'am,' said the deputy. He hurried away, not looking back.

'Potentially bright young fellow, I thought,' said Walker.

We went into the morgue, shutting the door behind us. It was big – there was room for several bodies – with bright lights and immaculate gleaming walls.

'This – is not normal for a small town,' said Honey. 'Maybe ten times larger than it should be. This is more the kind of thing you'd expect to find in a major city. Makes me wonder if they might have had to contend with . . . unusual situations before.'

'This was custom made,' said Walker. 'By someone expecting trouble.'

'Maybe something did happen here, back in the day, ' said Honey.

'And no one told you,' said Walker. 'Shame on them.'

'Never mind that,' I said. 'Look! They brought one of the bloody cows in here!'

Two mortuary slabs had been pushed together on the far side of the room, and a cow was lying across them, on its side. The four legs stuck stiffly out over the edge of the slab. We gathered round the carcass. The cow had been sliced open the whole length of its underside, from throat to udder. The sides of the belly had been pulled out and pinned back, to reveal the whole interior had been . . . rummaged through. Some organs were missing, others had been cut open and had pieces removed, still others had been moved around, rearranged. Large holes had been drilled through the hide and the head, to no obvious purpose. Both eyes were gone, and all the top teeth had been neatly extracted. The tongue had been sliced in half, lengthwise, and then left in place. One stiff leg had been dissected to show the nerves, another to show the muscles.

'Interesting,' said Walker, leaning in close for a better look.

'Extremely,' said Honey, leaning right in there with him.

'Gross,' I said, staying well away. 'I want to know how they got that thing in here, through that little door?'

We looked at the distinctly human-scaled door, shrugged pretty much in unison, and turned our attention back to the cow.

'The work looks professional enough,' said Walker. 'Definitely used scalpels, rather than knives. And since there's no damage from local predators, not long ago. Some burn marks on the internal tissues. Laser drill, perhaps? But none of this work makes any sense. It's not just a dissection. I feel sure there was a definite end in mind, but I'm damned if can make out what.'

'They practically strip-mined the poor creature,' I said. 'But why take some organs, and cut up others? Why open the beast just to move things around?'

'Presumably they were curious,' said Walker. 'Perhaps ... they'd never seen a cow before.'

'What?' said Honey. 'They came all the way here with their snazzy new stardrive, but couldn't tap into our computers to get the information they needed?'

'Maybe they like to get their hands dirty,' said Walker. 'Assuming they have hands, of course.'

'Seems more to me as if they were looking for something,' I said. 'And if they didn't find it in the cow, maybe that's why they moved on to the poor bastard on that slab there.'

We moved over to look at the middle-aged man lying naked and cut open on the next mortuary slab. Jim Thomerson, farmer and well known local businessman, who happened to be in the wrong place at the wrong time, and paid for his mistake with blood and horror. We leaned in for a closer look at the terrible things that had been done to him. His injuries were similar to the cow's, but so much more disturbing for having been done to a man. Organs missing, limbs dissected, his insides rearranged ... His empty eye sockets stared accusingly at us.

'Judging by the defensive wounds on his hands and arms, he was alive when they started,' said Honey. 'Though hopefully not for long.'

'Why now?' said Walker. 'Why start doing cattle mutilations to people *now*? What's changed?'

'Obvious answer,' I said. 'These are new aliens. A species newly come to earth. I'm going to have to teach them a hard lesson: you don't come waltzing in here unless you've cleared it with the Droods first, and learned the bloody rules. Someone's going to pay for this.'

'But even so,' said Walker, 'why take some organs, but—'

'I don't know!' I said. Walker and Honey looked at me, and I lowered my voice. 'I don't know. They're aliens. They don't think like us. My family have been dealing with aliens for centuries, and we still don't have a translation device that works worth a damn. Sometimes we don't even have basic concepts in common.'

'What do you do, if you can't communicate with a species?' said Walker. 'If you can't get it to follow your rules?'

'We kill them,' I said. 'And we keep on killing them till they stop coming. What do you do in the Nightside?'

'Pretty much the same,' said Walker.

'I've had some experience with aliens,' said Honey. 'Not really my department, but all hands to the pump when the river's rising.'

'What?' said Walker.

'It was an emergency!' said Honey.' And I was the only experienced agent on the spot. I was in the Antarctic, searching through Area Fifty-two for something important that had been shipped there by error (and you'd be surprised how often that happens), when something got loose from the holding cells. I swear, I've never heard alarms like it. I had to dress up in a total environment suit and go out on the ice to hunt it. Fortunately, it didn't get far. Stupid thing made the mistake of trying to go one on one with a polar bear. Took us ages to find all the bits. And we had to stomach-pump the bear.'

'Aliens aren't always the brightest buttons in the box,' I agreed. 'Just because they're smart enough to build better toys than us doesn't mean they've got any more common sense. Or self-control. Going back a few years, something crash-landed in the middle of a London park, and then disappeared into the sewers. I was called in and was ready to go down and pull the bloody thing out when the word came to leave it be. Apparently our Outer Space Beastie was eating the sewage, along with the vermin in the tunnels. So naturally our first thought was *Result!* And we left it alone, to get on with it.

'About six months later I was called back. The alien had eaten all the sewage, all the local underground wildlife and half a dozen people sent in to investigate the situation. And it was still hungry. It started sending extensions of its nasty protoplasmic self through the man-holes to attack whatever was in the street, and up through the pipes and plumbing into people's homes. People started disappearing; and given the state of their sinks and toilets I think I know how, though I rather wish I didn't. Had a Hell of a job keeping that one out of the news. In the end, half a dozen of us entered the sewers at different points and went after the alien with molecular flame-throwers. Burned our way through the whole underground tunnel system, end to end, until there was nothing left to burn. We still run chemical and DNA checks at regular intervals, just in case.

'Took me weeks to get rid of the smell.'

Walker shrugged easily. 'The Nightside is no stranger to close encounters. Any number of aliens have come slipping in through our various timeslips, from the Past, the Future, and any number of alternate dimensions. We had some Martians turn up last year on huge metal tripods, complete with heat rays, metal claws and poisonous black smoke. Nasty, squidgy things that fed on human blood, fresh from conquering some other Earth and keen for new lands to expand into. The fools. We blew their metal legs out from under them, dragged them out of their control pods, and ate them.'

'You *ate* the Martians?' said Honey, wrinkling her perfect nose.

'Delicious,' said Walker. 'Oh, we killed them first, of course. But for a while fresh Martian delicacies were all the rage in the very best restaurants in the Nightside. Some of us have been hoping rather wistfully that the timeslip to that particular Earth will open again before stocks run out.'

'I don't know why I talk to you,' said Honey. 'You always say the most disturbing things.'

Walker smiled. 'It's the Nightside.'

'Hold everything,' I said. 'I think I've made another connection. The aliens have moved from dissecting cattle to working on people at exactly the same time as the town's communications go down. I have an awful feeling these new aliens are planning something very nasty . . . Human mutilations on a grand scale. To a whole town full of people—'

'That's a Hell of a jump, Eddie, from one dead cow and one dead farmer,' said Honey.

'But what if I'm right?' I said. 'Work as a Drood field agent long enough, you get a feel for this sort of thing.'

'You're right, Eddie,' said Walker. 'Only alien technology could black out a whole town's communications so easily, never mind Honey's and yours. But what can we do? We can't alert everyone in town with the communications down, and even if we could spread the word, what good would it do them?'

'We can get the Hell out of here!' said Honey. 'Put enough space between us and the town and our comm systems should come back on line again, and we could get some reinforcements in here.'

'*Leave?*' I said. 'Run away, and abandon the people of Roswell to their fate? To be cut open while they're still alive, like that poor bastard on the slab? By the time we got back here everyone in this town could be dead!'

'And what if you're wrong?' said Honey, sticking her face into mine. 'Imagine the mass panic once word got out! How many would get trampled underfoot, or killed in car crashes? You could end up with hundreds dead and injured, all over a conjecture!'

'I'm not wrong!' I said. 'I won't abandon these people! That's not what Droods do!'

'Have you noticed it's getting darker in here?' said Walker.

Honey and I broke off from glaring at each other, and looked around. The overhead strip lighting was blazing as fiercely as ever, but a dark and heavy gloom was seeping in from all sides, soaking up the light. A blue tinge invested the other colours in the morgue, giving everything a strange and unhealthy look. I felt heavy, drained, with even my thoughts moving more slowly than normal. My torc burned coldly round my neck, trying to warn me of something.

And then both the cow's carcass and the farmer's body burst into flames – fierce blue-tinged flames that burned with such intensity that the three of us were driven back, holding up our arms to shield our faces from the intolerable heat. The flames snapped off, as abruptly as they'd begun, and conditions in the morgue returned to normal. The slabs were completely empty, with a few ashes floating on the air above them.

'Damn,' said Honey. 'Someone really didn't want anything left behind.'

'Which would seem to imply that someone was, and probably

271

still is, looking in on us,' said Walker. 'Three unexpected new factors, endangering their planned experiment.'

'So this was a warning to us not to get involved,' said Honey.

I had to grin. 'They don't know us very well, do they?'

And then our heads snapped round as we heard steady quiet footsteps in the corridor outside the morgue. They drew steadily closer, sounding louder and heavier all the while, until finally they stopped outside the closed morgue door. We stood very still, listening. The silence stretched on and on. Until finally Honey lunged for the door, with Walker and I behind her. She hauled the door open and we spilled out into the corridor ... but there was nobody there. The corridor stretched away before us, still and silent and completely empty.

'You heard it, didn't you?' said Honey. 'He was right outside the door!'

'I heard it,' I said.

'Told you we were being followed,' said Walker.

'Those were human footsteps,' said Honey. 'Nothing alien about them. So where did he go?'

'I don't see any other exits,' said Walker.

'Could someone in Roswell know what's going to happen?' said Honey. 'Some human Judas goat, perhaps, betraying his fellow humans for thirty pieces of technology?'

'There are other organisations who might have an interest,' said Walker. 'Black Air, Vril Power, the Xarathustra Protocols? Any one of them could have chanced across evidence of what's due to happen here, and struck a deal.'

'No,' I said flatly. 'There's no organisation on this planet better informed than the Droods, when it comes to aliens. If anyone had known, it would have been my family; and I would have been told.'

'Really?' said Honey. 'The Matriarch tells you everything, does she?'

'Everything that matters,' I said.

'Yes, well,' said Honey. 'You would think that, wouldn't you?'

'Children, children,' murmured Walker. 'We have to decide what we're going to do while there's still time.'

'Less time than you think,' I said, my torc burning cold as ice. 'Brace yourselves, people. Something's coming ...'

The corridor before us changed, altered, stretched, its far end receding into the distance. The kind of corridor you could travel all your days and never reach the end. The kind of corridor you run through endlessly, in the kind of dreams you wake from in a cold sweat. A strange glow replaced the normal corridor light, intense and overpowering, a light not designed for the tolerances of the human eye. Even the air was different, tasting foul and furry in my mouth, and so thin I was half suffocating. A different kind of air, for a different kind of being. Static tingled painfully on my bare flesh, and I could hear ... something. Something scrabbling at the outsides of the corridor walls, trying to get in.

'I recognise this,' said Honey. Her voice was harsh and strained, and strangely far away. 'I know this, from abduction scenarios. An intrusion of alien elements into our world. The aliens aren't waiting for us to track them down. They're coming to us.'

'Let them come,' I said, and armoured up. Immediately I felt much better, more human, more myself. 'Stay close to me,' I said to Walker and Honey, through my featureless face mask. 'Proximity to my armour should help ground and protect you, insulate you from the effects of this alien-created environment.'

Their faces cleared quickly as they moved in close, and they both stood straight, strength and resolve rushing into their features.

'I'm even breathing easier, now I'm close to you,' said Honey. 'How does that work?'

'Do you tell me your secrets?' I said, to hide the fact I wasn't entirely sure myself. 'Just stick close, and get ready to beat the crap out of anything that isn't us.'

'Good plan,' muttered Walker.

'No one takes a Drood anywhere against his will,' I said. 'Or his companions. Walker, why are you standing behind me?'

'Because I'm not stupid,' said Walker.

'I don't hide behind people,' Honey said haughtily.

'Bet you I live longer,' said Walker.

Wild energies crackled up and down the impossibly long corridor, seething and howling. They jumped from wall to wall, fast as laser beams, snapping on and off, leaving pale green trails of ionisation hanging on the air. Malevolent forces surged forward to attack my armour. I stood my ground, Honey clinging to my golden arm, Walker right behind me. The energies raged furiously around us, discharging on the air with blinding flares and flashes; but stopped dead, balked, unable to touch or even approach my armour.

As though they were afraid of it.

Lightnings rose and fell, pressing in from this side and that, searching for some weak spot in my armour that would let them in ... but I stood firm, and suddenly the energies fell away, retreating down the corridor, fading like the memory of a bad dream. I could hear Honey and Walker's harsh breathing in the sudden silence. I warned them quietly against moving away from me. This wasn't over. I could feel it.

And then the alien appeared. No door opening in space, no teleport effects; it was just there, in front of us, no more than ten feet away. Its appearance was so sudden that Walker and Honey actually jumped a little, and if I hadn't been wearing my armour I think I might have too.

'That ... is a really ugly looking thing,' I said.

'I've never seen anything like it,' said Honey. 'Walker? You ever seen anything like that?'

'Thankfully, no. Eddie?'

'Nothing even remotely like,' I said. 'It is quite definitely not one of the fifty-three alien species currently covered by the Drood Pacts and Treaties.'

'*Fifty-three?*' said Honey. 'There are fifty-three different kinds of alien currently wandering around our world? When were you planning on telling the rest of us this?'

'Fifty-three that we know of,' I said. 'The Droods don't know everything, though never tell anyone I said that. And there are always a few species coming and going we don't have any kind of agreement with, or control over. It's a big universe, and life has taken some really strange forms out there.'

'Fifty-three ...' said Honey.

'From other worlds, other Earths, higher and lower dimensions,' I said. 'They add up. Droods protect Humanity from all outside threats.'

'All right, I'll put you up for a raise,' said Honey. 'Now *what* is *that?*'

'Haven't a clue,' I said.

We studied the alien, as it presumably studied us. It looked like a pile of snakes crushed together, or lengths of rubber tubing half melted into each other. Each separate length twisted and turned, seething and knotting together, sliding up and around and over, endlessly moving, never still for a moment. The pile was taller than a man and twice as wide, and though its extremities were constantly moving and changing, the bulk and mass stayed the same. Lengths of it melted and merged into each other, while new extensions constantly erupted from the central region. It was the colour of an oil slick on polluted water, with flashes of deep red and purple underneath; and it smelled really bad. Like something dead that had been left in the hot sun for too long. The alien's basic lack of certainty was unsettling and painful to the human eye, and the human mind. We were never meant to cope with such things. We're not ready.

Shapes began to form, on the end of long writhing tentacles. Things that might have been sensory apparatus, or even organic weapons. And then a dripping bulge rose up through the top of the squirming pile, and sprouted half a dozen human eyeballs. A pale pink cone formed beneath the eyes, wet and quivering as it dilated.

'Communication,' said the alien through the cone, in a high thin voice like metal scraping on metal. 'Speak. Identify.'

And then it waited for an answer.

'I am a Drood,' I said carefully. 'I have authority to speak to other species. To make binding agreements. Talk to me. Explain what you're doing here. What you're planning. Or steps will be taken to kick your nasty species off this planet.'

'Drood,' said the alien. 'Name. Function. Not known to us.'

'Maybe I should try,' said Honey.

'Hush,' I said.

'You are unreachable,' said the alien. 'Explain.'

'Why did you injure, kill, and ... examine the human?' I said. 'For what purpose? Explain.'

'Necessary,' said the alien. 'Don't know Drood. Don't recognise Drood authority. Don't recognise any authority. We are. We exist. We go where we must, to do what we must. We dominate our environment. All environments. Necessary; for survival. For survival of all things.'

'Is it saying what I think it's saying?' murmured Walker.

'Damned if I know,' I said. 'At least it looks like we have basic concepts in common.' I addressed the alien again. 'What brought you to this particular world? What interests you in our species? Explain.'

'Potential,' said the alien. 'Experiment. Learn. Apply.'

'Experiment?' I said. 'Why the animal, and then the human? Explain.'

'Learned all we could from the animal,' said the alien. 'Limited. Useless for our purposes. Humans are more interesting. More potential. This will be our first experiment on your kind. On this town. This Roswell. Do not be alarmed. We are here to help you. This is for your own good. Necessary. See.'

A screen appeared, floating on the air before us. And on that screen the alien showed us what it and its kind were going to do. What would happen to the people of Roswell.

Scenes from a small town, undergoing blood and horror.

People ran screaming through the streets, but it didn't save them. They ran and they hid, and some of them even fought back; and none of it did any good. They were operated on, cut open, violated and explored, by invisible scalpels in invisible hands. Unseen forces tore the people apart; unknowable and unstoppable.

Cuts appeared in human flesh, blood spraying on the empty air. The cuts widened, and invisible hands plunged inside living bodies to play with what they found there. Organs fell out of growing holes, hands fell from wrists, fingers from hands. Some bodies fell apart, cut into slices. Men and women exploded, ragged parts floating on the air to be examined by unseen eyes. Discarded offal filled the streets, and blood overflowed in the gutters.

The screaming was the worst part. Men, woman and children reduced to terrified, helpless animals screaming for help that never came.

I saw families running down the streets, pursued by horror. One man had his legs cut out from under him, just below the knee, and he tried to keep going on bloody stumps. Until something opened up his head from behind and pulled out his brains in long pink and grey streamers. A woman clung desperately to an open door as something unseen pulled doggedly at one outstretched leg. She howled like a maddened beast as her ribs were pulled out one by one, examined briefly, and then tossed aside into the blood-soaked street. I saw children—

I saw a pile of lungs assemble, one by one, next to a pile of hearts, some still feebly beating. A man sat alone, crying bloody tears from empty eye sockets. A woman screamed her mind away, over what was left of her daughter. I saw whole families reduced to their component parts by unseen surgical instruments ... Cold clinical procedures that went on and on until the screaming finally stopped, because there was no one left alive to protest.

Everyone in the town of Roswell was dead. Butchered.

The floating screen disappeared, taking its views of Hell on Earth with it. I was so angry I was shaking inside my armour. My hands clenched and unclenched helplessly. Honey clung to my arm, making small shocked noises. Walker had come forward to stand beside me. His eyes were full of a cold, dangerous rage. I stared at the alien before me. I'd never hated anything so much in all my life.

'Why?' I said, finally.

'You wouldn't understand,' said the alien. 'You can't. You're only human. It limits you. This is necessary. You claim authority in this place, Drood; you threaten the success of the experiment. Leave. All of you. Remove yourselves from Roswell before we begin in six hours. Tell everyone. First there is a town, then there is a city, then there is a world. We will do more, as we learn more. We will remake you, and your world, and when we are done you will thank us for it.'

I charged forward, my fists studded with heavy spikes, reaching for the alien. It disappeared, gone in a moment, and the corridor returned to normal. No more strange lights, no energies, no distortions of space. I stumbled to a halt, and cried out in wordless rage. I spun round and punched the nearest wall with my golden fist, hitting it because I had to hit something or go insane. I hit the wall again and again, the plaster cracking and the brick crumbling. And then I made myself stop, reining in the anger and forcing it down, storing it for later. I armoured down, and stood before the wrecked and ruined wall, breathing harshly. Walker and Honey approached me cautiously. Honey touched my face with her hand, wiping away my tears. I hadn't known I was crying.

'We have to warn the local authorities,' said Walker.

'They wouldn't listen,' I said. My throat hurt, my voice a harsh rasp. I'd been yelling at the alien all the way through its presentation, but I hadn't realised. 'Would you believe something like this, without proof? And even if we could make them believe, what good would it do? I don't think the aliens would let them leave, and no one here has anything that could defend them against unseen forces and invisible scalpels. No, it's down to us. We stand between the townspeople and the aliens. We're all there is.'

'But what about the game?' said Honey. 'What about Alexander King's prize?'

I looked at her, and she met my gaze steadily.

'How can you think about that, at a time like this?' said Walker. 'After everything we've just seen!'

'It's my job to stay calm, and focused, and concentrate on the bigger picture, on what really matters,' said Honey, her voice perfectly reasonable. 'What we saw, what the aliens are going to do . . . It's not what we're here for. I have a duty, not just to the people of one small town, but to all the people. You heard that thing: after Roswell the cities, and then the world. I don't know of anything that could stop them, and neither do you. But maybe Alexander King does. Maybe there's something in his hoarded secrets that will do the job.'

'That's not why you want his secrets,' said Walker. 'You want to win the game.'

'We were sent here to solve the old mystery of Roswell, not this new one,' said Honey. 'There's no way King could have known about this. So it is irrelevant.'

'You're scared,' I said. 'Scared of what you saw. You can't cope with something this big, this important, so you hide behind the rules of a stupid little game that doesn't matter any more. We have to stand our ground here, stop the aliens from doing this. There'll be time for games later.'

'I'm sorry,' said Honey. 'I have my orders, and my responsibilities. The Independent Agent's secrets must end up with the right people.'

'And my duty is to ensure that people like you never get their hands on the prize,' said Walker. 'You can't be trusted with it.'

'And you can?' said Honey. 'Little dictator of a little world?'

'More than you,' said Walker. He looked at me, as calm and composed as ever. 'I'm sorry, Eddie. The game must come first. We can't be distracted by . . . lesser events, no matter how disturbing.'

'Let's not jump to conclusions,' I said carefully, holding my anger in check. 'Don't be so quick to assume these aliens aren't what we're here for. Why couldn't they be the answer to the Roswell mystery? The teleport bracelets must have dropped us here and now for a reason . . . So let's stop the aliens, save the town, and take evidence of that back to Alexander King so we can claim the prize. Screw "There can only be one." We can share the information.'

'No,' said Honey, and to her credit she did sound honestly regretful. 'The mystery of Roswell is what crash-landed here in 1947. And that had nothing to do with cattle mutilations. They didn't start until much later. And none of the descriptions of the original aliens was anything like the thing we just saw.'

'Then why are these new aliens here?' I said. 'Why choose Roswell, out of all the small towns in the world?'

'Perhaps because Roswell has such strong alien connections,' said Walker. 'To make what happens here more . . . visible. An alien atrocity in this town would be reported all over the world.'

'We're not here to be heroes,' said Honey. 'We're here to be agents. To discover the answer to a specific question. That has to come first. It's the job. And Eddie, I really don't think my superiors at Langley would approve of me sharing King's secrets with anyone else. They might even call it treason. So I will do what I have to do. I know my duty.'

'So do I,' said Walker. 'You cannot be trusted with King's secrets, Honey. Or your masters. I'm not sure anyone can. So I will win the game, take the secrets, and bury them deep in the Nightside where no one will ever find them.'

'And the people of Roswell?' I said.

'There will be time for revenge later,' said Walker.

'My duty is to protect people from outside threats,' I said. 'All people, everywhere. To Hell with games, and secrets, and politics. People come first – always. Get out of my sight, both of you. Go play your precious game. And when this is over, and I've stopped the aliens and saved the town, I will come and find you and take your precious prize away from you.'

'You do what you have to,' said Honey. 'And I'll do what I have to. I hope you do defeat the aliens, Eddie. I really do.'

'Yes,' said Walker. 'I'm sorry it has to end this way, Eddie. But we must all follow duty in our own way. Good luck.'

And just like that, we went our separate ways.

I walked slowly through the crowded Roswell streets, one man in the middle of unsuspecting crowds; all of them so much dead meat unless I could come up with a plan to save them. It was hard to keep from staring into their happy, innocent faces. How could they not know how much danger they were in? Couldn't they feel the tension on the air, the first echoes of the horror that was coming, so close they could almost reach out and touch it? Of course they didn't know, didn't even suspect; they lived in their world and I lived in mine, and it was my job to keep them from ever finding out my world even existed.

Five and a half hours now, and counting . . .

I strode on more purposefully, not going anywhere in particular, full of the need to keep moving, to at least feel like I was doing something. I concentrated on this idea and that, coming up with and discarding one plan after another, scowling so hard as I thought people hurried to get out of my way. I could leave Roswell. Commandeer a car and get the Hell out of town until I was out of the aliens' communications blackout. Yell to my family for backup and support. Throw enough Droods at a problem, and any enemy will go down in flames. The Hungry Gods found that out the hard way. Of course, there was no telling how long that might take; it could be over by the time I got back. And nothing left to do but contain the situation, and make sure the aliens couldn't repeat their bloody experiment somewhere else. As Walker said, there's always time for revenge. But there was no telling what I'd run into outside town. The aliens might stop me at the town's limits and hold me there; and then there'd be no one left to stand between the people and the aliens.

I couldn't risk that.

No. My only realistic hope was to locate the aliens' base of operations, and shut them down before they could start anything. One man against an unknown number of aliens, and an unknowable amount of alien technology . . . For anyone else that would be suicide; but I was a Drood, with a Drood's armour and training. And the aliens were going to find out what that meant. So . . . think it through. If the aliens were jamming all communications going in and out of Roswell, it made sense that the jamming signal was coming from apparatus somewhere inside the town. And a jamming signal that strong would have to be pretty damned powerful, and leave its own distinctive footprint on the local electromagnetic spectrum. Shielded from detection by Earth technology, of course; but not from me.

I concentrated hard on my torc, coaxing and bludgeoning it into doing something new and different . . . until at last a long thin tendril slid up my neck from the torc to form a pair of stylish golden sunglasses over my eyes. An absolute minimum use of my armour, hopefully not enough to set off any alien detection systems. I focused my Sight through the golden strange matter over my eyes, and Saw the town of Roswell very clearly indeed. I'd never tried parts of armour before and I made a mental note to discuss this with my family when I got back. Assuming I got back, of course . . .

My augmented Sight showed me a whole new Roswell. Dark shapes drifted through the streets like animated wisps of shadow, lighting here and there on people disturbed by a vague sense of menace or unease. Elemental spirits are always drawn to potential arenas of spiritual destruction. They feed like vultures on the fiercer, more distressed emotions. On the other hand, Light People were standing and watching all through the town: scintillating light and energy bound into human form, almost abstract living things. Their appearance at a scene was both a good and a bad thing. It meant something severely dangerous was about to happen, with many lives on the line; but also that they expected some agent of good to put up a fight. I always think of the Light People as basically good-hearted supernatural sports fans. There were ghosts too, and semi-transparent memories of places past, along with other-dimensional entities and travellers just passing through. None of them mattered. I looked slowly about me, sifting through the various information streams permeating the local aether, and soon enough, there it was ... A strange alien energy broadcasting from a location right near the centre of town.

I'd found them.

I headed straight for the source of the alien signal, and people grew increasingly scarce the closer I got. In fact, the few people still on the streets seemed to be actually hurrying away. I stopped a few and asked them why; and wasn't that surprised to find they couldn't tell me. They didn't know. They just knew they weren't supposed to be there.

The source itself turned out to be something very like a giant termite mound, thirty feet tall and almost as wide, pushing up from the broken earth of a deserted back lot. There were no people here at all, the surrounding streets silent and empty. I studied the alien mound from the shadows of a side alley, my augmented Sight feeding me almost more information than I could handle. The mound itself was a strange mixture of technology and organic materials. Grown as much as made, its vast sides undulated slowly, slick and sweating, as though troubled by passing dreams. There were shadowy entrance holes all over it, set to no discernible pattern. The cracked and broken earth around the mound's base suggested it had thrust up from below, and that there might be a Hell of a lot more of it deep under the back lot. What I was Seeing could be just the tip of the alien pyramid. I watched for a long time, but nothing came out and nothing went in.

Apart from the jamming signal, the mound was also broadcasting a powerful avoidance field. More than the usual *Don't look at me, nothing to see here, move along* suggestions; this was mind manipulation, a field strong enough that people couldn't even think about the alien mound, or anything connected with it. No wonder everyone in Roswell had seemed so unnaturally calm and languid; the alien signal was virtually lobotomising them, to be sure they'd stay in place for the great experiment. Presumably the signal would be dropped once the bloodletting began; so the aliens could observe the full spectrum of human reactions to what was being done to them.

My Sight punched through the avoidance field, but I knew I couldn't risk that for long, for fear of being detected. There had to be all kinds of surveillance going on within the mound. So I grabbed as much useful information as I could in quick looks and glances, ready to shut down my Sight at a moment's notice that I'd been spotted. I couldn't See any alarms, or proximity fields, or booby traps ... Only the mound, sitting there, sick and smug and serene, like an abscess on the world. So sure of its own strength and superiority over mere Humanity than it didn't even feel the need for protection. Fools.

I checked the time. Four and three-quarter hours, and counting.

I began to get the feeling I was being watched. At first I thought it was the mound, that some alien device had finally reacted to the presence of my torc and locked on to me. But it felt more like someone, rather than something, was watching me from behind. That someone had sneaked up on me while I was concentrating on the mound. Walker had been convinced that we were being followed through the streets of Roswell, and we never did find out what that was about. Could there be some unknown third party at work here in Roswell? Someone with their own agenda? Whoever it was, it felt like they were really close now. I let my hand drift casually on to the butt of my holstered Colt Repeater, took a slow steady breath, and then spun round sharply with the gun in my hand.

And there was Walker, standing a discreet distance away, leaning casually on his furled umbrella. He smiled easily at me.

'Hello again, Eddie. I've been here for some time, waiting for you to notice me.'

'I was busy,' I said. 'Concentrating on the alien mound.'

'Of course you were. I didn't know you carried a gun.'

'Lot of things you don't know about me,' I said, putting the Colt Repeater away. 'Even a Drood likes to have an ace or two up his sleeve. And I like aces that go bang. How did you find this place?'

Walker shrugged. 'I have my methods.'

'You've been following me, haven't you? And I was so taken up following the alien signals I never even noticed you.'

'Actually, no.' Walker came forward to stand beside me, curling his lip at the alien mound. 'Ugly looking thing ... No, I have a sense for these things, and it led me here. Like a bad smell. I did have a sort of feeling that I might have been followed ...' Walker looked over his shoulder. I looked too, but the streets were as silent and empty as ever. Walker sniffed. 'I haven't been able to catch a glimpse of whoever it is, and I'm really very hard to hide things from.'

'That suggests another agent,' I said. 'Someone of our calibre, with an interest of their own in what's happening here.'

'Let them watch,' said Walker. 'We have work to do.'

I raised an eyebrow. 'You've come round to my way of thinking, then? What about your duty to win Alexander King's prize, so the rest of us can't have it?'

He met my gaze steadily. 'I've seen too many good people die on my watch. I can't look away and let it happen again. You were right, Eddie; we can always take the prize away from Honey and her small-minded masters later on, and share whatever it turns out to be. We are professionals, after all.'

We shared a brief smile. On an impulse I stuck out my hand, and he shook it solemnly.

'Good to know I've got someone to watch my back while I'm in the mound,' I said.

'Hell with that,' Walker said. 'You can watch my back ... Are those sunglasses what I think they are? I didn't know you could do things like that with your armour.'

'You see?' I said. 'Being around me is an education.'

'It's certainly taught me a lesson,' Walker agreed. 'Can your Sight find us the best way in? We are on the clock here.'

I looked at the mound. 'There don't seem to be any obvious defences; no force shields, proximity mines, energy weapons. No chemical or biological agents. Nothing to stop us walking right in. They do have a really strong avoidance field, so maybe they're depending on that.' I gazed at Walker. 'Why isn't the field affecting you? You shouldn't even be able to tell the mound is here.'

'There are lots of things about me you don't know,' said Walker.

I had to smile. 'None of the openings seem any more used, or significant, than any of the others. So we might as well choose one at random at ground level and stroll right in. And hope my Sight can lead us to where we need to be.'

'You're not a great one for forward planning, are you?' said Walker. 'Let's do it.'

'Yes,' I said. 'Let us descend into the underworld, and show these alien bastards what Hell on Earth is really like.'

*

The moment I marched through the semi-circular entrance, and into the mound itself, things stopped making sense. The entrance became a tunnel, suddenly large enough to hold a tube train, and full of a shimmering light. The tunnel descended sharply, falling away before me. The walls were slick, moist, the surface slowly sliding towards the floor, which absorbed it. Strange protrusions rose and fell within the walls, indefinable things that might have been machines or organs or something Humanity had no name for. The air was thick and foul, but still breathable.

I set off down the tunnel, with Walker at my side. I was glad to have him there, someone I could depend on. As a Drood field agent I've seen more than my fair share of weird shit, but this place was seriously creeping me out. There were new gaps or openings in the tunnel every few feet or so, and it rapidly became clear we were in some kind of labyrinth or honeycomb. I kept heading down, following my Sight, towards the dark beating heart of the mound. I could feel its presence far below, like the monster that waits for heroes at the centre of every maze.

The monster that wins more often than the tales like to tell.

This much was familiar, but as Walker and I continued to descend things grew increasingly strange and odd, and subtly disturbing. It was hard to judge distances any more; things seemed to move suddenly forward and then recede, to stretch endlessly away and then suddenly be gone, or behind you. There were things in the curved ceiling that looked down on me, and turned slowly to watch me pass. The aliens knew we were there; but I didn't see one anywhere. The tunnels occasionally widened out into vast chambers whose shape made no sense at all, that actually hurt my eyes if I looked at them too long. Even with the protection of my golden sunglasses. I didn't know how Walker was coping. We didn't speak once we'd entered the mound. As though human speech simply didn't belong there.

There were objects in the caverns I couldn't look at directly, shapes without significance, forms with no function. Shadows flowed across the floor, slowly changing shape like oil on water, that didn't react as I strode through them. Gravity fluctuated, so that sometimes I bobbed along like a balloon on a string and other times it was all I could do to trudge along, as though I was carrying the Old Man of the Sea on my back. My sense of direction snapped back and forth, and I would have been hopelessly lost in minutes without my Sight and my torc to guide me. I didn't always know where I was going, but I always knew which turn or opening to take next. The floors sloped continually down, leading me on into the subterranean heart of the mound. To the place where all bad things were decided. I knew that much, even if I didn't always recognise the man walking beside me.

It was getting harder to breathe, harder to think. But every time my thoughts began to drift, all I had to do was remember the vision the alien had shown me at the morgue, and a cold rage would blow the cobwebs from my thoughts and let me think clearly again. I was here to bring the aliens blood and horror, and nothing was going to stop me.

Not even me.

An alien surged forward out of a side tunnel and stopped abruptly, to block our way. A great pile of writhing snakes, of twisting tentacles, of thick threads that melted and merged into each other. I stopped and stood very still, looking steadily at the alien. Walker stood beside me. The alien showed no signs of moving, or yelling for its security people. I tensed, half expecting the invisible scalpels, and then concentrated on how best to kill the thing. I was reluctant to summon up my full armour; the presence of so much strange matter within the mound might set off any number of alarms. I had my Colt Repeater; but even its many and varied bullets wouldn't have much effect on a heap of seething tubes.

'Allow me,' said Walker, his words a breath in my ear.

He took a firm hold on the handle of his umbrella, pulled and twisted, and drew from its hiding place a long slender steel blade. He strode purposefully forward and cut, hacked and sliced the alien into a hundred pieces, with cold, stern ferocity. The steel blade sliced keenly through the writhing tubes, severing and opening them up almost without resistance. The alien seemed more surprised than anything. It made no attempt to defend itself, just slid slowly backwards down the tunnel. Walker went after it, cutting it up with vicious precision, his arm rising and falling tirelessly. No blood flew on the air, just a thick clear ooze that dripped from the severed ends of twitching tentacle pieces as they writhed feebly on the floor of the tunnel. Soon enough the alien stopped moving, because there wasn't enough left of it to hold together. Walker finished it off, hacking away until there wasn't a length of alien tissue longer than a foot or two. Even at the end, there were no signs of any organs within the alien; just the endless pulsing tubes.

Walker stopped and lowered his sword. He stood over the last remnants of the alien, and looked slowly about him at the scattered pieces. He was breathing harshly, as much from emotion as exertion. He straightened up, flicked a few drops of clear ooze from the tip of his sword, and then slid it neatly back into the spine of his umbrella.

'A sword?' I said finally. 'Hidden inside an *umbrella?*'

'Don't show your ignorance,' said Walker, his breathing already back to normal. 'It's an old tradition in the British spy game. Mention it to your Armourer; he'll remember.'

'Why hasn't the alien's death set off any alarms?' I said, glaring about me into the painfully sharp light.

'Perhaps they weren't expecting such a basic response,' said Walker. 'There is such a thing as being over-sophisticated.'

'And if more aliens do arrive?'

'Let them come,' said Walker. 'I feel like killing more of them. I want to grind their bodies under my feet, and dance in their blood.'

'Good,' I said. 'I want that too.'

The centre of operations turned out to be a honeycomb of interlinked tunnels and caverns and what might have been other-dimensional spaces. There were openings and doorways that changed shape as you approached, tunnels that turned back on themselves if you didn't concentrate on your destination strongly enough, and floating viewscreens that popped on and off, showing glimpses of distressingly inhuman other worlds. It was getting harder and harder to be sure of anything. Just being inside the alien mound distorted my thinking, and filled my head with sudden thoughts and impulses that made no sense. I'd lost all track of time. My watch didn't work. But I had to believe there was still time to stop the aliens, or this had been for nothing.

I entered into a chamber like all the others, and stopped dead in my tracks. Walker stopped beside me, and swore softly. We weren't the only people in the mound. The aliens had abducted men and women and even children from the town of Roswell, and done things to them. For knowledge, or curiosity, or as a precursor to the experiment they were planning. Or maybe just because they could. For some alien purpose I could never hope to understand, or forgive. Some forty men, women and children lay scattered across the sticky floor of the great open cavern. More protruded from the walls, half sunk and immersed in the slick wet surfaces. There were no cages, no bars, no force fields. These people had been ... worked on, and then dumped here to live or die. Many had died, their broken and distorted bodies unable to accept the terrible things that had been done to them.

Most had not been so lucky. They were still alive, aware, and suffering.

Their bodies had been vivisected: opened up and changed, made use of for surgical experiments. Not the brute mutilations I'd seen on the farmer in the morgue, or even in the future vision the alien had shown me. There was purpose to some of what had been done here, even if its end remained unknown. These people had been opened up, had their organs removed ... and then put back again in different places, set up to work in different ways. Some organs had been replaced with alien substitutes, pulsing organic machines that wrapped themselves around kidneys and lungs and intestines.

I moved slowly forward into the chamber, like walking in a dream, a nightmare from which I wanted so badly to awaken. A man lay on his back, split open from crotch to throat, the sides pinned back with metal staples to reveal he'd been stuffed full of extra human organs. There were others like him, with several lungs or half a dozen kidneys connected together, or miles of added intestines threaded in and out of his skin, the whole length of his torso. Others had been hollowed out, with nothing left inside them but threads of alien tissues, performing unknowable alien functions.

The children were the worst. I couldn't look at the children.

'Dear God,' said Walker. 'What— what is this, Eddie? Are the aliens ... playing with them?'

'I think they're trying to upgrade us,' I said. 'According to their lights. Make us ... better. More like them.'

'Is that what this is about?' said Walker. 'Forcibly ... improving us?'

'For our own good,' I said, and I didn't recognise my own voice. 'That's what the alien said. Remember?'

'What are we going to do?' said Walker. He sounded lost. 'What can we do? I mean, we can't leave them like this.'

'No,' I said. 'We can't. That would be . . . inhuman.'

I armoured up and took on my battleform, covered with razor-sharp blades. And then I went among the suffering people, and gave them the only comfort I could. I killed them. I killed them all. I raged back and forth across the great chamber, cutting throats, tearing out hearts, stamping on heads; killing men and women and children as swiftly and mercifully as I could. I cut off heads, and stabbed alien organs, running them through and through till they stopped moving. I cut and hacked and stabbed, doing whatever it took to put a stop to this obscenity. It wasn't easy; the aliens had made their improved people very hard to kill.

Some of them still had voices. I think some of them spoke to me; but I've never let myself remember what they said.

I went screaming and howling through the chamber, ripping bodies out of the walls and tearing them apart with brute strength, shouting obscenities and prayers, and blood sprayed across my armour and ran away in thick crimson rivulets. I killed them all, every last one, and when it was over, when I had dispensed the only mercy left to me, I armoured down and stood shaking and crying in the middle of the piled-up bodies. Drood field agents are trained to deal with horrors, to survive acts and decisions no one else could, but there are limits. There have to be limits, or we wouldn't be human any more.

Walker had known better than to try and interfere. He came forward, stepping carefully over blood and offal, and put his arms around me, and held me as I cried. And for a moment, it felt like my father was with me again; and I was comforted. After a while I found the strength to stand up straight again, and Walker immediately let go of me and stepped back. He watched silently as I rubbed the drying tears from my face and took a deep steadying breath.

'Damn them,' I said, and my voice was cold, so cold. 'Damn the aliens to Hell for making me do that.'

'Yes,' said Walker.

'The aliens have to die,' I said. 'They all have to die. No treaties or agreements for them. No mercy. I have to send a message. That no one can be allowed to get away with things like this.'

'I never thought otherwise,' said Walker.

The centre of operations wasn't far away. My Sight led me straight to it. Another cavern, perhaps a little larger than the others, the slick curving walls almost buried under extruded alien machinery. And some things that looked to be at least half alive, studded with metal protrusions and lights like staring eyes. Long silvery tendrils hung down from the high ceiling, twisting and turning and twitching in response to unfelt breezes, or perhaps just the passing of unknowable thoughts and impulses. And there were aliens, whole bunches of them, working at unrecognisable tasks, lurching across the smooth floor like tangles of knotted ropes. They operated the unnatural technology with limbs or manipulators formed for each specific purpose, spouting sensory organs as needed in the shapes of eyes or flowering things or rippled sucking orifices.

They all stopped at the same moment, and then three of them rolled together to melt and merge into one great heap over eight feet high, hundreds of dripping tentacles piled on top of each other. Disturbingly human eyeballs formed on the end of bobbing tendrils, all aimed at me and Walker. A bright pink speaking trumpet extruded from beneath the eyes, flushing with rhythmic crimson pulses.

'Welcome,' it said. 'Be calm. You will not be killed; you are useful. Of use to us. You have demonstrated impressive capabilities. Your value will be incorporated into us, and when you have been improved we will send you back out into your world to prepare the way for us. You shall be our voice; our messengers and prophets.'

'I wouldn't put money on it,' I said.

'Their language skills are improving,' said Walker.

'Practice makes perfect,' I said.

Parts of the greater alien reached out to manipulate semi-organic machines that rose up out of the floor. The eyeballs still looked steadily in our direction. Creamy white eyeballs without any veins, and pure black irises.

'I destroyed your discarded experiments,' I said. 'The people you ruined, and threw away. They're dead now.'

'They were failures,' said the alien. 'Of no further use to us. You will be of use to us. There is much that we can do with you.'

'I'll die first,' said Walker. 'Better yet, you'll die first.'

'I represent the Droods,' I said, raising my voice so everything in the chamber could hear. 'No visiting alien species goes anywhere, does anything, on our world without our consent. We exist to protect Humanity from things like you. You should have come to us first. We could have worked something out. Prevented this.'

'No,' said the alien. 'This is necessary. You are small, limited, incapable of understanding what is best for you. We know. We are experienced in changing, upgrading species.'

'You've done this before?' said Walker. 'On other worlds?'

'On many other worlds,' said the alien. 'You must be changed; your species is inefficient. It will not survive the future that is coming. You are wasteful of your potential, but you can be made better. Remade. You must not try to interfere. That is wasteful, of time and energy and resources. We are doing important work here. You will thank us later. This is our work. Our responsibility. Our joy. We make things better.'

'Not here,' I said. 'Not to us. We decide our own destiny. The experiment you're planning is an abomination, and we will not allow it to happen.'

'You can't stop it,' said the alien. 'It is already in motion. Humans. You think so small. So petty. Your language is barely adequate for communication. You do not even see us clearly. We are not what you look at. This body. You talk with an extension. You are inside our body.'

'The mound,' said Walker. 'The whole damned mound is the alien . . . One massive organism. That changes things.'

'Yes,' I said. 'Don't suppose you have any explosives about you?'

'Nothing big enough.'

'You will be remade,' said the alien. 'Improved, made speakers of our purpose. You will convince others to do what is necessary. Conflict is wasteful. You will observe the results of our experiment, the greater things we will make out of those who survive. You will tell your world to cooperate, that it is for the best.'

'We'll never work for you,' said Walker. 'No one on this world will do anything but fight you to the last breath in their bodies.'

'You won't fight us,' said the alien. 'After a point, you won't want to. You will become greater. And it starts now.'

Dozens of aliens appeared in the chamber, rising up out of the floor, sliding out of walls, dropping from the ceiling. They blocked all the entrances to the chamber. More and more of them, too many to count, surrounding Walker and I as we moved quickly to stand back to back. He had his sword blade in his hand again. I called up my armour, and took on my battleform, bristling with weapons. Holding its form was a strain, but I was too angry to care. The aliens filled the chamber around us, packing the place from wall to wall, piles of slimy ropes sliding in and out of each other.

'Bad odds,' said Walker, his voice as calm and cool as always.

'I've seen worse,' I said.

'Really?'

'Actually, yes. Of course, I had reinforcements then.'

'Terrific,' said Walker. 'How powerful are those energy weapons protruding from your armour?'

'The blades are sharp enough to cut through a loud noise,' I said. 'Everything else is just for show.'

'No energy weapons?'

'No. I don't normally need them.'

'Well,' said Walker. 'When there's nothing left to do but die, die well. And take as many of your enemies as possible down to Hell with you. Get out of here, Eddie.'

'What?'

'I'll hold their attention while you make for the surface. Don't worry – you're not the only one with a few tricks up his sleeve. You get the Hell out of here, and do whatever's necessary to stop them. I'll buy you time. Go, Eddie. It's up to you now.'

'I can't leave you here! Not with them, they'll—'

'No they won't. I'll make them kill me first.'

'I can't—'

'You must, Eddie. It's the human thing to do.'

I was still looking at him, trying to decide what to do for the best, when a blast of searing energy slammed out of one entrance, incinerating a whole bunch of aliens. They blew apart, great lengths of burning ropes flying through the air. More energy blasts raked across the cavern, blasting aliens out of the way, as Honey Lake came striding in with her shimmering crystal weapon in her hands. She laughed cheerfully, a bright and wonderfully sane sound in that awful place; like a valkyrie come down to Hell to rescue her heroes. She fired again and again, and pieces of ragged tentacles flew this way and that as she opened up a space around her.

'Heads up, guys!' she yelled cheerfully. 'The cavalry just arrived!'

I whooped with joy and relief and ploughed through the nearest aliens, hacking them apart and kicking the pieces aside so I could get to the next. My golden blades tore through them as though they were made of paper. I waded through alien gore like a hungry man going to a feast. A cold and vicious rage burned within me, not just at what they had done, and planned to do, but at what they had made me do. I killed and killed, and it was never enough. Walker cut about him with his sword, deadly and elegant, and Honey fired her gun, and soon we'd cleared the whole chamber of living alien forms.

But more bodies slipped out of the walls and rose up out of the floor, and dropped from the ceiling; and again the entrance ways were blocked and the chamber was full. The alien was the mound, and we were just destroying the things it had made to fight us. It was distracting us, keeping us busy while the clock ticked down to the great experiment in the streets of Roswell. I had to stop the alien, not just its extremities. I called up my Sight, focused it through my mask, and made myself concentrate on what really mattered. The dark and secret heart of the alien mound, the one thing it couldn't live without. I glared around me, Seeing terrible things hidden in the walls and floor of the chamber, until finally I Saw, deep below my feet, something that blazed and burned like a dark sun: living energy sourced in alien flesh.

I yelled to Honey to blast the floor with her energy weapon where I pointed, and she nodded and hit the floor with everything she had. The floor rocked beneath our feet, splitting apart, forced open by the crystal weapon's implacable energies. They dug deeper and deeper into the alien tissues until finally I could see the dark heart itself. It wrapped itself in thick protective tissues, struggling to replace them as fast as Honey's weapon burned them away. I formed one long, slender and very deadly blade from my golden right hand, and sent it plunging deep into the dark heart of the alien mound.

It exploded. Alien flesh was no match for other-dimensional strange matter. Particularly when driven by the terrible cold anger of the human heart.

The individual alien forms collapsed, sinking in upon themselves; the long ropy tentacles already rotting and falling apart. The cavern shook like an earthquake, great jagged cracks opening up in the slimy walls. The floor seemed to fall away beneath my feet, in sudden drops and shudders. The whole mound was dying, rotting, falling apart. I ran for the nearest exit, Honey and Walker right behind me. I followed my Sight back up through the mound, heading for the surface even as the mound collapsed in on itself, sinking down into the earth. I ran through piles of dead alien bodies, kicking them aside, punching holes through walls where necessary. Strange lights flared around me, vivid energies spitting and crackling helplessly on the air. I ran for the surface, with Honey and Walker.

We burst out of the final exit and kept running, out into the fresh and human air of Roswell. We jumped over cracks opening up in the back lot, urged on by the sound of the dead mound slowly sinking down into the earth. Finally I decided I was far enough away, and only then did I let myself stop and look back, to see the last death throes of the alien mound. It was dry and cracked and corrupt now, disappearing into the hole it had made for itself. Walker and Honey and I watched till all of it was gone, and there was nothing left to show it had ever been there but a dark hole in the ground of a deserted back lot.

'Go down,' I said to it. 'Go to Hell, where you belong.'

I put away my armour, and stood there in the empty street, a man again. I was shaking and breathing hard, from exertion and emotion, and from relief that we'd stopped the filthy experiment before it started. Honey and Walker stood with me, breathing just as hard.

'So,' I said finally. 'You came back, Honey. Right in the nick of time. What changed your mind? What about the game, and the prize?'

'How was I going to be able to get anything done here, with all this nonsense going on?' said Honey reasonably. 'Besides, I didn't get into the spy game to turn my back on people. I serve the American people. As I decide best.'

'What are we going to tell the townspeople?' said Walker. 'Do we tell them anything?'

'Would they believe us, without evidence?' I said. 'They don't even have the farmer and his cow in the morgue any more, remember?'

'This is Roswell,' Walker said dryly. 'They'll believe anything – or at least enough to make money out of it. This time next year, this will all be a television movie. I wonder who they'll get to play me?'

'You were never here,' Honey said sternly. 'None of us were.'

'Right,' I said. 'This isn't the Nightside. We have to keep a low profile.'

'There could be more aliens from where those things came from,' said Honey, hefting her shimmering weapon. 'They could be back.'

'My family will take care of that,' I said. 'We have connections, in far away places. Treaties and compacts work both ways. Or we'll kick alien arse till they do.'

'I never knew you could do that,' said Walker.

'Not many do,' I said.

'And you wonder why other organisations don't trust the Droods,' said Honey. 'Your family has secrets the way other families have pets. Would it kill you to share information like that, so we could all sleep better at nights?'

'Possibly,' I said. 'We don't take chances. But I will talk to the Matriarch. Sharing can be good. What say the three of us go back to Alexander King, give him the answers we've accumulated, and then share the secrets he gives us?'

'Hell,' said Honey, 'I'm game if you are. Nothing like hanging out with a Drood to help you see the bigger picture.'

'Fine by me,' said Walker. 'But will the Independent Agent agree?'

'The man is dying,' I said. 'He doesn't have enough time left to haggle. He can give his prize to three agents who've proved their worth, or risk his precious secrets falling into unworthy hands after he's dead.'

'And Peter?' said Honey. 'How do we tell an old man that we got his only grandson killed?'

'We don't know he's dead,' Walker said 'He's just . . . missing in action.'

'Alexander King wanted his grandson in the game,' I said. 'He knew the risks.'

'Did Peter?' said Honey. 'He didn't operate in the same world as the rest of us.'

'No,' said Walker. 'He worked in industrial espionage. I'm pretty damn sure he wouldn't have shared the prize.'

'The game is now officially over,' I said. 'We've been to the five designated areas, investigated each mystery we found there, and come up with an answer. We may not have uncovered the answer to the original Roswell mystery, but I think this . . . is better. Certainly it's more than enough to prove our worth as the Independent Agent's successors, which was supposed to be the whole point of the game. Time to call it a day.'

'How are we supposed to let Alexander King know?' said Walker, glaring at the teleport bracelet on his wrist. 'How do we persuade these infernal contraptions to take us back to Place Gloria?'

I took out Peter's phone, and showed it to the teleport bracelet around my wrist. 'See this?' I said loudly. 'Proof, evidence and answers to the questions we were set. I know you're listening, Alexander! We can either give this to you or take it back to our respective organisations. So, beam us up, Scotty!'

And that was when Peter King stepped out of the shadows, stabbed Honey Lake between the ribs with a long-bladed knife, snatched the phone from my hand and disappeared; teleported away.

Honey made a shocked, surprised sound, and then collapsed as the strength went out of her legs. I caught her, and eased her to the ground. Her whole left side was already soaked with blood, and more ran down between our closely pressed bodies. Walker was saying something, but I wasn't listening. Honey made a pained sound and blood spilled from her mouth. I held her tightly to me. I looked up at Walker, to yell at him to get some help; but the look on his face stopped me. It confirmed what I already knew.

'It was Peter all along,' said Walker. 'The treacherous little shit. He killed Katt, and Blue, and—'

'No,' said Honey. 'That was me.'

'Hush,' I said. 'Hush.'

'No.' She forced the words out, past the pain and the blood. She needed me to know the truth. 'I killed Blue, and Katt. Tried to kill

Walker. Even sabotaged my own sub at the loch, so I wouldn't be suspected. I thought it was my duty. To win the prize, at any cost.'

'Honey . . .' I said; but the hard knot in my stomach wouldn't let me say anything more.

She smiled briefly, showing perfect teeth slick with blood. 'Never fall in love with another agent, Eddie. You know it's never going to end well.'

She died in my arms. I held her for a long time.

It all went bad so quickly.

CHAPTER NINE
The spying game

Why be an agent?

All right, you get to play with all the best toys, you get to see the world (though rarely the better parts), and now and again you get a real chance to stand between Humanity and the forces that threaten. You get to be a hero, or a villain, and sometimes both. But what does any of that buy you, in the end? Except death and suffering and the loss of those you care for. What makes a man an agent? And what keeps him going, in the face of everything?

Why be an agent?

Walker and I stood together, in a dirty back street, looking down at Honey Lake's body. I'd like to say she looked peaceful, and at rest; but she didn't. She looked like a toy that had been played with too roughly and then thrown aside. I'd seen a lot of people look like that, in the years I'd spent playing the spying game. When all the fun and games, all the adventure and romance, adds up to nothing more than bright red blood on a white jumpsuit.

'She was a good agent,' said Walker.

'Yes,' I said.

'She wouldn't want us to stand around, waiting to get caught.'

'No.'

'My teleport bracelet is gone,' said Walker, looking at his bare wrist. 'Yours too?'

'Yes,' I said. 'Honey's bracelet is gone as well.'

Walker shot his impeccably white cuff forward to cover his wrist. 'Peter must have taken them with him.'

'Only one way he could have done that,' I said, still looking down at Honey's body. 'Peter must have been working with his grandfather all along. The Independent Agent always intended for his grandson to win the game, to keep his precious secrets in the family. This whole contest was a set-up to establish Peter King as the new Independent Agent. I should have known. It's always about family. The rest of us were just here for show. Window dressing, for Peter's great triumph.'

'And we're left stranded in Roswell,' said Walker. 'With a dead body at our feet and the local law no doubt already on their way, tipped off by an anonymous source. How very awkward. Time to be going, I think.'

'We have to go to Place Gloria,' I said. 'Alexander and Peter must pay for this.'

'Yes,' said Walker. 'They must. I've always been a great believer in an eye for an eye, and a death for a death. Comes of a traditional public school upbringing, no doubt. Getting to the Independent Agent's private lair isn't going to be easy, though. We can't be sure Place Gloria is where or even when we think it is. Remember the flux fog? The exterior we saw may have no connection to the more than comfortable retreat we walked through.'

'You're talking to distract me,' I said. 'I appreciate the thought, but don't. What are we going to do about Honey?'

'We'll call her people,' said Walker, 'tell them what's happened and they'll get their locals to do what's necessary. The Company's always been very good at cleaning up after itself.'

I looked at Walker, and to his credit he didn't flinch. 'Walk away and leave her?' I said. 'Leave her lying here in the street, alone?'

Walker met my gaze unflinchingly. 'You'll pardon me if I'm not overly sympathetic, Eddie. She did try to kill me in Tunguska. And she murdered poor little Katt, and your friend the Blue Fairy.'

'I know,' I said. 'She was an agent.'

'Yes,' said Walker. 'And that's why she'd understand. In the field, you do what you have to do. She wouldn't have hesitated to walk away from you, and leave your body to be taken care of by the Droods.'

'Is this why we became agents?' I said, and was surprised by the bitterness in my voice. 'To play games, to chase after secrets that are rarely worth the blood spilled on their behalf? To end up stabbed in the back, just when you thought you'd won, bleeding out in some nameless back street, with most people never even knowing who you were, or what you did, or why it mattered?'

'You can't work in the shadows and expect applause,' said Walker. 'The right people will know, and sometimes that's the best we can hope for.'

'Anything, for the family,' I said. 'Anything for England. For Humanity. But for us? What about us, Walker?'

'Duty and responsibility are their own rewards,' said Walker. 'Old-fashioned, I know, but some things don't change. The things that matter. We do it because it has to be done. We do it because if we don't, who will? Who else could we trust to do it right?'

'She shouldn't have died here,' I said. 'Not like this.'

'It's always somewhere like this,' said Walker. 'That's the job. Did you ... love her, Eddie?'

'No,' I said. 'But she was ... special. If things had been different—'

'If,' said Walker. 'Always the harshest word.'

'Why did you become an agent, Walker? I had no choice; I was born into the family business. So was Honey, I suppose. But why you?'

'For the sheer damned glamour of it all,' said Walker.

I couldn't manage a smile for him yet, but I nodded to show I appreciated the effort. I turned my back on Honey, and walked away. Walker strode calmly along beside me, flourishing his furled umbrella like an officer's stick. Say what you like about Walker, and many people have: the man has style. We left the back lot and the empty street behind us and went into the town of Roswell to walk among sane things again.

'We can't let Peter take the prize,' I said. 'Not after everything we've been through. Not after what he did. He's not worthy.'

'I'll see him damned to Hell first,' Walker agreed cheerfully. 'And his bloody grandfather too. Peter must have been the one following us earlier. I said it had to be a professional. He probably changed the settings on his teleport bracelet while he was still in the Sundered Lands, leaving ahead of us so he could arrive here separately.' Walker frowned. 'Surely he couldn't have known about the alien threat in advance ... No. No, it must have come as a very nasty surprise to find he was trapped here with the rest of us. That's why he stayed well back until it was over, before making his move.'

I nodded. I didn't really care. It was just details.

Walker found a public phone, and told the CIA about Honey. I contacted my family through my torc. That wouldn't have been possible with the old torc, supplied by the corrupt Heart; but Ethel's upgrade to strange matter had gifted us with many new options, some of which we were still getting used to. The Drood communications officer was all over me the moment he recognised my voice.

'Where have you been, Edwin? We haven't been able to reach you for days! You know you're supposed to report in regularly.'

'I've been busy,' I said.

'But where have you been? It was like you'd dropped off the planet! We've had the whole family searching for some sign of you. Even Ethel couldn't locate you, and she sees in five dimensions!'

'Good for her,' I said. 'Now shut up and patch me through to the War Room. I want to speak to the Matriarch. The whole game's gone to Hell, and the Independent Agent has screwed us all.'

'I'm here, Edwin.' The Matriarch's cool and utterly professional voice sounded as though she was standing right next to me. 'Where are you? What's been happening?'

'The game was fixed from the start,' I said, doing my best to sound equally calm and collected. Even after everything that had passed between us, I still didn't want to let myself down in front of her. 'Alexander King never intended to let any of us get our grubby little hands on his treasure trove of secrets. So I'm going to be a very bad loser, and take them anyway. I need to know where his secret lair really is, Grandmother. Tell me.'

'If anyone in this family had even a strong suspicion where to get our hands on the Independent Agent, we'd have kicked in his door and shut him down long ago,' the Matriarch said. 'We don't like competition, we don't like people who change sides according to which way the wind is blowing, and we've never approved of his methods. We would also very much like to get back the records, trophies and forbidden weapons he's stolen and cheated us out of down the years. Alexander King is no friend of this family, and never has been. I'm sorry, Edwin. His present location is a complete mystery to us. The space/time coordinates he provided for your transport to Place Gloria were a strictly one-time-only thing. I did send three field agents after you on the off chance, but they ended up materialising halfway up an Alp with not even a climber's hut anywhere in sight. Callan in particular was very upset about that.'

'You know Alexander,' I said. 'You were close to him once.'

'I was younger then, and much more impressionable.' The Matriarch's voice didn't change a bit. 'And even back then, I would never have let my feelings get in the way of a mission. The family comes first, Edwin. You know that.'

'Yes,' I said. 'I know that.'

'Are you all right, Edwin?' said the Matriarch. 'You sound tired. Do you require assistance?'

'No,' I said. 'I need to do this myself.'

I shut down the contact, before she could start asking me questions I had no intention of answering. I looked at Walker, who'd finished his phone call and was waiting patiently for me.

'My family can't help,' I said.

'I can,' said Walker.

'You know how to find the Independent Agent?' I said, just a bit suspiciously.

'Not as such,' said Walker. 'But I can get us there. It's always been part of my job to be able to go where I'm needed. Of course, this will mean travelling via the Nightside. And Eddie, if I'm going to take you there, you're going to have to promise me that you'll behave. Droods are forbidden access to the Nightside for good reasons. Do you give me your word you won't start anything?'

'I'll be good,' I said. 'No matter what the provocation. I can do that, to get to Alexander and Peter. But how do we get to the Nightside from here?'

'I am about to reveal one of the great secrets of the Nightside,' said Walker. 'And to a Drood, of all people. What is the world coming to? Anyway, here it is: *timeslips don't just happen*. Well, actually, they do. Suddenly and violently and all over the place. Bloody things are always opening up, forming temporary gateways to the Past, the Future, and any number of alternate Earths. Apparently, it's the result of a major design flaw in the original creation of the Nightside ... But you don't really think the powers that be in the Nightside, the poor bastards who think they actually run the place, would let such a thing happen without trying to take advantage of the situation?

No, they found a way to tap into the basic energies involved, and made the energies work for them. The Authorities didn't just gift me with my voice, you know; they also gave me my very own portable timeslip. So I could come and go as I please, and be wherever I need to be, whenever I need to be there. And sometimes a little before.'

He produced a large gold pocket watch, on a reinforced gold chain, from his waistcoat pocket. He hefted the watch thoughtfully, and then held it out for me to see. The watch cover had an engraving of the snake Oroborus, with its tail in its mouth, surrounding an hourglass. Walker flipped open the cover, and inside there was nothing but darkness. Like a bottomless hole, falling away for ever. I pulled my head back with a snap, to keep from being sucked in. Walked smiled faintly.

'If you look into the abyss long enough, the abyss looks back into you. And sometimes it knows your name. I've been told there is someone or something trapped at the bottom of the watch, powering the portable timeslip. I've never felt inclined to pursue the matter.'

'My family has something similar,' I said, for pride's sake. 'A portable door. We've been using them for years.'

'Makes you wonder who had the idea first, doesn't it?' said Walker. 'And who sold what to whom? Droods may be banned from the Nightside by long tradition, but the Intelligence community has always had its connections, on many unofficial levels. Your portable doors operate in space and local time; my portable timeslip is more ambitious. The Authorities, in their various incarnations, have spent centuries studying timeslips, and slowly learning how to influence and manipulate them. Not the Authorities personally, of course; they have people to do that kind of thing for them. But this little watch can take me anywhere I need to be; and once it's been there it never forgets. Which means the exact coordinates of Alexander King's lair are safely tucked away in its memory core.

'Unfortunately, it's running low on power. There's just enough metatemporal juice left to transport both of us to a pre-arranged setting in the Nightside, where I can get it recharged.'

'I've always wanted to visit the Nightside,' I said.

'You only say that because you've never seen it,' said Walker.

He turned the fob on the pocket watch back and forth like a combination lock, muttering under his breath as he did so. He made one final dramatic twist of the fob, and the darkness leapt up out of the watch to form itself into a door, hanging on the air before us. A simple rectangle of impenetrable darkness, a patch of night sky with absolutely no stars, that could lead anywhere. Walker gestured for me to walk through. Only a few days earlier I would have refused, knowing better than to turn my back on Walker but I didn't care any more. I wanted justice, and revenge, and if I had to make a deal with the devil to get them, then so be it. I walked into the darkness and out the other side, and found myself in the dingiest, sleaziest bar I'd ever seen. Walker appeared out of nowhere to stand beside me.

'Welcome to the oldest bar in the world,' he said grandly. 'Welcome to Strangefellows.'

I have to say, I was not impressed. I'd heard about Strangefellows, of course; everyone in my line of work has. It's the place to go if you want to make things happen. Dreams can come true in the oldest bar in the world, whether you want them to or not. Miracles can happen and deals can be made, and if you sit at a table long enough, everyone in the world who matters will pass by. And while you're watching all this, someone will steal your wallet, your clothes, and quite possibly your soul. Strangefellows is where heroes and villains, gods and monsters, myths and legends go to sulk in corners and cry into their drinks.

I much preferred the upmarket, brightly lit and certainly more civilised ambience of the Wulfshead Club, which might have its share of disreputable customers, but always knew where to draw the line. The Wulfshead believed in security, good cheer and basic hygiene; all of which were ostentatiously lacking here. The lighting was not so much low as suppressed, probably so you couldn't tell what a dive the place actually was; and the air was thick with a whole bunch of different illegal forms of smoke. Just by breathing it in, my lungs were slumming. No one paid any attention to my sudden appearance; in fact I rather got the impression that the regulars were quite used to strangers dropping in unannounced. A lot of people were watching Walker carefully, out of the corners of their eyes. I was about to remark on that, when I spotted a number of small scuttling things in the shadows where the walls met the floor. I pointed them out to Walker, who shrugged.

'Don't mind them,' he said. 'They provide character. And the occasional bar snack.'

I tried not to shudder too openly as I followed Walker through the crowded tables towards the long wooden bar at the back of the room. I passed among vampires and ghouls, mummies wrapped in yards and yards of rotting gauze, a party of female horned daemons out on the pull, and even a few gods in reduced circumstances leant over their drinks and muttering how they used to be a contender. They all ignored me with a thoroughness I could only admire. They didn't know Shaman Bond, and with my shirt collar pulled as far up as it would go, they couldn't see my torc and mark me for a Drood.

None of them looked like people I'd talk to by choice, unless I was pursuing a case. I do have my standards. I've known my share of dubious dives in London – sleazy back-alley establishments where you have to mug the doorman to get in. Or out. I've strolled through my share of members-only clubs where the air of decadence and debauchery is so thick you can carve your initials on it. I've moved among spies and traitors, rogues and villains, friends and fiends and felons . . . and none of them had ever made my hackles stand on end the way this place did.

Strangefellows is where you go when the rest of the world has thrown you out.

A larger-than-life male personage was standing on a small stage, beneath a single spotlight, providing the live entertainment. He wore battered black leathers, left hanging open to show off the many scars covering his unnaturally pale torso. One of the Baron Frankenstein's creatures. He held on to the old-fashioned mike like he thought it might escape, while murdering an old Janis Joplin standard, 'Take Another Little Piece Of My Heart Now'.

'He's often here,' said Walker, though I hadn't asked. 'Appears on as many open mike talent shows as will have him; and let's face it, most of them have more sense than to say no. Seems he's not entirely satisfied with the Baron's work. He's saving up his pennies for a sex-change operation.'

I never know what to say when people tell me things like that.

So I just smiled and nodded vaguely, and fixed my gaze on the bar ahead.

'I need a drink,' I said firmly. 'In fact, I need several large drinks, preferably mixed together in a tall glass, but quite definitely not including a miniature umbrella or ragged slices of dodgy fruit I don't recognise. Any suggestions?'

'Yes,' said Walker. 'Whatever you do, don't let yourself be persuaded into trying the Merovingian cherry brandy. That's not booze, it is sudden death in a bottle. And don't try the Angel's Urine either. It's not a trade name. They have to bury the bottles in desanctified ground. I'd stick to Perrier, if I were you. And insist on opening the bottle yourself.'

'You take me to the nicest places, Walker.'

People made space for us at the bar without actually seeming to, or looking in our direction. Walker smiled charmingly at the blonde barmaid.

'Hello, Cathy. I need a favour. And you're not going to say no, or I'll send in a team of health inspectors with armed backup.'

She scowled at him with real menace. 'What do you want, Walker?'

'I need you to recharge my watch.'

'What again? I swear you only do it here so you can fiddle your expenses ... All right, hand it over. But if it blows the fuses again, you're paying.'

Walker and I stood with our backs to the bar, staring out at the crowds, drinking our Perrier straight from the bottle. Walker had his little finger extended, of course. The roar of conversation in the bar rose and fell, interrupted now and again by moments of music and mayhem. The place might be a dump, but it was a lively dump.

'What do you intend to do, when we finally catch up with Alexander and Peter?' said Walker. He didn't look at me.

'Kill them,' I said. 'No excuses, no plea bargaining. I'm going to kill them both.'

'For Honey?'

'For Honey, and Blue and Katt, and all the other people the Independent Agent and his games have screwed over down the years. Alexander King made himself a legend in our field by trampling over everyone who got in his way. He did good things, important things, there's no denying it. But only to build his reputation, so he could charge more. That's not what being an agent is about. The world's become too precarious to allow rogue operatives like him to run around loose.'

'You went to great lengths,' murmured Walker, 'to establish yourself as an independent field agent for the Droods.'

'I still am,' I said. 'It's not what you do, it's why you do it. I maintain a healthy distance from my family so I can see them clearly for what they are, and operate as their conscience when necessary. I'm an agent, not an assassin. But I will kill Alexander and Peter King, for the things they've done. Not only because of Honey. And Blue, and Katt. Am I going to have problems with you over this, Walker?'

'Not in the least. But Eddie, understand this: if it comes to the point, and you find you can't do it – you can't kill them – I will. And you had better not get in my way. I was never an agent, Eddie. I was a soldier.'

'For Honey?' I said.

'No. I never cared much for her. Typical arrogant CIA spook. No, some people just need killing.'

At which point a large, heavily muscled and more than fashionably dressed young man emerged suddenly from the crowds to loom over us. He planted himself in front of Walker and smiled nastily at him. He was handsome enough, in a blond Aryan steroid freak sort of way, and up close he smelled of sweat and testosterone.

'Hello, Georgie,' said Walker. 'You're looking very yourself, today. How are the bowel movements?'

'Screw you, Walker,' said Georgie. 'I don't have to take any shit from you any more. Not so high and mighty now, are you, without your voice? Not so powerful since you lost your precious voice in the Lilith War! All these years you've interfered in my business deals, humiliated me in front of my people ... well, you can't talk to me like that any more. It's my time now. And your time to get what's coming to you.'

'Friend of yours?' I said to Walker.

'Not even remotely.' Walker gazed calmly back into Georgie's fierce gaze, and if he was in the slightest bit concerned, he hid it really well. 'This appalling and slightly hysterical person is Good

Time Georgie. Your special Go To man in the Nightside for everything that's bad for you when you're working on a low budget. Whether it's drugs, debauchery or demonic possession, Georgie can get it for you at a lower price than anyone else. Of course, at such prices you can't expect guaranteed quality, or customer service. Never any refunds or apologies from Good Time Georgie. Buyer beware, and there's one born every minute.'

'That's all you've got now,' said Georgie. 'Words. No voice to back them up. I'm going to break your bones, Walker, and stamp you into the floor. No one here will help you. You've got no friends here.' He glanced at me. 'You keep out of this. It's none of your business.'

'You smell funny,' I said. I looked at Walker. 'Would you like me to—?'

'No need,' said Walker.

'Really, I don't mind. It wouldn't be any trouble.'

'It's only Good Time Georgie,' said Walker. 'I could handle Good Time Georgie if I was unconscious.' He smiled easily into Georgie's reddening face, completely unmoved by the man's size or presence or anger. 'Are you sure you want to do this? Are you really so sure I don't have my voice any more? Would I be here in Strangefellows, without my voice to protect me? Perhaps you've forgotten the terrible things I've done to you down the years. Or made you do to yourself. You're just a cheap thug, Georgie, whereas I . . . am Walker. Now go away and stop bothering me. Or I will tell you to do something deeply amusing, and so extreme that people will still be laughing about it thirty years from now.'

There wasn't an ounce of uncertainty in Walker's voice. He sounded like he meant every word he said. Good Time Georgie hesitated, his anger draining away in the face of Walker's calm certainty. Georgie glanced around. A lot of people had stopped what they were doing to see what would happen, but none of them looked like they had any intention of getting involved. This was Walker, after all. Georgie turned abruptly and stalked away. Walker took a sip of his Perrier, little finger extended even more than usual. And everyone went back to what they'd been doing.

'Awful fellow,' said Walker. 'I'd have shut him down years ago, but ten more would spring up in his place. There will always be steady business for those who come here to sin on a restricted budget.'

'Neatly handled, I thought,' I said.

'Thank you. I've had a lot of practice.'

'How long do you think you can keep this going, before people know for sure you're bluffing about your voice?'

'What makes you think I'm bluffing?' said Walker.

I didn't look at him. 'Can I ask . . . You lost your voice originally in the Lilith War? As in, the biblical Lilith?'

'Yes.'

'Forget it. I don't think I really want to know.'

'Very wise,' said Walker.

Behind the bar, the portable timeslip made a polite chiming noise to let us know its recharging was complete. The blonde barmaid unplugged the pocket watch from what looked like a battery re-charger on steroids, and slapped it down on the wooden bar before Walker with a violence that made both of us wince. Walker smiled politely, tipped his bowler hat to her, and then picked up the watch and turned to me.

'We have to do this outside,' he said. 'Too many built-in pro-tections and defences inside the bar.'

'To keep creditors from getting in?' I said.

'I heard that!' said the barmaid.

'I notice you're not denying it,' said Walker. 'Let's go, Eddie.'

Outside the bar, I got my first real look at the Nightside. Walker gave me a few moments to look around, and brace myself. The Nightside was everything I'd always thought it would be: loud, sleazy, brightly coloured, and steeped in its own dangerous glamour. It was like standing on a city street in Hell. Harsh-coloured lights blazed from the half-open doors of night clubs that never closed, along with every kind of music that made you want to dance till you dropped, till your feet bled and your heart broke. Shops and stores to every side, selling everything you ever dreamed of in your worst nightmares. Every sin catered for, every desire encouraged. The pavements were packed with would-be customers, hot for pleasures and secrets and knowledge forbidden by the outside world. Beasts and monsters moved openly among them. Anywhere else, I would have had to use my Sight to see so much, so clearly, but this was the Nightside. And this, all this, was just business as usual.

Everyone knows there's no law in the Nightside, only a few overseers like Walker to keep things from getting out of hand. Anything is permitted, everything is for sale. You can buy anything or anyone, do anything or anyone, and no one will stop you or call you to account. Or rescue you when things go bad. A place of casual sin and unchecked appetites, and no one gives a damn because that's what the Nightside is for. I ached to call up my armour, take my aspect upon me and bring justice and retribution to the only city where the night never ends.

'Now you know why we don't allow Droods in here,' said Walker. 'You're really far too simple and straightforward for a place like this. We do things differently here.'

'You can't have sin without victims,' I said. 'Who cares for them?'

'And you do take things so very personally ... Everyone who comes to the Nightside knows what to expect, Eddie. There are no innocents here.'

'You didn't answer my question.'

He sighed briefly. 'There are some, who do what they can. And that's more than most of those who come here are entitled to.'

'How do you stand it?' I said. 'Working in a moral cesspit like this?'

'It's my job,' said Walker. 'And I'm very good at it. Now, time we were going.'

His hands worked expertly on the pocket watch, and the darkness within leapt up and out, forming a great dark blanket above us. It slammed down like a flyswatter, and I didn't even have time to react before, suddenly, we were somewhere else.

The interior of Place Gloria was as I remembered it. Tacky, gaudily coloured reminders from the decade that taste disowned. I looked quickly about me while Walker put his pocket watch away, but everything was still and silent. I knew this room; it was where we'd all stood together at the start of the game, when we'd still thought we had a fair chance of winning. I caught Walker considering me thoughtfully, and made myself unclench my fists.

'I don't think we should go running through the rooms at random,' said Walker, 'in the hope of coming across Alexander and Peter.

310

There are bound to be protections, alarms, probably even booby traps for the unwary and those in a hurry.'

'Searching this place thoroughly could take for ever,' I said. 'I've a better idea. Make a lot of noise, and make them come to us.'

I drew my Colt Repeater, the gun that doesn't need to be aimed and never runs out of ammunition, and I fired it again and again, calmly and coldly destroying everything of value in the room. Anything that looked important, or expensive, or hard to replace. Ancient china blew apart, glasses and mirrors shattered, and the room was full of vengeful thunder. Photos showing Alexander's old cases and triumphs jumped off the walls, precious memories destroyed in moments. The photos showed him posing with the great and the good, the famous and the infamous. Smiling faces, blown away. I shot holes in objects of historical significance and artistic merit, and didn't give a damn. I destroyed antique furnishings and modern furniture, and stamped the pieces under my feet as I raged around the room. The continual roar of the gun in the confined space was almost unbearable.

Some things had their own protections. An oversized clock whose hands swept steadily backwards faded away before my bullets could reach it. An ancient black runesword mounted on the wall began to sing menacingly in no human language. My bullets couldn't touch it, so I moved on. And a huge stone hand in an impenetrable glass case gave me the finger. I didn't care. There were still many good things left to destroy.

It did occur to me that I was probably destroying, or at least vandalising, important relics of spy history, but none of that mattered. Not with Honey's blood still drying on my clothes, from where I'd held her close as she died. Not with the Blue Fairy's death message still fresh in my mind. And not while Alexander and Peter still lived.

I finally ran out of things to shoot, and slowly lowered the Colt Repeater. It felt heavy in my hand. The echoes from the continuous gunfire died slowly away, and Walker lowered his hands from his ears. The room was destroyed, bits and pieces everywhere, but no one came to investigate.

'Odd,' said Walker, entirely unmoved by the destruction around him. 'No alarms? No bells or sirens or those annoying flashing lights that always give me a headache? And no attempt to protect most of the items? Try this in the Collector's warehouse, and the security robots would be picking up bits of you for weeks afterwards. I think we have to assume that Alexander and Peter know we're here, and have no intention of exposing themselves to danger ... Which is understandable. If I was out here after me, I wouldn't show myself either. You know, this could be a trap.'

'I don't care,' I said.

'Don't care was made to care,' said an angry, familiar voice.

I looked round, and there they were, the three of them, standing in a tense threatening row on the other side of the room. Coffin Jobe, the Dancing Fool and Strange Chloe. My three fellow conspirators from the raid on the Tower of London. It seemed so long ago now, a different world. But here they were, and they were clearly not on my side. Coffin Jobe, the necroleptic, who died and came back to life so frequently he saw the world much more clearly than the rest of us. The Dancing Fool, who created his own martial art based on Scottish sword-dancing, and won every fight because he knew what you were going to do even before you did. Déjà fu. And Strange Chloe, the Goth's Goth with her black and white markings tattooed on her face, who could make anything in the world disappear if she hated it enough. And she had a lot of hate in her.

Friends, of a kind. Colleagues, certainly. All of them with good cause to want me dead. Life's like that, sometimes.

'Guys,' I said, 'this really isn't a good time.'

'What's the matter, Eddie?' said the Dancing Fool. His voice was harsh, vicious. 'Forgotten about us, had you? The three friends you betrayed and left helpless for the authorities in the Tower of London? The colleagues you stabbed in the back and then left to rot? If Alexander King hadn't stepped in to rescue us, we'd still be behind bars!'

'Alexander?' I said. 'Damn! How long has he been watching me?'

'Get over yourself, Shaman!' said Strange Chloe. 'This isn't about you, it's about us!'

'Only Shaman isn't your real name, is it?' said the Dancing Fool. 'Not even close.'

'Drood,' said Coffin Jobe, in his grey deathly voice. 'Bad enough that you betrayed us, Shaman, but you're a Drood too?'

'You have to admit,' said Walker, 'this is an excellent defence stratagem. Making you fight your way through your own friends to get to him. Alexander King made his legend by always being one step ahead of everyone else. It's almost an honour to see such talent at work.'

None of us was listening to him.

'I saved your lives!' I said to the three of them. 'Big Aus was planning to kill all of us, once he'd got his hands on what he was really after. You didn't seriously buy into that nonsense about the ravens, did you? He was after the Crown Jewels!'

'Yeah, right,' said Strange Chloe. 'And my arse plays the banjo. You'd say anything to save your own skin, wouldn't you?'

'I thought you were my friend, Shaman,' said Coffin Jobe. 'And you're a Drood?'

'How could you turn out to be one of *them*?' said Strange Chloe. 'The professional killjoys, the bullies and spoilsports, dedicated to taking the fun out of life! You pretended to be one of us, when you were really one of them ... Well, here's where you get yours, *Drood*.'

'Alexander brought us here so we could take our revenge on you,' said the Dancing Fool. 'He knew you'd try to smash in here, to steal the prize you couldn't win honestly. Typical Drood. And we jumped at the chance for a little justified payback!'

'You don't know what's going on,' I said, as steadily and calmly as I could. 'He's using you, just like Big Aus. You're only here as another way to hurt me.'

'This isn't about you!' Strange Chloe shouted, all but stamping her foot. 'Not everything is about you, just because you're a bloody Drood!'

'This is,' I said, and something in my voice stopped her. I looked at the three of them, and felt more tired than anything. 'Do you really think you can stop me?' I said. 'I'm a Drood, with a Drood's armour and a Drood's training. You know what that means.'

The three of them looked at each other, uneasy for the first time. They knew what a Drood can do.

'Always wanted a chance to show what I could do against a Drood,' the Dancing Fool said finally.

'Always wanted a chance to stick it to a Drood, the way they've always stuck it to me,' said Strange Chloe.

'I thought you were my friend, Shaman,' said Coffin Jobe. 'Friends are all I've got left . . .'

I could see the confidence growing in them as they talked themselves into it. The Dancing Fool was actually smiling.

'When word gets out I've taken down a Drood, I'll be able to double my fees,' he said.

'And have my family come after you?' I said. 'You never were the brightest button in the box, Nigel.'

Coffin Jobe and Strange Chloe turned their heads to look at the Dancing Fool.

'Nigel?' said Coffin Jobe.

'That's your name?' said Strange Chloe. 'Your real name? Bloody Nigel?'

The Dancing Fool glared at me, so angry he could barely speak. 'You bastard,' he said finally. 'You promised you'd never tell.'

'Sorry, Nigel,' I said. 'But needs must when the Devil's in the driving seat. And it's not as if you're a genuine martial arts master, either. Hell, you're not even Scottish! You added a minor talent for precognition to some moves you picked up watching Bruce Lee movies. Whereas I . . . really am a Drood. I'm here to kill the Independent Agent, for good reason. If you knew half the things he's done, you'd help me do it. Don't let him screw you over, like he did me. I will walk right through you to get to him.'

'Typical Drood,' said Strange Chloe. 'Think you can talk your way out of anything. Well, *Nigel* here may not be the real deal, but I bloody well am. I'm going to hate you out of the world, Drood; I'm going to stare you down until there's not one little bit of you left to remind me how much I hate you.'

Walker coughed politely. I'd forgotten he was there.

'Sort of friends,' I explained. 'More like colleagues. People I work with on occasion. You know how it is.'

'Only too well,' said Walker.

'Do you know who everyone is?' I said. 'I could introduce you.'

'No need,' said Walker. 'I know them all, by name or deed or reputation.' He studied them with his calm, cold gaze, and they shifted uneasily. 'Small-time operatives with minor talents. Their kind are always turning up in the Nightside, looking to make a reputation for themselves. They don't usually last long. Most of them end up like this – crying into their beer because the big boys play too roughly.'

'You bastard,' said Strange Chloe. 'I'll show you who's small time!'

'You stay out of this, Walker,' said the Dancing Fool, stabbing a finger at him. 'Our business is with the Drood. Don't get involved, if you know what's good for you.'

'And if I do choose to get involved?' said Walker, smiling a little.

Strange Chloe sneered at him. 'You don't have your voice any more. Everyone knows that.'

'And without the voice, you're just another killjoy in a suit,' said the Dancing Fool. 'So stay out of it.'

'Whatever you say, Nigel,' murmured Walker.

'Guys, please!' I said. 'Don't make me do this. I've already lost three colleagues to Alexander King. I don't want to lose any more.'

'See? We were never friends,' said the Dancing Fool. 'Only colleagues.'

'Then why are you so upset over the thought of being betrayed?' said Walker.

'Shut up! Shut up, Walker! You don't scare me any more!' The Dancing Fool's face was dangerously red with rage. 'Without your voice you're no better than us.'

'I don't have my voice,' said Walker. 'But I do have other things.'

'Oh, please,' said Strange Chloe, 'I could put you through a wall with my eyelashes.'

'Chloe,' I said. 'You don't want to do this. I'm the one who persuaded you out of that grubby bedsit, found you work, found you friends.'

'You didn't do it for me,' she said. Her voice was flat, cold, emotionless. 'It's all shit. Everything. Like I always said. Why should you have been any different? Everyone lies.'

'That's the Goth talking,' I said. 'I liked you better when you were a punk. You had more energy. And the pink Mohawk suited you.'

'Bastard,' said Strange Chloe.

'You were a punk?' said Coffin Jobe.

'Shut up, Jobe.'

'We all have our secrets,' I said. 'Get over yourself, Chloe. This is more important than your hurt feelings.'

'Nothing is more important than my feelings,' said Strange Chloe.

She stepped forward, and glared at me. I could feel power building around her. I hastily subvocalised my activating Words, and armoured up. Coffin Jobe and the Dancing Fool gaped at me; they'd never seen a Drood take on his armour before. Not many have, and lived to tell of it. Strange Chloe didn't care. Her rage seethed and crackled on the air between us as she took another step forward. The impact of her gaze hit me like a fist. That was her gift and her power and her curse: to make anything disappear that dared not to love her. Strange Chloe's stare slammed against my armour, terrible energies filling the space between us as she concentrated, the unyielding power of her fury straining to find some hold, some purchase, on my strange-matter armour. I took a step towards her, and her face became almost inhuman in its concentrated rage.

Things close to us began to disappear, driven out of reality by the overspilling energies of Strange Chloe's stare. Objects and trophies and pieces of furniture vanished, one after the other, air rushing in to fill the gaps left behind. Rich deep carpet faded away and was gone, leaving a slowly widening swathe of bare boards between us. Strange Chloe glared at me, scowling so hard it must have hurt her face, but all I had to show her in return was my featureless gold mask. I was almost close enough to reach out and touch her when her power broke against my armour, and blasted back at her. The full force of her gaze was reflected by my unyielding armour, and Strange Chloe screamed silently as she faded away, and was gone.

I armoured down.

'Sorry, Chloe,' I said to the empty air where she'd been. 'I hope you're happy now, wherever you are.'

'You killed her,' said the Dancing Fool.

'Her own power turned against her,' I said. 'And don't you dare sound so outraged, Nigel. You know damn well you never liked her. Not really. Don't you dare pretend she was ever your friend. You let her hang around because she was useful, a big gun you could pull on people who weren't impressed by your fighting skills. She was always more my friend than yours.'

'You were never her friend,' said the Dancing Fool.

'Sometimes you just don't have the time,' I said.

The Dancing Fool laughed briefly. There wasn't any humour in the sound. 'You've robbed me of one of my colleagues. Seems only fair I should rob you of one of yours. Never did like you, Walker.'

His long lean body snapped into a martial arts stance as he turned on Walker, clearly expecting to take him by surprise; but Walker was already waiting, gun in hand. He smiled briefly and shot the Dancing Fool, shattering his left kneecap with a single bullet. The Dancing Fool made a shocked, surprised sound as the impact punched his leg out from under him, and he fell to the floor. Tears streamed down his face as he clutched his bloody knee with both hands, as though he thought he could hold it together by sheer force. His breathing came short and hurried as the pain hit him in waves, each worse than the one before.

'How did you do that?' he said to Walker, forcing the words out. 'I'm fast. I can dodge bullets. And I always know what's coming! How could you do that?'

'Because you never met anyone like me before,' Walker said calmly.

I moved over to join him, giving the crippled Dancing Fool plenty of room. 'Was that really necessary, Walker?'

'I thought so, yes,' he said. 'We don't all have suits of armour to protect us.'

'Sorry, Nigel,' I said to the Dancing Fool.

'Shove it!' he said. Both his hands were slick with blood, and his ruined leg trembled violently from shock and nerve damage. 'I'll get you for this. Get you both! I'll never stop, never give up. You'll spend what's left of your lives looking over your shoulder, waiting for me to be there. And I will! I'll kill you both for this!'

'No, you won't,' said Walker. And he put a bullet through the Dancing Fool's other kneecap.

There was only the briefest of screams, and then the Dancing Fool passed out, from pain and shock and horror. I looked at him, and then at Walker.

'It was a mercy, really,' said Walker, putting away his gun. 'Revenge is such a waste of life. Besides, it's never wise to leave an enemy in shape to come after you.'

'There is that,' I said. 'At least they won't call him the Dancing Fool any more.'

We looked round for Coffin Jobe. He was lying dead on the floor. I got Walker to help me pick him up and settle him in a chair, so at least he'd be comfortable when he came back to life again. I left Nigel where he was; I didn't want to risk waking him.

'Well,' said Walker. 'This was all very distracting, but it doesn't get us any closer to Alexander and Peter. In fact, after this I think we have to assume that they've been observing us ever since we got here, and are therefore probably heading for the nearest exit, or locking themselves inside a reinforced secret bunker.'

'No,' I said. 'They won't leave. Not with so much unfinished business left between us. They know they haven't won until they've beaten me. Beaten me fair and square, to keep my family from coming after them. Because the other side of "Anything, for the family" is "Anything, for any member of the family". And the Kings' best chance for winning is here, on their home territory, where they have the advantages.'

'Would you still be willing to make a deal?' said Walker. 'Hands off, leave safely, in return for the Independent Agent's secrets?'

'No,' I said. 'But they'll believe they can persuade me to settle for that. Because that's how they think.' I raised my voice. 'I know you can hear me, Alexander! Talk to me! Tell me where you are, so we can sort this out face to face. You know you want to.'

A vision of Alexander King sitting at his ease on his great wooden throne appeared on the air before us. He looked exactly as he had before: an aged rogue in flamboyant clothes. But his smile was cold and calculating now, and it added years to his shrunken face.

'Walk straight ahead,' he said. 'I'm waiting.'

The vision snapped off. I glanced at Walker, and then leaned in close to murmur in his ear:

'Don't stand on ceremony. If you get the chance, kill him.'

'Glad to,' replied Walker.

We walked on through the Independent Agent's monument to his own genius, through room after room full of trophies and mementoes, and the museum he'd made of his life. Endless photos from his extensive career, from all places and periods, showing Alexander King as a young man, growing steadily older ... but not beyond a certain point. No photos of a more than middle-aged man, past his best, or an old man limping into retirement. Just endless portraits of the legendary Independent Agent, with famous faces from politics and religion, along with movie stars and celebrities, and even a few gods and monsters. (Though those last tended not to photograph well.) Alexander King really had got around, in his day.

I paused before one photo, nicely framed, but just one more set among so many. A young and handsome Alexander stood with his arm round the waist of a very young Martha Drood. A simple snapshot of a warm moment in the Cold War. Martha when she was a field agent, like me. She wasn't even as old as I was. She was beautiful, as everyone said.

Another photograph showed a middle-aged but still stylish Alexander, standing next to a young Walker dressed in what looked like his very first good suit. I looked at Walker, and he shrugged.

'When you have work that needs doing, you go to the best man for the job. And for many years, that man was Alexander King.'

'Have you noticed,' I said, indicating a whole wall of photos with one wave of my hand, 'all these photos of the man himself and his world, and the people he knew, but not one of his family. Not one of Alexander with his wife, whoever she was, or his daughter. Or Peter. What kind of a man has no family photos?'

'A man who lives for his work,' said Walker. 'You don't get to be the greatest agent of all time by allowing yourself to be . . . distracted.'

Soon after, we passed through a room full of evidence of Alexander King's more ruthless side. Stuffed and mounted exhibits of men and women from his past. Enemies he'd overcome, and then kept as trophies. At first I thought they were waxworks, but up close I could see the treated skin, and smell the preservatives. I tapped a fingertip against one eye, and it was glass. The exhibits were dressed in the very height of fashion from their times, from the 1920s onwards. Their faces were taut, emotionless, damned for ever to stand around the room in casual poses, as though at some awful cocktail party that would never end.

A museum to murder.

'Old enemies,' said Walker, striding casually through the carefully posed figures, and occasionally peering closely at certain faces. 'And maybe a few friends and allies who got above themselves. What better way to celebrate your victory, when you can't tell the world, than to be able to walk among your defeated foes and gloat as you please? I wonder if he talks to them? Probably. Probably the only people he can talk to, these days.'

'Anyone here you recognise?' The place was creeping me out big time, but I was damned if I'd show it in front of Walker.

'No one I know personally,' he said. 'I've only ever operated on the fringes of the Intelligence field. How about you?'

'Jesus!' I said suddenly, striding forward. 'This one's a Drood! He's still wearing his torc!'

I reached out to take the torc, and Walker grabbed my arm at the last moment and pulled me back.

'No, Eddie. Really bad idea. Booby traps, remember?'

I stopped, breathing hard, and then nodded curtly to Walker to show him I was back in control again. He let go of my arm.

'Later,' I said. 'I'll see to this later.'

'Yes,' said Walker. 'There will be time for many things, later.'

Finally, we ran out of rooms. I pushed open one last oversized door, and there before us was the room I'd seen in the background of Alexander's floating vision. A bare room with bare walls, nothing in it but a great wooden throne with its back turned to me. I stopped inside the door and took a good look around, but there was no one else in the room. Walker mouthed the word *Peter?* at me, and I shrugged. We strode forward into the room, and the door closed behind us. The throne began to turn slowly, spinning silently on some unseen mechanism and there, sitting on the Independent Agent's throne, was Peter King. He smiled at me, and nodded to Walker.

'Welcome to my home, both of you. Well, have you nothing to say to the legendary Independent Agent at the moment of his greatest triumph? I've been running rings around people like you for the best part of a century, but you have to admit this is one of my best! Oh, come on! Surely you guessed before now? Surely two agents of such vaunted skill and experience had the merest suspicion at some point that I wasn't who I appeared to be: that it was, in fact, me?'

'You've been masquerading as your own grandson,' I said, feeling numb and stupid. 'It was you all along, Alexander.'

'Of course, of course!' he said cheerfully. 'It was my game, my rules, and you never stood a chance.'

'Was there ever a grandson?' said Walker. 'A real Peter King?'

'Oh yes,' the Independent Agent said. 'Pitiful little fellow. No use to anyone, not even himself. No drive, no ambition, and not a single achievement of worth to his name. A dreary little man in a dreary little job. Industrial espionage. Is there anything lower, for such as us? I didn't really kill him, not exactly. Just relieved him of a life he wasn't using anyway. I took his life energy and used it to make myself young again, with a few nips and tucks here and there and a new face. It's not difficult, if you know what you're doing. An expensive process, certainly, but worth every penny. As a great man once said: what good is wealth, if you don't have your health? I feel so *young*! So *alive*! I feel . . . like myself again!'

He swung one leg elegantly over the other, and smiled condescendingly. I could feel my hands knotting into fists at my sides. I wanted to haul him down off his stupid throne and beat him to death with my bare hands. But I didn't. I made myself wait. He had more to say, more secrets to spill; and I needed to hear them.

'You didn't really think the legendary Independent Agent would give up his role and his secrets just because he was getting old, did you?' said Alexander, through Peter King's face. I decided to think of him as Alexander. It made it easier to hate him. 'The world needs me, needs the Independent Agent, needs my knowledge and experience and skills, now more than ever. Too many damned amateurs running around out there, screwing things up for everyone. When you've got a real problem, you need a professional. Someone who knows what he's doing.

'And don't get me started on the state of the official organisations! Bloody accountants have taken over, more concerned with balancing their budgets than actually achieving anything. And as for the Droods . . . I am lost for words, Eddie. You never should have meddled. All right, your family were corrupt. So what? They got the job done, didn't they? Did you know I offered to help you out during the Hungry Gods War, and some damned fool turned me down?' He leaned forward on his throne to glare at me. 'Did you really think I'd give it up, and go quietly into the long night? Lie down and die, because I got old? I didn't spend my whole life saving the world and putting it to rights just to grow old and feeble and die! People like

321

me aren't supposed to die! The world needs me! I have important things to do! Dying is for small people, for the little people who don't matter!'

'You're shouting, Alex,' said Walker.

'Ah. Yes. Sorry about that,' said the young Independent Agent, sitting back on his wooden throne. 'This new body is packed full of hormones. I'm still getting used to it.'

'The game never was what we thought it was,' I said. 'You set the contest up specifically so you could be in it, and win it. To beat us in front of the whole world. You needed to prove to yourself, and everyone else, that you were still the best. By taking on the greatest agents the world had to offer, and beating them.'

'Oh, please, you were hardly the best,' said Alexander. 'You were the five best up-and-comers. The ones most likely to be my competition, as I started life again. The ones most likely to get in my way as I built my new career as Peter King. I brought you into this game to show everyone I could beat you, yes; but mostly so I could kill you off before you became a nuisance.'

'Excuse me,' said Walker. 'But why me? I'm hardly an up-and-comer. I'm barely an agent. Why not choose the current champion of the Nightside, John Taylor?'

'You were my one indulgence,' said Alexander, beaming down on Walker. 'I wanted someone who could put up a good fight. Someone worth beating. And I wanted someone there who knew the old me, to see if they could identify me inside this new body. And you didn't! I fooled you completely!'

'That young blood is going to your head,' said Walker.

'I know,' said Alexander. 'Isn't it wonderful?'

'If all you wanted was to become young again,' I said slowly, 'there are any number of ways you could have become a young Alexander King. Not very nice ways, most of them, but that wouldn't have stopped you. The Independent Agent rejuvenated! Such things have been known to happen in our field. Rarely, and usually frowned upon, but not unknown. However, you didn't do that. You couldn't afford to. You've made too many enemies down the years, Alexander. Really powerful, really nasty enemies. You couldn't kill all of them and put them on display. No, they're out there, sensing weakness in your old age, jackals and vultures circling the dying lion.

'The only way you could hope to shake them off was by spreading rumours of your impending death, and then reappearing as your own grandson. Winning the game you set up would establish Peter King as a major player in his own right; and then you'd use the secrets gained from the contest as currency to get you back in the great game. You would become the new Independent Agent, with none of your old enemies any the wiser.'

'But why this desperate need for new secrets?' said Walker. 'Why play the game at all? Unless—'

'Exactly,' said Alexander. 'Knew you'd get there, in the end. There is no hoard of hidden secrets. Hasn't been for some time. There was once, along with whole vaults full of objects of power and forbidden weapons and the like. But I sold them off, down the years, to fund my wonderfully extravagant lifestyle. One at a time, and very discreetly, of course, but they all went. Sometimes I even sold things back to the very people I'd taken them from in the first place! Through a whole series of trusted intermediaries, of course; I couldn't risk any rumours getting out. Oh, I get almost giddy, thinking of how clever I've been . . . The last few items went in payment for my new youthfulness. Can't say I miss them. They were the past, and I must concentrate only on the future now.

'As befits a young man, with his whole life ahead of him.

'I shall be the new sensation of the age, and astonish everyone – once I've blown up Place Gloria, to establish Alexander's death. And yours too, naturally. A pity to have to blow up the old place; it's been good to me . . . But the world must believe the Independent Agent is dead if the new one is to rise from his ashes. And you have to die so you can't tell anyone what you know. Nothing personal – just business.'

'Wrong,' I said. 'This is personal.'

You don't think it's going to be that easy, do you?' said Walker.

'Oh yes . . . I believe so,' said Alexander. 'If you hadn't found your way here so quickly, I was planning to lay out a trail of breadcrumbs. I needed you to find me on your own, without calling in reinforcements. How did you get here so quickly? No. It doesn't matter. I haven't got where I am today by worrying over unimportant details. You're here, as I meant you to be. You know, you're very easy to manipulate, Eddie. I knew killing Honey in front of you would make you so angry you'd come charging after me without bothering to bring in any more of your annoying family.'

'That's it?' I said. 'That's why you killed Honey? Because of me?'

'No, Eddie!' said Alexander. 'Not everything is about you! She had to die, as all of you had to die. It's necessary. My game, my outcome, and no one left to contradict me. I killed her because of me, Eddie. This has all been about me. Get used to it.'

'You really think you can take me, in my armour?' I said. 'I've fought evil organisations, Hungry Gods, and my own damned family, and still come out on top. You stupid little turd! All of this, for your ego. You may be young again, Alexander, but you're still only a man, and I'm a Drood.

'I sentence you to death, by my hand, for the deaths of Honey Lake, the Blue Fairy, and Lethal Harmony of Kathmandu. And for the betrayal of your own legend. Because you were a great man, once.'

My voice was so cold even Walker looked at me uneasily. Alexander lounged on his throne, still smiling. He held up his left hand to show me a simple clicker in the shape of a small golden frog.

'Recognise this, Eddie? A device created by your own family Armourer. Designed to shut down your armour, and hold it inside your torc. An on/off switch, whose whole purpose is to give someone outside control over a Drood's armour. Your Uncle Jack felt it necessary to design such a thing, to be sure no rogue Drood could use their armour for evil, like Arnold Drood, the Bloody Man. He really did go bad, didn't he? Who would have thought such a well brought up Drood could do such terrible things?'

'I know about Arnold,' I said. 'I killed him.'

Alexander looked at me. He hadn't known that. He recovered quickly, brandishing the golden frog in my face. 'I persuaded your Uncle Jack to give me one of his duplicates. Partly so I could be there to take down a really bad Drood, if he couldn't, and partly in return for something he wanted so very badly that the family wouldn't let him have.'

'Like what?' I said. 'What could you possibly have that the whole Drood family couldn't get for him?'

'The Merlin Glass,' said Alexander. 'And if you knew why your dear old Uncle Jack wanted it so badly you'd shit yourself.'

I took a step forward, and he held up the golden frog admonishingly. 'Ah-ah, Eddie! One little click and your armour is trapped inside your collar, and then what will you do?'

I took another step forward. He frowned, confused. This wasn't the scenario he'd written in his head for this occasion. He clicked the golden frog once, with a large dramatic gesture. The small sound was very loud in the quiet. I subvocalised my activating Words, and my armour flowed out of my torc and covered me completely in a moment. Alexander King sat up straight on his throne, looking at me dumbly. He clicked the frog again and again, as though he could make it work through sheer vehemence. As though he could make my armour go away through force of will. He opened his mouth to say something, to call for help or activate some hidden defence. I didn't give him the chance. I lunged forward and punched him hard in the chest with my golden fist, crushing his heart. He slammed back against his throne, my right hand buried in his chest up to the wrist; and the last thing he saw with his dying eyes was his own horrified face reflected in the featureless golden face mask of a Drood.

I watched the light go out of his eyes. When I was sure he was dead, I leaned in close and whispered in his ear. 'New torc,' I said. 'New armour. Different rules. You really should have kept up to date, Alexander.'

Walker and I took our time, wandering back through the many trophied rooms and halls of Place Gloria. I'd already used my Sight to locate the hidden bomb, and turn off the timing mechanism.

'I think I'll take a good look around before I leave,' said Walker. 'Bound to be something here I can use to get my voice up and running again.'

'Can you do that?' I said. 'With the Authorities gone?'

Walker smiled. 'The voice isn't something the Authorities gave me, Eddie; it's something they did to me. All I have to do is find the right power source, and I can recharge it. Like the portable timeslip.'

'Be my guest,' I said. 'I don't want anything. Not from him.'

'What could he have that the Droods wouldn't already have?' said Walker generously.

'Still,' I said, 'don't take too long. When I leave, I'm re-setting the timer on the bomb. So no one ever has to know about ... all this. Alexander King was a good man, in his time. A real legend. No one needs to know what he was like at the end. A scared old man in an empty treasure house. Our field needs legends like the Independent Agent.'

'So he can inspire others to become rogue agents, like you?' said Walker. 'Standing alone and valiant, against the corruption of established organisations?'

'Something like that,' I said.

Walker shook his head. 'Heroes. Always more trouble than they're worth.'

'Somebody has to keep the big boys honest,' I said.

Why be an agent? To protect the world from all the other agents.

EPILOGUE

Walker went back to the Nightside. I went home.

I told the Matriarch what happened. Made a full report. She just nodded. She did, after all, know Alexander King better than any of us.

I went to see the Armourer. I told him I killed the Independent Agent. He was pleased. He asked how I got on with all the new toys he'd given me: the Chameleon Codex, the Gemini Duplicator, the new skeleton key. I told him I hadn't used any of them. I'd been so busy, I'd forgotten all about them.

His face went a colour not normally seen in nature, and I had to call some of his assistants to bring him a nice soothing drink.

And finally, I went home, to Molly. She was back in the wood between the worlds, back from her mission. We lay down on a grassy bank together. She didn't tell me about her mission, and I didn't tell her about mine. We just lay there, side by side, happy to be with each other again.

I never did tell her about Honey Lake, the woman I didn't love, and who didn't love me. Who died in my arms. But I will always remember her, and the time we had together, and how things might have gone differently, if only . . .